What readers are saying about the Warrington Legacy:

Great characters and interactions: This is a heartwarming and funny tale about two people who swore off love only to have it hunt them down when they least expected it. Leo and Gracie and excellent characters. They are developed well, and the author does a great job of making their interactions believable. The dialogue is written nicely and the narrative moves at a fast pace. Fans of romance novels and uplifting fiction will enjoy this story and the characters it contains.

A great love story! This beautiful romance novel leaves you teary-eyed. The story is of Leo and Gracie, two people who got hurt by love. These two broken hearts help to heal each other and finally find a second chance at love. I would recommend this book to everyone.

Finding love: A love story of two people that have loved before and are not really looking for a relationship at this point. Circumstances bring them together and feelings develop and grow. A sweet tale of discovery of themselves and each other with the help of those that love them. Story has well-developed characters in a tale with a few twists and turns and a surprise or two.

Sweet romantic story: This is the first book I've read by this author, and enjoyed it. It's a short and sweet romantic story. I loved the connections between the characters, and how they give themselves a second chance at love.

Sweet love story: This is the first time I read this author and enjoyed the read. Gracie was very entertaining pushing the limits. Leo was a pleasant surprise!! I can't wait to see where the relationship goes…

A book to recommend: I not only found a nice, well-written novel but also a beautiful message in this book. All through the narrative, I found myself immersed in the plot. This is the result of a great job done by the author as regards descriptions. She wrote such good descriptions for each scene that I felt part of them. I was left a nice message: When second chances appear, take them.

Loved every thing about it! I really loved the plot of this book. There is a lot going on and the author has written it in such a relatable way that is hard not to connect with the characters. I loved the fact that the lovebirds are podcast hosts as it adds so much to their love story and brings even more tension to their time apart. This author has an incredible way with words that will totally wrap you up and make you feel deeply connected to every chapter of the book. I'd highly recommend it.

Much more to discover: Second Chances is like a good soap opera, one that makes you laugh and cry, but overall it makes you think. It makes the reader reflect on past relationships, sad memories, lessons learned, and love. The characters are well-rounded; nobody is a saint, and nobody is a devil. The love story feels modern, relatable, and charming. This book is about going back to where you thought you had it all figured out and finding out there's much more to discover.

Great, realistic dialogue: A short and easy read — I love this book! The dialogue is great, and it feels authentic — as if I'm experiencing it in real life. The characters are very relatable, and I constantly found myself rooting for the characters in their journey of love.

It's All About Love

WARRINGTON LEGACY COMPLETE COLLECTION

MARSHA CASPER COOK

ISBN: 978-1-962402-37-8

For more about Marsha please visit

www.MarshaCasperCook.com
www.MarshasKidsBooks.com
www.MichiganAvenueMedia.com

Published by

Fideli Publishing, Inc.
119 W. Morgan St.
Martinsville, IN 46151

www.FideliPublishing.com

Dedication

To my family and friends, thank you for always being there for me.

As always, a very special thank you to Robin Surface, Fideli Publishing, and Jeff Fleischer, my editor, who have helped me achieve success with all my projects as an author.

Prologue

Leo Tucker had grown up with many superstitions handed down to him by his grandmother, and by her grandmother to her, and so on and so on. There was one superstition that Leo truly believed in — not that he didn't believe in hundreds of others, but this one stood out. Every time he found himself anywhere near a fountain, he tossed in all the coins he had in his pocket.

The story he was told was that spirits lived inside fountains, and if a person passed by a fountain without tossing in a coin, he or she would surely be followed by bad luck. Not a story a superstitious person wants to hear.

So when Leo found himself strolling the streets of Paris for the second time in his life, he was hoping to be inspired by the all of the romance novels he wrote in the past. There he was, a successful novelist trying to find his way back from losing his wife, Ellie, after her battle with cancer. He wasn't doing very well, even though he was trying.

Shortly before he was scheduled to leave Paris and head back to Chicago, he walked by one of the many popular fountains in Paris, Fontaine des Mers. It was so beautiful he could hardly speak. It was everything he imagined when he wrote about Paris.

He threw every coin he had into the fountain, closed his eyes, and made a wish. There she was. Ellie dressed in white, looking as beautiful as an angel and smiling at him as she stood in the water. He smiled back and said, "I love you Ellie. I always will."

By that time, a crowd had gathered around him. There were too many to count, but he heard them cheering him on, clapping their hands and shouting, "*Bonne chance, monsieur.*"

Then, in the most communal way, everyone tossed coins into the fountain and all Leo could hear was the coins hitting the water. It was exhilarating. Many of those watching were couples who were kissing each other after their tosses. Leo felt better, and smiled at all of them. "*Merci beaucoup.*"

Minutes after that, a young, beautiful blonde woman, Gracie Maxwell, couldn't help but wonder what was going on. She was fascinated by the amount of people standing there clapping and enjoying something she could not see. She jumped up, trying to see what was happening, but it seemed that there was no room for her to inch her way into the crowd.

Finally, when the crowd dispersed, she got a closer look at a man sitting by a bush close to the fountain. She didn't know what to do, so she tapped him on his shoulder. "Are you okay, sir?"

He never answered, and she never got a good look at his face. He left without a look or a word. She followed him for a few minutes, just to make sure he was okay, but he never turned around.

She walked back to the fountain, but found the crowd had dispersed. When she looked down at her watch, she knew she would be late for her flight home if she didn't hop into a taxi right then and there. She hailed one and was gone.

By the time Leo turned around and walked back toward the fountain to thank the woman who checked on him, all he saw was her getting into a taxi. He remembered her by her hat. It was white with black trim; a writer by nature, Leo remembered details.

Chapter One

Dinner at the Warringtons' was, at best, a challenge. That was even more true when something important needed to be discussed. Several months after Gracie graduated college, she and her father were still avoiding the inevitable topic: What was the rest of her life going to look like?

The first clue of the evening was when her mother, Francine, left the room. She was followed by their loving housekeeper, Ava, who immediately stopped serving whenever a serious discussion was about to happen, knowing they usually didn't go well. And at any sign of confrontation, Georgia, an adorable Labradoodle with big eyes and a furry golden body, either left the room or hid under the table.

Georgia was intelligent, quiet, and very loyal to everyone in the family, showing no favoritism. As a puppy, she immediately became a member of their household after Samuel Warrington — the head of that household, if only in his own mind — brought her home in a small cardboard box. He complained throughout the long ride home on the expressway during a snowstorm, but he had promised his daughters a sweet little dog for Hanukkah, and he was a man of his word.

The women in the household ran the place. Samuel knew he was outnumbered, but it was okay. He was CEO of a huge publishing house, and maintained his respect there. Father first, tycoon second.

Tonight, he was playing both those parts. It was time for an answer to the question he had been waiting to hear for months, and he wasn't usually a patient man. It was time to rock the boat.

Just as Gracie was about to get up from the dinner table, Samuel stood up. "Not this time, my dear. We have to talk, so sit down. This won't take long — but if it does, I have all night."

"Fine," she said, and sat down with a huff. "Okay, you've got my full attention."

"Gracie, let's get this settled. It's time to talk about your future at Warrington Media. You keep putting it off."

"I'm just not sure," she answered, realizing it wasn't going to stop the questions from coming.

"What's the hold-up?"

"Well, to be truthful, I don't think you're going to like what I've decided."

"Let's have it." Samuel's face reddened a bit when he was about to get angry. "Let's talk this over like two adults."

"Sounds fair. But I know what you want, and we're not exactly on the same page. In fact, we're not even close."

"Meaning what?"

"I still want more life experience before I root myself in one place. I feel like you're forcing me."

"Am I holding a gun to your head? Be reasonable."

"I'm just saying how I feel."

"You would be a great addition to the publishing house. I thought that was your goal. You've been working with Nicholas, and he tells me you're ready."

"He's telling you what you want to hear. Maybe he doesn't even mean it."

"You're smart and very capable. And you're my daughter. Like it or not, this could work out great for you. I'm not going to be around forever."

"What about Julianna? She's also your daughter."

"I know that, but you're the one who always wanted this."

"People change."

"Maybe I pushed too hard, but I know this could be good for you."

Gracie shook her head. "You just don't get it, do you? I want to build my own life. Can you blame me?"

"Yes, I can. Why start from scratch? I wish I had someone like me in my corner when I was growing up."

"I don't think I had a choice. I did what you wanted me to do, whether I liked it or not."

Samuel looked very unhappy. "I'm sorry you feel that way. I had no idea."

"That's just it. You've never taken me seriously."

"Does your mother know how you feel?"

"Somewhat. But you have both been very busy. Mom does her thing, and you do yours. Julianna does her own thing and no one ever says anything to her. And then there's me."

Samuel called out to his wife. "Francine, where the hell are you? I need you to talk to our daughter."

Francine, a beautiful blonde woman, sexy for her age, came back to the table. Even though dinner was at home, she was dressed as if she was going out, in a black fitted Chanel suit and pearls. No matter where she was, she was always the most elegant woman in the room — never the life of the party, but always the most stylish.

"Samuel, I told you it wasn't going to happen the way you wanted it to. I warned you years ago that Gracie had her own mind, but you didn't listen."

"Obviously not. Did you know about this?"

Francine sat down at the table. "Meaning what?"

"That she wants an adventure."

"As always, when you get something in your head, you don't listen. It's her life. I have told you that time and time again."

"Oh, so this is an ambush?"

"Dad, it's no ambush," Gracie interrupted. "I just don't want to stay here right now. I want to travel and have my own life. Adventures. Doing things that make sense to me. Learning things, meeting new people."

"Well then, excuse me. Look around. You're living in a ten-bedroom home, with a pool and a movie theatre downstairs. Is this such a bad life? You have everything. What more do you want?"

"I want to go places, see things. I'm leaving for Paris."

"And you can't explore all that life has to offer in Chicago? Or at least the United States?"

"I don't think so. I'm just too sheltered. I need to leave for a while."

"Nobody needs to go to Paris. You can go your whole life without ever going to Paris and survive. Many people actually live long, happy lives without ever traveling."

"You've traveled to so many places. And look at Mom; she' been everywhere."

"You can travel. But just to leave like that, without a plan—"

"I have a plan."

Samuel looked at his wife. "Francine, if you knew, why didn't you give me a heads up?"

"Because I knew this is how you'd react. You two are more alike than you realize."

"Maybe so," Samuel said. "Fine. I'll adjust. Maybe I'll bring Nicholas in to do more. He's aggressive and wants a bigger role."

Gracie agreed with that. Nicholas was a climber, always wanting more and more. He didn't care who he stepped over. She knew exactly what he was like, but she didn't care to elaborate. She was getting off the hook and wasn't about to push her luck.

"Yes," she replied, "Nicholas is always trying to expand his horizons. If you like that type."

"You're working with him, not dating him. Am I right?"

She didn't say another word about him, on the grounds that it might incriminate her. She didn't need to get into how she felt about Nicholas, but she didn't trust him one bit.

By the end of the conversation, Gracie had confused her father. She had managed to turn the tables on him.

"Fine, go and explore."

Gracie smiled, knowing she was now out of the woods; her father was waving the white flag whether he meant to or not.

"You know, Dad, I won't be gone forever."

"What if you meet some fascinating man and end up staying in Paris the rest of your life? We'll never see you."

Francine gave her husband a look. "Do you always have to do the 'what ifs?'"

"Yes, when it's about my children. I need to."

"Dad, you've got to be kidding," Gracie said. "I'll be back before you know it. Just give me some room."

"Is there something I'm missing here?"

"Well, to be truthful, I've gotten myself a modeling job for a new fragrance."

"And you're just telling us now? Couldn't you have said that first?"

Francine looked surprised. "Don't look at me. I didn't know that either."

"I just found out today," Gracie blurted out. "I wouldn't have kept that a secret. You know that, don't you?"

Samuel sat back and lit a cigar. Even though he claimed he was going to quit years ago, he took a few puffs every night to ease his nerves. One thing he knew for sure — this conversation with his daughter had given him reason to start smoking again. Like a lot of fathers, Samuel didn't like the reality of his daughters leaving. He knew it might happen; he just wasn't ready for it.

Gracie gave her father a kiss on his forehead before she left the room. "I knew you'd see it my way."

Samuel got the last word in. "That's not exactly true, but we'll leave it for now."

When the coast was clear, Ava brought in dessert and Georgia came out from under the table. The storm was over.

"There she is," Samuel said as he reached down to pet her. "Well, Georgia, you're always on my side. That's the best thing about having a dog. They love you and they don't talk back. They also don't leave."

"Can I have some black coffee, Ava?" Francine asked after taking a deep breath, now that the cyclone was averted.

"Sure, I'll be right back," Ava said. "That was a short one. It's a good day."

"Yes, it was. Amen." Francine smiled as she took another deep, relaxing breath. "Ava, honey, can you bring Samuel a brandy? I think he needs it."

Samuel shook his head. "No, I don't, but I do need some vanilla ice cream with a double dollop of whipped cream and lots of chocolate syrup. Oh, add a cherry or two, plus nuts."

"Wow, she really got to you." Francine smiled. "Just like putty in her hands. She weakens you, and you never see it coming. So, you trust she'll be alright?"

"Absolutely not. That's what private investigators are for."

"You're kidding, right?"

"No. She's my daughter, you know."

"And mine too. No investigator. Please."

"Fine," Samuel answered, knowing he had just lied to his wife. "Anyway, let's forget about that for now. I had a long conversation with Nicholas Sinclair. I'm planning on promoting him to editor. The guy's smart as a whip."

Francine smiled. "Plus he's very good looking. Do you think he can handle it?"

"He used to be an editor for *City or Country*. He's fairly young to have had such a job, and he could help move us in a new direction. I need some new blood, and it's obvious my family isn't interested in moving up the chain."

"There's always Julianna."

"She could care less about any of this."

"You might be surprised. One never knows; she might come around. She might realize you have to work and make money, instead of having your father put it in your account every week."

"Possibly." By that point, Samuel was nearly finished with his sundae.

"Just for the record, I loved that magazine *City or Country*. I read it every month for the last twenty years. Can't take the country out of me."

"Wow. I thought I knew everything about you."

Francine's eyes gazed into his as she sipped her coffee. "Guess not, darling."

Francine was happy that Gracie had decided to go for the adventures life had to offer. If she was being honest with herself, she wished she'd been able to do that after she finished school. Her plan was to go to Europe, but she found herself pregnant with Gracie. She and Samuel had lied about the date of their wedding, and only the two of them knew they had to get married. Some secrets were better kept private, and that was one of them — along with the obvious one that they were never in love.

Samuel had never been Francine's first choice, but they managed to stay married despite their differences. Their daughters were their common ground. Julianna was always a free spirit, and Samuel and Francine never pushed her the same way they did with Gracie. They learned very early to step lightly; one push too many and she would be gone.

Chapter Two

Minutes before Gracie boarded the plane for Paris, Samuel couldn't help but ask her, "Are you sure about this?"

"Yes and no, but I'm going. It's an experience I don't want to miss."

"I guess you have to do this, but please stay safe. I'll hold your job for you."

"Stop worrying. I'll be fine. You know me. Nothing stops me."

"I do. That's what worries me."

"Thanks, Dad. Now that's the father I love and admire. You always come around."

"Not always." Truth was, he was devastated. Gracie had spent summers at Samuel's office for years, and he had hoped she would follow in his footsteps. As he boasted to others — but never to her — she was one hell of a writer. That was why, after she graduated college, his hope had been to give her a job where she could use her expertise and possibly run the whole company someday. For the first time, he had a feeling that might not be the case.

Gracie hugged her father, holding on tight for a minute or two. As he watched her board the plane, he had a sinking feeling that she would be gone much longer than she had planned. He didn't want to let go, but he didn't have a choice. It was time.

Gracie had flown only a few times before, and never as far as Paris. She was scared to death, but she made the decision to "woman up" and forget her fears. She tried to relax, but thought about just how many hours she would be on the plane — and then she really started worrying.

Deciding that reading would be a good way to pass the time, she reached into her bag and found a book she'd started months ago. It was a romance novel a friend had given her.

Suddenly, her concentration was interrupted by the passenger sitting next to her. He was eagerly wiggling in his seat, trying to get her attention, but she wasn't all that receptive. She turned away from him, certainly not wanting to make friends. All she cared about was getting through the flight in one piece.

She was in no mood to talk, but her silence didn't stop him. "So, are you excited to go to Paris?"

She just nodded and turned away.

"Hi. I'm Leo." It was obvious he didn't get the message.

When he reached out for a friendly handshake, she had no choice but to shake his hand and hope all the pleasantries were over.

"Hi. I'm Gracie."

"I guess you're not a talker."

"I'm not."

"That's okay, I'll talk for both of us."

She realized she should have shut the conversation down immediately, but her nerves were getting the best of her. He wasn't just a talker; he was a chatterbox. She tried to block him out, but even earplugs wouldn't have helped. There was no way out for her, so she pretended to be listening.

Finally, she decided to try drastic measures. "I should warn you. I hate flying and I might throw up. So if I were you, I'd change seats."

"I always fly in the same seat if possible. Thanks for telling me. I just don't think it's possible. If you throw up on me, you throw up on me."

"You're kidding, right? You don't even know me. I wouldn't want to sit next to me."

"I have to stay in this seat."

"Why on Earth would you have to stay right here?"

"I'm superstitious. And if the plane crashes and I'm in a seat different from my assigned one, I might die for no reason at all."

Gracie looked at him as if he were crazy. "What are you talking about?"

"Well, let's take this as an example. If I take someone else's seat, and they were supposed to die but not me, I'll be the one who dies if the plane crashes."

"Not making me feel better." Gracie was getting nauseous. "Can we stop talking about crashing? I already have enough fears just sitting here praying to get to Paris with no mishaps."

"Sorry. I didn't mean to make your fear of flying worse."

"Maybe I'll move," Gracie said, about to get up.

"No, it won't be necessary. I can be quiet. I hope."

"Good. Then if you don't mind, I'll get back to reading my book. One favor. Please keep your superstitions to yourself. Okay?"

"Apparently you're not superstitious."

"I'm not."

"Do you ever walk under a ladder?" Leo asked, pretty sure he knew the answer.

"No, never."

"Well then, there you go. That's a superstition."

Gracie was hopeful that would be that, and he would be quiet. "Now that we've established that fact, I'd like to read a little, if you don't mind. I was planning on finishing this novel."

"Fine by me," he said as he closed his eyes and pretended to take a nap. After a few minutes, Leo tried to see what type of book she was reading, struggling not to be too obvious as he leaned over to look at the cover.

"What are you doing?" Gracie asked, losing her patience.

"Just interested in what seems to be holding your attention."

"And why would you care about this?"

"I'm an author."

"Really? I didn't peg you for one. Have you written anything I might know?"

"I don't think so. I'm going to Paris for a writing conference."

"Good for you."

"If you like reading romance, you're going to the right place. Paris is where love begins. I've always wanted to just sit outside at a café and watch lovers meet. The beginning of love is such a special feeling. I want to be there and see it all."

"Maybe you'll meet your true love there," Gracie said, before returning to her book.

Leo smiled. "I don't think so. I'm just going to watch and listen. I need the practice. Why are you going to Paris?"

Gracie didn't like answering questions, but he wouldn't take no for an answer. "I'm going for a modeling job."

"I can understand that. You're a beautiful woman."

Gracie looked at him, wondering if he was trying to pick her up. Leo quickly turned away, realizing he had said something that he probably shouldn't have. "Didn't mean to offend you."

Gracie laughed. "That's okay. I'm not offended. I'm a big girl."

"Good, then one more question. What are you reading?"

"Just some romantic trash for the plane. Keeps me occupied when I'm trying not to think about flying. I'm usually more of a mystery girl." She was lying; she loved a good romance story. When she was in high school, she read all the young-adult romance books she could get her hands on. She loved a happy ending.

"Really? I didn't peg you for that." He just played along, knowing many people didn't want to admit to reading romance books, and she was probably one of them.

She laughed and continued reading, hoping he didn't interrupt her, but he could not seem to stop talking. For the majority of the ride, he talked and she pretended to listen. He was finally quiet when their meal came. And soon after dessert, they both fell asleep.

Gracie was a little embarrassed when she woke up with her head on Leo's shoulder. "Oh my G-d — I'm so sorry. I don't know what happened."

"Well, I do. You took a few Dramamine because it got a little rough."

"I remember that now. So sorry." She felt her face flush.

"No problem. I was tired myself, and a little nauseous. I didn't want to throw up on you either."

They both laughed.

"So, Leo. I have to thank you for the conversation. I must admit this was quite a different flight than I expected, but you kept me busy."

Leo thought she was charming. And cute. "I'd like to take credit, but I think it was the Dramamine. Glad to be of service," he joked, thinking this could be why he was single.

He should have gotten over that feeling, because he went all through high school and college thinking he wasn't good enough to get a girl like Gracie. And now he had validated that feeling once again. Nothing had changed. Once a nerd, always a nerd.

After the plane landed and they were at baggage claim, Gracie and Leo shook hands as they said goodbye.

"Thanks again, Leo. My adventure begins now."

"So, that's why you're really here?"

"Exactly. Modeling is secondary. Adventure is my goal." Then she blew him a kiss and was gone.

Leo waved goodbye. Unfortunately, he wasn't confident enough to ask her if they could meet up for lunch or dinner while he was there. He should have. One more regret.

Chapter Three

Several months after Leo returned from his trip to Paris, he met the most wonderful girl, Ellie Meyers. She was adorable and smart, with short curly hair that perfectly fit her petite frame. She had a smile that could melt anyone's heart, and it did. Leo fell for her hook, line, and sinker. She was his destiny.

He first noticed her on one of his many trips to the library while he was researching his books. She worked there while she was finishing up her nursing training. She had decided after completing her journalism degree that writing didn't really interest her, but helping people did.

Even after weeks of smiling and waving goodbye, Leo couldn't work up the confidence to ask her out. Luckily, Ellie had more courage than he did.

She was putting away the books that had been used that day before closing when Leo came strolling by, pretending to be looking for something.

"Hello, Leo."

He smiled, happy she knew his name. Though it was on his library card.

"Hello, Ellie. Almost done for the day?"

"Yes, and I'm pretty hungry. Are you?"

"Actually, yes. It's been a long day."

"Do you want to join me for dinner?"

"Are you asking me out?" Leo was relieved she had asked.

"Well, you might say that. If I wait for you to ask, it might never happen."

"So, you know that I've been wanting to ask you out."

She smiled. "You checked out the same book for the last three weeks. Kind of a dead giveaway, don't you think?"

Leo couldn't help but laugh. "I try not to think, especially when I'm standing before a beautiful, charming woman who had the nerve to ask me out."

From that day on, he knew he would marry Ellie. Six months later, he did.

Besides being the greatest inspiration he could have ever hoped for, Ellie was someone his grandmother loved to pieces. He doubted he could have ever married a woman Lilly didn't like. She raised him, and any girl who married him knew she was still the other most important woman in his life.

Leo wondered how in the world he (or, more accurately, his alias Nicole Forrester) had become a romance writer — and a successful one at that — without ever really falling in love before, but he had managed it. He had lived his life mastering the art of telling a beautiful love story, thinking he was the guy who didn't get the girl. When he finally did, his writing became even more beautiful and meaningful. Until Ellie, he never considered himself the romantic type. She proved him wrong; to her, he was Prince Charming.

When he lost his princess to cancer, nothing could have been more devastating. Going on with his life seemed impossible.

After losing her, he vowed he would never let himself fall in love with anyone else. The pain of losing the love of his life was too hard. He didn't want anyone to ever take her place, no matter what. Ellie was his soulmate, and he knew he could never love anyone that deeply again.

Leo wanted to continue writing, but it was difficult. He would sit at his desk, face the computer — and then nothing. He had always been able to sit down and drink a cup of black coffee, and even on a bad day he could write. It might not have been his best work, but he would fix it up when he was done.

No matter how little he wrote, his publisher — Samuel Warrington — wouldn't give up. He seemed to call whenever Leo was struggling to write.

Leo didn't pick up the first few times that day. Finally, after the third phone call, he answered.

"So, how's my favorite romance writer doing today? I hope you're writing."

"I'm trying to write, but the words still aren't coming."

"Just write. Let me worry about whether the story works. Even on your worst writing day, you're better than any of my other authors."

"I appreciate your faith in me. You know I love you for it. I hope I can still do this. I just feel like I'm hardened and my emotions don't go where they need to be. The romance in me has disappeared. I still feel blocked."

"Of course. Something *is* blocking you. Your wife died."

"Maybe I should write a mystery until I get my sense of love and feeling back. Maybe I'll never be able to write romance again."

"Nonsense. Give yourself a little more time."

Leo was discouraged. "Okay, if you say so."

Right after he finished the conversation, his grandmother came into the room. "So, it's time for a break. I made your favorite."

Moving in with her after Ellie died was one decision Leo knew he had gotten right. He enjoyed living with Lilly, and helping out at the family bakery she still ran.

"Cinnamon buns. Oh, you're so sweet. What would I do without you?"

"Well, for now I'm here. Don't worry."

"Okay, I won't."

"Honey, do you want to talk about it?" She saw the pain and anguish in everything he did.

"No, but thanks for making these," he said as he bit into one. "Just like when I was little. Whenever I had a bad day, you made a batch of cookies or muffins. Man, these are good. Who said comfort foods don't work?"

"Certainly not a grandmother."

"I might go into the office tomorrow. Samuel wants to see me."

"Sounds like a plan." She kissed Leo's forehead. "You can do this. I have faith in you."

"Nana, you're the best."

***

The next morning, Leo had just finished getting dressed when the phone rang.

"Leo, it's me, Samuel."

"I was just leaving."

"You were deciding if you were going to cancel on me again."

"Well, maybe I was—"

"I gathered that much," Samuel answered. "Not a problem."

Leo sat back in his chair, feeling relaxed but also wondering why Samuel had taken the news so well. "Great, I'll see you in a few weeks. That should give me enough time to finish."

"Actually, I'll see you in a few seconds. Open your door. I'm outside your house."

"That's a joke, right?"

Samuel laughed. "No joke, my friend. I have a little something for you."

When Leo opened the door, Samuel was standing there holding a small gray-and-white Schnauzer. The dog was cute as a button and staring at Leo. They immediately made a connection.

Leo seemed to be a little off guard. "He's so cute." He cheerfully smiled.

"Leo, meet Bernie. I'm glad you think he's cute, because he's yours."

"Mine. Why?"

"You need a friend. Haven't you heard a dog is man's best friend?"

"Do you really think a dog is going to help me finish the book?"

"Call me crazy, but I do."

"So glad you have faith in me."

"Can I come in? Or are we going to just stand in the doorway?"

"Sorry. Come on in."

Samuel followed Leo into the study. His first thought was what a comfortable, warm feeling the room had. He always got that feeling when he visited Leo's house. He sometimes felt like just packing his bags and moving in.

The walls were covered with pictures, including many of Ellie. She was beautiful and kind. What a love they had; Samuel was a little jealous of anyone who had a love like that. He certainly didn't have that with Francine, though he did have two daughters he couldn't love any more than he did. He knew he was overprotective, but all he really wanted was to see them happy. Regardless of what they thought, they were his shining stars. He knew he should tell them he loved them more often, but he was as stubborn as they were.

"You do have a safe haven here, don't you?" he said to Leo. "It feels so warm and loving."

"It's my grandmother who does that. Lilly is a charmer."

"She sure is," Samuel said as he sat down, crossed his legs, and relaxed.

"Sam, do you see all these pictures? These are my life. They keep me on the straight and narrow and help when I'm lonely. I wish I could come in here and bang away on the keyboard, but I can't. I will try my best; I don't want to let my readers down. I know they would understand if they knew, but they don't know Leo Tucker. They just know Nicole Forrester."

"I'm sorry. I'm just not sure it would be in your best interest to come out and be Leo Tucker at this point. They love Nicole Forrester. Success like yours doesn't happen to everyone."

"I know—"

Samuel interrupted him. "Don't worry so much. Where's your grandmother? I smell the cinnamon in the air."

"I'm right here, Sam." Her walk was brisk and she was carrying a small tray; it was a wonder she didn't drop it. "Cinnamon buns right from the oven."

"Nana, did you know Sam was coming?"

"I did. Can't tell a lie."

"Your grandmother was the one who suggested getting you a dog," Samuel said.

"Really. You talked to her about this?"

"I did. I check in with her sometimes when you don't answer your phone. I worry about you."

"I'm fine, but I don't think I can take care of a dog right now."

Lilly smiled. "But I can. He'll be great company for both of us."

Leo seemed to accept that. "Sam, I can't believe you drove out here just to bring me a dog."

"Well, I do have another reason for coming," Samuel eagerly confessed. "I'm sending you on a trip. You need to feel inspired."

"I can get inspired by myself. I'll just try harder."

"That hasn't worked so far. You're going to Paris. When you come back, you'll finish what you started. It will be good for you."

"You know I can't. Nana, what about the bakery? I like helping you out."

"The bakery can do without you. The girls will handle it. Leona and Beverly are very capable."

"Maybe so, but I can't go. Not now. Some other time."

"Oh, I forgot to tell you. It's non-negotiable," Samuel added as he handed him a plane ticket.

Lilly nodded in agreement. "You're going. Believe me, it will make a difference."

"Then come with me."

"Nope. Who wants to go to Paris with their grandmother?"

Samuel laughed. "Listen to your grandmother. She's always right."

"Look," Lilly said. "You always say you want to go back to Paris. You talk about it all the time. It's been a few years since you've been there, and the last couple have been hard. So you're going."

Leo looked at his grandmother. "Do you actually think Paris will help me? What about the dog?"

"I do. I love you, but you need a little change of pace. Samuel's idea was Paris and mine was the dog. Bernie will be here when you get home." Lilly lovingly picked up the dog and held him. "See, he's already my friend. Come, we're going into the kitchen."

After Lilly left the room, Samuel patted Leo on the back. "Don't be mad at your grandmother. She loves you, but you already knew that. It's just five days."

"I have no choice, right?"

Samuel shook his head. "Let's go."

"I have to pack a few things."

"There's a bag with some things in the car. Everything you need. And what you don't have, you can put on your expense report. I've made all the arrangements, and Alex will take you to the airport after he drops me at home. Say goodbye to you grandmother and then we're off."

Chapter Four

It was morning, and Gracie had just finished cleaning the dishes while Jack was taking a shower. They had made love early in the morning and she was feeling safe, warm, and a little giddy. She was never going to be the girl who fell foolishly in love — but as smart as she imagined herself to be, she was often impulsive.

That changed when she received a call from her father.

"Honey, listen," Samuel began. "I know you love being in Paris, so please don't get all upset, but I have something very difficult to say. You know it's no secret I wasn't happy that you left Chicago, and I understand your need to see your adventures come to life but—"

"Dad, let me stop you there. Please don't do this."

But he went on. "The first time I checked out Jack, there was no record of him at all."

"Why did you did that?" She was angrier at her father than she had ever imagined possible.

"What do you think? You're my daughter and I love you. Would you rather he made of a fool of you?"

"Don't you trust me to make a good decision? After all, it's my life. Maybe you think I'm a fool, but I'm happy."

"Did you just hear yourself? You said you're a happy fool. What the hell is going on there? Are you brainwashed?" The conversation was moments away from explosion.

"It's been over two years. Get used to it. I'm not coming back to Chicago. There's nothing there for me. My life is here with the man I love."

"At first, I thought this wouldn't last. You left an opportunity of a lifetime. Does that sound like someone who is mature and has a lot of common sense? Who does that?"

"Me. I did it. Call off the dogs."

"Why don't I just send you the report?"

"I don't need a report. Throw it out."

"Please, let's just discuss this. I'll be calm."

"No, you won't. Once you decide something is so, there's no changing your mind."

"I could say that about you too," her father added. "When you come to your senses, we'll be here for you. But don't go too long."

"Right now, don't expect me to say anything you want to hear. When I get over what you've done, I'll call you."

After she hung up, she felt horrible. She had a feeling there was something missing, but she really didn't want to hear it. Jack was very secretive, and she was so open. They were opposite on so many issues, but it was always fun to disagree. They had great makeup sex. Still, she did question something Jack had never answered.

Every time she asked him about his family, he would change the subject. She just let it go, thinking he would eventually tell her. All he said was his life wasn't very interesting, but he occasionally hinted there was more to his story.

She let it ride for a time. Finally, one day when they were arguing about her family, Jack said he knew that Gracie's father hated him. "So, you tell me something about your father and I'll tell you something about mine." He said it in a joking manner, but she saw a chance to get some answers.

"Well, my father loves me. But when I was a teenager, he had me followed. I was mad, but I understood he was very neurotic about his children's safety."

Jack gave her a look. "Isn't that a little over the top?"

"He can be." She gave him a kiss to make him feel more comfortable; she could sense he was slightly nervous.

"My life was rather boring, maybe a little pathetic. But I grew up, and here I am with a beautiful, smart, and talented woman." He had a way with words. "My parents died when I was eight years old. They were in a serious car crash."

Gracie gasped. "I'm so sorry. You should have said something. It's no wonder you don't talk about them much."

"There you have it. Nothing much that you don't know."

After that, she never questioned him again. Looking back and thinking about what her father had said, maybe she should have.

After she cooled down and Jack left for an appointment, Gracie called her father. He didn't sleep very long and, even with the time change, she knew he would answer.

"So, Samuel Warrington, let's talk about this."

She could hear her father sigh in relief. "Fine. I'm ready to listen."

***

Right after she hung up with her father, Gracie had a good cry and quickly packed her bags. Samuel was going to take care of her travel arrangements and she would handle the rest. At the end of the day, Gracie and her father loved each other despite their differences.

She thought of just leaving, but she knew that was not the right thing to do. She would confront Jack in one final conversation. They were scheduled to meet for dinner at their usual place, the bistro. She got there early and took a table in back instead of their usual spot.

Jack was surprised when he walked in. "So, why the back table? You know how I like to show you off. And you look especially beautiful tonight."

"I don't think tonight's going to be one you want to remember. I've decided to go home to Chicago. I'm not coming back."

"What about our marriage? The children we were going to have? Most importantly, what about our love?"

"Our love? That's a joke."

Jack was shocked. "I don't understand any of this. You can't leave. *Notre vie sera belle.*" He reached for her hand and kissed it.

"Jack, our life together won't be beautiful. It's never going to be anything other than what it is now. We don't have a future. You know that."

Jack sat back in his chair, not knowing what to say. "Why not?"

For the first time, she saw nothing when she looked into his eyes. "Do you really not know what I'm talking about?"

"No, absolutely no clue. Please fill me in. Is it something your father said?"

"Yes, it is. Did you really think we could get married and have a family?"

"Of course. Why not?"

"I'm going to ask you again. Is there something you're not telling me?"

"Not that I can think of."

"Maybe you'd better think again."

"You can't leave. We planned a life."

"Whose life? Your family's? You know, your wife and daughter?"

His mouth dropped open. "Let me explain."

"Are you married?" Gracie wanted to be sure what her father said was true. "I'm asking you to tell me the truth. No lies, just one word. Yes or no?"

When he didn't answer, she stood up. She was trying her best not to cry, but that wasn't possible.

"Well, I guess I got my answer." Her eyes filled with tears. "You broke my heart. You lied to me. I feel like a fool."

Jack held onto her hand as if for dear life. "Please don't leave. I love you."

"Great. How were you going to manage having two wives?"

"Please sit down. We can talk about this. It's complicated."

"No it isn't," Gracie said on her way out of the bistro. "I have a flight to catch."

Chapter Five

Gracie got to the airport late and ran like hell to the gate. She called out to the attendant, "Please wait! I have to be on that flight."

"It's not possible." The flight attendant shook her head. "Sorry, Miss."

A feeling of desperation came over her. Gracie had to get on the plane. She began to cry, getting louder as the seconds passed.

"Fine, let me see what I can do," the attendant finally said in an irritated voice. "Can I have your ticket?" She looked it over. "It's first class."

Gracie nodded. "It is. Please—"

"What about your bags?"

"I just have this bag. I'm into minimal traveling. I need to get back to the States. I can't stay here tonight." Her anxiety took over. "Please see what you can do."

The attendant left for a minute. When she came back, she nodded for Gracie. "Come with me." She hurriedly moved her along. "It's okay. You're lucky it's a first-class ticket; those are the only seats available."

Gracie cautiously sat down. She had almost forgotten how much she hated flying, which explained why she forgot her Dramamine. She was anxious to get home and forget about the mess she created.

A few passengers gave her a look as she took her seat, but she smiled, trying to ease the tension. She didn't need enemies on a long flight. After situating herself, she laid her head back, but her memories kept her from sleeping. She cried a little, then fell asleep for just a few minutes during takeoff. When the seatbelt sign turned off, she relaxed, grateful to be on her way home.

She didn't want to be the woman who fell in love in Paris and came back with a broken heart. She had a sinking feeling about what her life might look like when she returned to a job she didn't want, without the man she was going to spend the rest of her life with.

While she was deep in thought, the flight attendant tapped her shoulder. "We'll be serving a light snack soon. Here's the menu. I'll be right back to take your order."

"I'm fine. Don't think I'll be eating. I think I'll sleep."

"If you decide you want something, just let me know."

Gracie smiled, glad that her father had booked her a first-class ticket. As the attendant moved on, she finally closed her eyes and slept.

She woke up in a panic when she heard the captain speaking to all the passengers over the loudspeaker. "I know you're all counting on a nonstop flight, but we're diverting to Kennedy Airport. The entire area in our path is going to be extremely rough, and Chicago O'Hare has closed until tomorrow evening at the earliest. We are very sorry for the inconvenience. We'll be back with more information as we receive it."

Gracie was scared. She was alone, depressed, and isolated. She hated flying in any situation, but there was no other way to get home. She noticed other passengers who were up and about going back to their seats as the seatbelt warning returned.

Once again, the voice over the loudspeaker interrupted. "The snowstorm is already in our path, and we're facing some turbulence from heavy rain and lightning. Please return to your seats and fasten your seatbelts. We'll keep you posted as things progress."

Gracie was breathing in and out trying to calm herself, but it wasn't working. She tried to wipe away the tears that were streaming down her face. She was whispering to herself, "Please dear G-d, just get me home."

Across the aisle, a young man close to her age was watching her, deciding if he should say anything. He thought she might get angry if he did, so he just sat there until she made eye contact.

"Can I ask a favor?" she anxiously asked.

"Sure. What can I do for you?"

"Would you mind sitting next to me? I'm so scared I could scream."

He smiled. "Of course. I doubt the other passengers would be happy to hear screaming. Don't you think? It's never good to hear someone screaming on an airplane."

"True." Her teeth were chattering as her level of fear was rising. "You're right. I can do this." She closed her eyes and gripped the seat as if she was getting ready for a crash landing.

The young man quickly unlocked his seatbelt and sat down next to her. After buckling up, he reached for her hand. "Hey, no worries. I'm here for you."

Gracie took a relaxing breath. "Thanks. You have no idea how much I appreciate this. By the way, my name is Gracie Maxwell. In case I die, you can tell them who I was."

"And I'm Leo Tucker. In case I die, you can tell them who I was. And if we both die, I'll see you in heaven."

Gracie barely looked at him. "That's not exactly reassuring."

The same flight attendant returned to check on them. "You guys okay?"

"You tell me," Gracie answered.

"I have to go back to my seat, but just watch me," the attendant said. "If I'm smiling at you, we're good. If I don't smile, we're not."

"And that's supposed to make me feel better?" Gracie called back to her.

"Hon, that's all I've got. We'll be fine."

Leo looked at Gracie and let her squeeze his hand. "I've got this."

"Okay. I believe you." She didn't.

The more turbulent the ride got, the harder Gracie squeezed. And the more she squeezed, the more this whole scene seemed familiar to Leo. He thought maybe he wrote it in one of his books. There he was, Leo Tucker, holding the hand of one of the most beautiful women he had ever seen…and then he realized who she was.

They were now holding hands, and Gracie hanging on tight. Leo didn't really know how else to comfort her, so he started to recite a poem, thinking it might calm her down.

Gracie stopped him. "Can we talk instead of the poem?"

"Don't you like poetry?"

"I love poetry. But right now, it would be better if we could talk. What's your favorite color?"

"Yellow. And yours?"

"I love red. But then again, I also love pink and purple. Oh, and I forgot black; it goes with everything. And in Paris they have the most unusual way of dressing. It's fun and carefree. I just loved going into some of the small shops."

By this time, Leo knew he had taken her mind off the rough flight ahead. "So. What's your favorite food?"

She smiled. "Chicago pizza. Lou Malnati's. That cheese is so good. And just for the record, I know what you're doing, and it's working. What about you?"

"I love hot dogs with relish and lots of mustard. That sounds damn good right about now."

"I haven't had a hot dog in years, but it does sound great. My father loves hot dogs. That's his favorite food. If we get out of this alive, I might ask him to take me for one."

"No worries. I got this. We will get out of this alive."

"Oh, you know someone up there?"

Leo smiled. "If I did, would I be on this flight?"

The turbulence had eased up but, just as the attendants were about to unbuckle their seatbelts, it suddenly returned and didn't stop for several minutes. Gracie's tears came streaming down her cheeks, and they weren't stopping anytime soon. Leo was trying to help by blotting the tears with a tissue. It wasn't working well, but it was the best option he had.

By this time, Leo actually thought they might be going down. He didn't know what to do. Gracie needed him, so he quickly turned on help mode and held her tight. It was nice to be needed. Until that moment, he didn't realize how much he missed having that feeling of being close to someone. Gracie squeezed his hand.

"Pretty good grip you've got there," Leo said, trying to make light of the situation.

"Yeah, maybe so. I used to play ball with my dad. What about you?"

"Nope. My dad died when I was pretty young."

"So sorry."

Once again, the captain made an announcement. "Thank you all for your cooperation and patience. We should be out of the woods now, so sit back and relax."

"Great news," Gracie said, taking in several breaths.

"We'll be landing at John F. Kennedy Airport very soon. We thought we might be able to sneak into O'Hare before the shutdown, but that isn't going to be possible. We will have a shuttle to a hotel, and will have more details about baggage and connecting flights once you check in."

Gracie let her head rest on the seat after sitting up like a soldier during the entire stretch of panic and uncertainty. "Leo, can you stay with me for the rest of the flight?"

"Sure." Minutes later, they both fell asleep.

They both woke up when the captain announced, "Please return to your seats and fasten your seatbelts. We'll be landing soon."

Gracie looked at Leo and smiled. "Well, at least we're almost on the ground."

Leo took a breath. "Yes, we are."

"Can I say something before we go any further?" Gracie asked, finally letting go of his hand.

"Sure, anything."

"Well, before things get too confusing as we leave, I need to say something. I'm not really one to do this but—"

"This sounds serious."

"It is for me. I really want to thank you for getting me through this crisis. I've never liked flying, and without you I'm pretty sure I would have made a fool of myself. I sometimes get scared shitless. My upbringing. Overbearing parents and all."

"No problem. I was happy to be there for you."

"Your wife's lucky to have a guy like you in her corner."

"I'm not married."

"But you're wearing a wedding band."

He smiled. "That was my father's. Every time I fly, I wear it for good luck." It was also the one he wore when he married Ellie.

"So, you're superstitious?"

"I wish I wasn't, but I feel like I was born this way. As long as I can remember, I never stepped on cracks or sneezed without pulling my ear. If a salt shaker tips over, I'm dead meat. I immediately throw some salt over my shoulder. What about you?"

"No. Never thought about it much." Then it hit her. "Did we ever meet before?"

Leo didn't answer.

Gracie was smiling. "We did, didn't we? You were the chatterbox on my flight to Paris."

"Chatterbox? Me?"

"Oh sorry. That just slipped out." Gracie was embarrassed, especially after how nice he was to her.

"Yep, that was me."

"I don't know what it is, but you have a way of calming me. Maybe it's your voice. And, if I might add, that's not an easy job; I'm a little high strung. Maybe more than just a little."

"You were scared."

"You might say that."

"I was scared too," Leo added. "Can I ask you a question?"

"Shoot."

"What gave me away?"

"You're superstitious. I remember that flight to Paris. You were talking so much I didn't throw up."

He laughed. "I had forgotten that part."

"Well, it's been a couple of years."

"Yes it has, and I'm sure a lot has happened to both of us."

Gracie didn't want to get into any long discussion about herself, so she just edited it down. "Let's put it this way: it's been a great learning experience. Some good, some bad. What about you?"

"Very good and very bad." He didn't choose to elaborate.

Gracie was taken aback. "Oh, so sorry."

"Me too," Leo said. As he turned away, Gracie noticed his eyes tear up.

"You know, I just thought of something. Were you at the Fontaine des Mers earlier today?"

"As a matter of fact, I was. Why?"

"You didn't happen to be the guy who caused all the commotion while throwing coins in the fountain?"

"I was. I threw a couple coins in and made a wish."

"What did you wish for?" she asked.

"If you tell someone your wish, it won't come true."

"There you go. Another superstition."

They both laughed.

Chapter Six

Once they got to the hotel, Leo and Gracie were separated by all the chaos. Luckily, her bag was pretty light. She had thrown away most of her things, wanting nothing to do with memories that belonged to her life with Jack. One thing she didn't have to worry about was buying clothes. There were plenty of stores in Chicago.

Her room was a lot nicer than she'd expected, but she really didn't care what it looked like. Her plan was to go downstairs, get something to eat, and then take a long bubble bath. If she didn't fall asleep right away, she would catch up on some of her favorite shows.

The only thing available at the hotel, as far as eating was concerned, was a bar that served food. It was quite busy and she didn't want to wait for a table, so she sat at the bar. She always loved to people watch, but she felt lonely as she looked around at all the diners. She used to have a plan, and now she had none.

As she drank her glass of wine, Gracie couldn't help but think about her future. She really didn't want to work for her father, but she was out of money. She had grown to love photography while she was in Paris, and had actually become quite good at it. She hadn't mentioned that to Samuel; she worried he would laugh and wonder where she came up with yet another idea about what she could do with her life. If she was being honest, she couldn't blame him.

After she finished her wine and a small salad, she took out a pad of paper and began to write down all the signs about Jack that she obviously missed. Then, out of the corner of her eye, she spotted Leo. She happily waved him over, then closed her notebook and threw it in her bag.

He smiled and walked over quickly. "I was looking for you."

She seemed surprised. "I thought of looking for you too, but I thought you might be tired. That was some flight."

"Can I sit?"

"Please do. I've never liked dining alone."

"I'm not sure we'll even be leaving tomorrow. My grandmother said they expect fifteen to twenty inches. It's not looking good, but Chicago works fast when clearing the streets, especially the airport."

"Are you close with your grandmother?"

"Very close. We live together."

"Really? That must be nice. I never knew my grandparents. I always wished I had them."

"She took care of me when I was young, and now I take care of her. She really doesn't need my help. She's quite self-sufficient, but I enjoy her company. Not to mention she's a spectacular cook and a phenomenal baker."

Gracie had never met anyone like Leo. He was so kind, while most of the men she had known were rough around the edges.

"Wine?" she asked, as she motioned for the server to bring her another glass.

He nodded in thanks. "Okay. I'll have whatever you're having." He noticed her notepad sticking out of her bag. "What have you got there?"

"Oh, just doodling."

"You don't seem like a doodler."

"Is there a look for a doodler?" She smiled, striking a pose.

Leo laughed. It felt good to laugh. "Now that we're safely on the ground, tell me about yourself." He found her captivating — not only was she beautiful, but she had a fascinating sense of style. He loved her look.

"Nothing to tell. I'm from Chicago and I'm very broke. I left Paris to come back home to live with my very rich father." Then she laughed. It wasn't the whole truth, but what was she going to say? *I gave my heart to a man I loved, and found out after two years of commitment that he was married with a child. How dumb am I?*

The wine suddenly hit her. She rarely finished a glass of wine and, well into her second glass, she realized she was getting drunk.

"If you have a rich father, he can help you out. That's good, right?"

"It's good and bad." Gracie took a couple more sips. She had no cares and was in the moment. "Oh, I forgot to mention. I did modeling and photography."

"That's a big something to be a by-the-way comment."

"Maybe so." She hoisted herself up on the barstool, and briefly lost her balance.

As Leo carefully lifted her up, Gracie forgot herself and almost kissed him. It caught him off guard.

"Ooops, sorry," she said.

"So, Gracie, what shall we do now?"

"I think I should go upstairs and sleep this off. I'm not feeling all that great."

"How about going for a walk?"

"I don't think so. This has been a long day."

"Come on. It's cold but beautiful."

"Okay, I'm in," she answered, wondering why she said yes.

"I think we need to get our coats," Leo said. "Meet me in the lobby in a few minutes?"

"Sounds good. Not planning on freezing to death."

They took the elevator together, and soon realized they were on the same floor.

"Where's your room, Leo Tucker?"

"Right here."

"Mine is next door."

"Convenient, don't you think?"

"Maybe others from the plane are on this floor," Gracie said as she struggled to get the card in the slot to open the door.

"Let me help you," Leo said as he gently took the keycard.

"I actually don't think I would recognize any of them."

"Me either," Leo admitted. He had been looking at Gracie and no one else.

"I think I had too many glasses of wine, especially since I haven't had much in the way of food. Two feels like ten."

"I'll watch you so nothing happens."

"Thanks so much. Do you always pay such close attention to people you don't really know?"

"I feel like I know you."

"Well, sadly you don't. I'm not sure I know me," Gracie added, not pleased with herself.

After she got her coat, Leo put his arm around her to make sure she didn't fall. He was surprised in himself. He felt like a teenager when he looked at her.

"Maybe we shouldn't go." Leo was trying not to push.

"No, let's go."

***

As soon as the air hit Gracie's face, she became lightheaded. She almost fell over again, but Leo caught her.

"Maybe we should go back inside." Leo was thinking about her welfare.

"No, I'm fine. I think a little fresh air will help."

"Are you sure? We can go back in. I think they have a coffee bar in the lobby."

"No, let's stay outside."

"Whatever the lady wants." He smiled easily.

Gracie felt like she was having an out-of-body experience. Something she had never felt before. It was either that or too much wine.

She looked into Leo's calming eyes and kissed him once. Then she kissed him again. It shocked her, but she didn't care. She was at peace, or drunk — or both. It somehow felt right, but he was a stranger. She read books about women who had these kinds of unexpected kisses that meant nothing, but she never imagined herself doing such a thing.

Leo was hesitant to kiss her, but he did. He immediately felt guilty. He couldn't bring Ellie back no matter what he did, and he knew he had to live again, but somehow he put up a roadblock every time he did something that reminded him of his love.

"I'm sorry, Gracie. I shouldn't have done that."

Gracie kissed him again, with more feeling than before. "You have the softest lips I've ever kissed. Don't apologize. You're a good guy."

"I try to be."

Then, without warning, Gracie threw up. Leo carefully took her hand and helped her sit down on a bench outside the hotel.

"Stay here," he said. "I'll be right back."

She was shivering and everything seemed a little fuzzy. For a moment, she almost forgot she was in New York. She took a few deep breaths and closed her eyes. She started to get up, but everything around her seemed to be spinning. She sat back down, reminding herself that Leo said he'd be right back.

Leo ran into a small grocery store nearby and grabbed some paper towels and wipes. He threw a twenty by the cash register. "This should cover it," he said as he rushed out.

When he returned, Gracie was crying.

"Everything will be fine," Leo said, not knowing what had her so down.

"Will it?"

"Yes. You have to believe in yourself and the power we have inside us to overcome almost anything."

"Sounds like you've been to this place."

"Does it feel like no return?"

"It sure does," Gracie said as she sat there, too cold to move but too queasy to stay.

Leo continued. "Somehow you come back to life. You don't know how you did it, but without warning you're back." Gracie realized he was talking about his own experience. After that, she didn't remember much more.

Leo gently moved Gracie's bangs away from her face so he could see her eyes. "You will feel again. It might not seem like it, but the old you will be back. You'll know it."

"What if I don't want to be the old me? What if I don't like her?"

"Then you'll change. Life has a way of letting us rebuild what we have lost. Just give yourself some time." He wished he actually believed his own words.

"You sound so smart."

"Believe me, I'm not." He knew she probably wouldn't remember anything, so he decided not to elaborate. He was still careful about opening up to anyone.

As Leo gently wiped Gracie's face, tears fell from his eyes. He was reminded of his wife and how he was there for every session of chemotherapy. Cleaning her up was something he did quite often during those sessions. They were tough, but Ellie fought like hell to stay alive until she couldn't. After more sessions than he cared to remember, Ellie made a decision to stop. A few weeks later, she was gone. As devastated as Leo was, it was her choice.

By the time Ellie was diagnosed with breast cancer, it had spread. They tried everything — clinics, hospitals, doctors in different countries — but nothing worked. They fought the battle together. After her death, Leo promised himself he would never open up to anyone again. The pain of losing her was too crushing.

He snapped himself out of his own trauma, realizing Gracie needed to go back to the hotel.

"Let's go."

"Go where?"

"Back to your room."

When they got back, Gracie took off her clothes and Leo turned away. When she was done, Leo gently laid her on the bed and took off her boots. She looked so sweet. He could tell she had been through something very painful. He knew that she wouldn't remember anything after he left the room, but he would.

In the morning, all the passengers received messages saying that O'Hare had opened and it was safe to leave. Leo knocked on Gracie's door. When she didn't answer, he assumed she was downstairs checking out and he would see her there, but when he got to the lobby she wasn't anywhere to be found. He hoped they would finish their conversation and say their goodbyes at the airport. He would ask for her number, and hopefully she would say yes to seeing him. When she didn't show up at the airport, he was disappointed. But he understood. It was probably for the best.

Chapter Seven

On the flight home, Leo couldn't stop thinking about Gracie. He hadn't expected to have any thoughts about anyone other than Ellie for the rest of his life, so the interruption was welcome. However, if Gracie hadn't even said goodbye or left him a message, she probably had no intention of ever seeing him again.

He really didn't know if it was just one of those things that happened to two strangers in an unusually scary incident. He thought if he ever had a chance to be with her again, he would show her the difference between a guy who cared and a guy who didn't. Had she been on the flight home, he would have made the effort to get her number. But he never found her.

Once the plane touched down in Chicago, he was thankful to be home. As soon as the key was in the door, he had a welcome committee: his grandmother and Bernie.

Samuel was right about taking some time away — and about coming home to a dog. Whatever the reason, it worked. He felt better about everything.

It was also great to smell the aroma of blueberries that filled the house. His grandmother had made a batch of scones for him. He loved them, and she was always happy to bake them. She knew her grandson better than anyone ever could. Because, unlike his mother, she was there for him.

"Wow, I missed these," Leo said as he bit into one. "These are especially great today. How is it you always know exactly what I need?"

"Because you're my favorite grandson."

"I'm your only one."

They both laughed.

"Listen, honey. You know I'm always in your corner. Tell me all the details. Did you meet anyone there? Paris is the place where romance begins."

"No beginning this time. Sorry, Nana."

"I think it's time for you to start looking around for someone to spend the rest of your life with. Ellie was wonderful, but you're young. It's not good to be alone."

"I'm not alone. I have you."

"I'm flattered, but you know what I mean."

"I want to meet someone, but—"

"No buts. Just think about it."

Leo nodded, knowing that would make her happy. He was deciding if he should tell his grandmother about Gracie, even though he really had nothing to say other than she was beautiful and smart. And he did want to see her again. He had no idea where she lived or anything else about her, other than she was unhappy.

After pouring cups of coffee for the two of them, his grandmother took a seat right in front of him so she could see his eyes. That was always her barometer of his happiness. Sometimes it was like pulling teeth, but she had patience and she knew he would eventually tell her what was on his mind. She had a tendency to push the envelope just a little when the time was right. "So, what are you keeping from me? I know there's something, so let's have it. And don't tell me nothing."

"Well, I enjoyed Paris. It was beautiful and I watched people in love. Some of the nights I spent crying because I missed Ellie so much."

Lilly hated seeing her grandson so sad. She grabbed his hand and held onto it with a tight, loving squeeze. "Honey, if I could take away the pain I would."

"I know. I'm okay, really I am. Glad to be home."

"You'll find someone. You're a great catch."

"What else would you say? I'm your grandson."

"You seem calmer and a bit more focused. Did you meet someone in Paris?"

"Nope. We met on the plane going home. She was a basket case. It was a pretty bad flight."

"You're not exactly the best flyer."

"Compared to her I was a champ."

"That's the best time to meet someone. Did she like you too?"

"I don't think so. At least not in that way."

"How do you know that?"

"I'm not her type."

"How did you leave it?"

"We didn't. She wasn't on the flight coming back from New York."

"Call her anyway."

"I can't. We never exchanged numbers."

"So, try to find her."

"I don't think so. She could have said goodbye, but she didn't. Something happened to her in Paris and she didn't say what. We were two strangers in a tough situation. Nothing more, but there was something about her." His smile indicated a spark.

"Something is not nothing. I'm just glad you went and gave yourself the time to relax and unwind. You've been having a very difficult time yourself. Sounds like you could help each other."

"We didn't talk about our stories. We just knew each of us had one."

"Maybe you should have. "

"No, it wasn't appropriate."

"Where's your romantic side?"

"I don't think I have one anymore. My characters do, but I don't."

"Says the greatest romance writer ever."

"Not exactly."

"Would I lie?" She laughed.

"Meanwhile, how are you and Bernie getting along?"

"It's great to have him in the house. He keeps me company. He's a keeper."

"On that note, I'd better go write. Samuel only has so much patience, no matter how much he likes me. Bernie, let's go finish this book." Leo was surprised when Bernie followed him into the office, but he was glad he did.

In no time at all, Leo was writing faster than usual and his thoughts were clear. He began to feel as if he could finish the book and make Samuel a happy man. He was surprised by how easily the words were coming. He was starting to feel like the old Leo was coming back. Maybe going to Paris really had helped.

For the next week, he wrote like a madman. But when he was close to finishing, he got stuck. He still seemed to be missing the feelings he used to have that made his stories ring true. He felt something was off. *He* was off.

He just couldn't write the ending when he knew damn well that his story was not up to par. The last thing he wanted to do was disappoint his readers; after all, they were his priority.

From the day he met Ellie, she was his entire world. He wrote stories before he met her, but she inspired his writing to become beautiful prose. Ellie had always been there to talk when he needed help. She was the consoling reality who inspired his beautiful, romantic fiction.

But the secret he was keeping bothered him. His fans never knew that Nicole Forrester was really Leo Tucker. There were so many times over the last few years that he wanted to reveal himself, but he didn't. Samuel's favorite saying was "if it's not broken, don't fix it." So, for the time being, the publishing house got what it wanted.

While Leo admitted going to Paris had been good for him, he was surprised he was still thinking of Gracie. He didn't know much about her, but he couldn't get her off his mind. She was the first person he thought of when he woke up in the morning, and the last person he thought about before he closed his eyes at night. It used to be Ellie, and that somehow made his new feelings feel disrespectful. But Gracie seemed to light up his life without knowing it.

Chapter Eight

For the first few weeks after her return from Paris, Gracie woke up, had breakfast, watched TV, and waited for lunch. Her thoughts were on her bad choices in men. She had decided she would give them up for good. That was the only way she could assure herself she wouldn't allow anyone in to hurt her.

Ava set down her usual — a grilled-cheese sandwich with tomato and a small bowl of tomato soup. "Gracie, it's time."

"What does that mean?"

Ava sat down next to her, took the remote, and shut off the TV. "Your mother called and wants to speak to you when you're done."

"I'm not ready. And where is she anyway?"

"Italy."

"That's good. Maybe she'll meet a charming gigolo like I did."

"She went there to write. You know your mother."

"Actually, Ava, I don't."

"Listen, get dressed. We're going for a hair appointment and a manicure."

"Maybe tomorrow. I look okay."

Ava put the remote in her sweater pocket and reached for Gracie's hands. "Come on. I'll drive."

"Like you did when I was five."

Ava handed her a mirror. "Take a look."

Gracie reluctantly looked at herself. "Oh my. I look like something the cat dragged in."

"Right, so get dressed."

Gracie got up and went upstairs. "I'll be down in a few minutes."

Ava walked back into the kitchen and called Samuel. "She's going."

***

After her day of beauty, Gracie reluctantly went to the *Daily Times* newspaper downtown. Her new job was not exactly where she thought she belonged. Before she left for Paris, she was prepared to work with her father, but everything changed when she decided to stay in Paris. He gave the editor job to Nicholas Sinclair, who seemed to be on track to eventually become CEO.

If Gracie had her way, she didn't want to be anywhere near him, but it wasn't her decision. Nicholas was a good journalist but a little raw around the edges — just like her father. He was able to get people to do the impossible. Gracie always had her own mind, and wasn't as pliable as her father would have liked. People had come to know her as confident, but she wasn't sure she was that person anymore. Time would tell.

Patience was not one of Gracie's top qualities. She knew Nicholas was the man her father preferred for the time being, even though she knew she could do his job with her eyes closed. When she was a little girl, she used to sit at her father's desk and imagine herself as the boss. That was a far cry from where she stood now.

The only job available to her when she came back was one she wouldn't wish on her worst enemy. She was the voice of "Dear Hannah." Giving advice to unhappy, disappointed lovers was definitely not on her list of things she wanted to do. Especially now that she was one of them.

She hoped her father would see the light and stop punishing her for leaving, but she admitted jumping ship to stay in Paris now seemed childish. Back then, she thought she was on top of the world; now, she didn't know who she was, but she would keep that to herself. Falling in love with a married man and not knowing it? How stupid. She behaved like a foolish schoolgirl.

Just like her changing her name. She didn't want anyone to know her father was Samuel Warrington, so she always used her mother's maiden name. He wasn't happy about that either, but she did it anyway. She could quit, but she wasn't stupid. With declining sales and the downside of advertising, other newspapers weren't rushing to hire her. Her father's media dynasty was on top as always, probably because he ran a tight ship.

Like it or not, she had no choice but to try to change her course by talking with Nicholas. She hated having a history with him. Before she left for Paris, Nicholas was writing an article for one of Samuel's magazines and she was doing research for the story. At that time, Gracie's career was all about journalism and staying on course after college.

They had never worked together before, but Gracie was excited about the challenge as much as the opportunity. One thing about her father — he may not have said it, but she wouldn't be doing any assignment he didn't think she was up to. Samuel Warrington knew everything that was going on at his company at all times, and no one could argue that.

When Gracie was first introduced to Nicholas, it was hard to get past his looks. He had a movie-star quality, handsome and sexy. What a combo. His profile spoke of power. She immediately developed feelings for him. She knew she had to be cautious with her attraction to him because rumors were always flying around the office about his affairs. He had gone from one assistant to another, and through all the women in the secretarial pool. He was a busy guy, especially when it came to extracurricular activities.

Gracie had dinner with him several times, but never alone; one time her father joined them. Then Gracie made the mistake of accepting an invitation for a short business trip. She was young and eager, and he was smart and well established. It was all on the up and up, but their first dinner at a small but elegant resort in Lake Geneva, Wisconsin, turned into more than an assignment.

She was already well aware of his charm when Nicholas knocked on her door right before their dinner engagement. There he was, one of the finest-looking guys she had ever known, standing before her holding one red rose. That's when she knew it would be more than just dinner.

His smile caught her completely off guard, but she could tell he knew she was weakening. Her eyes were always very expressive, and he knew she was interested but trying to seem reserved. He studied her for a moment. "How about one dance for the road?"

"I don't think that would be a good idea."

"I do," he said as he moved toward her and into her room. She moved back and took a deep breath, deciding if she should push back or stay in the moment. "From the minute your father introduced me to you, I've wanted to do this." He took her in his arms and passionately kissed her. She wanted to kiss him back with the same passion, but she stopped herself.

"Wait. Nicholas, we can't do this."

"Why not? We're adults. Shouldn't we be able to kiss whoever we want?"

"We're working together."

"So what? We can still work together."

"This is going to end badly."

"Why are you saying that? You don't know that will happen. Maybe we'll get married, have kids, and live happily ever after."

"Does that line work?" Gracie asked as she stopped herself from kissing him.

"Every time." He kissed her again, but this time she kissed him back. "You know you take my breath away."

"I've never taken anyone's breath away," she whispered in his ear

"Well, you have now."

"You're not serious. We don't really know each other."

"We know enough."

He inched his way toward the bed, holding her as if they were dancing. "We don't need music."

Gracie didn't like feeling vulnerable, but she knew she was weakening. Nicholas brought that out in her. She knew that the minute they met. She didn't like him, but she wanted to kiss him. And now the only thing she could think of was to just do what came naturally.

There was one kiss, and then another and another. For a moment it felt right, and after that she didn't care. He was so passionate and good looking; she felt as if she was dreaming. But when they woke up next to each other in the morning, she was disappointed in herself.

"This can't happen again," she said as she woke him up.

"Why not? I thought we were good together. If you remember, we—"

Gracie waved her hands in front of his face. "Stop stop stop. There's no we. We can't do this and you know it."

"Gracie, we didn't do anything wrong."

"Yes we did."

"By whose standards?"

"Mine. For G-d's sake. My father would be devastated."

"He doesn't have to know."

"He'll know. Samuel Warrington knows everything that happens, whether you think so or not. We work together and he won't get rid of me. He's my father."

"You're saying he'll get of rid of me?"

"Exactly. He loves you, and he knows you have potential for great things. I've heard him talk about you."

"What about you? Don't you think we could be good together?"

"If you were someone else, it might be possible. But you have women falling over for you. I'm not good at sharing."

"No one's like you. It could be different with you."

"Does that line ever work?"

"Yes, actually it does."

She laughed. "You think I'm going to believe that Nicholas Sinclair is going to be a one-woman man?"

"That does sound strange. Maybe you're right. What should we do? You know I really like you. I was hoping for more than just a one-night stand."

"I'm sure you were. Does that have to do with me, or the fact that I'm the boss's daughter?"

"That's a low blow."

"So, is it true?"

Nicholas didn't answer; he just kissed her in a delightful, romantic way. She found him hard to resist, but she decided it would be best to leave. That was the realistic side of her. The wilder side usually won, but not this time. It was difficult, but for the best. She packed her bags, rented a car, and left Lake Geneva.

She couldn't stay with him because, if she did, she would never want to leave. Right then and there, she decided she was never going to get involved with someone she worked with, which was why she applied for the modeling job in Paris. She could have used a recommendation from Nicholas, but she decided to try it on her own, and the rest was history. She got the job. She was speechless. If she was honest with herself, she was a little heartbroken when Nicholas wished her goodbye and good luck. Their one-night stand was just that, one romantic night with a charming guy.

***

A few years later, she was right back where she started, working with Nicholas Sinclair. And he had the job she would have had if she'd stayed.

Nicholas was charming as always, and even better looking than he was before she left, if that was even possible. This time around she enjoyed getting under his skin; it was amusing. He was a bit more stressed than she remembered, but now he was the editor of several of her father's magazines.

That was how she wound up being the voice of "Dear Hannah." As she sat there in her small, closet-like office, she pretended to enjoy her job — which was difficult at best.

She was reading another email from an unhappy woman. Her answer was supposed to help, and she hated giving advice — especially since her own track record wasn't fabulous. She reread what she had written, then printed it out and reread it again. It was horrible. It was almost as if someone else wrote it. Everything she had written was boring. It was a stock answer, and a bad one.

Gracie straightened her leather skirt and paraded down the hall to Nicholas's office. Instead of knocking on his door or having his receptionist announce her, she burst into his office and stood directly in front of him with her arms folded.

"I'm ready to move on to a position that would be more suited to my talents."

"Hello to you too, Gracie dear."

"Remember when I asked you not to refer to me as 'dear?'"

"Yes, actually I do."

"Great. Then don't."

Nicholas loved when she got mad. She was even more beautiful and sexy when she was angry. "So, what brings you here, Miss Sunshine? Time for a little temper tantrum? It's been a few weeks." He laughed.

"This is no time to laugh. I can't possibly sit around all day and answer these stupid 'Dear Hannah' letters. I want something I'm more suited for."

"What would that be?"

"Your job."

Nicholas laughed again, which really made her angry.

"What? Don't you think I can do it?"

Nichols decided it would be best not to answer if he ever expected to get anywhere with her. He knew she didn't like him, but that made him want her even more.

"Well, I guess now that I've said what needed to be said, I should go, because it's never going to happen. I just wanted to get it off my chest."

"What makes you think I won't give you anything else to do?"

"Just because you're you and you like to be one up on me."

"How do you know that?" Nicholas asked as he offered her a seat.

"I don't want to sit."

"Fine. You look more beautiful that way."

"Nick, don't go there."

"I'm not going anywhere with that. I'm just trying to be nice."

"Well, well, well. You haven't changed one bit."

Nicholas smiled. "Have you?"

"I most certainly have. I'm more assertive."

He laughed. "I didn't think that was possible. Anyway, your career is out of my hands. Your father wants it that way. Ask him for another assignment."

"Does he always have to get what he wants?"

"You know the answer to that. Your father is a powerful man with his own ideas. I just work here."

"You're kidding, right? You do more than just work here." Gracie thought for a second or two before giving Nicholas a pitch. "If you ask him, he might see the light. Tell him I'm ready."

"Honey, he's already seen the light. It's called a spotlight show, with you as the host of your own podcast. I just hadn't figured out how to ask you yet."

"What are you talking about?"

"A podcast. You know, a broadcast. Like radio."

"I know what a podcast is. I just don't want to do one."

"They'll love you."

"No, they won't. They don't know anything about me. I'll be boring with nothing to say."

"Oh, that's a laugh. You walked into this office a few minutes ago and you haven't stopped talking."

"That's different."

"It will bring in so much revenue."

"Was this really my father's idea? Or is this your pitch so I fail?"

"It was his idea, trust me. All his."

"And you said no, right?"

"I said I would ask you."

"Well, you did, and I said no."

"Gracie, can you be reasonable for just a minute? Everything is changing. I think you can be good at this."

"How in the world do you think that could even be a possibility?"

"Because you're smart and you have enough of an edge that makes you unique."

"I don't even like to talk to you that much, let alone talking to strangers."

"You're really good at giving advice. No one would guess you—"

"Don't even finish that. You and I both know relationships aren't my specialty. I'm sure my father filled you in."

"Not really. I have my own theory."

"And what is that?"

"Let's not go into that. I may have had a few bad ones but…never mind. You're not a psychiatrist."

"True." Gracie assumed he was thinking about his own personal failures, and how he never got past the sex in his relationships. A deep conversation for him was asking a woman if she'd be staying for breakfast.

He smiled as he got back to work. "Anything else I can do for you? If not, I have to finish this report."

"No. But just for the record, I'm not the right one for a podcast."

"Maybe we can discuss it at dinner."

Gracie laughed. "You're kidding, right?"

"We can talk about old times."

"Not happening. I'm not your type."

"Your mother thinks I'm your type."

"At this point in my life, my mother would think a frog is my type. She just wants grandchildren."

"If you play your cards right, I can give her what she wants."

"Did my mother say something to you?"

"Nothing other than she wanted to fix us up."

"When was that?"

"Since the first day I met her. I just wish you would say yes."

"Not going to happen. No date, no dinner, and definitely no sex."

"I just thought dinner might be nice."

"No, it wouldn't. I don't like you."

Nicholas nodded. "I figured that. Is there more?"

"Yes, there's more. Second reason: I don't like you."

"Go on, seems like you have more coming."

"The third reason is I really, really don't like you."

"Maybe we can talk about a plan for you to work with me."

"Now that's funny," Gracie said. "I was thinking you could possibly work for me."

Nicholas laughed. "You never stop, do you?"

"Never."

As persistent as he was, she wasn't going to give one inch. She loved shooting down his ego. She'd missed that.

Every time she was in a meeting with him or he was giving her direction, she couldn't help but wonder what might have happened if she had stayed. Would they now be a team? Or friends? Or the couple that was and got divorced?

There was no turning back for her. If she was to rate him, it would be an eleven out of ten in looks, but maybe a three for personality. He was far too aggressive for her taste, but she did have an eye for a hard-nosed man every now and then.

Nicholas sat there, trying not to get up and give her a kiss. She was more beautiful than ever. He thought it might be nice to get closer to the boss, which was why he'd asked her to dinner years ago. She left for

Paris thinking he was going to use her, but he proved himself without her around.

"Nicholas, what on Earth are you thinking about? You seem a million miles away. Did you hear what I just said?"

"Of course." He was lying.

"Nicholas, one question. Doesn't it bother you that I don't like you?"

"A lot of people don't like me."

She finally smiled. "I can see why my father chose you over me."

"Enough about me. Forget dinner, forget about a drink. Let's just do what we need to do to take you up a notch."

"I don't think so. I never listen to podcasts, and certainly don't think that's for me."

"Since you took over 'Dear Hannah,' we've doubled our traffic."

"Isn't my father rich enough? Why a podcast?"

"That's not for me to answer. Ask your father. And maybe you'd better take a look at your shoes and bag before telling him you don't care about money."

"Very funny. Look who's talking. I bet your Armani suit and Gucci loafers cost twice as much."

When he didn't answer, she knew she had made her point. She loved doing that to him.

"Just sleep on it," Nicholas said as she was about to walk out the door. He had a huge grin on his face. He did wish she would sleep with him again.

She smiled back at him. "You wish. Why don't you sleep on it? And when you wake up, please talk to my father and tell him there's no way."

She pranced out, wiggling her derrière while Nicholas sat there enjoying the view. He reminded himself how he missed her cute tantrums. She was still the same headstrong Gracie.

Nicholas thought again about joining the Warrington family, especially now that he remembered his chemistry with Gracie. Samuel Warrington was an icon, and just working with him gave Nicholas every opportunity — but being the boss's son-in-law would work seamlessly in his continuation up the ladder.

Even though he had a tremendous amount of work to do, he couldn't help but think about the conversation he'd had with Gracie's mother right before Gracie came back.

"Guess who's coming home?" Francine had said as she walked into his office looking picture perfect. Her expensive red pumps and white leather suit made her look ten years younger — though if she *had* been ten years younger, Nicholas would have invited her for a drink and let the chips fall where they may.

"Francine, how nice to see you. What brings you here?"

"My daughter."

"Tell me more."

"She dumped her lover."

"You're kidding. I thought it was the perfect relationship. She's been gone for almost two years."

"Does that bother you?"

"No. Why would I care either way?"

"Because the mere mention of her name caught you off guard, and Nicholas Sinclair doesn't get caught off guard too often."

"How do you know that?"

"I keep my ears open when I'm here."

"Tell me more."

"Gracie's coming back. I think she'll be back at the company. I have talked to Samuel and mentioned your name."

"Come on, Francine, you know your daughter. She's not coming back for a relationship and she doesn't even like me. I'm not sure she ever did."

"No, but she needs someone like you to keep her on her toes. My daughter gets bored easily. I remember that she talked about you all the time before she left."

"And you think I should give it a try?"

"I do. She's worth it."

"That I know," Nicholas said. His tone was eager.

"Good for you, Nicholas Sinclair. I always knew you were smart and wanted a future that's permanent. I love my daughter and Samuel loves you. He would be happy to have you as a son-in-law. However, he can't know any of this."

"You don't really think I'm marriage material, do you?"

"That verdict is still out. My daughter likes adventure and you can give her that."

"What about love?"

"What about it? It's highly overrated."

"My lips are sealed, but I'm not sure about this. Your daughter is quite savvy."

Francine grinned. "Don't tell me I made a mistake. I can usually read men so much better than women. I have faith you'll do the right thing."

Nicholas beamed. "I don't think you made a mistake. I'm your man. This can work."

"Then it's a done deal. Go for it. And remember, we can never speak of this again. The ball's in your court," Francine added as she made a quick exit.

Chapter Nine

Though Leo's life without Ellie had been very lonely, his grand-mother tried everything she could to hold things together. Lilly was known for her patience and understanding — and when it came to her grandson, she was all in.

She knew the loneliness he felt because she had been a young widow, which was why she decided to take matters into her own hands. Samuel and Lilly were good friends when they were young. Actually, they had been more than just friends; they had a breathtaking affair that neither of them ever forgot.

Looking back, Samuel sometimes questioned why he wound up with Francine instead of Lilly. He had always wished he could love his wife a little more than he did, but that never happened. Francine was a tough cookie, and love wasn't enough for her. Samuel didn't always give her what she needed. But then again, she had some issues being the wife of a man who ruled wisely and was sometimes uncompromising. He was always the executive, and she was a socialite with ten books under her belt. Samuel didn't publish any of them. That, in itself, was a statement of independence.

Right after Francine had written her first book, she found a small publishing house to release it. The editor in chief, Wyatt Hamilton, had been her lover for years. Though Samuel suspected she was having an affair with Wyatt, he never said one word about it. How could he? Especially when he had loved someone else his entire married life.

Lilly had been an exceptionally beautiful young woman. She had long, blonde, wavy hair, as well as a wonderful smile and a personality to match. She understood Samuel as no one else did or could. They were lovers and friends. Though they regretfully stopped seeing each other, their friendship still mattered. Whenever things got rough over the years, they secretly relied on each other for support.

When Ellie died, they were thrown together by Leo's grief. Samuel was so involved and caring. He helped make the plans and set everything up for the funeral and the shiva, a week of Jewish mourning. Traditions were as important to Lilly as they were to Leo, and she was just as appreciative of Samuel's help. Leo never suspected Samuel and his grandmother had a long history — or any history at all.

The day of the funeral, Leo was devastated and so was Lilly. After the ceremony, Lilly went upstairs to take off her heels and her dress, wanting to get more comfortable. She was wearing the one black dress she owned, which she called her funeral dress. When she bought it, she had no idea she would be wearing it for the granddaughter she had come to deeply love.

She had no idea Samuel was behind her until she heard the door open. Samuel had been in that room once before, but this time he locked the door behind him just to be safe. Lilly didn't say a word; she just stood there and stared at him.

"Are you okay with me being here?" he asked.

"It's been a long time, hasn't it?"

"Too long." As Samuel moved closer to her, she didn't stop him. He threw his arms around her and hugged her so much tighter than ever before. "Let me help," he said as he wiped her tears away.

Lilly looked up at him. She was a little over five feet tall, and he was more than a foot taller. "You know we decided long ago we wouldn't do this again, but I'm glad you're here. I need you."

He kissed her with all the sweetness she remembered. When he was with Lilly, Samuel was a completely different person. They both knew it, but sometimes it was just too late to change things.

***

Several weeks after selling the house where he and Ellie had lived, Leo moved in with Lilly. He couldn't bear walking into an empty house, and his grandmother insisted he join her in the beautiful home he'd bought for her.

Once again, he needed his grandmother and, as always, she was there for him. He felt comfortable with her. That was something he lacked with his own absent mother, Nora; they spoke every few weeks, but it was never enough for him to feel the closeness he would have liked.

Nora Tucker had her own ideas of what a mother should be and, as far as Leo was concerned, they definitely fell short. Leo always felt his life would have been a lot different if his grandmother hadn't taken over after his mother left to travel the world. She was there to kiss the bruises and to understand some of the bullying he went through when he was younger.

She was the one who took him to baseball games, swimming, and park outings. Once she even helped him build a tent for an overnighter. That didn't work out very well, but after going to sleep in a nearby hotel, Lilly made sure he was back before breakfast and no one was the wiser.

As Leo grew older, he became his own man. When he met Ellie, Lilly couldn't have been happier. And when she died, Lilly also lost someone she loved.

She kept hoping for Leo to be focused and to feel somewhat better, but that wasn't happening. That was when she called Samuel for help. They met at a restaurant where they used to go years ago. It had been remodeled and had new owners, but the ambiance hadn't changed — small tables with red napkins and checkered tablecloths. The music in the background was classic, and each table had a vase with a mixture of white and red roses blended to perfection. It was their place.

Lilly got there on time and was surprised when she noticed a small blue box waiting for her at the table. When she neared the table, Samuel couldn't take his eyes away from her. She was always a beautiful woman. She was wearing a black wool suit and white satin shirt. She didn't look her age, but she never did.

"Lilly, why do you look better than ever?" He patted his stomach. "And why have I not aged as well as you have?"

"Honey, to me you look as handsome as ever. And one thing shocked me — you're early. Mr. Samuel Warrington, as I live and breathe."

"Don't tell anyone. It might ruin my image."

She smiled as she sat down. "Thank you so much for meeting me."

"Are you kidding? A call from you made my day. I've got a little something for you."

Lilly looked down at the Tiffany box. "What's this for?"

"It's just a little something for you. Everyone needs a little something now and then."

She opened the box and couldn't believe her eyes. "You remembered."

He nodded as she took out a pin she had admired years ago. It was a small diamond rose with layers of leaves surrounding it, all done in diamond pavé. It was breathtaking.

"I love it." A few tears rolled down her cheeks as she put it on. "I can't believe you bought this for me."

"I was delighted that you called. I'm not sure why you did, but I'm here for whatever you need." Samuel took hold of her hand and gently held it for as long as he could. He was feeling happier than he had felt in years.

"It's about Leo. I'm worried sick. I want to help, but I don't know what to do. I'm not the best at showing my feelings, except when it came to you. I guess you already knew that."

"I did."

"Sam, you know how I love my grandson. I just don't know how to help him."

They spent the rest of the afternoon chatting about many things. The entire time they were together, Lilly kept touching the pin and reminding herself of what she had lost. She lied to herself, thinking she didn't still love Samuel. He was thinking the exact same thing.

Chapter Ten

Gracie continued her daily routine of reading messages. Every day, the same thing. Boring, boring, boring. She really wasn't the right person for the job, but she just assumed that she would do it for a little while and move up the chain. But somehow, she got stuck in a rut.

Knowing her father liked to prove a point, she was certain he wasn't about to move her into another position. She knew she had to pay her dues. And if she couldn't handle it, he would probably show her the door.

Her first message of the day was from Missy in Chicago:

Dear Hannah,

I'm kind of in love with a guy who wants to marry me. But whenever we talk about the wedding date, I keep putting it off. He's a great guy, but when I tell him I love him I really don't mean it. He's nice and he's rich, which at first seemed doable, but now I'm not so sure. My question is: should I settle?

Gracie sat there for a few minutes, deciding how to answer. She knew if she gave the answer that she really wanted to write, she could be fired, family or no family. Her father didn't have her sense of humor. And he was watching her like a hawk, even if he pretended he wasn't.

Dear Missy,

When I first read what you wrote, I was going to give you the same old advice about finding a way to work things out. But then I decided to just give you my real reaction. Listen, if you don't love him, leave him. It sounds like you need some excitement in your life, so break up with him and travel. If you never find the right guy, at least you'll have one great adventure. Go for it. Say goodbye and don't look back. The right guy is out there waiting for you. Good luck.

Hannah

Gracie sat back in her chair, feeling good about her answer. She broke the mold and felt terrific. It was almost worth getting fired. For the next week, most of her replies were over the top. But as long as no one was editing her, she continued. She was free at last.

If Nicholas thought she was edgy before, there was no stopping her now. She laughed after writing each answer, and her job suddenly seemed so much better. She was beginning to enjoy it. She loved that she could finally be in charge of her own writing.

***

As she glanced down at her watch, Gracie reminded herself of the meeting she was scheduled to have with Nicholas. It could go either way. He could be mad and tell her to take a softer approach — or maybe he would just fire her, with her father's okay. She didn't care.

It was late and his assistant had left for the day, so she knocked on the door. She wanted to compose herself rather than just push her way in. She was trying her best to be responsible.

"Come in," Nicholas called out.

"Hi. Shall I sit? Or are you firing me?"

"Sit down. You're a Warrington; I can't fire you. Only your father can do that. You know the world would be a lot easier for you if you used the name Warrington."

"I go by my mother's maiden name for just that reason. I don't like favors. This way I have my own identity."

"Okay, but—"

"Whatever you're going to ask me to do, it's a no."

"I'm not asking you anything. I'm just saying you've done a great job so far with your replies. Lots of good feedback."

Gracie smiled. "Really? That's surprising. So no podcast?"

"Not right now. It's on hold."

"My father's okay with that?"

"He wasn't exactly committed to a podcast; he was just thinking about it."

"So, it worked?"

"Damn right it did. You're quite good at helping people. Who knew?"

Gracie was happy. "Well, thanks for pushing me. But don't get any ideas about us."

Nicholas laughed. "You've made that clear."

"Good. There's no shortage of women for you."

"None like you."

"I'm sure you'll always have a girlfriend. Or two or three."

"What does that mean?"

"You know. You like to wake up with someone next to you."

"And I wish it was you."

"Now if that's not complete BS, I don't know what is."

"Have I ever lied to you?"

"That's because I've never given you the opportunity to lie."

He loved the passion in her eyes. And if he was honest with himself, he was still more than a little attracted to her. He never could resist a beautiful blonde, and he knew she was so much more.

Chapter Eleven

Leo had cancelled the last two meetings with Samuel. It wasn't that he had writer's block; he just wasn't sure if he wanted to write as Nicole Forrester or Leo Tucker. He was thinking of possibly writing a mystery or two, or maybe even a series. It sounded like a challenge he would enjoy. He had spent so much of his time writing beautiful romance stories, and he thought a change would be good for him. Maybe killing off a few characters would make him happy. He wouldn't know if he didn't try.

Leo decided not to drive to the office, so he called a taxi. He didn't want to be uptight on his way back home; he usually needed a nap after a meeting with Samuel. It wasn't easy to please Samuel. And even after working together for years, every book was different. Samuel liked some more than others, but he published them all.

Valentina, Samuel's assistant, smiled when Leo entered the office. He was a little wet because, for the first time in his life, he forgot his umbrella. He hated the rain since he was a little boy. That trait came from his grandmother; she never went anywhere without an umbrella.

"Sorry, Leo, he's late as usual," Valentina said. "He just called and said he'll be here in a few. Make yourself at home."

"Thanks so much."

Leo glanced down at the table covered with magazines. They were all outdated. "Valentina, do you think Samuel can get some new reading material? After all, he owns several publications."

"Thrifty, isn't he?" Valentina said as she brought out some new magazines. "I brought these from home. You know Samuel. If it's important to him, he takes care of it; if not, he doesn't."

Samuel came zooming into the office like a tornado. "Leo, good to see you. Follow me."

Leo did just that as he waved goodbye to Valentina.

Once they got into Samuel's office, the publisher took off his coat and threw it on one of the chairs. Then he lit a cigar.

"Samuel, isn't this is a smoke-free building?"

"It is, but that's the nice thing about owning the building. I can break the rules."

Leo sat down. "Yes, you can. So, did you read the pages I sent?"

"Leo, don't look at me that way."

"What way?"

"I know I'm not supposed to smoke, but I can't help myself. It helps me think."

"So, what do you think so far?" Leo repeated, slightly apprehensive.

Samuel smiled. "I think Nicole Forrester is back. And I realize that you always change your ending, but don't."

"My books usually end on a much higher note. I brought some pages because I know you would rather talk to me while you read."

"Well, things change. I think this one works. It's more about reality in life. Besides, this story is going to be a series."

"Samuel, you know I like standalone stories better."

"Let's take a leap. It's time to change. We can't keep doing the same thing. And, my boy, in real life everything doesn't always work out."

"True, but—"

"Let's not do buts," Samuel said. "Let's be positive. Can you take this story further?"

Leo thought for a moment. "Yes, I think I can. That's why I was about to write a new ending. I had more to tell."

"Think about this. Use what you thought would be your new ending as the beginning of your new book."

Leo nodded. "I might be able to do that."

"Might?"

Leo realized he might not have put that the right way for Samuel to sign off and relax. "Samuel, I can do this. Don't worry. I'll begin today and keep you posted. It's a great idea and I'm excited to go for it. I'm all for moving on with some new ideas.

"As long as we're talking about new and different, I was thinking." Leo took a deep breath and decided to shoot for the moon. "As soon as we finish this new series, we could think about Leo Tucker writing with Nicole Forrester. Just so we bring it in slowly."

"You're one of the best romance novelists I've ever published."

"Coming from you, that's quite a compliment."

"I only speak the truth. You know that."

"I'm grateful for all you do. It was just a thought."

"No more thinking. I'm hungry. How about a hot dog?" Samuel rubbed his overweight stomach. "I haven't had one for a few days. Francine's got me on a little diet."

"Really? How's that going?"

"Well, I'm on a diet when I'm home. When I'm not, well, you know the answer to that. I haven't lost a pound in years. Let's go. We can finish talking while we eat."

***

Just as Samuel and Leo hit the pavement, Gracie came running out of the building. She didn't see Leo — but he saw her. He was prepared to walk on without saying hello, thinking she might not remember him. He didn't feel like being embarrassed.

Samuel called out. "Gracie, hold on! Come here for a minute. I want you to meet someone."

"Can't!" she yelled back.

"The hell you can't. Don't be rude," Samuel added with a wave to come over. "Come on, we're going for a hot dog."

She gave up and ran over.

"Gracie, meet Leo. Leo, meet my daughter, Gracie."

"Leo, it's nice to see you again." Gracie's attitude immediately changed.

Samuel was surprised. "Do you know each other?"

"We do. Remember I told you about the guy who saved me from making a fool of myself on the airplane?"

Samuel smiled. "Yes, I remember. Leo, she couldn't stop talking about you when she got home."

Grace was a little self-conscious, and that was something she rarely felt.

Leo smiled. "That's me. The guy from the plane."

"Great. You're coming with us for a hot dog."

"Can't," Gracie said. "Nicholas is waiting for me."

"Forget about Nicholas. Let's go."

As they walked toward the hot dog stand, it finally stopped raining. Leo couldn't help but wonder who Nicholas was. Maybe her fiancée? Her boyfriend, or just a friend? He figured it was no use wondering. If he knew Samuel, he would learn exactly who Nicholas was by the end of lunch.

"Leo, what a small world this is."

Leo nodded. "You could say that again." Leo was very happy to see her, but was surprised that Samuel was her father. All along, all he had to do was ask. But, of course, he hadn't even mentioned her to Samuel.

"My daughter works with me. She's moving up the chain. Her boss is Nicholas Sinclair. You'd like him. Good guy."

Gracie snickered to herself. If Nicholas was anything, he wasn't a good guy.

"So, Leo, what brings you here?" Gracie asked. "I had no idea you knew my father."

Samuel quickly chimed in. "We worked together on a couple of projects."

Leo sighed in relief. Thank goodness Samuel answered, because he wouldn't have known what to say. That was the challenge of writing under a different name, and he was never good at lying. Even when he was a little boy, both his grandmother and mother could always tell.

After lunch, Gracie raced back to the office, realizing she was very late. Just as she was about to scoot in the revolving door, she fell. She knew better than to run in four-inch heels, especially when they were new.

She sat down in the lobby for a minute, examining the damage. One split heel and a rip in her tights. Then the phone rang.

"Where are you?" Nicholas asked in an annoyed tone.

"Nicholas, sorry. Something came up."

"Well, I set up a meeting with your new marketing staff. I thought it was time to put our money on you."

"I don't get it." Gracie was confused. She had no idea Nicholas actually believed in her. She thought she was just the boss's daughter and they were stuck with each until one surrendered.

"What's to get? I'm trying to help make this publishing company a significant media source."

"Isn't it already?"

"Yes, but this is your moment."

"What's the rush?"

"Didn't you want to advance?"

"I did, but—"

"No room for doubt. If you're not here in ten minutes, we'll just toss this idea. This was your time to shine. I thought you really wanted it, but now I'm not so sure."

"Didn't you tell me I was doing great?"

"I did."

"So, you lied?"

"Do you always have to ask so many questions? Just get here." Then he hung up.

There were times when Nicholas wasn't half bad, but then there were others when she didn't like him at all. That call was one of those times. Gracie knew she had better think fast.

She refused to get lost in the shuffle, so she held it together by going into the ladies' room and straightening her clothes. She took her scarf and wrapped it over her hips in a stylish manner to hide the rip from the fall. She snapped the heel off her other shoe, turning her heels into flats. She stood up straight and confident.

Gracie didn't want to be the poor daddy's girl who needed a job because she lost the love of her life. She was more than that. She was the girl who said, "Here I come world!" For the first time in a long time, she felt like Gracie Maxwell and didn't think about her failed relationship with Jack. She could do this.

By the time she got to the meeting, Nicholas was just about to close the discussion. "So here she is, the one and only Gracie Maxwell, 'Dear Hannah.' Too busy for us, I assume?"

Gracie half smiled and took a breath. These must be the people Nicholas had mentioned on the phone. There were two young adults, probably just out of college. As Nicholas introduced them, Gracie kept thinking how young they were and how old she was getting. The guy was movie-star handsome, while the young woman had curly brown hair, big eyes, and a pleasant smile.

"Gracie, meet Drake and Mae. They're here to handle your computer needs and social media presence. Drake's an expert in podcasts.

The guy's a genius. And Mae's going to be your right hand. She's a social media queen."

Gracie nodded. "Hi. I definitely need your services. I know nothing about podcasts other than I don't like them. But we're in it to win, right? I'm so happy Nicholas hired such a competent team."

She quickly shook their hands. Nicholas had no idea how she successfully captured the moment, but she managed to get them in her corner. He thought he was the only one who could do that; obviously, he was wrong.

Chapter Twelve

Once Leo got home, his mood improved as he smelled the pleasant aroma throughout the house. He knew his grandmother was up to something. Bernie met him at the door and followed him into the kitchen.

Leo hugged his grandmother. "Looks like someone's been busy."

"I thought you needed some cheering up."

"You always know what I need."

"It's a grandmother's job."

"You're the best," Leo added as he snatched a tiny piece of brownie and popped it in his mouth. "So, so good."

"Just like when you were little. You could never wait until they cooled. Also, your mom called."

"And?"

"You know your mom."

"Not as well as I should. If it weren't for you, I don't know how I would have grown up. Her parties and travels are her life, not mine. I don't mean that in a bad way, but you know she could have done better."

"She wasn't always that way. When your father died, it was so traumatic for her that she fell to pieces. That's when I moved in. I started to cook for you and I cleaned the house. She was so depressed and no one could get her out of it. She had doctors who wanted to help, but she didn't want their help, or anyone's. It wasn't a pretty picture. But you were a normal, healthy kid with a grandmother who took you to school, doctors, dentists, restaurants, kids' parties, playdates, everywhere you needed to go. I loved doing it."

Leo smiled at his grandmother. She was his shining light. And when she smiled back, he knew they were in sync. For a boy to lose his father at nine was a very serious blow, but he never forgot how lucky he had been to have a grandmother who had such get up and go.

"Nana, why didn't she tell me how she felt?"

"It's not in her DNA. She isn't a bad person, just a woman who couldn't handle tragedy. That's why I'm here for you. I want to make sure you have a life after Ellie. You know she would want that for you."

"I know. I'm trying. I will have a life, I promise you that. So stop worrying." He wished that were true. "When it's all said and done. I guess l lucked out by having you pull me through all the tough spots."

"And remember, your mom loves you. She's just not able to be there for you. Besides, she knows you always have me."

"Yes, to sugarcoat everything. It does help. I guess you don't have to be with your children twenty-four hours a day to have them feel loved. But when you're home, you're supposed to give them all you've got. Apparently, my mother never got the memo. Anyway, what did she have to say?"

"She's got another guy. Ten years younger."

"Wow." Leo was a little shocked, but he shouldn't have been. His mother had quite a few lovers.

"There aren't too many men your mother's age who can keep her pace."

"She needs a party happening all the time," Leo added with regret.

"Some things you can't change," Lilly admitted, "but she missed it all."

"You're right. She missed it all, but I was the one who lucked out. I have you."

Chapter Thirteen

Samuel knew he was in trouble with Gracie. Everything he said made it worse. He really wanted the best for his daughter, but their relationship seemed to only become more complicated.

He would stay up late at night, trying to work out a plan. Day after day, he noticed Gracie moping around the office and home. She never even tried to contact any of her old friends. He was concerned because this was not his fearless daughter; usually, adventure was her middle name.

He finally came up with a plan that could help both Leo and Gracie. It was obvious to him that they were both missing out on all life had to offer. Each had their own reasons, but they both needed a friend.

Samuel invited Leo out for dinner and wouldn't take no for an answer. After their bellies were full and they had a brandy or two, Samuel sprung a favor. "Leo, you know I treasure your friendship, so I feel we can discuss this difficult subject."

"Are you firing me? Was this a wonderful dinner to take my mind off the end of my career at Warrington?"

Samuel laughed. "Of course not. I'm not firing you."

"Well, I know it took me a long time to finish my last book."

"It's nothing like that. I just need your help."

"Sounds serious," Leo said, waiting for the other shoe to drop.

"It's Gracie. She's miserable and I can't seem to get through to her."

"What can I do? I barely know her."

"You know enough about her."

"Not really. I don't even know why she calls herself Gracie Maxwell."

Samuel laughed. "It's her mother's maiden name. She doesn't want people to know I'm her father. Hell of a thing. You raise a child, give her everything, and then at the end of the day she changes her name. Kids."

"Oh, I get it."

"You do?" Samuel seemed surprised. "Well, anyway, I was wondering if you could help her with her column."

"What column?"

"'Dear Hannah.' That's my daughter."

"I had no idea."

"She likes to keep everything to herself."

Leo sat back in his chair and sipped his brandy. He didn't even like it, but he knew Samuel didn't like to drink alone. "You're kidding, right? What do I know about writing a column?"

"You know quite a bit about love."

"Does she know I'm the guy behind Nicole Forrester?"

"Of course not. I love you like a son. I wouldn't jeopardize that."

Leo was relieved. "Thanks, I appreciate that. Sometimes I hate that I have to lie to people. Actually, I hate it all the time."

"It's not really a lie. It's just not using your real name. You're still the same person."

"Am I?"

"Listen, I know I'm not your father. But if you were my son, I would tell you to look forward and start to live again. That's why I sent you to Paris. You've been dealt a rough hand. Ellie was a wonderful woman, but the next card is when your life changes. That why I'm asking for your help. I think doing something as you, and not as Nicole Forrester, will help."

"Maybe you're right."

"How's this? Think about it overnight. If you're okay with it, please come to the office tomorrow afternoon. I could really use some help with this. Gracie's quite miserable. I know she thinks I don't understand, but I do. At least I want to."

Leo had never had this kind of conversation with Samuel. It felt good, almost like he finally had a father to watch over him.

Samuel continued. "I love my wife, but she's not in love with me. Never has been. She's an elegant woman who's married to a regular Joe who isn't her type. We have a good life together, but you need more. Love matters."

When they shook hands and said goodbye, Samuel hoped he would be able to count on Leo. But if he didn't show up, he wouldn't hold it against him.

***

The next afternoon, Samuel was delighted when Leo strolled in five minutes before the scheduled meeting. He had hoped Leo would take the bait, and it looked like he had.

Samuel didn't think he made a mistake when he watched the way Leo and Gracie looked at each other. If they didn't see it, he did. It was very similar to the way he and Lilly used to look at each other.

"Okay, I'm reporting for work," Leo said. "Maybe I'll get some ideas from some of the letters."

"Maybe so." Samuel smiled in a reassuring way.

"I'm still pretty shocked that Gracie is Hannah, but I guess it's like me and Nicole Forrester."

"Possibly. Only time will tell. Sometimes things have a way of working out without you ever seeing it coming. When Gracie started college, I thought she would be my replacement one day. I'm not sure she even likes working here, but for now it's a job. Just don't tell her I said that."

Samuel looked down and checked his watch. "Oh, geez. Come on, we're late."

No one was surprised that the meeting was starting late; whenever Samuel was involved, it always did. Gracie smiled, reminding herself that her father was always late picking her up from parties or from school. Nothing had changed in all these years.

She figured something was up when her father came barreling in with Leo. Samuel may have thought he knew his daughter, but she also knew him pretty darn well.

Then there was Nicholas, who had no idea what was in the works. He had remembered seeing Leo in the building several times, but they were never formally introduced. "Hey, who are you?"

"Leo Tucker. Samuel asked me to be here. I didn't mean to intrude."

"I confess it was me," Samuel admitted. "I think Leo will make a great addition to the team."

Gracie was suspicious. "Dad, what's going on?"

Nicholas was even more skeptical. He liked calling the shots, even though Samuel was ultimately the boss. At that moment, he had no idea what was going to happen.

"Samuel what's going on? Did I not get a memo? What am I missing?"

"Maybe I'll go outside for a few minutes and leave you three alone," Leo said, already regretting being there.

Samuel looked at all three of them with stern eyes. "Hold on. Let's not get ahead of ourselves. This isn't anything that will hurt any of you, so sit down and let me talk."

Nicholas was trying to stay cool, but he was ready to lose it. Not a surprise to Gracie. She had seen him in action and it wasn't pretty. Obviously, her father had never seen this side of him. Everything Samuel did was a test, one way or the other. "Samuel, I'm not sure what's going on but I need to make a call. You can start without me," Nicholas said, and then he left.

Samuel was concerned, and went after Nicholas. "Hold up, I need to talk to you."

"Can we talk later?"

"Please, Nick, come to my office."

That left Gracie and Leo staring at each other.

"I know you're wondering why I'm here," Leo said.

"Yes. Maybe you can tell me what's going on. I was wondering how you even know my father."

"Does it bother you that I'm here?"

"Of course not. Should it?"

Leo took hold of her hand. "Can we talk about the elephant in the room?"

"There's no problem."

"Why weren't you on the plane going home? I thought we could talk. I never realized I wouldn't see you again."

Gracie didn't look him in the eye. She just kind of slipped away and slid toward the door.

"Gracie, wait."

She turned around. Gracie didn't pull any punches. "Did we sleep together?"

"Where on Earth did you get that idea?"

"When I woke up in the hotel, I was undressed and ready for bed. Did you dress me after we, you know—"

"Know what?"

"Slept together? We did, didn't we?"

Leo snickered. "No, we didn't sleep together. We just met."

"When did that ever stop a man from sleeping with a woman?"

"I can't speak for all men, just me. And no, we didn't. What is wrong with you? Do you clump all of us together? I had no intention of sleeping with you."

"Same here."

"Really?"

"That's just it. I didn't remember anything and, when I got up, I wasn't sure what happened. I'm done with men. All of you."

"Nothing happened. I swear."

"I've heard that before," Gracie added in a cynical way. "You're all alike."

Leo was taken aback. "Before we go any further, let me tell you something about me you might not know. My wife is gone. She died, and sleeping with other women is not something I think about."

"I'm so sorry, Leo."

"You're beautiful. And if we did sleep together, I wouldn't want you to be drunk and unaware of how amazing it would be. I would want you to feel pleasure, not regret."

Gracie just stood there speechless. She'd had no idea, and she felt about as low as one could feel. How selfish of her to think every man was insensitive. She felt like a jerk.

"Now that that's over, let's sit back down and wait for your father and Nicholas to come back. If they don't, we can go for a hot dog. That usually solves everything."

Finally, a smile appeared on Gracie's face. "That's my father's solution to everything."

"Well, you've got to admit it's a good one."

Gracie's smile was so inviting. "Deal."

Leo put out his hand for a quick handshake and Gracie took it. "Deal."

"And one last thing," Leo added. "You undressed yourself and I looked the other way. I didn't want you to be alone, so I stayed and sat in the chair beside you just to make sure you were okay." Then he cautiously smiled.

Gracie wanted to walk over to Leo and kiss him, but she didn't. She had never met anyone like him. He was kind, considerate, and so not her usual type.

She still sometimes found herself wondering what her life would have been like with Jack. Maybe they would have gotten a divorce. Maybe it would have been better if he was honest with her — but then again, he had a child. He wasn't a good man, and that was why she was never going to put herself in that position again.

"Can I ask you something? Why weren't you on the flight going home? Did you stay away intentionally?"

She smiled. "No. I decided to take a train. That plane ride was too scary; I just couldn't do it again."

Leo felt relieved. Not that he could see any chance of anything happening between them, but at least it wasn't about him. His confidence level was quite low, but hearing her reason made him feel somewhat better.

Nicholas and Samuel were on their way back to the meeting when they saw Gracie and Leo talking. Samuel felt a sudden sense of love in the air, but he had been wrong before. "Not that I want to interrupt the two of you, but I think we have a meeting to begin," he said. "You know I'm a busy man."

"Yes, sir!" Gracie said in a sassy way. "Are you always the only one who has work to do? We all work, you know."

Samuel shook his head. "Did I raise you to be like this?"

"Sure did." Then she kissed her father's cheek. "You made me who I am."

Samuel weakened just enough to smile. Whatever his daughters did, he still loved them to pieces. That would never change.

Finally, the meeting began. Gracie sat between Leo and Nicholas. The couch sat three comfortably — but even if it was bigger, it still would have felt uncomfortable. Gracie crossed her legs and found her foot touching Leo's leg, but when she crossed them the other way, her foot knocked into Nicholas's leg. Not a perfect fit for any of them.

"Now that I have your attention, I have an idea that will work for everyone," Samuel began. "And once my daughter stops crossing her legs, we can begin."

Gracie gave him a strange look. "Fine. I'm done."

"So glad you're comfortable." Samuel's tone was sarcastic. Not a surprise. "I wasn't aware of many of the problems my news division had before we needed to change the whole system. But Nicholas pointed me in the right direction with things like 'Dear Hannah,' so I have opened my eyes to new ideas."

Gracie looked at her father. "Let's have it. I have a column to write."

"That's why we're here. Leo was gracious enough to pitch in for the time being. It's right up his alley, and I think you two will be a great team."

Gracie looked at Leo. "Did you know who I was when we met?"

"Of course not."

"So why on Earth would the two of us be better than just me?"

Leo glanced at Samuel, waiting for him to chime in, but he didn't.

"Your father thought it would help."

"Are you replacing me with Leo? And Nicholas, why are you just sitting there?"

"Gracie, let me worry about that," Samuel said. "I have made many decisions in my time."

"But this? Something just doesn't sound right. I think you're getting rid of me, but you don't know how to tell me."

"Have you ever known me to pussyfoot around?"

"No, but—"

"No buts right now. Just let me finish."

"Dad, what the hell does that mean?" She was getting pissed.

Samuel chuckled. "So now it's dad."

Leo was confused. "Sam, I'd like to hear more."

Gracie sat back, realizing the relationship between Leo and her father was more than a hello-goodbye one. Not many people called her father Sam, but now Leo was added to that list.

"You're both going to be doing it. A team. If you think about it, you might consider how great it will be. I think it's time to rename the column and the podcast. We'll call it 'It's All About Love.'"

Nicholas was in shock. "Samuel Warrington, have you lost your mind?"

"It's going to be a great team. You'll see."

"Samuel, what are your plans for the two of them? Gracie's been doing great with her column. Why add another person?" He sounded like a jealous lover.

"She's doing great, but it would be good to have both a male and female opinion."

Nicholas was beginning to find this whole situation precarious. "Are you back to the idea of a podcast?"

"Okay, everyone stop," Samuel said. "Gracie, just hold on for a minute. Let me explain the plan."

By this time, Leo was certain he was in the wrong place at the wrong time. "Sam, I think I should let you all figure this out. I'll call you later."

"Leo, please stay. If my daughter will calm down, we can work this out."

Gracie frowned. "Fine, tell us."

"Just so you know, I'm in charge of this project," Samuel continued. "Gracie, you're my daughter and I love you, but this is going to be a great way to get even closer with your readers. This is the updated version. You two will be the toast of Chicago. Leo's a very calming and understanding guy. They'll love the two of you. You'll be the conversation at everyone's dinner table."

"So, you're saying I'm not calming?" Gracie was uneasy about being pushed into something so fast.

At first Samuel didn't answer, but then he just lowered his reading glasses and peered right at his daughter. "Is that outburst from a calm individual? You have the passion and Leo has the tranquility. Perfect match for the column and the podcast. Chemistry matters, and you'll get there."

Leo hadn't signed up for a podcast; he had no idea that was why he was helping.

Nicholas had a lot to say, but he assumed it would be in his best interest to limit his words. "Samuel, can I something?" he asked.

"Of course you can. Shoot."

"What makes you think Leo's right for this job? We can do better. Sorry, Leo." Nicholas sounded arrogant because he was.

"I think I'm capable," Leo replied with confidence. He wasn't going to just sit there and take whatever Nicholas said in stride. He was a best-selling author, and a good one at that.

"You're dead wrong, Nick," Samuel said. "I asked Leo to join because he's a very skilled author. Don't think for a minute that I don't know exactly what I'm doing."

"Okay, Sam, you're the boss," Nicholas said with a sense of obedience and subtle anger. "Why am I here?"

"Because you're a big part of this publishing house. I have something more in mind for you, but we can talk about that later."

"Later, right. I guess I have no choice."

"Come on, Nick. The three of you look as if I just sentenced you to life in prison."

Gracie was uneasy. "Maybe you just did."

"Listen, we can talk more about this new project at dinner. I'd like all three of you to join us tonight at the house."

"All of us?" Nicholas asked.

"Mom is free tonight?" Gracie asked. "Does she know about this?"

"Of course she does. What kind of a man do you think I am? I know better than to get on the bad side of Francine. I've been there before, and it's not a pretty picture."

Gracie shook her head in disapproval. Leo had no clue as to why he was invited, and really hadn't planned on crashing a family thing. Nicholas just didn't want to go.

Right before Samuel walked out of the room, he smiled. "See you all at eight."

Leo was a gentleman, and reached for Nicholas's hand. "Nicholas, nice to meet you. I guess we'll be seeing each other again very soon, whether we like it or not."

"I guess we will," Nicholas replied as he left. "But not tonight. I can't make it."

Gracie seemed at a loss for words, but Leo decided to stay for a minute or two. "Is there something going on with you and Nicholas?"

"Nothing other than he's my boss."

Leo couldn't help but laugh. "I guess that means you don't like him."

"I don't. Never have, never will." Gracie smiled. "Well, all things considered, that's a good thing."

"Have you known him for a while?"

"Yes, longer than I care to think about. Before I left to go to Paris, we worked on a few projects together. My father gave him what would have been my job. It wasn't his fault, but just the same, anyone else would have been better. So goes life."

"You might be wrong. Your father loves you and wants what's best for you."

"I lost that war when I left for Paris. Anyway, who are you? My father has never mentioned your name to me, ever. But you seem to know quite a bit about me."

"I hardly know anything."

"Now you're lying. Just like all the others. One lie after another."

Gracie was baffled by Leo. He was a nice enough guy, but he seemed to know too much about her, and she didn't like it one bit. "Leo, what don't I know? Maybe you'd better tell me exactly who you are and why you're here."

He was saved by the bell when his phone beeped. As he looked down at the number, he knew he didn't have time to talk. Samuel wanted to see him in his office ASAP. "We can talk about this tonight at dinner. Got to go. Let me just say one thing first."

"Fine. I'm listening." By this time, Gracie was annoyed at the whole situation. Everything was happening so fast that her head was spinning.

"You're a natural at this. You're funny too."

"You have actually read my column?"

"I do read it. Even before I knew who you were."

"I'm shocked."

"You have an edge. I think that's a plus. You never know what you're going to come up with. I find it refreshing. You're definitely not the same old, same old."

Gracie was surprised — that he listened, and that he thought she had her own style. She smiled at Leo, thinking it might actually be great to get to know someone like him. He was honest, and she liked that about him.

"I wish I was adventurous like you," he continued. "You don't seem to be afraid of anything. Well, other than flying."

Gracie found him amusing. Another quality she wasn't used to.

"Me, on the other hand, I'm afraid of everything. Maybe that's what your father wants for the podcast. Opposite ways of seeing relationships."

Gracie shrugged her shoulders. "Maybe so. Okay, see you tonight. I'll think about that."

As Leo was leaving, he bumped into Nicholas. "Oh, I see you're still here."

"On my way out," Leo said as he turned back to wave goodbye to Gracie.

Gracie walked over to Nicholas. "What's so important?"

"Let's go to my office. We can talk there."

"Why not here? It's just you and me. Or do you need your desk to hide behind?"

"My office, please."

"I'll be there in a minute."

***

Gracie made herself comfortable on his couch. She had been there so many times before, but usually she was too mad about something to care about what was on the walls of the office she thought should be hers. While she waited, she was impressed by all the awards, along with some very expensive contemporary artwork. There was probably a lot she didn't know about Nicholas, but she forced herself not to care. One thing she knew for sure was that he wasn't good for her.

"Sorry to keep you waiting."

"Aren't you the polite on these days? So, why am I here? Any pearls of wisdom, now that my fate isn't in your hands?"

"You know, Gracie, you might have this all wrong. I've never been in control of you."

"Well, you act like it."

"Your father's the boss. This is Warrington Media, isn't it?"

"I know you always have something to say. So, let's hear it."

"You think you know me, but you don't."

"Let's put it this way. I don't want to know any more than I do."

"Well, now you're on your own. Doesn't that sound good to you?"

"It should, but you know my father. As long as I'm here, he's the boss. He's not impressed with my work. That much I know."

"You're wrong. Your father is very impressed with you. He's not good with compliments. You know that. But he knows the media world."

"Did you know about any of this?" Gracie asked, certainly not one to hold back.

"I was as shocked as you are. But your father usually makes good decisions. He's a smart guy. That's why I like being here. It would be even better if you would give me a second look."

"What are you saying?"

"The way you were looking at Leo was something I would love to have. You know I think you're beautiful and smart."

"You could have mentioned that before. I thought you were just putting up with me because I'm the boss's daughter."

"That never mattered. I just wanted you to be the best you could be. You're quite a woman. Maybe I don't tell you that enough."

Gracie was stunned. It was like seeing him for the first time. "I didn't think you felt that way."

"Well, then you were wrong. Oh, and one more thing. Your father's moving your office upstairs. He wanted to surprise you, so don't tell him I told you."

"You're kidding?"

"He made that decision right away. He might never tell you, but he appreciates your skills. And he's very proud of you."

Gracie was taken aback. The pieces of this puzzle didn't match up with anything she was hearing. There were probably several things she had yet to find out. Samuel Warrington liked to make her work for everything she got. It was a test, all of it. Always had been.

"Why aren't you coming tonight? Don't you want to see what's up my father's sleeve?"

"I don't think so. I hate family things."

"Nicholas, don't be silly. It's not a family thing. It's just dinner."

"It's never just dinner at your house."

Gracie acknowledged that comment by nodding. "So, you've heard. I guess our family is known for disasters."

"I went to a few of those dinners while you were gone."

"Really?"

"They were a little intense, but I got through them."

"I see."

"Anyway, enough about me. You've got your boyfriend coming."

"He's not my boyfriend. I'm single and staying that way forever. Besides, I don't know much about him."

"Maybe, but he sure as hell likes you."

"How do you know that?"

"He never took his eyes off you. And for the life of me, I have no idea who he is or why he is here with us at Warrington."

Gracie was a little troubled by his words. "There is no us."

"There could be if you let me show you the real me."

Gracie laughed. "Oh, I've seen the real you. And sorry, hon, that ship has sailed. Actually, that ship sunk. The last thing I need is a man with no morals."

"You know that's not true. Maybe you haven't noticed, but I've changed. Can't you give me a tiny, tiny little break? Maybe you're wrong about me."

"I don't think so."

"Wait one minute. There's something I've been meaning to do since you got back."

Nicholas had been fighting his feeling for Gracie, but it seemed as if he was running out of time. It was now or never. He wrapped his arms around her waist and kissed her. The kiss caught her off guard. She attempted to move back, but she found herself moving toward him instead. *What is wrong with me?* she kept thinking as he got closer.

When his lips touched hers in such a tender, caring way, it shocked her. She expected him to be as aggressive as he had been before, but maybe he was right. Maybe he had changed. It was just one kiss, but it was a kiss worth remembering.

"See you tonight, Nicholas. It won't be as bad as you think. Once my father has a drink or two, he's mellow and almost fun."

"Still a no," he said as he walked back to his desk, sat down, and pretended to work. He was always so cool and calm with every move he made, except for that kiss. He actually seemed vulnerable. *Probably an act*, she thought.

Chapter Fourteen

Dinner at the Warringtons' was never dull. No one ever knew what to expect. When Samuel initiated a family dinner, there was a fifty-fifty chance things would go bad.

On more than one occasion, Gracie's sister Julianna would heat things up, but she hadn't been around for quite a while. She started most of the turbulence and then left the table, leaving everyone wondering what would happen next.

Gracie and her sister were close growing up, but they were as different as night and day. Being the oldest, and usually the wisest, Gracie set the example. But when Gracie changed course and left to live her adventure in Paris, Julianna took her own path to freedom. For her, that meant packing her bags and not telling anyone where she was going.

Julianna had a great sense of humor. When she was a kid, the dinner table was far less intense, unless she had one of her famous tantrums. Julianna was a redhead with a hot temper, while Gracie was always considered the beauty of the family and the sensible one — though she lost the second title when she left for Paris.

At least Samuel and Francine knew where Gracie was, but Julianna vanished with just a letter explaining why she was leaving. Samuel and Francine hired a private detective, but even the best in the business couldn't find her. She called every now and then just to say she was alive.

Samuel tried his best to accept what he couldn't change, but he never stopped trying to find her.

Samuel assured himself that this dinner would end up like no other. He was good at keeping secrets, and nobody else knew why he had planned this special dinner with Ava's help. Ava was one of the few people Samuel never screamed at. From the time Gracie and Julianna were young, he knew he needed someone competent and cool headed. That was Ava, and she never let him down.

The kitchen smelled fabulous. Ava was stirring the gravy when Samuel snuck in. "I knew you could do this," Samuel said as he handed her a bouquet of fresh flowers.

"No need for this."

"Of course there is. I know today's your day off, but I appreciate your help."

"Are you going to tell me what the surprise is?"

"Of course not. It's called a surprise for a reason."

Knowing the family dynamics, Ava planned a dinner menu that she knew would be safe: chicken, roasted potatoes, cooked vegetables, and a salad. Dessert was cheesecake with strawberries, then coffee, tea, or hot cocoa. If everyone was still talking by then, brandy was on deck.

Ava always had her fingers crossed before a dinner like this. Just then, she felt Georgia at her leg. The dog was her best friend, and she was thankful to have her around when things got tough. "What are the chances of a fight-free meal tonight?" Ava asked. On that note, Georgia left the room.

***

After Francine got word that Nicholas wasn't coming, she made a call to remind him of their conversation. If he wanted her help trying to win over Gracie, he needed to get there as soon as possible. She wasn't taking no for an answer.

Once dinner was served, and after Francine checked her watch dozens of times, the doorbell finally rang. Francine quickly went to answer the door. She didn't like missing a thing.

There he was, standing in the doorway. Francine felt like a schoolgirl staring at Nicholas, acknowledging his stunning appearance. "Thank goodness you're here. You look great tonight, if I must say so myself."

Francine smiled, admiring how he looked. She could never resist a handsome guy dressed for a special evening in a casual blazer and jeans. The white shirt made him look like he just stepped out of a magazine.

"Thanks for coming. When I heard you said no, I just couldn't have that. Especially after our little talk."

"Didn't we say we should never discuss this again?"

"We did, but sometimes I lie."

"That's not true, is it?" He hoped she was joking, but he didn't know her well enough to be sure.

"No, my lips are sealed. You're perfect for Gracie, even if she doesn't know it. But she will."

"I hope this isn't a mistake. I don't like family dinners. Too much fuss. I don't like complicated."

Just as she was about to close the door, there stood Julianna. "I don't like complicated either. Still up to your old tricks, Mother?"

Francine was surprised and embarrassed, hoping her daughter hadn't heard too much of the conversation. "I had no idea you were standing there."

"Obviously." Arrogantly smiling, Julianna couldn't help but find this whole thing a little weird. "Francine Maxwell Warrington, you're brokering your daughter. Nice to see nothing has changed."

Francine got her answer; Julianna had heard it all.

"Mother, isn't this a little beneath you? Does Gracie know about this?"

"Nothing to know. Just conversation."

"Then why do you look like a little kid who got caught with her hand in the cookie jar?"

"No cookie jar here. Come and hug your mother." Francine hugged her daughter. "I'm really glad to see you. I was just so surprised. I don't know what you're thinking, but this isn't what it looks like."

Nicholas didn't know what to say. "Francine, maybe we can do this another night."

Julianna smiled and held out her hand. "I'm Julianna. The bad seed. Don't be silly. My lips are sealed. I love a good secret."

Nicholas smiled, a little intrigued by this whole scenario. "Hi, I'm Nicholas Sinclair."

Julianna was impressed. "Oh my G-d, you're way up the ladder, aren't you? I read a few articles written about you. You're a big deal, and obviously trying out for a bigger deal. I like you already."

Francine took a deep breath. "Why don't we take this into the dining room?"

"Good idea. I'm starved," Julianna said as she picked up her pace, almost dancing in. "Well, look at this. The gang's all here."

"Oh, my G-d! Julianna, you're home!" Gracie ran over to her sister and gave her a bear hug. "I didn't realize just how much I missed you until you walked in. I'm so glad you're here." She squeezed harder.

Samuel stood up. "Well, well, well, as I live and breathe. So happy you said yes."

"Hi, Daddy," she said as she kissed his forehead. "I thought it was time."

Samuel gave her a big hug. "I'm glad you're home."

Francine was annoyed. "Samuel, you knew about this?"

"I did, but I didn't think she would come."

Georgia came out from the kitchen and jumped all over Julianna. "At least someone is happy to see me without any questions," Julianna said as she bent down to hug her old playmate.

Ava ran over and gave her a kiss. "How's my little Julianna?"

Nicholas smiled, relieved to realize the pressure was off him. He was just there as an innocent bystander — well, maybe not an innocent one.

When Leo looked over toward Nicholas, they immediately knew what the other was thinking. They both wished they weren't there.

Gracie was amused by this whole charade. She had known something had to be up. "So, Sis, what brings you to this neck of the woods? Dad, right?"

"I'm damn happy to have my girls home," Samuel said.

Julianna was just about to sit down when she noticed Leo. "And who might you be? A friend of Dad's? Oh, don't tell me. You must be Gracie's guy from Paris. Dad filled me in."

Gracie gave her a look, reminding herself of what her sister was really like. She spoke her mind no matter what.

"Just Leo from Chicago," he said.

"Oops," Julianna said as she reached for a sip of water. Julianna was never known for her discreet behavior. "And you expect me to believe that? Now sell me a bridge."

Leo stood up and reached over to shake her hand. "Anyway, nice to meet you."

"Nice to meet you too, Leo," Julianna said as she pushed the chair in, making herself comfortable. "So what's the occasion? Who's getting married, or whatever it is you're all here for?"

"Can't we just have a nice dinner?" Samuel asked as he began to eat.

Julianna looked around the table. "If that's what you say it is. But for my money, something very strange is happening here tonight."

"Okay, here's one strange thing," Gracie hesitantly admitted. "Leo and I will be working together. We're going to do a podcast."

Francine stopped eating and looked at her husband. "Samuel, what's going on?"

"Just some new changes. It's time to move into the new world. I think Leo and Gracie are going to be a great team. And there is one more thing. Julianna is coming to work as an assistant to Nicholas."

Gracie was surprised. Her sister had never been much for reading or anything related to the publishing industry. Something must have changed.

Francine's eyes nearly popped out in shock. "Samuel, have you lost your mind? This isn't anything negative about Julianna, but why would she work at a place she's hated since she was a little girl?"

Julianna answered for her father. "Don't blame Daddy. It was my idea."

"And since when does your father do something just because you asked him?"

"Oh, I see. So my sister who hates talking just for the sake of talking is doing a podcast." Julianna looked at Gracie, wondering what was really going on. "And I am being called out for thinking about my future. It's about time, don't you think?"

Samuel began eating as if the conversation was put on pause. "Everyone enjoy."

Francine pretended to smile. "Okay, I get it. I think this family likes change, so that's what we're all going to do. Including me."

Samuel stopped eating. "Does that mean you're going to be working with all of us? And publishing too?"

"No. I'm going on a long trip to catch up on things I've missed. Now that your dad has his girls home, it's my time."

Samuel ignored the conversation and went on eating. As for Gracie, she wasn't that shocked. She knew her mother felt trapped in a life she didn't plan.

"Mom, I think that's great," Gracie said, remembering their conversation before she left to go to Paris.

Everyone continued to eat, wondering who would be the next to drop something ridiculous into the mix.

"So, Leo how's your grandmother doing?" Samuel asked. "We should have asked her to join us. Next time."

Leo smiled. "I'm sure she would love it. She doesn't get out much. I try, but it only works on occasion." Then he thought to himself how odd that question was. Why would Samuel say that, and why did Francine turn her eyes away from him?

Samuel sipped his wine, realizing he shouldn't have brought up Lilly at all. Then he raised his glass. "Let's toast this wonderful evening with family and friends. And thank you, my dear Julianna, for coming home. I'm so glad you did. To life."

Glasses clicked and eyes were on everyone. Gracie couldn't make heads or tail out of this whole dinner party. She didn't sip; she gulped.

Francine smiled. "So what's the big meeting about?"

"No meeting," Samuel said. "Just enjoying time with family and two great guys."

Gracie laughed. "Are we supposed to believe that?"

"You should," Samuel said. "The more I think about the new podcast, the more I think it's going to be successful. Nicholas, what do you think?"

Nicholas, who usually had a lot to say, didn't say much — an indication that everything wasn't exactly paradise. He just shrugged his shoulders and took a sip of wine. "Time will tell."

Julianna smiled. "Wow, I wish I could read minds. This crowd is tense. Glad to see nothing's changed. We've just added a few new players."

Gracie smiled back at her sister. After a family dinner, they used to have private talks that were especially fun when other guests were present. They used to sit on the deck and talk for hours about life, family, and how they saw their future. Where they all were at this point in their lives had not gone to plan.

Samuel sat down and looked around the room. He was pleased. He took another sip of wine and stood up again. One more time, he lifted his glass.

Gracie and Julianna looked at each other, anxious for the evening to end so they could relax and talk.

Samuel began again. "We're all here because, after a long hiatus, this family is finally back together. Before the jury decides how this evening happened, it was me. I saw the future, and I plan to see it through with my girls happy and safe. And let me say one more thing before all of you go bananas. I didn't know Julianna was coming back for sure until a few days ago. Now everything seems a lot clearer than it has for a very long time."

Looking right at Gracie, Samuel said, "I'm certain it's going to be a great chance for my girls to help grow what is already a substantial business."

Gracie didn't want to cause waves, but she was ready to walk. None of this made any sense, but sometimes her father liked to confuse people so he could get the most out of them.

Samuel continued. "Gracie, whether she knows it or not, will be terrific. Now on to Leo. Leo will be there because I asked him to help. We've been friends for years, and he has a warmth to him that is rare. He will help Gracie find her strengths. I know — and she knows — that she is capable of just about anything."

Gracie managed a smile.

"And, just for the record, Julianna called me and wanted to come home." He smiled at his daughter. "Do you have anything to say?"

Julianna nodded. "Well, I'm not stupid and I know it's time for me to get into the real world. I knew it would happen eventually, but not this soon. I've made quite a few bad decisions, but that's part of life. It's time for me to get serious. I actually want to have a somewhat normal life."

Francine looked at her girls and wondered how her two adorable children had gotten into so much trouble as they entered their adult lives. Naturally, she didn't want to take all of the blame, but deep down she knew she could have done better.

Gracie was impressed by how much her sister had grown up in the years they were both gone. She had also made some bad decisions and was ready to grow up. She held up her glass. "I second that."

Nicholas could hardly wait to leave this insane dinner. There was so much going on. He was thankful that his family didn't have any of these get-togethers. Then he noticed Gracie looking his way. She smiled at him, causing him to rethink leaving. Was she warming up to him, or was he just imagining it?

Ava smiled when she brought in the coffee. She had seen many chit-chats go bad, but everyone seemed to be on their best behavior. No fights, no tantrums, just good old-fashioned conversation. She looked under the table and Georgia wasn't there, so she knew the dog also assumed nothing bad was going to happen.

After dinner, they had their brandies on the deck. It was a lovely time of year, and it had been such a long time since the girls were both seated at the table.

Leo helped bring the dishes into the kitchen. "Oh, that's okay, Leo," Ava said while tying a garbage bag. "No one ever brings dishes in. I'm used to doing it myself."

"My grandmother always thought it was a good idea to learn to be in the kitchen. Good practice for life."

"Sounds like a smart woman."

"She's the best."

"Can you cook?"

"Absolutely. My grandparents had a bakery. Actually, we still do, but my grandmother only works part time. Let me tell you, she can bake."

Gracie stood there, watching Leo converse with Ava. She liked the way he treated everyone. She hadn't been exposed to men like him. Then again, she was never attracted to anyone remotely like him — not that she would admit being attracted to him in any way. She might have had a hint of interest, but she wasn't going to act on it. She continued chanting silently in her mind, *No, no more men.*

She thought it was the sweetest thing when Georgia entered the kitchen and Leo bent down to pet her. He was so kind. If Georgia was comfortable with him, that was a good sign.

Back at the dinner table, Nicholas whispered to Julianna, "Do you want to go for a drink later?"

"I don't think so. It's been a long day."

"It will help you unwind."

"Does it look like I need one?"

"No. Well, maybe just a little."

Julianna bit down on her lip, questioning his motives but leaning toward going. He just needed to make his case a little better. "I shouldn't, but maybe I will." Then she whispered in his ear, "What about your deal with the devil?"

Nicholas smiled. "As far as I know, I'm a free man. So let me ask again. Would you like to go for a drink?"

"Okay, I'm in. But not tonight. Soon."

Francine was eyeing the two of them. What could her daughter be thinking? Julianna definitely hadn't changed.

***

When everyone left for the evening, Francine walked into the bedroom and turned off the television Samuel was watching.

"What are you doing?" Samuel asked, perturbed. "I was just relaxing."

Francine sat down at the edge of the bed. "What exactly are you trying to do? Pick out the men you think our daughters should be with?"

"Maybe I should ask you the same question."

"What does that mean?" Francine was annoyed. "Are you trying to fix Gracie up with Leo?"

Samuel tried to give her an innocent look, but that wasn't going to work. "Are you crazy? Why would I do that?"

"Because you like to be in control. Gracie came back and now Julianna's back, and you think you can keep them from leaving again."

"Let's talk about crazy. You're pushing Nicholas toward Gracie. Let me tell you, that will never work. Gracie's polite to Nicholas when I'm around, but word has it in the office that they bicker like schoolchildren."

"Well, I think they'd make a great couple."

"Forget about that. It's not going to work."

"Because you think Leo's the right one for her. Now that's a laugh."

"Can I watch TV? This conversation is going nowhere."

"Just promise me you won't push them together. It's not a good thing. Just because you're still in love with Lilly."

Samuel's face reddened. "What the hell does that mean?"

"Do you think I don't know about Lilly? How naïve do you think I am?"

"What's Lilly got to do with this?"

"Lilly isn't just Leo's grandmother. She's been your lover for years."

"Francine, you've gone mad. That's not true at all."

"I've known about her for years."

"And yet you're bringing her up now?"

"It matters. I think I'm going to travel for a while. When I come back, we'll see what happens next."

"Meaning?" Samuel was surprised. There he was, thinking he should have told his wife everything, but the timing was never right. He never imagined she knew anything about Lilly. He was stone cold wrong, but happy it was out in the open. "Maybe that's a good idea. We might even miss each other."

"I think it sounds like a plan. I'll leave in a few days. But why don't we make a pact? Let our daughters do their own thing. It's important that they find love on their own."

A few quiet moments passed before Francine left the room. "Sam, do you still love me?"

He didn't answer at first, but then he couldn't help but wonder. "How about you. Did you ever love me?"

They both got their answer when neither of them said another word.

Chapter Fifteen

Gracie took a few deep breaths just before the show was ready to air. She was now sure this endeavor would fail. A podcast was nothing she ever wanted to do. How did she let her father talk her into doing this? She was supposed to be an adult.

Five, four, three, two — live show. She was on the air. And she totally froze.

Luckily, Leo was there. "Good morning, Chicago. Welcome to 'It's All About Love.' My name is Leo Tucker and with me is my co-host, Gracie Maxwell. Call in and let us know what makes you happy and what makes you sad."

As Gracie watched Leo, she began to feel as if this was really possible. He knew what to do, and she was in good hands. Gracie was going to do the unthinkable for a woman who would rather read a book than talk.

Leo was calm as could be, and she was listening to his every word. She was shocked when he started talking about them.

"Gracie and I met each other on a plane, and then my life changed."

Gracie smiled as he motioned for her to join in. "Well, that's right. I was just about to throw up when Leo talked me through a rough plane ride. And then my life changed too." She laughed.

She was a little shaky, but she decided to trudge ahead. She breathed in and out several times; her Tai Chi was helping.

"And what made you feel that way, Gracie?"

"Beats me. But luckily we didn't crash and we're both here."

"It wasn't that bad, was it?"

"Yes, it was. But here we are, and it's smooth sailing with a fun show for all of you listening." Right then, something clicked. She would use her sarcasm to get through this. Leo could be the sincere one, because he obviously was. "So, gang, we're here for you. If you have any questions, call in. You might not like what we have to say, but you're going to enjoy us. Come along for the ride. It's going to fun."

Leo felt happy to be there with her. A podcast? Who would have thought? Something clicked, and he knew it. He wondered if she felt that way too.

"And look at this — our first day, and all the lines are lit up," Leo added with a silent clap of his hands. "Gracie, do you want to take the first call?"

"Gentlemen first." She smiled, and he was mesmerized. She was so beautiful, and he was there with her. Maybe he wasn't the nerd he thought he was. If his friends could see him now.

Leo hit the button. "Hi, welcome to 'It's All About Love.'"

"Hi Leo. How do you know it's not just wishful thinking when you start to believe that the guy you love is truly falling for you?"

"Well, does he look at you as if you're the only one in the room, or does he look around and you know he's not looking at you at all? Does he ask you how your day was and actually mean it? Does he kiss you goodbye when he leaves, or is he in a hurry to go somewhere else?"

Gracie sat back in her chair and just listened.

The caller answered. "Well I'm not sure, but I sometimes feel like he's not in the same room as me."

"If you feel that way, he's probably not the one. When the right one comes along, you will feel his eyes on you. The warmth coming from him will be real, and that will show you he's the one for you. He will look at you and know there's nowhere else he'd rather be."

Gracie nodded, impressed with his answer.

"Next caller."

"Gracie, I have had a few relationships, all ending the same way — very badly. How do you know when it's time to leave?"

Gracie wasn't prepared for a question to hit so hard on her first day. It was one thing to respond in writing, but another to hear the questioner's voice. She was silent for a moment. Leo waved his hand, motioning for her to answer.

"Now that's a good question. One way to tell is to ask him a question about his life. If he won't answer, or if he does but you know it's not true, you'd better think twice and run, run, run. Life is too short to be lied to. When a man lies once, he will lie again and again and again."

Leo laughed. "So, there you go." He looked right into Gracie's eyes. "Remind me never to lie to you."

"You seem to be a guy who knows it's not a good thing to do. Am I right?"

When Leo didn't answer, Gracie wondered if she'd hit a sore spot. She had been known to do that on occasion.

"Next caller," Leo said as he smiled back at Gracie, knowing he'd have to come clean about Nicole Forrester at some point.

Chapter Sixteen

Though the numbers shifted back and forth for the first couple of weeks, the podcast became highly successful. Leo had been having the time of his life and Gracie, to her surprise, felt the same way. Neither of them had expected the show to last more than a few weeks.

Their marketing staff was a big help. They were respon-sible for getting so many posts and emails sent out. Nicholas did have talent, because he found a way to get the message out and the team did a fantastic job. Gracie and Leo owed them a lot.

Samuel was so pleased he even took a weekend off. He was very relaxed, and it certainly wasn't because he wanted to spend time with Francine. She was somewhere in the Mediterranean, having the time of her life. Samuel, meanwhile, was out several nights in a row. Maybe no one else noticed, but he seemed to be down a few pounds and was much happier. He even declined a hot dog lunch. Gracie knew there was something going on.

The days were passing so quickly that Gracie didn't realize at first that Leo always seemed to leave the building before she had a chance to say goodbye. After every podcast, it was the same thing. They finished the show, had a few laughs, and then he disappeared.

Their show had no prepared topics, but so many calls came in day after day that there was never a lull. It was fun.

Leo began that day's show. "Well, here we are again, happy to be with you. This is 'It's All About Love.'"

"Hi, I'm Lexi from Chicago. This is for Gracie."

"Hi, this is Gracie."

"There have been times when I want to walk out of my relationship with this gorgeous guy with tons of money and a fabulous home, but I stay. Sometimes he goes away on business trips and he never calls to see how I'm doing or if I need anything. Let me add that he goes away for weeks at a time."

"Do you work?"

"No, he doesn't like me to work."

"Do you live there full time?"

"Yes, I do, but I've been saving up money. I've saved quite a bit."

"Enough to live your own life?"

"Yes. I have quite a nest egg."

"Can I be blunt?" Gracie hesitantly asked.

"Yes, please do."

"Leave your man. If he loves you, he'll find his way back. And if he doesn't, well, the hell with him. It's his loss. If you want a normal life, there should never be anything standing in your way that doesn't make sense. If you think there's a problem, that's because there is one."

"Gracie, that sounds doable."

"One more thing. Are you afraid to leave?"

"No, not really."

"Good. Is he out of town?"

"Yes, he'll be back tomorrow."

"Start packing. And, honey, good luck. You've just made a great decision. Your life is just beginning. Have fun! And remember, if you're really in love, nothing ever stands in your way. Money comes and goes, but love should be forever."

Leo smiled. He liked that thought.

***

After a month or so, Gracie asked Leo to meet her in the office they shared but rarely used. She wanted to run some things by him. She didn't know if he would show or not, because it seemed as if he was trying to avoid her.

When Leo knocked on the door, Gracie called out to him. "It's your office too. Why are you knocking?"

He walked in holding a beautiful bouquet of roses. He knew she liked them. "I have a peace offering."

"What's this for?" Gracie asked as Leo handed her the bouquet. She smiled, smelling the beautiful aroma. "I love roses."

"I know you do. But I haven't been completely honest with you."

"Join the crowd."

"Can I sit?"

"Of course."

"Remember during our first show, I talked about how lying is never a good thing?"

"To tell you the truth, I don't remember much about that day, except that I froze. And if it weren't for you, I would have been a one-show wonder."

"Well, it was about lying and how lying is never good in a relationship."

"Okay, but why the flowers?"

"I've been keeping a secret that only two people know — your father and my grandmother."

"Sounds intriguing. I like secrets."

"That's what we need to talk about. You once asked me how I met your father."

"And you never answered me."

"I know. That's why I'm here. I love Manny's Deli. I used to eat there almost every day."

"So does my father. He's a deli man."

"Exactly. Your father always got a corned-beef sandwich with extra mustard on rye, with fries and pickles. I usually ate a turkey sandwich on a bagel with mayo on the side. Simple, but good. I always found it easier to write with background noise."

Gracie didn't know what to make of this story.

"One day, your father came up to me and asked me what I was doing. He admired my concentration and said he wished he could do that. He got distracted easily."

"Well, that's true. Sounds like him."

"At first I didn't answer, but then he sat down next to me. I figured, 'Okay I'll answer or I'll never get any work done.' I told him I was a struggling author. Your father laughed and said, 'But it's such a busy place with so much going on.' I told him I tune out the noise, and that I loved the food."

By this time, Gracie hoped he would get to the point.

"He didn't say much for a few minutes, but then he asked another question. 'What do you write?' I thought he was just being nosy. I had no idea who he was, other than a guy who loved corned beef with mustard. I told him I wrote romance, and he asked if he could read it. I didn't want to be rude, but I told him I never let anyone read my work until I'm done."

By this time, Gracie was laughing. "You said that to Samuel Warrington?"

"I did. He smiled. As he got up, he turned back and handed me his card."

Gracie was fascinated by this story. "So, what happened next?"

"He told me that when I was finished my story, I should bring it to his office. I didn't think much about the card yet because I wasn't finished, and you know how people do things just to be polite."

"Not my father."

"I didn't know that at the time. But the card was on my dresser. When my grandmother asked me where I got it, she told me who your father was. She also said to say hello when I talked to him. Apparently, she knew him years ago."

"That's so funny. I guess you never know who knows who." Gracie was laughing. "What a small world."

"There's more."

Gracie was ready for just about anything, other than what he was about to say.

"Leo Tucker is Nicole Forrester."

Gracie didn't say another word. She was too shocked to speak on many levels — especially because he was one of her favorite authors. Now she realized why her father partnered her with Leo for "It's All About Love." Now that she knew, she worried she would be intimidated. That usually didn't happen to Gracie Maxwell, but this could be a first.

Chapter Seventeen

Nicholas had been pleased with how the podcast had found an audience — and a loyal one. He let Gracie and Leo make their own decisions, which pleased Gracie. Because they made such a great team, their listeners sent emails, texts, and letters to rave about the two of them.

Gracie and Leo ate lunch together every day, but they never talked about anything other than the show. Despite their feelings, they were not coming clean to each other; it was less complicated if they left romance out of it. Gracie didn't want to ruin their friendship with romance, and Leo was afraid to let himself feel anything that might hurt him.

Nicholas was preoccupied with a secret his own. He wasn't prepared to talk about it with anyone, but he thought he might want a woman's opinion. Gracie seemed like the logical choice, because it was about her sister. So he did the unthinkable and asked to meet with Gracie to get her advice.

Gracie wondered why she had been summoned. "The ratings are good, so what's up?"

"Well, there's no other way to say this, so—"

"Oh, this is serious."

"It is. It's not something I'm particularly good at."

"You mean telling the truth? Just go for it. I can handle it."

Gracie sat there, waiting for the other shoe to drop. *I knew it*, she thought. *My father is having Nicholas do the hard work because he can't face me. Me, his own daughter. So sit up and be the old Gracie; take it like the woman you are.*

Nicholas had no idea what she was thinking, which was par for the course.

"So just fire me. Get it over with."

"What in heaven's name are you talking about?"

"I just assumed that's why I'm here. If it's not to fire me, then what is it?"

"You and Leo are a terrific team. This has nothing to do with that. I need to ask you for a favor, and to confess something to you. I never thought these words would come out of my mouth."

"Okay, just spit it out. I don't have all day. You know me, all work and no play." Even she laughed at the thought of that being true.

"I'm in love with Julianna."

Gracie had no idea. "I think I should sit down."

Nicholas sat beside her. "So, what do you think?"

"I had no idea you were seeing her."

"We've been together every night since the dinner at your parents' house. The minute I first laid my eyes on her, I had that feeling."

"You had that feeling? Really?"

"You know. The one where nothing else matters and that person is the only one you see, even in a crowded room."

"I get it, but I must say it's mindboggling."

"I thought you might say that, given our history."

"Now that you've told me the good news, is there more?"

"Has she mentioned me at all?"

"Actually, she did. She thought you were a pain in the ass, and that my mother handpicked you for me."

"I doubt that would have ever happened."

"You're damn right it wouldn't have." Just because he was handsome, charming, and very smart, that couldn't make her fall in love with him. Besides, she was planning on being single for the rest of her life.

Then, to top everything off, Nicholas opened a little box. "Do you think she'd like this?"

"Wow, that's a beautiful ring. Isn't this a little fast?"

"When love hits, it's best to just go for it. Who knows what tomorrow brings?"

"That doesn't sound like you at all. What did you do with the old Nicholas Sinclair?"

"He's in love. This is the new me. To be truthful, I'm working on it. It will take a little time."

"How did this happen? You never just do something. You usually think about it and think about it."

"All I know is she looked at me and something happened. I fell for her like a ton of bricks. It's not that I haven't been with lots of women."

"Can't argue with that." Gracie smiled. "This isn't your first rodeo."

"So, do you think she'll like it?"

"She'll love it. Is that why I'm here?"

"I just wanted to run it by you."

"And you did."

"I hope she'll realize how happy she makes me."

"No doubt in my mind she will. It's beautiful. I'm sure she'll love it. She's marriage material, not me. I'm a free spirit and I love it."

"So you say. There's someone for everyone, and I think you found your guy."

"Not yet I haven't. I'm not looking, and I'm not sure I'll ever start."

"Well, as far as I can tell, you have an admirer."

"What are you talking about?"

"Leo. Don't you see the way he looks at you while you're talking? I've watched the two of you during shows. He's still captivated by your answers."

"You've got it wrong. He had a life he loved and it's gone. Believe me, he's not looking."

"What are *you* talking about?"

"He tragically lost someone he loved. I doubt he'll be falling for anyone in the near future, if ever. Let's just leave it at that for now." She quickly changed the subject. "So, when's the big night for you and Julianna?"

"Don't know yet, but I'm going to do it soon. Maybe tonight."

"How often are you seeing each other, besides at work?"

"We've been practically living together, but she usually goes home by morning."

"No wonder I haven't seen her much these days. Actually, I haven't seen anyone home lately except Ava and Georgia. That's always the best company anyway. They don't judge me; we just have fun. Popcorn, a movie, and control of the remote. Who can ask for more?"

"Gracie, it's not like you to do a 'poor me' speech."

"Not poor me. Lucky me. I didn't say anything like that. I don't need a man to make me happy. Most of you don't like to commit until we push so hard it turns you off. Forget about me not being happy. Just worry about yourself. And you'd better not hurt my sister, or you know who's coming after you."

Chapter Eighteen

Gracie could hardly wait to tell Leo the good news about Julianna. But when she got to the office, Leo was standing at the window just staring out at the city. He seemed a million miles away.

"Penny for your thoughts?" she said as she tried to pep him up, seeing his eye were red from crying.

"I didn't think people said that anymore."

"Well I do," she said. "Are you okay?"

"Just an off day."

"Are you having those a lot?"

"No, but today was Ellie's birthday."

"So sorry."

"That's okay. I'm trying to get used to her not being here. Obviously I'm not trying hard enough."

"You want to go to lunch with me?" Gracie blurted out.

"Not today. I already have a date."

"Oh," she said, a little disappointed. "I wanted to keep you posted on some news."

"If it's bad news, don't tell me until tomorrow."

"It's nothing like that. It's good news."

Leo half smiled. "Okay, let's have it."

"Nicholas is asking Julianna to marry him."

"You're kidding, right? I didn't even know he had a thing for her."

"Me neither. My sister never mentioned she was even seeing him, although she has seemed a little distant lately. Sometimes she gets like that, and I have to pry things out of her. And she never discusses her love life with me. Never did."

"Is this a good thing?" Leo asked.

"Yes, I'm glad, but I hope she knows what she's getting herself into. He's kind of a player."

Leo was surprised by the news. He always assumed Nicholas and Gracie were a secret duo. But now that he knew they weren't, he felt relieved. He was starting to care about Gracie more than he wanted to.

"As long as you're here, why don't you come join us for lunch?" Leo asked.

"I don't like being a third wheel. It's not my thing."

"It's not like that. Just come."

"Really?"

"Yes, there's always plenty of food."

"Okay. I'm in. Where?"

"It's a surprise."

"Okay. I guess we can take the time. I doubt we'll get fired." Gracie smiled, feeling surprisingly comfortable with him. "Or maybe getting fired wouldn't be that bad."

"No, maybe not," Leo said, not certain he would be working with her for a long period of time. He was already doing the podcast far longer than he had imagined. He was only supposed to be there for the launch, but he was enjoying the show and was good to stay for the immediate future.

✳✳✳

Leo took the scenic route home. As he drove, he could sense Gracie was losing her edge and becoming softer. He loved the way she smelled. He didn't recognize the fragrance, but there was something familiar about it.

"I forgot how beautiful Sheridan Road is," Gracie admitted. "When I first got my license, my friends and I used to take this route. Some of the Northwestern fraternities had parties and we used to prance in as if we were princesses."

"Were you?"

"Yes, I guess you could say that. We always left after a few minutes. I was never the girl who liked frat guys. My friends did, but I was the one driving and I made the decision. Frat boys were so into themselves. You now, like Nicholas." She stopped herself from saying any more. She knew if she kept talking, she would sound jealous of someone who might be her sister's husband.

"I was never the fraternity type."

Gracie smiled. "I figured that from your Jack Madison series."

"You know that series?"

"I guess I should admit something to you. I'm a Nicole Forrester junkie. I love your books. I loved the ending of that series. What a family! And Stephanie! It was a good thing she dumped Randall. He was a bad guy. And that Michael, he was such a pain." Then she laughed. "Now look who's the chatty one."

Leo smiled, thinking the day seemed to be getting better.

"Sorry, I didn't mean to go on and on."

"That's okay. It took my mind off things," Leo said as they drove down a beautiful garden path that led to a phenomenal home. It looked like a castle.

"Who lives here? Man, I thought we had a nice house, but this is breathtaking."

"It's a house I bought for my grandmother. She loves gardening, and she worked hard to put me through college, so I always promised her she would live in a castle one day."

"Do you always keep your promises?"

"I do. Or at least I try to."

"That's impressive. This house is extraordinary. Oh, excuse me, this castle." She felt like a schoolgirl talking to a guy for the first time. There was something about Leo that made her feel calm. She reminded herself of their flight home from Paris. He was the only good thing about that flight. His voice, his charm, and his wit kept her from going totally off the rails.

Gracie wandered around the back to look at the garden Leo mentioned. It was spectacular: red, white, yellow, and pink roses everywhere. She felt like she was reading a book and this is where it took her. Now that she knew Leo was Nicole Forrester, she understood his imagination, but this was reality.

Sitting on the large deck was a beautiful woman with silver hair twisted in a fashionable bun. She was having coffee at a table filled with sandwiches, fruit, and pastries. Everything looked fabulous.

"Is that your lunch date?" she asked Leo.

"She sure is. She knew this is a hard day for me, and she didn't want me to be alone for lunch. Come meet her."

"Are you sure it's okay? Maybe she wanted to be alone with you."

"You'll see. She'll be quite happy. You'll like her."

When Leo had mentioned his grandmother and her advice on the show, Gracie had no idea she was this elegant woman with a sense of timeless style.

"Nana, can we join you?"

"Please. Who is this lovely woman?"

"Gracie, meet my favorite person, my grandmother Lilly."

"It's good to meet you," Lilly said, nodding in approval. She thought it was about time he had some fun. He worked day and night, and she was getting concerned. She was happy he brought Gracie home. Since Ellie died, he had never talked about anyone else except Gracie, and now she could see why. She was charming and beautiful, and Lilly sensed Leo meant something to her. They already looked like a couple.

"I hope you're both hungry," Lilly said after looking down at her watch. "I know the two of you are on a schedule and I don't want you to be late. I love your podcast."

Gracie was flattered. "You listen?"

"Of course. My friends do too. We look forward to it. And after the show, we have a little coffee gathering and chat about all the subjects you discussed."

"That's terrific. It's so good to hear your friends listen."

"It's not the questions as much as you and Leo chatting. It's delightful."

"I'm so happy you like it. I had no idea our banter would be so well received by different generations. That makes me so happy. I wasn't sure I could do this. Leo, on the other hand, is a natural-born talker."

Lilly beamed. "So true. Even when he was a baby, he was chattering all the time. By the time he was five, he knew every neighbor on the block."

Gracie laughed as Lilly poured her a cup of coffee.

"Cream or milk?"

"Black."

"Me too. Cream, milk, half and half, not for me."

Leo bit into one of the brownies. "This is so good."

Lilly laughed. "Even as a little boy, he wanted dessert before dinner." She handed Gracie a brownie. "Why not?"

The moment Gracie bit into the brownie, she smiled. "This is really great. I love these."

"Your father loved them too."

Lilly made a mistake, and she knew it. She pretended as if no one heard her, but they did. "Anyway, what will it be? Tuna or chicken salad?"

It was a lucky break when Bernie pranced in. Gracie bent down and petted him. "How cute is he?"

After they quickly finished lunch, Gracie checked the time. "Maybe we should go back."

As they walked back to the car, Gracie breathed in the air and the picturesque beauty of the garden. "I love roses," she said. "And your grandmother; she's wonderful. Thanks for taking me here. It was a beautiful lunch. You're such a lucky guy to have such a wonderful person in your corner."

Gracie began walking down another path that led to a small pond. "Are there fish in this pond?" she asked.

"Yes. I always liked to go fishing when I was young, so we added one when we built the house. My grandmother used to take me fishing every weekend."

"Can we sit?" Gracie asked.

"Sure."

"This place makes you forget all your troubles."

"I wish that were true for me," Leo admitted. "I haven't been able to enjoy anything as much as I did before. Except I really like doing the podcasts with you."

Gracie smiled his way. "Me too. I've surprised myself so many times since we met. I don't know how you manage to do it, but you always make me feel as if everything is going to be alright. In fact, I've never met anyone like you."

"Is that good or bad?"

"It's good. It's very good." Her smile was contagious.

"You know my grandmother was happy to meet you. She's heard about you for months now. I talk about you quite a bit. I haven't smiled or laughed as much as I do when we're together."

Gracie seemed happy. "How do you know your grandmother approved? You haven't had time to talk with her alone."

"I could see it in her eyes. We have this thing where we know what the other is thinking. She's been my rock; without her, I would have fallen apart when Ellie died."

Gracie clasped his hand. "Look, I'm not the best at understanding love, but your wife was lucky to have someone who cared about her so much. You're a good guy, and that's why I like you. There's something about you that makes me feel safe. I'm sure she felt the same way."

Leo didn't say much. He just listened and closed his eyes, trying to clear the sadness from his mind. He wanted to be happy again, but he was scared. He looked at the pond and saw Ellie waving at him just like he saw her at the fountain in Paris. She was all dressed in white and smiling. She nodded as if in approval of Gracie. Leo felt sure this was a sign. It was almost as if she was saying goodbye. Tears were slowly streaming from his eyes.

Gracie reached inside her jacket and handed him a tissue. "I'm so sorry. It's my fault. I shouldn't have said that. It was wrong of me to presume to know anything about how Ellie felt."

"It's okay. You're being my friend."

"Maybe we should go," Gracie suggested, but Leo just sat there without saying a word.

"I'm so sorry. I'll be back by the house."

Just as she got up to leave, Leo grasped her arm. "No, don't go. Please. Let's just sit here for a minute or two."

"Okay, I can do that."

Gracie looked back toward the house and saw Lilly smiling. Lilly nodded to her, as if to say it was okay. Gracie felt peaceful.

"Can I ask you something, Leo?"

"Sure. You know more about me than most. We're friends. I've always been so busy that I never really had friends. Your father has been my friend. He's always there for me."

"I'm his daughter and I love him, but I haven't felt like he's always been there for me. Do you think he's proud of me?"

Leo looked at her in a slightly different way than he had before. He was concerned that she didn't know how much Samuel thought of her. "It might not be my place, but your father loves you so much. Before I knew you, he would talk about his children and how he hoped that they would be part of what he built someday. He did it for you and your sister. All of it."

Gracie was amazed at what she had just heard; it felt good to hear. Of course, she would have liked it to come from her father, but Leo had done a great job of making her feel better.

As strange as it was, she was there to help Leo get through the day. Gracie realized he was a man she could love. He cared about making her feel good, and she loved that about him. So much for her not wanting love again.

They both sat there, listening to the rhythm of the water in the pond.

Gracie moved slightly closer. "I want to kiss you, but I'm afraid it will ruin what we have."

Leo wasn't expecting her to say that. "You want to kiss me?"

"Yes. Why are you so surprised?"

"You're so beautiful, and you've had so many wonderful adventures. I'm just plain old Leo Tucker, not the most romantic guy. And a sad one at that."

"Aren't you also Nicole Forrester, the most romantic romance writer I've ever read? Your words are magical. They soothe me when I'm down. You are that man."

"Nope. I'm not that man."

"You certainly are. The Leo who I do a show with is a man who answers with his heart. I want to know that man better."

"Ask me again."

"Do you want to kiss me?"

He smiled. "I have wanted to kiss you from the moment I laid eyes on you. I should have asked to see you again on your first trip to Paris, but I walked away thinking it wasn't possible."

Gracie sat there speechless.

"And then again in New York, when you weren't on the plane going back, I never thought I would see you again. I had no idea where to find you."

"Maybe you should kiss me now."

His lips brushed against hers as he spoke. "I can do that."

There was a dreamy intimacy to their kiss. Leo's lips were warm and sweet. The first two kisses were special, but the third one was the charm. He was wonderful and she knew it.

"Are you sure this is what you want?" he asked.

Her smile answered him.

Second Chances

Chapter One

Samuel couldn't help himself. Once again, he thought it was time for a family dinner. A Warrington dinner could go either very good or very very bad. Few were middle of the road. Dinner that night was family: Francine, his wife of more years than he liked to think of, his daughters, Gracie and Julianna, and of course his son-in-law to be, Nicholas. He had invited one of his favorite friends too, Leo Tucker. He was hoping Gracie would give him a second look.

He knew Leo was quite different than her other boyfriends, but that is why he had high hopes for Leo. Leo was a good man who had suffered a great loss and was now coming back to life, and he knew Gracie could be a part of that recovery.

Gracie referred to Leo as a good friend and nothing more, but Samuel thought if they could work together on the podcast, something more than just a friendship would be in the cards. Gracie was not interested, she had said repeatedly to Samuel, and he knew that was a fight he wasn't going to win. So, he didn't argue with her because he hated to lose.

It usually started out peaceful, but then, on occasion, it would go south. He was hoping to stick to the subject he wanted to briefly go over, the wedding of Nicholas and Julianna. One he wholeheartedly approved of.

Ava was busy in the kitchen, trying her best to stay to herself. She didn't like committing to an opinion because on occasion she stirred the pot in the wrong direction and someone got mad. They didn't stay mad, but it was uncomfortable at best. So, over the years, she didn't discuss her feelings out loud unless asked, and even then, she was cautious.

She knew everyone's secrets, or at least the ones they shared with her. Ava prided herself with a hazy memory if necessary. She tried to be like Georgia, their Labradoodle, who didn't outwardly show favoritism, but she had one, Gracie. No one outwardly discussed it, but everyone knew it.

Samuel lifted his wine glass and everyone else followed. "To my new son-in-law to be, Nicholas Sinclair, who if anyone would have told me this was possible, I would have laughed in their faces. However, he's a good man and the kids have my support. To a life of love."

Francine smiled as she lifted her glass in joy. "Yes, to life with a man you love." For once, she was happy with Julianna's choice. Her toast was appropriate because she had wished she had married a man she loved.

Ava entered with a platter that held a beautiful turkey. It wasn't Thanksgiving yet, but Francine picked the menu. Everyone loved turkey and the wonderful mashed potatoes, Ava's best dish. Already on the table were rolls and butter, substitute salt for Samuel whose blood pressure was higher than necessary. Ava was certain he didn't know, but he did. Also on the menu were some of the old familiars, olives, pickles, and applesauce. Samuel didn't like any of those. He asked about what was for dessert because he always had room for that.

"So, any ideas of where you two would like to get married? As long as it's not in a church, I'm good with that."

Francine kicked her husband under the table.

Samuel laughed. "Just kidding." Already conscious that Nicholas had planned to convert. It was Nicholas who decided. His parents were gone, and he liked the Jewish traditions.

Samuel had initiated that conversation as soon as Nicholas had asked to marry his daughter. Surprisingly, Nicholas was old school. Not the womanizer Gracie had said he was. Although Samuel wasn't stupid, and he knew all the talk in the office, but that was then. Now he was engaged to his daughter and all of that was behind him. Samuel also had that discussion with Nicholas, but no need to tell the family about that little talk. After all, Nicholas was marrying his baby.

Julianna gave her father the, *you can stop now look.* And Samuel did.

"We don't know yet. We just got engaged. I haven't decided what month or what year," she announced with conviction. "I promise you'll be the first to know. So, stop planning. I'll give you plenty of time."

"Maybe you could elope. That might be fun," Gracie added jokingly or at least pretending that was a joke when she saw her father give her that *not now honey* look.

"When you said what year, you were kidding, right?" Samuel was surprised but not shocked.

He knew his daughter's secret, but he was certain that would all be cleared up soon. He was working on straightening out her mess. She was very good at putting herself in situations that required his help, actually both girls did. They wouldn't admit to it, but all the same it was the truth. His mission in life was to make sure they were happy, even if it killed him. *Got to love those girls.*

Samuel was watching Leo, thinking maybe he shouldn't have had Leo join them. He didn't want it to be obvious how much he would like to see Gracie and Leo become a couple.

He knew his daughter was a handful, but when he watched them, they had that special spark. They were good together, and not only during their podcast, but it was the way they looked at each other when they didn't think the other noticed. He had that with Lilly, but not with Francine. One of the things he desperately missed.

Leo had also been thinking as to why he accepted the dinner invite, although he knew he loved spending as much time with Gracie as he could without being too obvious. So far, it was more or less a kiss and then nothing. He was disappointed, but he understood Gracie's hesitation because he also was reluctant to become attached. For now, friendship was enough.

Samuel knew he had to get this party going. It wasn't a party; it was turning out to be another crash and burn dinner. Looking around the room, he watched Francine gloat because she told him this wasn't a good idea but as always, he did what he wanted.

"So kids, the podcast is going well. Leo, my boy, and Gracie, you two have outdone yourselves. I'm proud of you. You are making a killing. People just love you guys."

Gracie almost spit her food out. Praise from her father was not an easy task. "Well thank you, Samuel, so glad you approve."

"Gracie, you know I don't like it when you call me Samuel."

"Yes, I know that," she added as she took another sip of wine. She was pleased with herself.

Francine gave her daughter a look. She didn't say anything because Gracie and her father were very much alike. Sometimes fewer words would work, but both of them loved to get the last word on any subject on any day. If you put the two of them in a room, it spins.

"So, Leo, I was wondering if the news about your grandmother is true. She's got the bakery up for sale?" Francine asked just for the fun of it. She liked to put Samuel on edge. It was a goal she loved achieving.

"She does that every year, and then once she gets an offer, she changes her mind and it's business as usual."

Samuels continued to eat without a comment. Very unlike him. This time, he kicked Francine under the table. She nodded, realizing she pushed the envelope too far. She didn't care. She was smiling inside.

Ava was on her way in from the kitchen, as well as Georgia, who headed under the table, feeling the hostility in the room. "Dessert tonight is chocolate cake with pistachio inside. Any takers?"

Samuel smiled. "Nothing better than that. Ava, what would we do without you?" He took a deep breath, glad the previous conversation died out.

"Order out," Francine was quick to answer. "Ava, without you I'd be lost." The girls laughed, knowing that to be the whole truth and nothing but the truth.

"That's absolutely right." Samuel smiled, thinking of dessert and trying not to think of how unhappy he was that once his girls left, he would be alone. He assumed Francine might be thinking that exact thought.

What they needed was a heart-to-heart talk. Francine and Samuel were very good at pretending they were happy, but both of them knew it was time to be honest with each other. They weren't getting any younger, but hopefully they were wiser.

For now, dinner was going, going, gone! Tomorrow would be brighter.

Chapter Two

It had been a very long time since Samuel and Francine had gone out for dinner by themselves. They were usually entertaining business associates, but this time they both knew why they were there. It wasn't to discuss business or to have a relaxing evening together. It was to discuss their divorce.

Samuel picked Gibson's Steakhouse, not only because it was his favorite, but he was certain Francine would be on her best behavior. On more than one occasion their marital quarrels ended up as a free for all battle of the fittest. Each declaring themselves the winner. If one were to say what the outcome would be after their dinner, it would be a tie. They were both going to get what they wanted. A fresh start.

Sensitive subjects never went well, but with a full belly Samuel could handle almost anything, except defeat. He didn't even like that word. Defeat meant weak, and he wasn't some tragic story that others would laugh at. He was Samuel Warrington and he deserved to win. Sometimes he was a little full of himself, well it was a little more than sometimes.

Francine looked gorgeous as always. Once she put on her expensive pearls and her huge diamond ring, it didn't matter what she was wearing. She liked to be in the spotlight, to wave to her friends, pretending she was the happy wife of Chicago's favorite publishing guru. Samuel was very liked in the community. He never said no to a donation or a request to make Chicago a better place to live.

People loved him. He was known for his pleasant smile and a warm handshake, but just don't cross him. Then things could get ugly, but luckily that didn't happen often. Samuel wasn't there to make enemies; he was there to make friends. That usually worked in his favor and helped with his image.

He was a very successful businessman, a tycoon, would be the best way to describe how the publishing world viewed him. But to his daughters, he was just a father who was very hard to please. He loved them to the moon and back, but to be truthful, he wasn't sure if either of his girls were up to the task of replacing him. That always made him feel unsettled, but he never let on to anyone that was how he felt. Everyone assumed his girls were next up, but not even his daughters thought it would happen.

They each had master's degrees, but to him that wasn't the end all to his decision, especially since he didn't finish college. So much for the diploma, even though his daughters didn't have the option of not finishing. They weren't him, and the world was a very different place than the one he grew up in.

The servers knew both their orders. For Samuel, a large steak, potato, shrimp cocktail, and their fabulous Macadamia Turtle Pie for dessert was his order. Francine would be having her usual tossed salad with salmon, dressing on the side, no dessert. No added calories for her.

Right after they sipped their wine, Samuel, who didn't like to beat around the bush, asked. "Who's going to talk to the girls? Or possibly we should do it together. They'll have questions and if we're both there we can answer them together."

"I think it's better if you do it."

"Why? You're their mother."

"Right, I got that, but you're their father. You always handle them better than me. You know that."

"That's nonsense."

Francine raised her eyebrow. "Is it?"

"I really hate to rock the boat by myself. They're finally getting over me bringing them back to Chicago."

"Wouldn't you say the boat has been rocked and the passengers are drowning?" Francine sat erect and agitated. "You're the one that keeps them on a tight leash."

"Is that what you think? I love them, and their happiness is my number one priority. I try to protect them, but as of late I feel that I could have done better."

"I get that, but in some circles that would be a little bit too possessive."

"Not in my circle," Samuel added.

"This is pretty much coming out of left field for them, don't you think?" Francine questioned. "I don't think they're expecting this. They're smart girls, but they have their own lives. Samuel, face it. They're not two years old. They're women now. They don't watch our every move."

Samuel knew she was right, but his protective side took over. "Well, haven't we waited long enough to finally do the right thing? I know I'm not always easy."

"Now that's an understatement."

"Maybe, but we're still their mother and father no matter what age they are. They'll be upset, no doubt."

"No doubt. But shouldn't this be our time now. We're not going to live forever."

Samuel obviously didn't see it the same way. It was no secret his daughters were his life. He had a drawer filled with every birthday card, Father's Day card, camp letters, notes from their teachers, and anything else his girls had given him. They were reminders of how lucky he was to have them.

He loved Gracie and Julianna more than anything. He had always been their protector. Would they understand when he told them the truth? Maybe he would only tell them half the story. Lilly would come later. He didn't want to push them.

"Are you planning on telling them about Lilly?"

"Not yet. I don't even know what to say to them."

Francine stared at him for what seemed like an eternity. "Why don't you ask Lilly what she thinks." Francine was being sarcastic.

"She doesn't know," Samuel added with honesty.

"She doesn't know what, that you love her and we're getting a divorce?"

"We haven't discussed any of this. This is between us, you and me. Not Lilly."

"I'm sure you'll be shouting it out from the rooftop. After all these years, you're finally going to be able to be with the woman you've always loved. That must be a relief. It's a dream come true. I'll be out of your life very soon. You'll finally be rid of me."

"I never thought of it that way. We had a life together and we've accomplished so much. We have two daughters. That's what we share. Doesn't that account for something terrific? Even if they do give us grief now and then."

"Now and then? I'd say we've had our fair share."

"Has it been that bad?" Samuel asked, not really understanding her comment.

"You don't know half the things those girls were up to."

Her honesty was troublesome to Samuel, but he assumed it was accurate.

"Look, It's not too late for happiness. Wouldn't it be nice to finally wake up to the woman you've loved? I knew you never loved me, but that was okay. You did the right thing and stepped up to the plate. Like it or not, you married me, pregnant and unhappy. That made you one of the good guys."

"I know, but I'm no saint. I could have been a better husband."

"And I could have been a better wife, but here we are."

"If this really is what you want. I'm fine with it, but you know you've said you were leaving before. You've been known to change your mind."

She smiled. "Not this time. This is for real."

"Okay, I just don't want to involve the girls if it isn't going to happen."

"It is. I promise you, this will happen."

Francine's answer was welcomed by Samuel. "Fine, what about the house? We can't both live there."

"We can let the lawyers take care of that. I never liked the house anyway," she confessed with certainty.

"You could have fooled me. If I remember correctly, you were involved in every step of the architecture. You hired everyone from the bottom up. Remember?"

"Vaguely." She was lying. She remembered greeting the contractor every morning with coffee and bagels. Every day she had new ideas and loved every minute of the time making sure the house felt like a home. She had an eye for color, and her style was impeccable. She did a great job, and when it was all done, both Samuel and her were pleased.

And as the years went on, everything changed. It was shortly after Julianna was born when she started to feel unhappy and inadequate. Samuel was busy making deals and making lots of money. That part she liked, but she didn't like the role she played. Being a mommy hadn't quite satisfied her needs, and the fact that Samuel was never home didn't help.

That's when she began to write books and think for herself. She joined book clubs and the country club where she met men, handsome, confident, rich men.

At first, she was just a golfer having fun, but after she got better at playing golf, she became a lot more than just a golfing partner. She became a sexy dinner date to a lot of single older guys, and of course a few younger men sprinkled in the mix. Samuel didn't notice, and after a while, she didn't care if he did. She was a free spirit, a married free spirit. All of that had contributed to them having their goodbye dinner. *So far so good.*

And for Samuel, he couldn't have been happier. He sat back in his chair watching several of his friends waving and smiling at him, totally unaware of what was really going on. He had imagined this night a hundred times before, but now it was reality. A smile on his face at that moment was not for what was happening, but for what was yet to come.

He was going to be a free man, and for that he thought Francine deserved a healthy goodbye package. He was treating it like a business deal because for him it was. It appeared that she had thought this out, so the last thing he wanted was bad blood between them. He had a legacy that he protected from day one, and that was something she didn't know.

She only knew half of his net worth. After all, he started with nothing, and he was a generous man but he wasn't stupid. Some of his associates had almost lost everything to divorce. He wasn't going to be one of those guys. After all, he was Samuel Warrington.

You don't get to be number one without drive and commitment and stepping over a few others to get there. He wasn't always proud of that but, just the same, he did what he had to. Francine didn't have to know everything. And he was certain she didn't.

"Okay, so let's decide what to say to the girls. Both of us. Together. It will be better that way."

"I can't do it," Francine declined with a sense of remorse.

"Let's be realistic, it's our daughters, yours and mine. Let's do this together. If we do it together, they'll understand. If we don't, they may not realize we both want this."

"I'm leaving tonight. I'm really sorry, but my flight is leaving soon. You're so much better at handling the girls then I am. You know that. It's no secret you've always been the one they go to. You and Ava are far better than me at any of this."

"Ava's not their mother, you are. She's always been wonderful with the girl, but this is different. She can't fix this for them."

Francine knew she was wrong, but still she was on her way to be with the man she had loved for years. "Just explain it to them the best you can, and I'll handle it at my end."

"Are you going alone?"

"No, I'm not."

"Are you going to tell me who he is? Shall I guess?"

"No, you don't have to guess. You know exactly who he is. You know it's Wyatt."

"It's always been him, hasn't it?" Samuel asked, knowing he knew where she was and who she was with at all times.

"Yes, but I didn't need to talk about him with you. I never thought you earned the right to know my personal thoughts and wishes. Just as I knew who you really loved. I knew we were always being followed. You're slipping."

"I'm not slipping, but I just wanted to let you know I'm still on the top of my game. But you know that. I'll tell the girls myself, but I'm not going to lie."

"And you. Are you going to tell them about Lilly?"

"It depends on how the conversation goes. I love them, and I'll see if it's going to be too much at one time. They're our daughters, and they will know about me soon enough. But you're their mother, and that will be a big blow to them."

"I guess you're right." There was a trace of sympathy in her voice, but not enough for her to change her mind.

Samuel was disappointed in her behavior, but he knew there was nothing more he could do. She always did things in her own way. He guessed if he could come to terms with this chaos, so would Gracie and Julianna.

"Before you leave, let me write you a check. Whatever you need," he added.

"No worries. I was at the bank before we met for dinner. I made a withdrawal." Her smile was beguiling.

"How much, Francine?"

"It was substantial." She grinned.

"How much, Francine?" He took a deep breath in rather than start a shouting match. They had plenty of those in their almost thirty years of marriage. He thought after everything they had been through. Finally, they might be able to end what probably should have never been.

Francine could tell her husband was getting angry. His face was red, and that was when she knew she was wearing out her welcome.

Francine cautiously smiled as she stood up. "Let's put it this way, if you write any checks, they might very well bounce." She laughed. With that being said, she left.

Samuel sat there for a very long time deciding how in the world he would tell his girls what had just happened. He would tell them as soon as he found the right words, if in fact that was possible.

Chapter Three

For Gracie, the thought of a new relationship was off the table for now. She may have shared a few kisses with Leo, but it appeared that neither of them was ready for commitment. They never spoke of their kiss, and it appeared to be just a moment.

On occasion, they each wondered what it would be like if they were a couple. Being single and alone wasn't ideal for either of them, but for the time being their work together would be enough to get them through the bad times.

The podcast was a smashing success, so every Monday through Friday Leo and Gracie sat in the studio and helped others make the right love decision. Actually, it was a relief for both of them. No pressure, just fun. And when they left the studio, they left each other. No dinners, no coffee, and definitely no kissing.

One problem Gracie faced was getting up early in the morning. It was a challenge, but Ava being the greatest housekeeper managed to get Gracie up and running. Not an easy task.

Gracie instantly woke up when she saw Ava staring down at her holding her morning coffee. "I think you might need this."

"Did something bad happen?" she asked as she took a few sips. "G-d, this coffee tastes great."

"It's decaf."

"Really, you think I'll be too wired or something? Are you trying to sedate me? I need the real thing."

"Later, honey. Right now, you need to stay calm."

"So, tell me the news and cut to the chase. I don't like the way you're looking at me. Am I going to freak out?"

"That's a possibility."

Gracie's silky blonde hair was a mess, especially after she scrunched it with one hand. "Okay, let's have it." She was starting to get nervous. "How bad is the news?"

"Not sure. You tell me."

"It's not like you to be so suspenseful. Let's have it." She was ready, smeared make-up and all. All she remembered from the night before was being so exhausted she fell on the bed, closed her eyes, and fell sound asleep. And now this.

Ava had been both a nanny and housekeeper since forever. In fact, Ava was more of a mother to her than her own. She was the one she went to when she had a school assignment that troubled her, and Ava was the one who got her through her first love. She was her main go to and nothing could ever change that.

"Have another sip," Ava said as he sat down beside her.

"Fine, if you insist. What did Julianna do or say? It's always about her."

"It's nothing she did. And why in heaven's name can't you give that girl a break. You two have been this way since you were little. I think it's time to give it up. You're sisters for heaven's sake."

"As you know, she has been known to get a little bizarre at times. I love her, but sometimes it's like walking on eggshells. Can't imagine what her wedding will look like."

"Yes, I know that, but I also know she looks up to you. You're her role model."

"Not anymore. I'm hardly a role model. I can barely get through a day without being mad at myself for doing incredibly stupid things."

"So, you're not perfect. Look at you now. You've picked yourself up and got back on the horse."

"Tell my father that. He doesn't trust me,"

Ava laughed. "You know your father. He takes his own sweet time to forgive. I think he's come a long way."

"Maybe," Gracie added. "But it still seems far away. I can keep on delivering, but it seems as if it's never happening. I blew it. Some legacy. Actually, I'm pretty sure my time has come and gone."

"Maybe not. Your father's just stubborn. You know that."

"I know it, but I don't have to like it."

"Well then, you'll just have to prove him wrong. You can change his mind by just doing what you've been doing. You've got it in you. I know that. Look how successful your podcast is."

"It's Leo. All him. He's special. People love him. My father loves him. And that's not an easy feat."

"Let's not argue who's better at it. You're both great. A fabulous duo."

Gracie frowned. "Do you really think so?"

"Where's the confident Gracie I know and love."

"I'm working on it. Paris did me in. So, for now, tell me what you came to tell me. If it's not Julianna, what is it?"

"Okay, here goes. And don't shoot the messenger," Ava said, trying to lighten what was to come next.

"Let's have it. I'm a big girl."

"Okay, but don't scream, it's Jack. He's here."

"My Jack? Jack the jerk Gigolo? Jack, the married man who doesn't deserve me? Jack, the married man who proposed to me while not mentioning he had a wife and child? That Jack?" Her voice was growing louder by the second.

Ava nodded. "Yep, that would be the one."

"Did you tell him I'm not home?"

"I didn't say anything other than wait here. And then I came up to see you."

"Why? You could have said I don't live here anymore or something like that."

"Didn't you just say you're a big girl now?"

"I did, but obviously I'm not," she said quickly as she jumped up, spilling the coffee all over herself and the bed. "Oops, sorry. This is why I don't have breakfast in bed. Anyway, for news like this you should have brought me vodka, not coffee."

Gracie grabbed a few pieces of Kleenex from her nightstand and haphazardly tried to blot the coffee. Meanwhile, Ava grabbed a towel from the bathroom. "I got this."

"Thanks so much. You're the best. What would I do without you?"

"You'd be just fine. May I remind you that you were gone for a few years. Who cleaned up your messes?"

"Jack did, of course."

"Good to know." Ava added, trying to straighten up the bed. "You need to get dressed. He must be here for something important."

"I can't see him now. I'm just getting over his lies. Just tell him I left the country for parts unknown."

"So, you hate that he lied to you, but you're asking me to lie for you."

"Yes, it's just a white lie. A little one. You used to lie for me."

"That was a long time ago, and I told you never ever again. And besides, he's gorgeous."

"Oh, I do know that. That's how I got into trouble." Gracie closed her eyes, picturing him kissing her. "Yep, he's definitely a fine-looking man. His dazzling appeal is charming, I can vouch for that but, unfortunately, he's a liar. What kind of man doesn't tell the woman he wants to marry that he's already married?"

Ava smiled. "You can't have everything," she added sarcastically. "In my day, looks were enough."

"You sound like you're a hundred years old when you talk like that."

"Well, I'm not young, sweet pea." She smiled at Gracie with love.

"Since I have been listening to hundreds of hard luck stories, I've been trying to be on the right side of love. I'm actually beginning to believe Leo's advice."

"Seems like you're beginning to like him more than just your podcast partner."

"Nope, that's not happening. We work together, that's all."

Ava knew there was more. "If that's what you say, then that's what you say."

"That is what I say." She was lying. "And besides, he's just not my type."

"Well, my dear, don't pass on a good thing because you're afraid. Take it from me. I missed my chance. I had a good man, and after that nothing mattered."

"You never talked about this before," Gracie added, wondering why.

"Nothing much to say. It's water under the bridge."

"You've never talked about what you did before you came here."

"Not much to say. I came from an agency, and was just about finished with horrible interviews and mean people and promised myself I was going to find another profession."

"Glad you didn't."

"Well, I took the job here as a last resort and was going to move back to Ohio. I needed money, and this job was just to hold me over until I found a better job."

"But you stayed. Why?"

"Because you came into this world, and for me it was just what the doctor ordered. I was now part of a family."

Gracie seemed genuinely happy. "Lucky me. You're always there for me, you have no idea how much I appreciate you. I'm sorry if I don't tell you that enough. Guess before I left for Paris, I was a bit immature."

"It's all part of growing up." Then she hugged her. "Now get yourself dressed and I'll entertain Jack. You know he speaks English very well."

"Yes, he does. Amazing, isn't it?"

Actually, the only person Gracie was looking forward to seeing was Leo. When she was on air, she couldn't remember enjoying anything as much as doing the podcast with him. Leo changed her life in so many ways. She kept her distance for a good reason. She was afraid. She didn't want any more heartbreak. Loving the wrong man was brutal, so for that reason, she was taking a pass.

And now to ruin it all, Jack Monroe, her ex-lover, almost husband, was downstairs and she had no idea why. And she really didn't care. He was bad for her. Even if she did want to see him, she knew he was bad for her.

"Ava, he shouldn't have come."

"But he did. So, my suggestion would be to get dressed and come downstairs. You can be a bigger person. Since you've been home, you've made yourself quite a household name. You know your new favorite saying, *woman up*. You need to be that woman now."

"You're right. I'm Gracie Maxwell. I host one of the most favorite podcasts among millions, *It's all about Love*. How's that?"

"Good, now say it again with more feeling."

"Fine. I'm Gracie Maxwell, and along with my co-host, Leo Tucker, we are podcasters extraordinaire." Then she laughed. "How funny is that?"

Just as Ava was about to hit the stairs on her way back to Jack, she heard Gracie whispering her name. "Ava, come back. Quick. Can you keep a secret? I have to tell someone," Gracie whispered.

"Right now?"

"Yes. Don't tell anyone what I'm about to tell you."

"My lips are sealed. As far as I can tell, the majority of your life has been a secret from your parents. So yes, I can most definitely keep a secret."

"Leo Tucker is Nichole Forrester."

"What on earth are you talking about? That's a joke, isn't it?"

"Nope, no joke. My father has been his mentor for years. He's the guy that writes all of the Massey Leamington steamy romantic books, and you know the others. We've read them all."

Ava laughed. "That's who he is? Are you sure?"

"He told me himself. My father had his identity pretty well locked up. He's been secretly publishing with Warrington Publishing."

"All of his books?" Ava's tone was one of shock.

"Maybe not at the very beginning."

"Wow, that's headline news. Are you sure?"

"He told me himself. My father doesn't know I know. It's a hush hush secret. A big one at that."

Ava was stunned. "Wow, I thought I knew just about everything there was to know about this family?"

"Me, too," Gracie added. "I don't even think my mother knows."

"Talk about the best kept secret in town," Ava said as she hurried Gracie on to get going. "I'll be downstairs staring at Jack. Try to make it fast. I have no idea what to say to him."

"Something will come to you." Gracie laughed.

"I'll stare at him and make him feel uncomfortable. How's that?"

"Perfect. Maybe he'll leave." She kissed Ava on the cheek. "That's why I love you. You always have my back."

"Maybe I'll run away with him." She laughed.

"You could do better," Gracie added with a smirk on her face, *and so could she.*

Chapter Four

As Gracie looked at herself in the mirror while applying her lip-gloss and mascara, she recited the words, "Woman up, and don't fall for his charms. Once was enough. Remember, woman up."

She then proceeded downstairs to the guillotine. She couldn't think of one good reason why he would show up unannounced. He never mentioned he would ever be coming to the states again. He said he didn't like Chicago. She wasn't buying whatever he was selling. So she said, but when she saw him standing in her home, everything changed. She knew she was weakening.

Gracie was caught off guard when he kissed her hello on both cheeks and then surprisingly embraced her. "It's good to see you. I wasn't sure you would even see me."

"Well, to be truthful I almost didn't, but my curiosity got the best of me," she said, as she drew herself from his arms. "I assume you have a good reason for showing up here. You might want to fill me in, and hurry up, I have a life."

He smiled devilishly. "There's the Gracie I missed. Straightforward and to the point."

On that note, Ava excused herself and left the room. Georgia followed. She was curious, so she listened in. She had one little flaw: she loved handsome men and the stories behind their charm. That's why every day at lunchtime she would be sitting at the TV having lunch and watching soap operas. Come hell or high water, she parked herself on the couch and didn't move until they were over. Nothing worse than missing an episode or having it preempted by some breaking news.

Gracie was trying her best not to succumb to his charms. She had made a promise to her father not to see or speak to him, ever. It was easier if Jack was in Paris and she wasn't able to feel the fire that was still burning inside her, but there he was standing in her living room, looking exquisite. She was doomed. *Maybe not.*

At that moment, Gracie had so much going through her head she felt as if there was no air in the room. She refused to pass out, stubborn as she was, so she inhaled a few times. Would she melt to his charms? If she was the strong woman she thought she was, she should have thrown him out before he said anything. The big question was, why didn't she?

She was desperately trying to ignore what she was thinking, especially because her heart said *put your arms around him and kiss him like you're happy to see him.* But her mind was saying *go away and leave me alone. We have no future.*

While she was busy thinking of all the reasons to tell him to go, Jack couldn't stop staring at her. She was simply stunning. He loved when she wore her hair down with wispy bangs that brought out that special sparkle in her eyes. He could never resist her, even on a bad day. And at that moment he didn't want to.

He couldn't figure out why he was so foolish as to let her leave Paris, not that he had a choice. She was going to leave no matter what, and he knew he deserved it. He lied one too many times. He could have told her the truth while she was still living with him, but he didn't. Another bad choice.

"Gracie, you look incredible."

"Okay. Stop. None of your charm, please. I'm not in the mood."

"It's not charm, it's the truth. You're still the most beautiful woman I've ever been in love with, not to mention your wit and intelligence."

"Jack, please let's not do this. I'm not impressed."

"I didn't come here to impress you."

"Good because you're not."

"You can't stop a guy from trying."

"Yes, you can," she said with conviction. "Anyway, forgetting about how wonderful you think I look and how smart I am, why are you here?"

"I have something for you."

"What could you possibly have that I would want?"

"You left so fast you didn't take your photos, so I took the liberty of getting them published under your name."

"Why on earth did you do that? And in my name. Isn't that illegal?"

"Well, I doubt once you see the beauty in your photos you might not have me locked up."

Disgusted by his arrogance, she had questions. She hadn't expected him to ever do anything for her again after their rocky goodbye. She made it clear she never wanted to see him again, but then again, she didn't throw him out yet.

"So, why the importance of this whole thing and coming to Chicago? This really doesn't seem like your style."

"Because they're fascinating and brilliant and I wondered why you never showed most of them. Why didn't you show them to me?"

"Well, to be truthful, you didn't seem interested in what I was doing."

"That's not true. You know that."

"I don't know that. When I first got to Paris, you were always attentive to everything I did, and then as time passed. I was just someone to sleep with. Nothing I did seemed to matter."

"That's ridiculous. That's far from the truth." He then handed her a beautiful book with all her photos.

Gracie was more than shocked as she flipped through the album "You did this for me? Oh, my G-d. Thank you." Immediately she backed off. "Maybe you're really not as selfish as I thought."

"There's a lot you don't know about me. I'm not who you think I am."

"I thought I knew you, but obviously I didn't. Jack, it was two years of my life. And then I found out you had a wife and child? I appreciate what you've done with my photos, but I still don't understand why you lied to me the whole time."

"You never really gave me a chance to explain. I loved you and I still do. I want you back. We're good together."

Gracie couldn't help but snicker. "You're kidding, right?" She wasn't prepared or impressed by his declaration. She was done. There was no turning back. She had promised her father she wasn't ever going to talk to him again. Not that she hadn't gone rogue sometimes and did a complete flip flop as to her promises. But she was confident she wouldn't fall for his colossal appeal. He did have that magic that was undeniable.

"Let me take you dinner tonight and I'll explain everything. We can do this."

"No, Jack, we can't. There is no we."

"Gracie, I'm dead serious. Can't a guy make a mistake?" Jack argued.

"Jack, whatever you were expecting when you came here clearly isn't happening now or ever. We can't go back."

"Why not?"

"Jack, you're married. What do you want from me? Let's just let it go and pretend you never came here at all."

"What if I don't want that?"

"What if I do? When I left it was for a very good reason and nothing has changed. So, while I do appreciate the photos, maybe you better tell me why you're really here?"

"You do know me, don't you?"

"I thought I did, but it turns out I didn't know you at all, and guess what, I don't want to know anything more about you or better yet, let's just forget I asked the last question. It doesn't matter anymore."

While he was just standing there, she kept looking at him, not really understanding anything about him. One nice gesture certainly didn't change anything. A liar is a liar. And Jack, no matter how gorgeous and charming he was, he was a fake. End of story. She took a breath in. *Yes, woman up, Gracie, woman up.*

"Gracie, it does matter. We loved each other."

They were interrupted when Ava came back into the room with a tray of cookies and was haphazardly placing mugs onto the tray. "How about a snack?"

"So sorry, Ava. Jack was just about to leave. Right, Jack?"

"I can stay for a while. I have nowhere to be," he claimed.

"Well, actually I do. I have to go to work. It's a work day."

"Oh, I didn't realize."

"What, that I work or that I think we don't have much to say to each other? So, are you going to tell me why you're here or not?"

"Maybe you're right, we can talk about this another time."

Just as Gracie was about to tell him there wasn't going to be another time, Ava came back in realizing her timing was bad. Too late to go back now. Should she serve or should she leave? She saw the way Jack was looking at Gracie, so she did what all soap operas stars do and she continued pouring as if nothing was happening. "Coffee or tea, Jack?"

Sarcastically, Gracie added, "How perfect. We can have coffee, but then Jack is leaving." She gave Ava a questionable look as to why they needed this little coffee get together.

"Cookie for you, Gracie?" Ava elbowed her way in, feeling very uncomfortable, but neither Jack nor Gracie seemed to notice. Probably because they were too deep in their game of one up. So far, the score was tied, but Jack was losing ground fast.

He did have a cookie, and offered Gracie one. "These are terrific."

Ava smiled with pride. She knew if there was one thing she could do well, it was baking cookies. She used to teach the girls some of her baking tricks when they were younger, but Gracie was never interested in cooking, and Julianna on the other hand was a wiz in the kitchen. She did miss those days. Everything seemed a lot simpler back then.

"Fine, I'll have a cookie. Thank you, Ava, so sweet of you." Once again, her tone was sarcastic.

Ava didn't blink at the sarcasm because over the years, she had plenty of practice. One thing about the Warrington's, they were masterful at family drama.

Chapter Five

Leo didn't always know the right thing to do when it came to women, unless he was writing about them. So when he decided to hop in the car and visit Gracie without asking, he had no idea what he was about to enter into. They were friends, and they did share a couple of kisses, but as far as just showing up, that wasn't in the book of Etiquette 101.

He was slightly flustered when he was greeted by both Ava and Gracie. Right off the bat something seemed strange. "Good morning to both of you," he said as he handed Gracie a beautifully wrapped box. "These are from my grandmother's bakery. I thought you'd like them."

"How sweet." Gracie smiled, quickly debating on her next step. She hadn't told Leo too much about Jack, other than he was a jerk and a homewrecker. And she did expect a bit of apprehension as to why he was sitting in the living room chit chatting with Ava, but of course it was too late to make excuses. Jack was there, and so was Leo.

Gracie didn't know what to do because if she invited Leo in, he might get the wrong idea seeing Jack there, but then again, she couldn't just let him leave. "Ava, can you give me a minute with Leo."

Ava left realizing this was a little more complicated than she imagined. She could tell by the way Gracie looked at Leo he mattered. "Okay, I'll handle everything. No worries."

Gracie closed the door behind her. "Let's take a walk."

By this time, Leo realized he should have called. He was never very good at handling his love life. He could write about it beautifully, but personally, he was awkward at best. "I'm sorry. Did I interrupt something?"

"Not really. I just wanted to explain a few things before putting you into the fire."

"That bad?"

"You might say that. Jack, you know, my ex? Well, he's here."

"Paris, Jack?"

"Yep. Who would have thought?"

"Maybe I should go?"

"No, please stay, but follow my lead and maybe he'll just leave and never come back. If my father finds out, he'll go crazy."

"That part is true. That much I know."

"Great," she added as she hugged him and gave him a sweet kiss. "Thanks, I owe you. And please, no matter what happens, just follow me. "

By this time, Leo was confused but decided he could do this. "Okay, I'm in. Are you sure about this?"

In the meantime, Ava was sitting next to Jack having a cookie and some tea. "I think this is my cue to leave." As she walked out of the room, so did Georgia. Georgia hated conflict and being a member of that household for a long time, she could sense trouble. *Dogs can do that.*

Gracie nodded as she motioned for Leo to sit. "Jack, this is Leo Tucker, my Podcast co-host and well, you know…"

Jack pretended not to understand. "What are you talking about? Are you two together, like, *together*-together?"

Gracie laughed. "Well, yes, we are and we're very happy."

Jack stood up and they shook hands. "It's nice to meet you, Leo." He was trying to be polite, but the words were forced. He was disappointed because he was there to reconnect with Gracie, not to be standing there defeated. However, just because they were together didn't mean he was out of the game. *So typical of him.*

"I know. I'm one lucky guy." Leo added with a smile on his face that he hoped looked genuine because it perhaps was. He was able to do this because he was pretending to be writing the scene as he spoke. Then he kissed her. Not a real smoochy kiss, but a substantial one.

"So, Leo, where did you and Gracie meet?"

"Oh, now that's a funny story. I'm superstitious, and well, that part is a longer story, but to make a long story short, from the moment I laid eyes on her I couldn't help but fall in love. At first, she couldn't stand me, but I was persistent. A woman like Gracie can't be pushed into anything."

"Don't I know that," Jack confessed.

Gracie was caught off guard. She felt as if she wasn't in the room and actually, she wished she wasn't. But Leo was a brilliant romance author, and she knew he was playing it out like a scene from one of his books. That would be because she had read every book he had ever written. She knew his style and she loved his writing and she might even love him if she let herself. *Let's save that thought for a later date.*

Gracie handed Leo the book. "Look, honey. Jack brought me a present. It's all the photos I took in Paris. I guess when I left, I left those behind."

Leo smiled. "Wow." Leo sat down and flipped through all the pages. "These are terrific."

"Leo, we can look at them later. No rush."

"Of course, there's a rush. This is a part of you I had no idea existed. These are breathtaking."

Gracie shouldn't have been surprised by Leo's remarks. It appeared that he could lie. *Well, he* is *human.*

Leo wasn't lying. He was fascinated. Each photo was better than the next. The more he knew about Gracie the better. He was interested in everything she did, and that was the whole truth and nothing but the truth. This game she was playing might not be a game at all for Leo. He found her to be truly amazing, and that was his reality.

While Leo was trying to be this wonderful, charming man of the hour, Jack was trying his best to understand how Gracie could have fallen in love in such a short period of time. That was his arrogance talking.

"I guess you were right when you said there was no we," Jack whispered to Gracie.

"Yes, that's true, so I think you might want to leave." And then Gracie gave Leo a huge bear hug. He was surprised, but enjoyed the drama. It was something he might have written in one of his novels. Thinking back, he did, *Memories Left Behind.*

"I'm not so sure I want to leave without telling you the truth about why I really came here. It's wasn't about the book," Jack explained. "I can't leave without telling you something I should have told you from the beginning."

"Maybe we could talk about this another time," Gracie said as she held Leo's hand. "It really doesn't matter now."

"But it does to me," Jack added with a bit of anxiety, which for him was not common. Actually, from the moment Leo entered the picture, the entire scenario was odd. Jack couldn't put his figure on it, but he knew something was off.

Gracie did owe him that, but at that moment, Jack leaving was for the best. She knew he was right. She never let him say anything to her after she told him she was leaving. There were bits and pieces that never quite fit, but when she left Paris, she was so upset, anything he said to her would have probably made it worse.

But she had never for one second expected him to come to Chicago. Yet, here he was. *Although living through his lies wasn't easy,* she thought, *sometimes it's better to let sleeping dogs lie. Funny I always hated that expression.* Her mother always said it, and now there she was thinking maybe her mother was right. But, no need to bring up the past.

"I think I should be going," Leo said. "Maybe you two can finish whatever conversation you were having before I came in."

Gracie kissed Leo's cheek. "No secrets between us. Right, dear?"

"Right … It's fine. I'll meet you later at the studio. I have some work to catch up with."

"Are you sure?"

"Positive. You two should talk."

Leo didn't want to leave, but he knew if he ever had any chance of being with Gracie, she had to finish what obviously wasn't over between Jack and her. He couldn't move on with Gracie if there was a wall between them.

It was quite possible Gracie had some things to work through before she could let go of the past. But as of that moment, it didn't seem like it would be any time soon. Gracie was also suffering from extreme loss as he was, but to what extent, he really didn't know. Who was he to judge loss?

If he was truthful to his grief, maybe he wasn't quite there yet either. *Better to be safe than sorry.* That saying always sounded better than it actually was.

Chapter Six

What Gracie should have done was leave with Leo. Sometimes leaving well enough alone was better than diving in when you don't know what the outcome will be. But her curiosity did get the better of her. Standing before her was a man she had so deeply loved, but could she forgive him? No was the sensible answer, but love was not always logical.

"So, tell me why you're here? I know there's more to this friendly gesture. I'm happy now. What we had is just a memory. It's over."

"Gracie, do you actually think that show you just put on was believable? You don't look happy. I *know* happy."

"No, I'm afraid you don't. You know infatuated. And besides, Leo is a wonderful person."

"I can see that, but he's not your soul mate. I am."

"Well, you're wrong. He's a terrific partner in every way."

"So, you're telling me you're not happy to see me?"

"That's exactly what I'm telling you. When I left Paris, it was difficult, but I've managed to make a really good life here. I'm productive, and everything seems to be going in the right direction."

"And you don't miss Paris?"

"I miss Paris, but not you." She was lying, but no way could she let herself be captivated by his magic. *Been there, done that.*

Jack cleared his throat a couple of times, knowing he was about to shock Gracie. "I know your father checked me out and came up with a profile that wasn't mine. It was thorough, but the man he checked out was Jack Monroe."

"Okay, and that's you. So now what?" Gracie blurted out.

"It's not me. And that's the truth. This whole thing is a bit messy."

"A bit messy? You're kidding, right? It's a lot messy. Jack, why don't we just stop right here, so I can say something you need to know."

"Fine, you go first." Jack wasn't surrendering just yet.

"My dad is overprotective, but it's usually for a good reason. He doesn't make mistakes. "

"This time he did. I'm not married and I don't have children."

"Is this another one of your lies? I'm really over this. We were a mistake from the beginning. My father warned me before I left that I might end up staying there with someone like you."

"I'm not a bad guy. Really."

"You nearly ruined my life. So how can you come to my house and tell me you're not a cheat, instead you're really a good guy? How dumb do you think I am?"

Jack was a little taken back by her comment. "I thought we were good together. I know you thought we were perfect for each other. We still are."

Gracie tried not to be too graphic, but she called it like she saw it. "I just wanted to leave, so that's what I did. It wasn't all my father. I'm not just my father's daughter, I'm a grown woman who can make a decision, and I made one. The right one."

"You were wrong to leave. I did love you and I still do."

Even that bit of honesty didn't change Gracie's mind. If he still loved her, it was late to hear about it. "You lied to me."

"I promised myself years ago that I would never disclose my true identity, even if and when I fell in love."

"Jack none of this is necessary. Next, you'll tell me you're FBI or James Bond or something. I'm fine with the way things turned out. If things weren't this way, I would have never met Leo. But you're French. You're a lover not a fighter. You don't want to lose."

"No, I don't want to lose."

"Sorry to burst your bubble, but we're done."

"At least let me explain."

"Fine." Gracie was losing her patience. "Go ahead. I'm listening."

"Okay, here goes nothing. Jack Monroe is not my real name. I'm Jack Weiss from Chicago. After my parents died, I was young and depressed. They left me a lot of money, so I studied abroad and never came back to the States. I fell in love with France and the beauty of the language. I made a decision to speak French most of the time, that is until I met you."

Gracie wasn't quite sure if this was just a story he made up or if it really was true, so she didn't interrupt. Hard as it was, she stayed quiet.

Jack continued his plea. "I wasn't a very happy guy. It may have looked as if I was some sort of socialite when we met, but I wasn't. I didn't have a family. But then I met you, and you became my family. Life was finally beginning to make sense."

"So, you changed your name? Why in the world would you do that?"

"I could ask you why your name is Gracie Maxwell and not Gracie Warrington."

"That's different."

"Why is that? Because it's you, not me?"

Gracie wasn't going to lose this argument. "You knew about my family, and I never lied to you about who I was after we got serious. So why didn't you trust me enough to tell me the truth?"

"I really don't know."

"That's not a good answer."

"I did it on a whim. I waited for the right time to tell you, but it never happened. I continued the lie and then when we planned to get married, I knew you would be furious, so I didn't say anything. I was waiting for the right time."

"What about the marriage license? You know you need one no matter where you live. Were you planning on lying on the marriage certificate?"

"No, I wasn't. I would have told you before we went through with the wedding."

"That sounds even worse. So, you're not married, and you don't have a child. And you weren't going to tell me your life is completely fictional until we were ready to say 'I do'? That's something you might see in a movie, not in real life."

"I'm so sorry, Gracie. I really am. I'm ashamed of what I did, that's why I'm here. I had to tell you the truth."

He seemed sincere, but Gracie wasn't warming up. His words, even if he was being honest, weren't helping him plead his case. In fact, he was making it worse, if that was possible.

"No wife, no child. So, you took someone's identity?"

"It wasn't like that."

"That's what I'm hearing. What about your parents? Did they die in a car crash or is that a lie too?"

"That's true, but I was eighteen not eight."

Gracie was getting angrier by the minute. "What in the world is wrong with you? Was everything I knew about you just one big lie?

"No, of course not. I love you. That never changed. From the very moment we met I knew I wanted to spend the rest of my life with you. That's why I'm here. And that is the truth."

Gracie just shook her head in disgust. She wondered how in the world she hadn't seen through any of the lies. She thought she was smarter than that.

"After you left, Jack Monroe contacted me. I had never met him. I didn't even know there was a Jack Monroe. It seemed like your father wasn't kidding around with his threat."

"What threat?"

"It doesn't matter now. It's all good."

"Says who?"

"Your father loves you, and I spoke with him the other day, but we decided not to tell you."

"*We?*" Gracie was steamed. "So, you and my father talked this over without telling me?"

"We did. However, he had no idea I would get on a plane and come to Chicago. He said you were doing well and were happy with the life you made when you returned. I really didn't believe that for a second."

"And now you do?"

"No, not really."

"Did he offer you money to stay away?"

"He did, and he also said if I discussed this with you it wouldn't be a pretty picture. You know the power your father has. However, I have plenty of money. As I said, my parents were very wealthy and I invested wisely when I was old enough to do so. Money is of no concern to me."

"Is that supposed to make me feel good about any of this?"

"Probably not, but would you consider giving me a chance to prove myself. Come back to Paris with me. I want you in my life. What do you say? I can tell you miss me. I'm right, aren't I?"

Before Gracie could answer, Jack began to kiss her. The first kiss was on the tip of her nose, then her eyes, and finally he kissed her right smack on the mouth. There was no doubt he was a good kisser, and she immediately felt her knees weaken. Her emotions whirled and then skidded to a complete stop. She drank in the sweetness and the familiarity of his kiss, but when she opened her eyes, she didn't see Jack, she saw Leo. And that shook her.

"So how was that? Is that not a kiss from a man who loves you?"

Gracie smiled. "No, it's from a man who lied to me."

Chapter Seven

Gracie barely made it to the studio. Leo took a deep breath. He was so glad to see her. He imagined all kinds of things, such as her never coming to the studio at all, or hopping on a plane and going back to Paris with Jack. His imagination was running wild.

When she smiled and placed her hand on his forearm in a caring way, he hoped the worst was over. The worst meant she wouldn't be going back to Paris, but he couldn't be sure. After all, they'd had a kiss, but nothing serious really happened. It didn't go very far, probably never would.

"Do you want to talk about it?" Leo asked, trying to be supportive, but slightly afraid of what she might say. Sometimes less was more.

"No, thanks. Believe it or not, I'm good. Not happy with my father, but what else is new."

"Is Jack going back to Paris?"

"I'm not sure. We can talk about it later. I think we have a show to do now. Look over there."

The discussion was postponed when their producer Charlotte motioned for them to get a move on it. "Guys, whatever's going on here, we have a show to do."

"We can do that. Just two friends having a little conversation," Leo said casually.

Gracie half smiled. "Right, two friends."

Even after all the shows they'd done together, one would think Charlotte would calm down. But she was a great producer, and they both knew it, even if she was anxious before, during, and after every show. Plus, her anxiety got the most out of them for each and every show.

They were now number two of the top podcasts in Chicago. Having Warrington Publishing behind them, as well as a fabulous PR team, made everything click. Advertisers were their friends, and their listeners sent them gifts all the time. Chicago loved them, and their podcast went full throttle worldwide.

Leo bit down on his lip, a little frustrated when he noticed Samuel was seated outside the broadcast room. He took a few deep breaths, hoping Gracie wouldn't turn around and see her father. She always got a little uneasy when he was around.

Five, four, three, two — live show. They were on the air and Gracie motioned for Leo to start. It was always easier when he did the intro. It gave her a couple of seconds to take a deep breath and relax into the show. She had never quite forgotten the first show when she froze. Since then, it took her two minutes before she was good to go.

"Good Afternoon, Chicago. Welcome to "It's All About Love." My name is Leo Tucker, and with me is my happy go lucky woman of the hour, Gracie Maxwell."

She smiled as he said that. She liked the way he always made her feel as if she was the one with the style and know-how, when in all reality it was him.

"Call in and let us know what makes you happy *and* what makes you sad. Let's talk about your relationships, good as well as bad."

"So, Gracie, I can see you're full speed ahead. I saw you rush in."

"Hi, Leo. What a day. You're so right. I barely made it to the studio. So much to do. It seems like every day something happens and I lose track of time."

"It's almost like you have another job. Do you?" He was kidding.

"One job is quite enough for me. It's my own fault. I think I watch too much TV. Actually, I know I watch too much TV. Once I turn on the TV, it's never ending clicking. I love series shows and binge watching, that's me."

"So, you're a clicker?"

"I hate to admit it, but I am. I bet you're not."

"I'm not. Once I decide on what I'm watching, I finish it no matter what. I'm the loyal type," he said, giving Gracie a questioning look.

She didn't know where the conversation was going, so she quickly moved on. She was good at that.

"I started holiday shopping." She didn't, but it was a great way to change the subject. "What about you?"

"I like to wait until the last minute. It's so much fun. Speaking of Holiday time, Thanksgiving, what's the plan?"

"Well, are we working or taking off?"

Leo laughed. "Good question. Charlotte, are we working?"

As they both turned their heads her way, she nodded. That's when Gracie saw her father. He waved good-bye as he left the studio, and that was the first time she noticed him being there. That was a good thing. Leo took a calming breath, thankful there was no drama in the works.

"Well, I guess we're working," Leo added as he waved to Charlotte, who was nodding yes.

"As long as we're working, why don't we ask our listeners to call in and tell us their plans. It's always fun to hear holiday stories. We all have them. I know *I* do. Family dinners can be daunting."

"And they can also be fun." Leo picked up the beat a little after that scary comment. "So, everyone save up your holiday stories. It will be fun, but nothing too heavy, we need to keep it light during the holidays."

"Good idea Leo. Fun is good."

"Yes, it is. If you don't want to call in, just message us and we can talk about whatever it is that you're looking forward to or whatever you're not. We all have that aunt who pinches our cheeks and kisses our foreheads."

"We do?" Gracie asked in innocence. "My relatives don't do that, they just give an air kiss the right, and then one on the left, then they go straight to the family bar in the dining room where my father cautiously gives them drinks. He waters them down. We've had a few close calls."

Leo laughed. "Is that true? Waters them down?"

"No, just kidding." Gracie nods her head yes because that's what happened at most Thanksgivings. Some guests drank too much. She smiled, thinking back to when one of her aunts took to the floor after she mixed wine with her medicine. It wasn't funny at the time, but after the fact, it was.

Gracie motioned for Leo to start the phone calls. "So, that about wraps up our holiday plans. Let's talk love."

Leo hit the button. "Welcome to, 'It's All About Love.' Do you have a question or comment for us?" Leo asked as he hit the call button.

"I do," the caller said, then paused for a moment. "I know this might sound crazy, but do you believe in love at first sight?"

Gracie pointed for Leo to take that one.

"No, I don't think that's a crazy question. I did fall in love at first sight. I'm not great at expressing my feelings head on, but she won over my heart immediately. I was scared to ask out the person I hoped would be the love of my life. But, she was confident enough to invite me to dinner first."

"So you went?" the caller asked.

"I did, and after that we spent every day of our lives together. We were a couple till death do us part. Every day was one filled with love."

Gracie jumped in, realizing the subject was too close for Leo's comfort zone. "So, caller, does that answer your question?"

"It does, but I seem to fall in love with every girl I've ever taken out. I've even asked several of them the big question."

"And that was?" Gracie knew, but she thought it would be cute to hear the answer.

"Will you marry me?"

"So did you marry any of them?"

"Nope, not a one. That's why I'm asking for advice."

Gracie motioned for Leo to answer. She knew his answer wouldn't be as sarcastic as hers would be.

"What on earth am I doing wrong?" asked the caller.

"I just think you might not have found the right one. Don't rush love, because sometimes it takes a little time. And, on occasion, it takes a long, long time. Some people fall faster than others, and some are complicated," Leo answered, looking right into Gracie's eyes.

"That sounds like great advice. Yes, love is quite complicated."

Leo chimed in, "But when you do find the right one, and she loves you back, there's nothing greater than that. Life is short and it's up to you to make it sweet."

Gracie was charmed by Leo's answer. *What woman wouldn't be.*

Chapter Eight

Five minutes after the broadcast was over, Gracie stormed into her father's office. This was nothing she hadn't done before. She hadn't needed to lately because her father hadn't tried to interfere in her life. However, after her conversation with Jack, she could barely get through her show. She was as mad!

Her father's assistant, Roseann, was sitting at her desk, filing her nails and listening to music. That was a dead giveaway her father wasn't in.

"So, where's my father?"

"Good afternoon to you too, Gracie."

"Sorry, Rosie. Didn't mean to be rude."

Roseann nodded. "So, what's he done this time?"

"How did you know?"

"It's been that way since you were a teenager. Every time he upsets you, you have that look in your eyes."

"What look?"

"The look that says I can't believe what my father did."

"Am I that obvious?"

"Pretty much," she said as she handed her a letter. "Your father's not in, but he left this for you. He said you'd be coming around after the show."

Gracie shook her head in disbelief. "I can't believe he knew."

Gracie plopped down on the reception area couch to read the letter.
Honey,

I know you're mad, but you know I love you. I didn't know Jack would show up at the house. I was wrong. Don't laugh. You know I hate being wrong, but this time I was. I just can't seem to let you girls grow up. We can talk about this soon, but not tonight. Please believe me, I really am sorry. Talk soon.

Love you no matter what,
Dad

Roseann watched Gracie for her reaction. "So, are you still mad at him?"

"I'm not really sure." And with that, Gracie left the building.

Chapter Nine

Julianna was people-watching, waiting for her sister to join her for a late lunch at their favorite restaurant, RL. This place was both elegant and relaxed at the same time. It was also one of their father's picks. He said it reminded him of home while being out. He loved the grilled cheese and tomato soup. Those things mattered to him because he was a family man at heart.

When Gracie finally arrived, she was out of breath with her usual, I'm sorry but … excuse. Julianna was used to it. There was nothing new about her sister's tardiness. She wasn't sure if Gracie was actually running late or if she enjoyed being that fashionably late person everyone notices. Not that people wouldn't notice Gracie. She was a gorgeous blonde with a beautiful smile who never could just walk into a room without all eyes being on her.

"That was pretty good, Gracie. You're only 30 minutes late. Good thing they know us here, otherwise I wouldn't have gotten a table."

"Could have been worse."

Julianna laughed. "Could have been better."

"I know. I needed to talk to Dad after the show, but I guess it can wait. He was gone for the day."

"Gone for the day? That's not like him." Julianna was a bit puzzled, realizing her father was doing a lot of strange things as of late. "Seems like he's got a lot going on."

"He always has a busy schedule. I don't even know how he does it." Gracie commented. "He's on high alert every day for one thing or the other."

"He loves every minute of it." Julianna smiled. "He likes being the man of the hour, every day. Haven't you heard? He's Samuel Warrington."

Both girls laughed.

"Do you think he'll ever slow down?" Gracie asked, already knowing the answer.

"Nope," Julianna said as she took a piece of bread out of the basket and smacked her lips. "Sorry. I'm starved and this so good. I wish I could eat here every day."

"You could. You have a rich fiancée." Gracie laughed, still not used to the fact that Julianna and Nicholas were a couple — an engaged couple to boot. How that had happened was beyond her. It happened super quickly.

"Hey, do you think something's going on with Dad? Mom's been away quite a bit, and Dad, well, he seems to be having a lot of business meetings."

"I don't know. Tonight, I know he's got some sort of important business dinner. He's going to Lake Geneva."

"Really? Lake Geneva? What's up with that?" Gracie asked as she bit into a roll. "You're right. This is *so* good."

Julianna seemed amused. "Right? "

Gracie wasn't going to say anything about Jack, but she felt like it. She needed to get it off her chest. She was a lot calmer since she read her dad's letter of apology — a first for him. "Guess who was sitting in my living room this morning?"

"Don't know, but do you want me to guess?'

"No, probably not. Takes up too much time, and you wouldn't be able to guess. It was Jack."

"What? Why is he here? Oh, my G-d!"

"Exactly my sentiment. He came to bring me a book of my photos. Actually, it was pretty nice. The book I mean, not him sitting there looking at me. Although he looked better than ever."

"What kind of photos?"

"One of my hidden talents. I started taking photos and got pretty good at it," Gracie confessed as she laughed. "Well, that's not the half of it. I'll make a long story really short. He came to the house, he confessed his love, and told me the truth. He told me Dad found him, and it really wasn't him, but Dad thought it was him, and he wasn't married and didn't have a kid and a bunch of other unnecessary facts."

Julianna placed her elbow on the table, listening and trying to put the pieces of her sister's conversation together, wondering if that was even a possibility. Gracie was going 'round and 'round in a circle.

"Anyway, he's a liar and Dad made me mad and… Oh, never mind. We can talk about that another time." Then she laughed. "Oh boy, that sounded like a Leo story."

"Yes, it did." Julianna smiled, not understanding any part of what had been said, but it looked like that was all her sister was going to say. So she prompted, "Finish the story. Don't stop there."

"Forget about it. I'll handle it. I'm here to talk about you, not me."

"Okay, got it. I think." Julianna looked at her strangely. "Are you sure?"

"Certain. So, what did you want to talk to me about?'

"If you're not finished, we can talk about Jack."

"Oh, I'm finished, all right. Definitely finished." *She wasn't.*

"I don't know where to begin, but first, will you be my maid of honor? That's a good place to start. No date yet. Don't know where the wedding will be held at or anything, but there will be a wedding."

Gracie was touched. "There's nothing else I'd rather do." She was lying, but she wasn't going to tell her sister it would be her very special honor if she was marrying someone else. She still didn't trust Nicholas. However, maybe he did turn over a new leaf. In her opinion though, it was highly unlikely. But in all fairness, everyone deserved a fair chance, even Nicholas.

"That's great. It's all so exciting. Thank you. I'm so happy. There's no one else I'd rather have at my side. Even if we have differences, we have each other and we always will."

Gracie was happy she could do this for her sister. "Good, that's what counts. If you're happy then so am I. You are sure, aren't you?"

"I'm sure. *Very* sure."

Gracie felt a little guilty for not being as happy as she would normally be, but she knew Nicholas might not be satisfied with just one woman. She couldn't say anything to her sister because that would break her heart. She seemed to be so happy being a girl in love, she didn't want to burst her bubble. But Gracie knew Nicholas had quite a spicy life, one she was part of. But that little bit of info was never going to be open for discussion.

"So, is that what we're going to be celebrating today? Maybe we should have a glass of wine."

"Let's skip the wine for now."

Gracie had no idea why. "Okay, not a wine day. Now you really got me curious."

"Well…"

"Not a good beginning. Well, is like but. There's more coming and it isn't good."

"When I left Chicago, I didn't go anywhere fabulous like you did. Now Paris, that's exciting. Ohio was where I decided to go."

"Ohio? Why there?

"It was pretty scary at first. I'm not like you, but I thought I wanted an adventure like the one you were on."

"My life isn't that glamorous. Believe me, I made my share of mistakes. I was infatuated, and fell hard, for a liar no less, who now says he isn't a liar. Paris was secondary, Jack was the one. Or so I thought."

"You've always been so savvy. As long as you brought it up. How did it happen?"

"Well, it didn't end well, as you know. My life is like an opened book, and not a good one if you ask me. I thought I could handle everything, but turns out, I can't. My story isn't that unique. Girl meets a gorgeous, sexy guy and falls in love. Boy turns out to be a jerk. Nothing new. Girl leaves the guy, comes home, and gets a G-d- awful job because she missed her chance. Nothing against Nicholas, but he got the job I wanted. I may call myself Gracie Maxwell, but I'm Gracie Warrington in real time."

"I know. You always seemed to know what you wanted, but me, I never knew. Who would have thought we'd both be working at Warrington?"

"Let's forget about me. Tell me what's going on? Come on, I can't wait one minute more. Out with it."

"I was pretty careful to go to a place where Dad couldn't find me."

"And that's way up there against all odds. He usually gets whatever he wants, some way or the other."

Julianna smiled. "It took him a while, but he found me, and I wouldn't come back."

"You're kidding me, right? You're Daddy's favorite."

"That's what I say about you."

Gracie laughed. "So, go on."

"I fell hopelessly in love."

Gracie's jaw dropped. "I don't believe it. This is a joke, right?"

"No, it happened. I fell in love and we got married."

Gracie was almost too shocked to speak, but then when she began to process her sister's words. She had so many questions. "And you're just telling me now? How is that possible? Why in heaven's name didn't you say anything to me?"

"I really don't have an answer for you. Please don't be mad."

"Easy for you to say that, but wouldn't you be mad? Do you tell me everything?"

"Mostly."

"Well, then I guess we're even." Gracie added.

"Not really. I know for a fact you've been keeping one major secret from me."

"And what does that mean?"

"It means you slept with Nicholas."

Just as the server was about to approach their table, Gracie motioned for him to go away and he did. She held up her hand, meaning come back in five.

"Do you hate me?" Gracie asked, almost afraid what the answer would be.

"No, silly. I love you. I know it didn't mean anything, and it was a long time ago."

"And who told you that wonderful piece of old news?" Gracie asked, half sarcastic, half irritated. When Julianna didn't answer, she knew who told her. "Nicholas, right?"

She nodded. "But don't be mad at him. He thought it was best to get everything out in the open. And that's why I needed to talk to you. It's not about him, it's me who hasn't been truthful."

"Okay, I'm listening."

"Oliver Walker, that's his name. He's handsome, very rich, and an incredible lover." She blushed.

"What is going on here? Is there more? Seems like you've got a lot more to tell. So, spill."

"You might say that. One thing's for sure, I love Nicholas more than I've ever loved anyone, including my husband. Oliver was there for me when I needed him. I just wasn't ready to be what he needed. He has a daughter, Sophie. She's ten."

"And are you ready now?" Gracie questioned.

"I sure as hell hope so. Nicholas and I have something special. That's what I know. He's been pretty straight forward about all the women in his life, and there were quite a few."

"You might say that." She muttered to herself. She didn't like being included on his list. He didn't have to tell, but that was Nicholas. Sometimes he talked without thinking.

Gracie didn't say another word, wondering if she could stay quiet forever, at least until she had a conversation with Nicholas. She added that to her mental to-do list.

The server was back. "Ladies, are you ready?"

Gracie looked at her sister, eyeing the menu. "The usual?

Julianna nodded. "Yep. Sounds good to me."

"Okay, we'll each have a toasted cheese sandwich and tomato soup. I'll have coffee, my sister will have… " She pointed to Julianna to continue the order.

"Nothing for me, thanks. Oh, wait a minute, I'll have green tea."

Gracie gasped. "Green tea, what's happened to you?"

"Nicholas happened to me. It's calming. He loves tea."

"That's exactly why I don't like tea. I don't want to be calm," Gracie added with a laugh.

"Well, ladies. You've made a good choice." The server smiled. "In Chicago, tomato soup and toasted cheese at RL is a classic. Although, coffee would be my choice. We have terrific coffee."

Julianna laughed. "We love it here. You don't have to sell us."

Gracie smiled, "It's one of our dad's favorite places to go for lunch. He's here several times a week. Samuel Warrington."

"Sam is your dad?"

They both looked at each other, not surprised by his comment. There weren't too many people in Chicago who didn't know him.

"He's such a good guy. He always brings us free books and magazines. That's his order too. Toasted cheese and tomato soup. Such a regular guy. He does love his desserts. We all love serving him. He's the biggest tipper we have."

Just as soon as the server left, Gracie started to finish the conversation. "Okay, let's get one thing straight. Nicholas and I don't really see eye to eye on many things, but I know he loves you."

"I hope so," Julianna acknowledged her sister's comment. "He acts like he does. Do you really think so?"

"I do, because I asked him point blank. I wanted to make sure he didn't hurt you. And he was clear about how he felt. I believed him, well not at first, but I think he really does love you. I also told him I was perfectly happy giving him a second chance, but if he lied to you, even once, I would make his life miserable. And you know I can do it."

A faint smile appeared on Julianna's face. She was still holding back.

"So, continue, and let's hear about you, and leave me out of it. Please?"

"Okay. I thought Dad would never find me, but his detective buddy did. Dad thought he was being very persuasive, but I was ready to come home. I had already told Oliver I was leaving. But you know Dad — he thinks it was him, but it wasn't. He thinks he saved me."

"Yes, I do know Dad. He likes his girls close by," Gracie admitted. "I'm not always happy about that, but he's been a terrific dad other than that."

"I can't argue that, but sometimes it's a little too much, and other times it's not enough. He tried to make up for Mom never being around, but nothing can make up for that."

"So, that's why you showed up for dinner shortly after I returned? Dad ended up getting both of us back. Wow. He's good at getting what he wants."

Julianna smiled. "Guess so. Samuel Warrington is who he is. We have quite a legacy to follow. I don't think it's for me, but I might be wrong."

Gracie nodded. "Maybe someday we'll share the job. We could, you know?"

"True, but Dad's not going anywhere. Believe me, he's not ready to give it all up. At least not to us. I think he's got his eyes on Nicholas. That's my guess."

Gracie didn't argue the fact. She nodded in agreement. "Okay, tell me what you really wanted to talk about. I doubt it was about Dad's legacy. You keep skating the issue."

"I'm not divorced yet. Nicholas thinks it's over, but Oliver has never sent me the paperwork."

"Why don't you just call him? It's pretty simple. Just pick up the phone and say, *'Hi, Oliver, this is your ex-wife to be. Where are the papers? I need them. I'm engaged and I want to make some plans.'*"

"Easier said than done."

"Oh, boy. You haven't told him about Nicholas, have you?"

"Nope. He actually thinks I might go back to him. In fact, he's waiting for me to tell him just that. I can't have him coming here."

"Does Dad know about all of this?"

"He does, but he promised to let me do this on my own."

"And you think he will?"

"Yes, because he knows if he pulls his tricks, I'm gone."

"You don't mean that, do you?"

"I absolutely do. It's time he let me grow up. I got myself into this little triangle. I'll get myself out."

"Maybe it's better if you go to Ohio and talk to him … unless you're worried you'll stay. Sounds like you had a life there you might eventually miss."

There was a quiet pause as they both thought for a moment before Gracie asked, "Where's Sophie's mother?'

"She died in childbirth. It's sad, but Oliver is a terrific father. He's like Dad, but not as demanding. Although, she's still young and he's in control. I did love her. In fact, I still do. I didn't want to hurt her but…"

"You love Nicholas more. Most likely you didn't expect to fall in love so quickly. So, that's why you haven't set a date yet."

"Exactly, but I'm not going back. I'm happy here."

Gracie held up her coffee cup and clicked Julianna's cup in a toast. "Here's to us growing up on our own terms. I think you'll make the right decision, but you need to do it soon."

"So, girls. What's the occasion?" a familiar voice asked as she neared the table.

Gracie jumped up when she realized who it was. "Avery, what are you doing here in the middle of the day? Come sit down and join us."

"Looks like you guys were in a deep conversation. I was waving to you and you didn't even flinch."

"Sorry. We're just talking. You know us, we never stop. Anyway, why are you here? It's not like you. I've tried to get you out of the hospital so many times that I finally I gave up," Gracie admitted.

"I'm meeting a few friends from the hospital."

"Doesn't sound like you. Chit-chatting at RL."

Julianna took her bag off the chair. "Sit for a minute."

Avery looked around to see if she was the first one there. With no sign of her friends, she said, "Sure. You might as well hear it from me."

Gracie was confused. "We just talked last week. What's going on?"

"I gave my notice."

Gracie's eyes opened wide. "You what?"

"I've decided it's time to change my life. I need to get away from all the hustle and bustle. Every day's the same. It's non-stop. I need a change of scenery. I'm moving to Wisconsin."

"I can't believe it. Why Wisconsin?" Gracie gasped.

"I'm renting a beautiful place in Lake Geneva and I took a job at Geneva North. Actually, it's a good thing. The ER is smaller and that's what I need now. I won't be on call every weekend, and maybe, just maybe, I can have a life. I'm exhausted. And as you know, my divorce took a lot out of me."

Gracie looked sad. "I'm happy for you if that's what you want, but I'll miss you. After all, we haven't had much time to get together since I got back. When are you leaving?"

"Soon — in a few days," Avery added with a touch of regret. "I'm hoping I won't chicken out. It's scary leaving a place I always loved."

Gracie took a deep breath. "Wow, I don't know what to say. Maybe you shouldn't be going. Why not just take a little vacation?"

Avery laughed. "I don't think a few days out of here will do it. I guess I'm just getting cold feet. I'm going. At least that's what I say to myself every night for the last week or two when I look in the mirror."

"Okay, congratulations to my best friend, Dr. Avery Hunter, who is leaving one of the finest hospitals in Chicago. Is that really what you want?"

"I haven't had a decent night's sleep in probably over a year. I haven't gone to a movie, a play, or treated myself to a massage or manicure. I haven't had a date since the divorce. I feel like a nun."

Gracie felt horrible. "I'm sorry. I never thought about that. I'm just so proud of you. I guess I was just thinking of the MD after your name. Not to mention how important you've become. And just for the record, you can't be a nun, you're Jewish."

"I know, sweetie." Then her eyes scanned Julianna's finger. "So why do I not know about this? When did Mr. Gorgeous propose? It's pretty fast, isn't it?"

"It is, but he's worth it." Julianna's smile was ear to ear. One thing about Julianna, when she was happy, there was no hiding it, and when she was sad, the world knew that too. Julianna didn't censor herself like Gracie.

Gracie didn't say much about the wedding, but Avery knew the story behind the story. Not many people knew about Nicholas and Gracie.

Avery waved to her hospital team as they came in, motioning she'd be right there. "Guess I shouldn't be rude. I'm going to miss those guys. I've known some of them since my internship."

Gracie stood up and hugged her friend. Then she whispered. "We'll talk soon. Love you, honey. Good luck, really."

As soon as Avery left to meet her friends, Gracie looked at her sister. "So, before we call it a day, I want to finish my story real quick. He wants me to go back to Paris with him."

Julianna's eyes popped open wide. "Are you going to go?

"No."

"Thank goodness. Is there more? Because it seems like there's more."

"Let me lay it out for you. He wasn't married, never was, and his name is Jack Weiss, and he's from Chicago."

Julianna motioned for the server to come back. "I think this is a dessert day. We both seem to need it."

Gracie nodded in agreement. "Today we gorge ourselves with sweets. Tomorrow we stay off the scales."

"So, what can I get for you ladies?" the server asked, not expecting what came next.

Julianna replied, knowing exactly what she meant. "We'll have a brownie with vanilla ice cream, coconut cake, and apple pie with caramel ice cream and a lot of whipped cream. And if you have a few cherries, put them on top."

Gracie smiled. "That sounds about right."

Chapter Ten

Samuel's office was just as one would expect it to be. It was the largest office in the building, and beautifully designed. The room was divided into office and conference room that contained a long wooden table and ten chairs. His office featured traditional furniture, including a leather couch and a few comfortable oversized leather chairs and a large Aubusson rug under his desk.

He liked to conduct business on his own terf, thus the conference room. He also didn't like huge meetings. He preferred smaller ones that allowed everyone to speak and not be intimidated.

He redecorated from time to time, as his company grew and he acquired more space. Eventually he bought the entire building. He'd never finished college but, somehow, he got to the status he desired without a college diploma. Of course, it took years and a lot of hard work, but he did it.

He had come close to finishing college, but when he married Francine, they had Gracie to think of, so he started his career off slowly but efficiently instead. Some would call him ruthless, but those who really knew him well knew he didn't become a legend by accident. It was because he was logical and very hard working.

He was waiting for his daughters to arrive, trying to figure out just how much he was willing to tell them about the breakup with their mother. He knew Gracie was mad as hell at him, and while he did deserve it, he liked to pretended he didn't. And then there was Julianna. He'd pushed too hard with her, but he knew no other way. All he wanted was for his girls to be happy, but sometimes he got in the way with one of his well-meaning gestures.

There were a lot of obstacles in his life right now, and even he grew impatient thinking about it, but he still carried on business as usual. How long could he keep up the pretense that everything was fine when he damn well knew it wasn't? The only good thing that seemed to be sliding into place was his love for Lilly. *True love never runs dry,* he thought. *Will the girls understand? Probably not.*

The girls were late, and when the door opened and they pranced in, it reminded of him of back when they were in grammar school. They had absolutely no idea that what they were about to hear would probably break their hearts.

Gracie kissed her father's forehead. "Sounded important, so here we are. What's up?"

Samuel pointed for them to have a seat. "I heard you two were at RL yesterday. How was it? Neither of you have been there for a long time."

"And you knew that because Julianna and I are so popular or are we being followed?" Gracie smiled, wondering if he was up to his old tricks. She didn't really care, but when the opportunity to give her father a one-line zinger arose, she took it. Like father, like daughter.

Samuel chuckled. "Do you actually think I'm having you followed? Am I that bad?"

He had his answer when neither of his daughters answered, instead giving him a blank stare. When they did that, they knew it caught him off guard, and that's definitely why they did it.

He realized that each of them had figured out a little bit about the power moves he used to meticulously control them. He didn't like that one bit, but they were his daughters, and they'd learned from a pro. *Shouldn't be surprised.*

Julianna sat down and crossed her arms, ready for some pivotal point as to why they were there waiting for a shoe to drop. She hoped it wasn't about her wedding because she specifically told him time and time again she would let him know when she and Nicholas planned to tie the knot. "Why were we summoned?" she asked, curiously getting the better of her.

"Girls, I *asked* you to come. I didn't *summon* you. There is a difference, you know."

"Good to know," Gracie quipped. "So, what's this little get-together about?"

"Okay, I'll get to the point. I've been trying to figure out just how to tell you, but nothing seemed appropriate."

Both girls looked at each other, realizing this was something their father didn't feel comfortable talking about. That was so not like him.

"Out with it, Samuel Warrington," Gracie kidded, breaking the ice.

Julianna suddenly became uneasy. "Is it about me and Nicholas?"

"No, honey. You're fine. This is about me and your mother. We're getting a divorce."

At first, Gracie was too shocked to speak, but then after a long pause, she tried to make light of it. "So, Dad, what did you do this time?"

"Nothing. Really. Trust me, it's not me. Your mother decided it was time to go our separate ways. You girls are grown, and she feels it's her time to explore some of the things she thinks she missed."

"It's not like she couldn't do that without divorcing you. She's always gone on excursions all over the world without you. She seemed perfectly happy with that set-up. Who wouldn't be?"

"That's true, honey, but there's a lot of complicated history to our lives that you don't know."

"Maybe we should wait to discuss this with Mom. She should be here. Why isn't she?" Gracie asked. This all seemed so strange to her.

"She thought it was best for me to talk to you. You know how she is."

"I guess we really don't," Gracie said morosely, annoyed with her mother. "So, you're saying she just decided to not show up? What kind of mother does that?"

"I guess our mother does," she said, with disappointment in her voice.

Samuel knew it was wrong. Francine should have been there. Looking at his girls, he felt terrible that he had to be the one to burst their balloon. After all, he and Francine had play-acted most of their married life, and apparently the girls had no inclination that anything like this could ever happen. She should have known how this was going to go. And that was probably why she left without a word to her daughters.

Julianna took a deep, aggravated breath. "I can't believe this is happening, and the fact that Mom isn't here is absurd. What are you not telling us?"

"She's found someone else," Samuel tossed the truth out casually. He probably shouldn't have, but he did because the looks on both their faces let him know he had to say something or they wouldn't let it go. It had always been his job to protect them, but the fact that he couldn't this time was very unsettling.

"And that doesn't bother you?" Gracie asked with a sense of confusion.

"Girls, your mother's a grown woman. She's not happy being with me, and to be truthful, I'm not happy with her. I'm so sorry about this. It just couldn't be helped."

You could hear a pin drop. Samuel shouldn't have said that, but he did. The words just flew out of his mouth. He wanted to tell them about Lilly and that he had been in love with her his entire married life. This was one secret too painful to speak of at that moment. He would tell them soon.

"Why now?" Gracie asked as she uncomfortably pulled her hands through her hair. "I can't imagine you ever holding back like this. It's so not like you."

"I'm sorry, it's been painful for me. I never thought it would go this far, but I'm okay with it. Your mother has a right to be happy."

"What about you?"

"I'll be fine. This may be shocking to you two, but I've been living with it for many years."

Tears were running down Julianna's face. "I just can't understand why Mom didn't have the guts to sit here with her husband and her daughters, who love her, and tell us the truth."

"She just wanted the dust to settle," Samuel said, but he knew that didn't cushion the blow his daughters were feeling.

Gracie was angry. "The dust to settle? What the hell does that mean?"

Julianna stood up. "It means she didn't care enough to think about how we would feel. And Dad, you can pretend this is smoothing things over, but you know it's not. Let's get out of here and discuss this."

"If it's okay with you girls, can we talk a little bit more in a few days. This way you can digest this whole thing better, and I can too."

"Is there more?" Gracie asked, feeling as if they were some missing pieces.

"Yes, there is, but that's not up for discussion today." He hugged each of his daughters in a very loving way. "I love you guys."

Neither of his daughters said another word as they walked out. It did seem as if Gracie, who usually liked to have the last word, didn't have anything to add that would change the situation. Samuel knew he had hurt his girls, and if he could have changed the sadness he saw on their faces, he would have. Once again, Francine had failed her daughters.

Chapter Eleven

Samuel's discussion with his daughters didn't go well, and he knew he couldn't make up for Francine not being with him to tell them. Maybe they would understand more when he told them about Lilly, that or would get worse.

Maybe they would blame him, and maybe to some extent it was his fault, but there was a lot they didn't know. And, maybe there was no blame. Life changes and love happens, but trying to explain to his girls how much he loved Lilly was not going to be easy.

He would tell them about Lilly as soon as he told her that Francine had left him. He'd waited a lifetime to be with her, and now as happy as he was, it was going to be complicated at best. Thank goodness Lilly was such a kind, warm-hearted person. She would help him. At least, he hoped she would. What if she wasn't prepared for any of this, and instead of planning their future, she said no. That was a possibility he didn't want to think about.

He had a limo pick up Lilly. All he'd told her was they would be having a romantic dinner at Lake Charlemagne and they would be spending the night together.

He wanted to go back to where it all began. Lake Charlamagne was a quiet, out of the way place with one tiny fast-food diner, a bowling alley, and a drive-in theatre back then. It had become more commercial as years went by, but the beauty and the calmness still existed.

Years before, Samuel had rented a small cottage for the evening. They were quite young then, but Samuel wanted their first night together to be special. He didn't have much money back then. In fact, he'd spent his entire paycheck making sure Lilly would have a night to remember. It turned out to be their last night together.

Both of their lives had changed, but he was now able to do the things for her that he'd promised her so many years before. Now he owned the entire property around the lake. The grounds were spectacular and peaceful. It was going to be a great place to go when he wanted to turn off the world and relax, if that was possible. He never really made time to just sit and enjoy what he had accomplished. He just kept going as fast as he could, buying companies and selling off whatever wasn't profitable.

He was very good at what he did, but it took a toll on his health. He knew he could've taken better care of himself, but he didn't. So, now that he had finally made the decision to enjoy his life, he intended to marry Lilly as soon as he could and then follow the plan his doctor laid out for him. This included making better choices when he ate, and exercising to get rid of the extra pounds he'd accumulated over the years.

He wasn't one for long vacations, and for most of his life he had stayed close to home. It hadn't been until recently that he discovered there was a lot more to life than just looking at your checkbook and watching the zeros multiply.

This was the first time he'd ever brought anyone to his new property. In fact, he hadn't even told his family about this magnificent getaway. The property was zoned for a bed and breakfast, but he wasn't sure he would ever have guests or rental rooms. He liked the fact that it was his, and hopefully soon it would be his and Lilly's.

Lilly had the limo driver pick her up at a coffee shop close to her home. This was the first time she had lied to her grandson. She decided this trip wasn't going to be something she wanted to discuss with Leo. Quite frankly, she didn't think he would understand the frustration she felt about her love for Samuel. He would ask questions she wasn't prepared to answer.

When the car slowed, she didn't recognize where she was at first because everything had changed so much. But then as the driver rounded the curve, she saw the lake. The memories became as clear as if it were yesterday instead of so many years ago. A few tears fell as the memories came rushing in. The memory of the last time Samuel and she were together before they each married other people was bittersweet.

They'd had a few private encounters over the last several years, but nothing too romantic. They were just friends who missed each other. Samuel wasn't prepared to hurt Lilly a second time, so they kept it simple, with a dinner here and there, and few lunches

When the car finally came to a stop, the driver got out and took her suitcase while she looked around. She had never been back to this area, and she admired the large estate that now existed. The smell, the sites, and the beauty of it all were breathtaking.

It looked as if the small cottage they'd stayed at was still there, and it looked like someone lived there. She imagined it was a caretaker, but that was just speculation on her part. Flowers surrounded the outside of the cozy abode, along with the white picket fence just like she remembered.

As she was escorted to her room by a lovely gentleman, she couldn't quite comprehend the whole story of it all. She began to feel the flutter of butterflies in her stomach. How could she be this nervous? She wasn't a young school girl anymore, and the fear of being too old to have an encounter like this plagued her mind.

The ambience was a little taste of Paris. She used to dream of the two of them going there and sitting outside a hotel, sipping wine while people-watching. They had missed so many things that could have been.

Everywhere she turned was elegant and stunning. Floral arrangements adorned the hallway and the staircase. She was impressed by all the beauty and the charm here. *How lovely*, she thought. Even at her age, the excitement of being with the man she had loved for her entire life was incredible. It was something she'd waited a lifetime for. It was their chance to be together with no interruptions. They had nowhere they had to be and no one to check on, it was just the two of them.

A short while after she bathed and unpacked her bag, there was a knock on the door. "Be right there," she called out. She was nervous, but disappointed when it wasn't Samuel at the door.

Standing before her was a tall, sturdily-built woman. She was probably twice Lilly's size. "Are we ready, madame?" she asked in a French accent.

Guess that's what I'm about to find out, Lilly thought nervously. "Monsieur Samuel m'a demandé de vous faire un massage," she said, then she proceeded to open the closet door and take out a massage table. "Plaisez," she added, indicating Lilly should lie down on the table.

Lilly smiled, deciding to just go with it. "Thank you." She had never had a massage, but here was her chance. Today was proving to be filled with unexpected extravagances. First the limo and now a massage.

As she lay there, her mind whirled. *What would Leo think? Would he be disappointed in me for having an affair with a married man? A man who was his boss! There are so many reasons I shouldn't do this, but yet here I am.*

After an hour, Lilly was as relaxed as she had ever been. When the masseuse left the room, she took a deep breath, trying to center herself. She felt at least twenty years younger, but still nervous. She didn't want to disappoint Samuel. He was married to a gorgeous, elegant socialite whose fashionable style had worked as brilliant strategic PR for Samuel. She felt like she couldn't compete with that.

What if I'm a disappointment to Samuel? I'm not young anymore. As she slipped into her new lace robe and soft velvet slippers, she decided she felt confident in who she was. She also knew that this was a day that would define the rest of her life, good or bad.

Another knock on the door made her jump up. "My G-d, this is a busy place," she muttered.

When she opened the door, she was greeted by a friendly face. She'd seen this man when she arrived. "Hello again… Josh," she said, reading his nametag.

Josh was holding a large basket filled with a collection of chocolates and champagne. "Mr. Warrington said he will be here soon. Enjoy these treats while you wait."

"Looks delicious. Candy's my weakness."

"Mine too," he shyly admitted.

"Well then, by all means, have one. Please."

He shook his head no, smiled and left. "They're for you. Enjoy."

As Josh left, she walked out to the balcony and smiled as she breathed in the fragranced air. To her, nothing was more satisfying than the aroma of flowers. She couldn't believe she was there waiting for Samuel to arrive. It all seemed too perfect.

Then the door opened with a click, and there was Samuel, holding flowers. It looked exactly like the bouquet he had brought to her on their very first real date all those years ago. These were nothing as fancy as the flowers in the room and lobby. *He remembered the yellow daisies,* Lilly thought happily. "Don't tell me they're from Florence's."

"Yes, they are."

"They're beautiful. I love them."

"Florence passed away a few years ago, but her daughter took over."

"I don't believe all of this. I feel like I'm dreaming. Why now, Samuel? What has changed?"

"Please, sit," he said as he handed her a small Tiffany box. "Go ahead and open it."

Her hands were shaking, but she opened the box, and there it was, a magnificent pear-shaped diamond ring. It was stunning. "Samuel, what's going on?"

"It's about us. This is the only place I want to be, here with you. I've waited for this to be a reality. I never thought our time would ever come, but it has."

"You know, Samuel, I was going to say no when you asked me to come today."

"But you didn't."

"Remember when Leo's wife Ellie died and you followed me to my bedroom?"

"Of course, I remember that night."

"We decided we couldn't ever do anything like that again. Even if we still loved each other."

"I know we said that, but I wasn't sure I could keep that promise. You know that."

"We didn't want to hurt our children." Lilly couldn't help but bring that up.

"Tonight is different. We have our whole lives left to live. We're not young, but we can be happy. Say you'll marry me."

Tears were streaming down her face. "What are you doing? We can't do this."

"Oh, yes we can. Our life begins today, right now. You and me, forever."

"How is that possible?"

"It appears that Francine and her lover have decided to move further in their relationship. She's leaving me. She has someone else."

"Did you know?"

"I did. It's her publisher, Wyatt Hamilton. They've been together for years. They always travel together, among other things, and I've known from the very beginning."

"Is it serious?"

"Yes, I think it's always been something special."

"Always?" Lilly was a little surprised.

"Yes. We never talked about it, but I knew he was in her life. I was busy, so it never mattered."

"Does it matter now?"

"All that matters is that we can have a second chance at happiness. I'm finally free, and we can be together for the rest of our lives, if you'll have me."

Samuel slowly placed the brilliant diamond on her finger. Moments later, they were in each other's arms, sharing what was always there — their love for each other.

Chapter Twelve

In the morning, Samuel arranged for the two of them to have breakfast in a small dining room off to the side of the large banquet hall. "I feel like royalty," Lilly said as she was attended by two handsome young servers. One was pouring her coffee; the other was placing a fruit plate that looked divine in front of her. She loved fresh fruit, especially strawberries. "I could get used to this."

"I hope you do. Our life together is going to be everything it should have been had we married years ago. Except this time, money is no object."

"You remembered how much I love strawberries. I'm more than flattered."

"I never for a second forgot anything about you. I've spent a lifetime dealing with regrets about what we've missed. Sometimes, when I found myself alone, I would daydream about you."

"I did the same," Lilly confessed. "Samuel, we can't go back. We both had lives, and each of us have a family we care about. What are we going to tell them? How could this possibly work."

"It will work itself out. We're going to have our second chance. We deserve it, don't we?"

"It seems simple, but it's really not. You know that."

Samuel reached for her hand. "I know but…"

Lilly interrupted, "What if our kids don't understand? You know there's a very good chance they won't."

"Then we're going to jet off to some island and live the rest of our days together."

Lilly smiled. "And Warrington Publishing? Are you just going to walk away from something that took you years to create? You're Samuel Warrington, self-made publishing tycoon."

Samuel laughed. "It sounds a whole lot better when you say it. I have two daughters. They're my legacy. They're just not ready, but Nicholas Sinclair, my son-in-law to be, is incredibly smart. He knows exactly what to do. I've been training him for years. He actually wants to be the boss. I won't have to ask him twice."

"What's he like?" Lilly wondered.

"You'll like him. He always sticks to a plan. He's not afraid of anything, and he works non-stop if he has to. He always gets the job done, no matter what."

"Sounds a lot like you." She smiled at Samuel, hoping he got the drift.

"Actually, you're right. In many ways, he is. However, in many ways, he's not."

"And the girls. They'll be okay with that?"

"No, they won't be. They will be absolutely furious with me. But I'm not ready to leave this world yet, and my hope is that one or both of them will be up for the task when the time comes."

Lilly looked at him, a little shocked. "You know better than that. We have no control over how long we stay on this earth or when we go."

"Well then, I think Gracie could do it if she would ever stop being mad at me for advancing Nicholas to the top position."

"Why did you do that?"

"Because she up and went to Paris on a whim. I had hoped by now she would be further up the company ladder. I finally got her back, and then you know the rest. She really loves doing the podcast with Leo."

"Yes, but that might not be forever. Leo has a lot more books in him. Surprisingly, he enjoys the podcast, or maybe not the podcast so much as being with Gracie. Have you noticed?"

"I have. But I haven't said a word to her. They have a great bond," Samuel remarked with a smile. "Leo has brought out the best in her. She came home from Paris heartbroken and angry, but now she's happy. I love it."

Lilly smiled. "Samuel, behind that corporate genius the world sees, there's a wonderful man that I see. That's why I love you. That's why I've always loved you. And beside anything else, when Leo needed you, you were there for him. That made me love you even more."

"I love him like a son."

"I know you do. I guess I'm just worried about our kids and what they will think."

"Well, I can tell you I'm going to be happy as a lark knowing I'm finally going to be with the love of my life. I know I should be thinking more of my legacy and what I built, but if I'm honest with myself, you're the one I need by my side. However long we have, I want us to be together."

"And we will be, but let's be honest, Samuel, I know how hard you've worked your whole life. It is about Warrington."

"I'm hoping one or both of the girls will be up to the task, but right now I'm not really sure they even like being at Warrington. They may not be ready now, but I'm sure as hell hoping that will change. A man can dream, can't he?"

"I hope for your sake that dream comes true."

Samuel felt like a million bucks being there with Lilly. "Thank you for being you. You're just what I needed. We missed so much. Didn't we?"

Lilly kissed him sweetly. "Well, we may have missed a lot, but we have time to make it right. I love you."

"Truer words were never said. We won't have to make it right because it's already right."

They kissed again, and they both knew it was more than right. "This is going to be ours. Our private getaway."

Lilly inhaled the sweet aroma of freshly mowed lawn one as they toured the magnificent grounds. It was lovely here. She secretly wished she could be in this moment forever, but she was afraid it wouldn't last.

Samuel had hurt her before, and maybe he didn't realize just how much. As she followed his lead while they walked back toward the entrance, she could only hope things would be different this time. That was her problem to deal with. She was always very practical, and for most of her life, she'd played it safe. *I've learned that whenever something seems to be too good to be true, it usually is.*

Chapter Thirteen

After their podcast was over, Leo waited for Gracie outside the office. "If you're not busy, there's someplace I'd like to show you. That is, if you have the time."

"I'm available. What did you have in mind? I could use a distraction." She couldn't stop thinking about her parents. She was sad about it, but she knew if they weren't happy with each other it was probably for the best. Hopefully they could find happiness, and maybe love.

"It's a surprise. It's going to be fun."

"Let me just go home and change my clothes."

"No need, this place has no special requirements. You'll see."

On the way to the car, Gracie couldn't help wondering why Leo didn't mention Jack. For some strange reason, she wanted to know what he thought, but if she brought it up, it might make him uncomfortable.

"Leo, I'm so glad you're not mad at me for putting you in a bad position with Jack."

"That's what friends do. No worries. I'm sure you would have done the same thing for me."

Gracie didn't quite understand what he meant, but she nodded that she would.

Leo drove around the back of his grandmother's bakery. "So, this is it? Your grandmother's bakery? This is a surprise, but a good one. I was hoping to see her again."

"She's not here today. She's out of town and the girls that work for her just left for the day. It's just you and me, and I'm going to bake something for you."

"You're kidding, right?"

"Nope. Let's go inside."

Gracie couldn't believe how quaint the bakery was. It looked like a vintage movie set. When you stepped down on the floor, especially with high heels, the floor squeaked. The counters were long and wide, and were covered by a protective cloth.

Leo ran his hand across the table. "Everything is prepared for the next day. That's why the tables are all set to go. My grandmother likes every day to start on time, and having things all set to go the night before works out fine."

"She sounds precise."

He laughed. "You could say that. They start at five and open at seven a.m. She doesn't like to keep the customers waiting. So, many of them come here before they start work each day. It's tradition."

She laughed. "This is the cutest place I've ever seen. And it smells terrific."

"I know. The aroma of chocolate is so sweet and calming. When I was a little boy, I could hardly wait for school to end, because after school I would meet my grandmother here. She always had something very special she'd made just for me. It was always terrific. I'm lucky to have her."

"Yes, you are. I can tell by the way you talk about her. You have such a special bond. That's so nice. I see it in your eyes every time you mention her name."

Leo smiled as he continued showing Gracie the bakery. He took her hand. "Come around to this side and look over here. There's a beautiful garden in the back. In the summer, there are tables and chairs so the customers, or 'friends' as my grandmother refers to them, can have their morning coffee with a fresh roll, croissant, donut, or whatever their favorite is."

"That's so sweet."

"And one of my most favorite items are the daily specials. They start the day with a special bread that they give out as samples to all the customers. I actually think people come here just for that. It's always something fabulous. It's warm and ready to eat."

Gracie smiled. "I'm getting hungry while you're talking."

"That's good," Leo said with a plan in place.

"She has customers from generation to generation. And she even ships out of town for those loyal customers who moved away."

"Wow. That's really something. This is incredible. It's like a piece of history."

"It gets better. I really am going to make something for you. Is that okay?"

"Are you kidding? I'd love it."

Gracie was taken back as she listened to Leo talk so fondly of his grandmother. She had never met anyone so charming. She knew she was lucky to have met him because there had never been a guy in her life who was this wonderful. If she was looking for love, he would be first in line. But, of course, she had made the decision that it was going to be a long time before she went down that road again.

"So, what'll it be?"

"You choose. I'm sure it'll be wonderful. It smells so terrific in here, I'm excited. Thank you for bringing me here. I actually didn't think anything like this existed."

"Well then, sit back and relax. The show is about to begin."

Leo carefully took out everything he needed to make a chocolate cinnamon roll. He seemed to be having such a good time, and Gracie was amazed that he had another hidden talent she didn't know about. She was becoming more and more impressed by him. He was filled with surprises.

"You know I'm not that great in the kitchen. Ava has been with our family since I was a baby, and with her being such a great cook, I never bothered learning. Well except in Paris, I did cook a little when I was there. However, it wasn't very good."

"Ava is a great cook. I agree. Not that I've been there that many times, but whenever I have been, what she cooks is always top notch. Your father loves her cooking, especially those desserts — he really goes to town on those."

They continued their conversation as Leo whipped everything by hand and then put it in the oven. The things he was mixing smelled amazing. Gracie was having so much fun. Strangely enough, she was happy just watching Leo.

"So, while we're waiting, how about some hot chocolate?"

"Do you have marshmallows?" Gracie couldn't help but ask.

Leo laughed. "Is there any other way to have hot chocolate than with marshmallows? I love marshmallows. In fact, when the weather was bad, my grandmother and I used to put them in the oven on broil. When they were toasted and a little crispy, we would eat every last one of them."

"Ava did that for us too. It's like a campfire in your kitchen."

"You got that right."

Gracie was feeling relaxed and quite happy, which for her was a novelty. She had an edge about her, but when she was with Leo, she seemed to lose her cynicism.

She was a little confused by her own emotions, but for the most part, she never gave into anything too sentimental. She actually blamed her mother for that. Francine Warrington wasn't exactly the warmest person in the world. That was a terrible thing to admit, but her mother seemed to be missing in action when emotions were involved.

"Do you like music?" Leo asked as he pressed a few buttons, looking for some of his favorite songs from his playlist.

"I do. When I was little and feeling alone, I used to turn up the volume and dance my heart out."

Leo laughed. "Really?"

Leo switched to a soft beautiful song. "May I have this dance?"

Gracie smiled. "You're kidding, right? Elvis?"

"Let's dance, his songs bring out the romance in anyone."

"Even me?"

"Even you. It's good for the soul, especially slow dancing."

Leo reached out for Gracie's hand and held her tightly. They locked, and they did a spin.

"You're serious, aren't you?" She felt a bit excited. He knew his way around the floor, even if it was a bakery.

Then she reminded herself he was a romance writer and she remembered a few beautiful scenes where the couple also kissed when dancing together, but she wasn't going to let that happen. Unless, of course, he meant something when he kissed her. *What am I thinking? It's just a dance.*

"When it comes to dancing, I'm very serious. There is no other way."

After the dance was over, they hugged, but they didn't kiss. Each of them was disappointed, but neither of them pushed it to that level.

Gracie grinned. "I must say, you're pretty smooth. I didn't take you for that kind of guy."

"Let's put it this way. There's a lot you don't know about me."

For a moment, Gracie let her guard down. "Same here."

The hours seemed to pass quickly, but it appeared that neither of them was in a hurry to get anywhere else. The chatter was fun, and Leo seemed at peace, while Gracie was a little uptight about her Jack situation. It appeared that Leo, as usual, was sensing her anxiety, but he knew he was making her laugh, and that was a good thing.

Leo was anxious to know what had happened with her and Jack, but he knew Gracie would tell him when she was ready. Waiting was okay. After all, she was there with him, not Jack.

On the other hand, Gracie knew exactly what he was doing, and it was working. "Leo, I have a question that you may or may not want to answer. You know me, I'm not shy."

"Go right ahead. Anything. You know more about me than anyone else."

"Really? You don't seem like you hold back."

"I do. My characters don't, but I do. Anyway, I'm not that interesting."

"You're kidding, right? You're so successful, and your books have brought so much happiness to those of us who read them. You're kind and considerate, and believe me, I don't know many guys like you. Do you have *any* bad qualities? I'm not sure. Since we've known each other, you seem pretty consistent in your behavior."

"Of course, I have some bad qualities. I'm human, aren't I?"

"Maybe not. I've been around you for a while now, and for the life of me, I haven't seen any."

"Well, for one thing I talk too much. And I'm very superstitious. Oh, and I hide behind a fake name, as you know. Leo Tucker is nothing like Nicole Forrester."

Gracie laughed. "I know that, but that's just your job. Your brand, as my father would say. That's what counts"

"Did you tell him you knew?"

"Absolutely not. I can keep a secret."

Leo smiled. "Good because your father doesn't want anyone to know. Even though you're not just people. You're my partner. "

She liked the way that sounded. "Your partner?"

"You know what I mean." His face flushed a little. "You're the better half of the podcast. You've got what it takes."

"I doubt that. I think the chocolate has gone to your head," Gracie added, amused. "Look at you, you're not the least bit rattled, whether it's here or on our podcast. Every show seems to work, but without you, no way it could be good."

"Not true at all. You're very engaging and free spirited."

"I don't know about engaging, but free spirited, yes. That's me. It drives my father crazy. And I love it. That's the fun of it."

"You two do have a special relationship."

"Yes, he drives me crazy, and I do the same to him."

"That much I know." Leo also knew how much Samuel loved his daughter. He wanted to tell her that, but every time he did, she didn't believe it.

"The one thing I know for sure is I'm not the one he thinks he can hand over the reins too. I doubt I'm anywhere near gaining enough of his respect to carry on his legacy."

"Maybe he'll surprise you someday. You know you two are more alike than you think."

"I don't see it."

Leo wasn't sure if he should continue, but he thought he knew Gracie well enough to make a mini observation. He didn't want to go too far though. Samuel had confided his feelings to him about his daughter many times. He didn't think the time was right to let that slip, so he let it go. *Better safe than sorry.*

"Do you think there's something's wrong with my father? He took off a few days and didn't say where he was going."

"He's fine. I'm sure. Maybe he just needed some time alone," Leo said with confidence. "Anyway, this is about you having some down time too. How about another cinnamon roll?"

"I'm stuffed, aren't you?"

"Yes, but I want to be a good host," Leo said as he cleaned up. "I better make sure everything is in its place for tomorrow."

"I can help. You've been a great host, so that's the least I can do. I think I needed this wonderful evening. I feel pretty relaxed."

"That's what I was aiming for," Leo confessed as he handed her the mop. "Are you sure about this? A date where a mop is involved isn't really a date."

"Leo, are you saying this is a date?"

He shrugged his shoulders, not really knowing how to categorize what the night was. "Yes, I guess it's a date."

Gracie and Leo didn't realize they were a bit more than just podcast co-hosts. It's too bad their anxiety got in the way of their happiness, but with a little bit of luck, one of them would make the first move. So far, nothing gained, nothing lost, or so they thought. They were wrong — dead wrong. They were a perfect match, but until they each realized it, it didn't matter.

Chapter Fourteen

Just as they were leaving the bakery after hours of chatting and really getting to know each other, Gracie got a call. She wasn't planning on picking up, but something felt wrong. At first, she didn't recognize the voice on the other end. "Hi, this is Gracie."

"Gracie, it's me, Lilly. Leo's grandmother."

She was a little confused as to why she was getting this call. "Are you looking for Leo?"

"No, honey, I'm looking for you."

"Okay, how can I help you?"

"Honey, I need you to come to Lake Geneva."

"Why?"

"They think your father's had a heart attack."

Gracie's face went white and she leaned up against the wall so she wouldn't pass out. The phone fell to the ground and Leo picked it up.

"Hi, this is Leo. Who is this?"

"Honey, it's me. You need to come to Geneva North. They think Samuel had a heart attack. They're not sure how bad it is."

"What are you two doing in Lake Geneva?"

"It's a long story, I'll talk to you when you get here. I'm glad you're with Gracie. Can you pick up Julianna? She'll be waiting for you."

"Sure, we'll be there as soon as we can. What happened?"

Lilly didn't want to say too much because the doctors hadn't told her much of anything. If you're not related and don't have medical power of attorney, no one tells you anything. "Please, honey, no questions right now. Just come as quickly as you can."

Before they left, Leo could see Gracie was shaking. He put his arms around her. "Everything's going to be okay."

Gracie nodded. "I can't believe it. My father's had a heart attack. He's always seemed as healthy as a horse."

Tears were falling from her eyes, so Leo grabbed a Kleenex and dabbed them as they fell down her cheek. "You don't have to seem sick, sometimes it just happens."

"Just like that?"

"Yes, but I am wondering why my grandmother was with him. I guess that's a good thing."

Then a spark of anger hit Gracie. "It's my mother's fault. It was quite a shock to hear that she was leaving. He was never great at being alone. Maybe he needed a friend."

Leo nodded, "Maybe, but why my grandmother? Well, we'll see, I guess."

Leo was always cool headed in an emergency. That's who he was. And that was a good thing because he could sense Gracie was falling apart. "I'm sure he'll be fine. Maybe it's not a bad one. They're pretty good at dealing with heart attacks. You know that, right?"

"I know, but right now whether it's a bad one or not, It's my father. He had a heart attack. It's not good."

Leo grabbed her bag, and when she was safely in the car, he called Julianna. "Hi, it's Leo. We're on our way."

"Leo, why are you using Gracie's phone? Is she all right?"

"She's in the car and she's fine. She's shaken up, like all of us. I just wanted to let you know we'll be there as fast as we can."

After they picked up Julianna and had an initial, worried conversation, no one spoke during the rest of the trip — not even Leo. When they got there, he dropped the girls off at the ER entrance and went to park the car. He was pretty shaken himself, but he managed to keep it together, at least while the girls were around.

He sat there in the car for a few minutes, reminding himself of his grandfather's death and not being able to go in the ambulance with his grandmother. He never even got to say goodbye. That always upset him, and as he got older he understood, but he didn't back then.

Being upset about this was natural. After all, Samuel was like a father to him and he and his grandmother had been the ones who helped him pick up the pieces of his broken heart when Ellie died. He loved Samuel, so he sat there for a few minutes trying to get his feelings in check. He wanted to be there for Gracie, but first he had to stop the tears from running down his cheeks. He took a few deep breaths and reminded himself of the wise words Samuel's once told him: "Love does hurt sometimes, but it's also very beautiful. Never be afraid to love."

After a few minutes, he'd pulled himself together enough to get out of the car. He wanted to be the strong one. He knew this was going to be difficult, but he wanted to help and the only way that was going to happen was by taking himself out of the picture and thinking only of Julianna and Gracie. Samuel was *their* father. With that in mind, he went inside.

Nicholas had just made it to the hospital when a young thirty-something doctor came out to speak to them. "Hi, I'm Dr. Jacob Levitt, I'm Samuel's physician."

It sounded as if he had seen Samuel before, which seemed a little curious, but at the time, all they cared about was Samuel's condition. G-d knows their imaginations were getting the best of them.

Dr. Levitt sat on the edge of the table next to the couch where Gracie and Julianna were sitting. "He's doing fine right now. We're waiting for a few more tests to come back, but I knew you were all out here waiting for some answers, so I thought I'd come out to reassure you."

Gracie couldn't help herself. She was scared. "He's not going to die, is he?"

Julianna started to cry and Lilly put her arms around her in a comforting way, even though they had just met. "Thanks, Lilly. I'm sorry. I just…oh, never mind, I don't even know how I feel."

"That's okay, honey. It's your father in there."

Lilly sat there staring into space, completely dazed. One minute she and Samuel were sharing their love, and the next minute he was clutching his chest. She knew the look. Her husband had the same terrified look on his face when he had his fatal heart attack. Thank goodness she didn't listen to Samuel's protests and called an ambulance. He was reluctant at first, but when the pain got worse, he agreed to take a ride to the hospital.

There she was, comforting his daughters who had no idea why she was there and what she and Samuel meant to each other. Her heart was breaking, just like theirs. And then there was Leo, every time she looked at him she felt dishonest. They were always up front with each other. She'd always told him everything, except for this one part of her life — the one before his grandfather. She wasn't actually lying, she just kept Samuel out of the equation. What happened to their love and why he married someone else was water under the bridge.

She was happy she had taken the engagement ring and put it in her bag because this was not the place discuss it. Luckily, there was very little conversation while they waited, and no questions. She knew there would eventually be lots of questions, but hopefully Samuel and she could answer them together.

She had missed some of the conversation while she was preoccupied by these thoughts. From what she could gather, the test results weren't in but things weren't exactly good.

"Please, just tell us the truth. Is he going to die?" By this time, Gracie was quite upset.

"I know how difficult all of this is, that's why I wanted to come out. He's resting comfortably, and we're taking great care of him."

"That's good news, right?" Leo questioned.

"Yes, it is. The heart attack was not as severe as I originally thought. But we're not quite out of the woods yet either."

"What should we do now?" Gracie asked, holding her sister's hand.

"Hold onto good thoughts," Dr. Leavitt said as he got up and took hold of Julianna's hand. "I'm going back in, and I'll keep you posted. He's making progress. Your dad's quite a fighter."

"You don't know the half of it." Finally, she could smile.

"Doctor, can we stay here for now?" Leo asked, knowing that no one wanted to leave, or would leave for that matter.

"Of course. I promise to report back soon. There's coffee and some cookies in the lounge. Help yourself."

Gracie forced a smile. "Thank you. We're good for now. And Doc, one more thing, could you give him our love and tell him we're all out here waiting to see him?"

Chapter Fifteen

After a rough couple of hours, Samuel began to feel a little better. He realized there would be questions about why he was in Geneva, and with Lilly no less. But, first things first, he was thankful he didn't need surgery. He took that as a good sign.

He'd had a check-up a few weeks ago in Geneva instead of with his regular Internist because he didn't want anyone to know he wasn't feeling up to par. He had blown it off, thinking it was stress. He wasn't planning on listening to the advice Dr. Leavitt had given him, but he would now.

Changing his life wouldn't be easy, but the alternative wasn't an option. With a better diet, some exercise and medication, it could make a big difference. Time would tell. Giving up salt and rich foods wasn't his idea of a good life, but death was an unacceptable alternative.

He sat up, waiting for his girls to ask one question after another, but he was happy that he was alive to be able to answer them. *Wow,* he thought, *I'm a new man. I'm not going to let anyone treat me like an old, sick man, though. I'll still be the same guy who is tough as nails when I'm dealing with people, even though I know I'm not quite that guy at the moment. I can act, though, so no one will know.*

After the nurse finished cleaning him up, he looked at her, smiled and asked, "So, how do I look?"

"Pretty good for a man who just had a heart attack."

"I want to look better than that."

The nurse smiled. "Okay, you look terrific. You look like a guy that just had a baby. How's that?"

He laughed. "Better, but not great. You've got spunk. I like that."

He looked at her nametag and asked, "So, Dawn, how long have you been in this line of work?" He always liked to call people by their names when addressing them.

"Today's my first day."

He laughed. "I hope you're kidding."

"Mr. Warrington, I've been doing this for most of my life. Feels like all of it."

"Samuel's my name. Mr. Warrington sounds like I'm old. I'm not that old."

Dawn smiled. "Samuel, my friend, you also have spunk."

They both shared a laugh, realizing neither of them were new at this game.

"Are you ready to see your family?" Dawn asked, realizing he was trying to get his "I'm fine" act going and she thought he was doing a pretty good job.

"Ready as I'll ever be."

He wasn't a religious man, but he was praying for a speedy recovery and that his life wouldn't be over. He actually made a promise to G-d that he would eat better, exercise, and do everything he could to keep his blood pressure down. He was lying just a little, well more than a little. He knew he wasn't perfect, but he was very good at making deals. Making them with G-d, now that was another story. *I might even relinquish some of my duties to the girls, but then again, maybe not.*

Dawn came out of his room smiling. "Your father wants to see all of you at one time."

"Is that okay? Isn't there a limit of visitors?"

"There is, but your father's very persuasive."

"You might say that," Gracie said with certainty.

"We also give Samuel a bit of special treatment, since he's given us several large donations. I doubt when he made them he ever thought he would be a patient here. Either way, he won't take no for an answer."

Gracie smiled. "Okay then. I'll get everyone together." *Looks like Samuel Warrington is back to business as usual.*

Chapter Sixteen

Samuel's hospital room was quite large. Not that anyone expected Samuel to be in a small cubicle like everyone else. There was a round table and three chairs at the far corner of his room along with a large screen TV. Apparently, making donations earned you some nice perks.

There was orange juice, coffee, and muffins for everyone, sitting on the table, just like what he provided for his meetings at the office. It took a little compromising, but Samuel was used to getting what he wanted, even in unusual circumstances. He nodded to Dawn, thankful for her help.

He was being monitored, so if he ran into a problem, the staff would know immediately. If that happened, his visitation rights would be revoked, whether he liked it or not.

It was difficult for Gracie and Julianna to see their father lying in a hospital bed, but he didn't look as bad as they'd imagined. He had called in a few more favors to make sure he looked presentable, instead of like a man who had just suffered a heart attack.

He had a robe over the obligatory blue hospital gown that every patient wore. One thing he couldn't change were the wires attached to him and their corresponding beeping machines. He didn't have the power to change that. He did just have a heart attack.

"So, I guess you all know by the grace of G-d I'm going to survive this ordeal. I made some promises to G-d, but we can talk about that later. First, I'll just say it's good to see everyone, but I can tell by the confused looks on your faces you can't figure out exactly why I'm here in Geneva with Lilly."

Gracie couldn't contain herself one minute longer. "Dad, look it's obvious we're all here because we love you and are thrilled you're going to make a full recovery. But—"

"Okay, hold on." Samuel interrupted. "Before we go any further, let me address the elephant in the room. And Lilly, please don't be mad, it's just a figure of speech."

Lilly smiled and nodded, as did Julianna, Gracie, Leo, and Nicholas. They had no idea what was coming next.

"Okay, I hate to admit it, but I'm a little tired and I promised the doctor this would be a short visit." He motioned for Lilly to come closer. "Your mother and I have been married for so many years I've lost count, but unfortunately, we weren't very happy. In fact, we were quite miserable, but we both kept extremely busy so it didn't matter much."

Julianna interrupted. "Thirty years, Dad. Thirty years." Her voice was emphatic.

"I know, honey, but we weren't happy. I wasn't planning on telling you like this, but I think you need to know now because I'm not going to lie to you. Lilly and I met years ago. In fact, I met Lilly around the same time I met your mother. I'm not going to get into all the details right now because my time to talk is limited. If you look back to the door, there's a Nurse Dawn is motioning for me to get to the point quickly. And she means it."

Gracie didn't know what was coming next, but she was hoping that was all her father was going to say for the time being. But just in case he wasn't done, she wanted him to know this was enough for today. It was nothing he wouldn't have done if it were her going on and on. "Okay, this can all wait. You need to rest."

"Gracie, stop. I love you, but I have to do this now. Just let me finish."

"Fine. I guess you're about to tell us something important."

"It is, honey. Sorry, but I need to do this now."

She nodded and took a deep breath, not sure of what was coming her way. It didn't look promising.

He took hold of Lilly's hand. "We are in love, and I've asked her to marry me."

For the first time ever, Leo didn't say anything. But by the look on his face, he was shocked into silence. Nicolas shook his head in disbelief. Julianna cried, and Gracie left the room. It seemed no one was overjoyed at the news. This was not exactly what Samuel had been expecting.

Samuel went on anyway. "I love Lilly and she loves me, and if by the grace of G-d I get through this ordeal, we're going to get married. We're not asking for your permission, but we would be happy if you accept our decision and are happy for us."

Julianna wiped her tears away on her sleeve. "I don't know what to say."

Nicholas smiled. "I do. Congratulations. I can't say I would've ever imagined this whole scenario, but here we are and strongest man I know is telling us he's in love. So, I guess if you're happy, Samuel, I'm happy too."

Julianna gave him a weird look, surprised by his comment.

Leo couldn't help but feel a little disappointed in his grandmother as he gazed her way. "You never said anything. Why? All our heart-to-heart talks and you never mentioned being in love with someone other than grandpa."

"Honey, I'm so sorry. I wanted to tell you, but I never imagined Francine would leave Samuel, so there was nothing to say. It was just an old, deep wound that, frankly, I didn't want to think about."

Julianna stared at her father. "Daddy, this seems so unreal. You and Lilly Tucker. How did this happen? I don't mean anything bad, but this is all so shocking."

"I guess I might not have made it clear. This isn't up for debate. This is reality, mine and Lilly's. I've loved her forever and now we finally have a chance to be together."

Julianna was trying to understand. "It's just a lot to handle so quickly. And please, Lilly, believe me, this isn't anything negative about you. You raised a wonderful grandson and we all like Leo, but you have to know how difficult all of this is to take in."

Lilly nodded. "I do, and I'm really sorry you had to find out this way."

"Me, too." Samuel's voice was sincere. "I love all of you, but try to understand."

Samuel continued trying to justify himself. "You know how in life nothing is set in stone and sometimes, especially with parents who have had lives before our children were born, we don't always tell them everything. We don't tell them because it doesn't matter what our life was before them. I love Lilly and she loves me. For however long we have, we're going to make it count."

"I get it, but getting engaged so quickly? I know Mom has had her issues, but this has my head spinning," Julianna said with concern. "Sorry, Lilly."

Samuel answered for Lilly. "I want you to understand how much Lilly means to me. How much she's always meant to me. I might not have been able to get my one wish, but your mother wanted this divorce now, and I said yes."

"Does Mom know about Lilly?" Julianna asked, not sure what the answer would be, but she wanted to know.

"She does. She's always known."

"Shouldn't we call her?" Julianna asked.

"The nurses already did."

"Is she coming?"

Samuel shook his head no. "She's already out of the country. I've talked to her. It's fine."

As Samuel stared at the tubes in his arms and the machines beeping with his every breath, he knew he was on a slippery slope. "Let me say something, and please don't take this the wrong way."

They were all listening, trying to make sense of all that just transpired. "I want you to look at me. Sometimes, people don't get a second chance, but I'm finally going to get mine. I did love your mother, in a different way, and the most important part of my life has always my girls. So for that, I am forever grateful to your mom."

Lilly moved closer to his bed and held onto Samuel's hand. "I just want my grandson and you girls to know, I will never stop loving Samuel. I never have, and I never will."

Samuel felt good about what Lilly had just said. "I know this is confusing and we can have a better conversation later, but for now, I'm a little tired."

Lilly squeezed his hand, while Julianna and Gracie each gave their dad a kiss on the cheek. "We love you, Daddy." Gracie said as she walked away.

Samuel smiled back at his girls. He never got tired of being called Daddy. Sometimes, when he looked at them, he still saw them as little girls. He was content for the time being, especially having Lilly by his side. He was lucky enough to have escaped a serious heart attack, and he would forever be thankful for a second chance at love.

Leo took his grandmother's hand and walked her into the waiting room. "Are you happy?" he asked.

"Yes. I'm happy and sad all at the same time. I'm just so worried about Samuel."

Leo didn't want to hurt his grandmother, so he didn't say much. He loved Samuel, but this whole scenario was very hard to accept. "Did you love Grandpa?"

"I did. He was a good man, but he had flaws like everyone else. I can tell you he loved you more than anything else. And if the next question is one I think you want to ask but you're afraid to, I'll answer it. No, he never knew about Samuel. There was no reason for him to know."

He kissed her cheek. "Okay, but I have to say, this is more than a surprise. It's life changing. You know, I had no idea any of this was going on."

"Nothing was going on. I assure you. We barely saw each other over the years. There were three men in my life, your grandfather, Samuel, and of course the most precious one, you. I don't think I could ever love any man the way I love Samuel."

Leo understood what she meant. He hugged his grandmother and kissed her cheek. "I'm really lucky to be one of those men."

Chapter Seventeen

Samuel found it difficult to think about his legacy, but after his recent heart attack, he couldn't seem to think about anything else. He began to realize he wasn't infallible. His last will included provisions, but he knew he should talk to his girls and make them understand that although he loved them to pieces, he didn't think either of them were even close to ready to take over the business. He'd have to find a diplomatic way to say that if he ever wanted to talk to them again.

Francine called too. It was lucky for her when she called he was by himself because, had Lilly been around to see his face turn red in anger, she would have quickly stopped the conversation.

"I understand from my lawyers you've asked for something I'm not willing to give you. Why do you think you deserve any part of the company? You made the decision to leave, allowing both of us to have new lives. You're going to have plenty of money when this is over, you don't need more."

Francine laughed out loud. "Samuel, my dear, without my parents, you would have nothing."

"Is that where this conversation is going?"

"Yes, of course this is where the conversation is going. Why wouldn't it?"

"Because that was over thirty years ago, and I paid them back with interest. Did you forget that?"

"No, I didn't forget, but what I'm asking for is a percentage that would be mine, not the girls', mine. You can help them in other ways. You know neither of them is up for the job. The only one that can do this is Nicholas."

"I get it, but it's my decision to pick my successor."

"Maybe not."

"Why are you calling me when you should be talking to your girls? They need you."

"I doubt that. They have Ava. I know I'm not mother material."

"And where are you? What kind of a mother does this to her children? You're calling me, but they need you. Believe me, there's nothing I need from you."

"Samuel, first of all, I'm certainly not telling you where I am because if you haven't found me yet with your team of investigators, I guess you could say I've done a good job of disappearing."

"I'm not looking for you, and I'm sure by now you know what happened to me. The hospital contacted you, right?"

"They did. I knew you were home, so I'm sure Lilly is there to help you," she said sarcastically.

"She's not here now, but she's been very supportive."

"Such good news. Anyway, this is food for thought. Just give me what I want and I'll leave you alone. If not, this won't be the last time you hear from me. I was hoping we could get this accomplished before it gets out of hand."

"Why am I not surprised. Call your daughters and then we'll see."

"Fine, I'll take care of it."

Chapter Eighteen

Gracie hadn't been spending as much time in her office since her father's heart attack, but she hadn't missed a show. She would do a show and then leave immediately. Some of her behavior was a little childish, but she didn't want to stick around and have any lengthy discussions with anyone, especially Leo. She knew it wasn't his fault about his grandmother and her father, but still, she remained silent.

When she woke up that morning, she knew it was time to return to some of her normal activities, like early morning coffee and donuts, and then preparing for the show. But now she relied on Leo to ease her into the conversation, which he did effortlessly, but it wasn't fair to take him for granted, which she so easily did.

So, with coffee in one hand and a donut in the other, she was just about to sit at her desk when two of her favorite employees, Brooklyn and Dolly, followed her in. Both had been her friends for years, and after college she got them both jobs at Warrington. They were happy and doing a great job.

"Now that's what I call a welcoming committee. How's everything going? Is there a problem?" Gracie sensed there was. "Okay, don't keep me in suspense. Isn't it a little early for you guys to be here? I expected to be alone for a couple of hours."

Brooklyn laughed. "We didn't want to miss you."

"So, you asked me the other day if anything was going on with Sir Nicholas."

"I did. You know I don't trust him."

She laughed. "I think I should tell you what I was planning to tell you, but I decided against."

Dolly interrupted. "I told her she shouldn't wait any longer. You need to know."

Gracie motioned for them to sit. "Okay guys, spill it. I'm a big girl. So, let's have it, however bad it is. Don't soften the blow."

Dolly kidded around. "That's why we love you. You're straightforward and to the point."

"Okay, enough flattery. What's going on?"

When Dolly stood up and closed the door, Gracie knew she wasn't going to like what they said. "I guess this is serious. Okay, let's have it. He's cheating on my sister, right?"

Brooklyn nodded. "Well, that's what we hear, but you know how it goes around here. There's a lot of new young ones. They're nice, but fresh out of school. They like to brag about men. And then there's Nicholas Sinclair. He's always ready for a new conquest. Sorry, hon, I know your sister's engaged to him, but I think you need to know so you can keep an eye on him."

"I know all about that, as you well know," Gracie said, getting angry with Nicholas. There was nothing knew about that. "How many?"

Dolly tried her best to make it short and sweet. She held up three fingers.

"Are you sure?"

Brooklyn nodded. "Maybe not all three, but at least two."

Gracie was not happy. "I'll talk to him. But first, thank you both, you know I love you." They had a group hug. "I'll call RL, lunch is on me."

Brooklyn added before leaving, "Hon, so sorry, but we had to tell you."

"You did the right thing. Thank you."

It wasn't shocking to hear, but it was unpleasant. Gracie suspected Nicholas of unscrupulous activities, so after Dolly and Brooklyn left her office, she took a few minutes to calm down and take several deep breaths. It didn't help.

She was mad. He was just like Jack. She was beginning to hate all men, well not all men, just men she was attracted to. But then there was Leo, who was a truly good man. Why couldn't she just take down the wall between them? If she could answer that question, it would be easier and a lot less stressful. *Someone's going to get a great guy in Leo. Probably not me because I'm done with men. I mean it. And then again, maybe I don't.*

When she had cooled off sufficiently, she headed to Nicholas's office. He was an early riser, and she knew he would be there already. She knocked, just in case he was otherwise engaged in one of his extracurricular activities. *Once a bad apple, always a bad apple.*

She knew he couldn't keep his hands off other women. She wanted to be the one to tell him that Julianna was still married, but she wasn't going to betray her sister.

The thought of him being in charge of her father's company was sickening. She wanted his job, but more than that, she wanted to stop pretending she didn't want it.

Maybe Julianna is infatuated with his looks. After all who wouldn't be? He's gorgeous. He looks like a model, and his best attribute is his contagious smile. Equally aggravating is the fact that he always knows the right thing to say, whether it's true or not. Knowing that both she and her sister fell prey to his charm infuriated her.

"Come in, Gracie."

"How did you know it was me?"

"I know your knock, and besides, I went by your office a few minutes ago and saw Dolly and Brooklyn paying you a visit. You know your private eye pals."

"They're my friends."

"Don't I know it. If they weren't, they'd be gone."

"You know they're smart."

"I do, but they watch every move I make."

"Someone has to."

"Aren't you here a little early? Actually, I'm surprised you knocked instead of just storming in. I miss those days."

Gracie closed the door and sat down. "Do you really want to know?"

"Yes, I do. But first, can you give me an update on your dad?"

"I guess I can do that. He's ready to come back to the office, but his doctor doesn't have the same opinion."

"Well, your father's resourceful. He'll figure it out. You know he'll win."

"I do, but for now he's home with Lilly."

"And how's that going?"

"Surprisingly well. She's really quite nice, but it's hard for us to see him with another woman. We're in the process of trying to accept what we can't change. I'm sure Julianna filled you in."

"Actually, we haven't been spending as much time together. She's been sticking close to home these days."

"Yes, she has. That's what I wanted to talk to you about." She paused for a moment, letting her intentions settle in the air before continuing. "I think we need to talk about that path you're going down. It seems eerily like the one you were on when we first met."

"Will you ever give that memory a rest? It happened, and it was over before we did any damage. I got the message loud and clear. And then you left for Paris."

"Let's not make it about me. Just tell me the truth, are you cheating?"

Nicholas laughed in his devilish way. "Cheating, are you crazy? I wouldn't cheat on your sister, unless, of course, it was with you. I'm ready if you are."

Gracie laughed. "You've got to be kidding."

"Yes, actually I *was* kidding. I'm not cheating on your sister. Guess you got some bad info. I'm a little busy trying to run this company."

"You know I said I would help."

"I know. Your father gives me a daily agenda, and then I follow it."

"That's not true, you do exactly what you want and he knows that."

"That, my dear, is not the case this time. He's still running this place, not me."

Gracie laughed. "There it is, right there. Lie number one. I, for one, know you've made a few changes that he doesn't know about."

"Well, it's just like you to doubt everything I do. Any changes to the day-to-day activity were made with your father's approval." Nicholas wasn't surprised she'd brought it up. In fact, if she hadn't, he would have been shocked.

"Let's get down to the nitty gritty. Have you been up to your old tricks? I heard there's a few new beautiful women working here."

"There's a lot of beautiful women working here."

"But they know your track record. The new ones don't."

"Believe me, there's nothing going on. But if you're available, that's another story. Ready to give up Leo? He's not your type."

"And you are? There's nothing going on between us.

"And what about Jack, the guy that almost got you. I heard he paid you a visit."

"Remember what I just said. Let's not make it about me. I'm not that interesting."

"That's not true at all. You're very exciting. There's no one here that can even come close to you. When you walk in a room, there's excitement in the air. The listeners love you."

"I'm here to talk about Julianna. Please control yourself. She's the best you'll ever find."

"I love your sister, and I'm not on the market. How's that for a truthful statement? So, can you call off the watchdogs?"

"They're my friends."

"Gracie, it's time. Haven't I proven myself?"

Gracie was silent for a long moment, studying him as she tried to decide whether or not to truly answer that question.

"Gracie, why are you staring at me like that?"

"Before I leave, you have to promise me that you won't hurt my sister."

"Your sister doesn't need you to protect her. She's all grown up now."

She laughed. "I know that, but it's you that might need to grow up. So, for now, we'll forget this conversation."

Before Nicholas could respond, she was gone.

Chapter Nineteen

Samuel didn't tell Lilly about Francine's phone call. In fact, he didn't tell anyone. He thought the day he came home from the hospital he would be fine, back to normal. But when that didn't happen and his recovery was slower than he imagined, he wasn't happy.

He just hadn't yet recovered that get-up-and-go confidence that always got him what he wanted. He hadn't experienced anything like what he was feeling, and he was mad at himself for never taking care of himself in the first place.

Luckily, he had a great doctor who didn't sugar-coat his condition, and offered good advice. Samuel wasn't exactly cooperative when he was warned his blood pressure and cholesterol were too high and he needed to give up salt, but now that he'd gotten a second chance, it was up to him to get everything squared away, especially his legacy.

Even though he put up a brave front, he was scared. Dr. Leavitt was the perfect doctor for him. He reassured him as they joked that he would once again rule the world.

Samuel wasn't anywhere near calling it quits, and the best medicine was having Lilly at his side. Their time had finally come and they weren't going to waste a second thinking anything other than the best years were yet to come.

It was challenging for Gracie and Julianna, having Lilly around so much, but it wasn't difficult to understand why their father loved her. She was comforting, in a very pleasant way, and within a few days, they began to like having her around.

They'd never really had a mother figure in their lives. Even when their mother was home, she was either planning an event for the country club or planning her next trip. But Lilly was different. She listened to them. Gracie began to understand how lucky Leo was to have Lilly in his corner. In a few days, Julianna came to feel that way, too.

After that, watching their father smile and ease into a relationship with Lilly meant the world to them. However, it wasn't one big happy family. Things weren't going to be quite that easy. It would take some work on all sides. But it was going in the right direction.

Ava had made a new friend in Lilly and she enjoyed having her around because Lilly was also a great cook and a much better baker than her. Not surprising for a woman that owned and operated her own bakery for decades.

They spent hours together in the kitchen, finding appealing foods and discussing ways to cook so Samuel wouldn't miss the lack of sugar and salt in his new diet. The good news was Samuel had already dropped quite a few pounds. While he wasn't happy about what he called "tasteless" foods, he was happy about this progress, as was his doctor.

Samuel hadn't had a hot dog or hamburger since he left the hospital. He knew at some time or another, he would eventually have to have one or both. He didn't think he could be the perfect patient forever. He could just about smell those hot dogs with fancy relish and mustard dripping down the bun. However, one thing he didn't want was bypass surgery, or worse — a stroke. He had no plans to leave this world any time soon, especially while Lilly was by his side. He wasn't about to lose his dream this second time around.

One would think a man like Samuel would've left his wife years ago, but he made a promise to honor and cherish his life with Francine, even though he loved Lilly. His family was everything, but now he had love in his life again, and he was not going to take it for granted. He had nothing to feel guilty about either, since Francine had initiated this very exciting new chapter of his life. So, come hell or high water he was going to make the most of it.

He had just gotten back from his daily walk when he decided to take a peek into the kitchen. He watched for a few minutes before entering, which he had been jokingly warned not to do. Cooking was now a top-secret mission in the Warrington house. There was lots of comparing notes between Lilly and Ava about what he should eat.

"Well hello, ladies. Is this where all the magic happens?"

"You've got that right," Ava said as she laughed, shoving a few of the condiments in her pocket.

"You can take whatever you just shoved in your pocket out. I know what you two are up to. And I want you to know I'm okay with it. But don't think for a minute I'll never have another juicy hotdog with ketchup, mustard, and relish, and a pickle or two. Let's not forget an order of nice, thin cut, French fries — the greasy ones. Those are the best."

Both Ava and Lilly gave him a look that said he wasn't fooling anyone but himself.

"Ladies, no worries. Everything in moderation. Isn't that what people say?"

Lilly smiled. "Right now, it doesn't matter what people say, it's what your doctor says."

"I got it, chiefs." He laughed. "It's for my own good."

Lilly nodded. "Okay, at least you're agreeable."

"Well, anyway, I was thinking if we can get the kids to agree to join us for Thanksgiving, we can go to Lake Geneva."

Lilly seemed surprised. "Why there?"

"Why not there? I'm going to see the doctor on the Wednesday before Thanksgiving, so we might as well stay there and celebrate. The kids haven't seen what I've done to Lake Charlemagne yet. I'd like to show them."

Lilly smiled. "It was beautiful, but maybe they're not ready."

"I didn't like the way they found out about us. A hospital emergency room isn't exactly what I had in mind. Maybe I'll invite Dr. Leavitt. I don't think he has any family in Wisconsin."

Ava looked disappointed. "Are you sure you're up to it? I'm happy to cook all your favorites." She was feeling sad about missing out on one of her favorite holidays.

"I most definitely am ready. Why wouldn't I be? I have the two of you watching my every move. Who wouldn't like that?" His sarcasm rang loud and clear.

Lilly smiled and took hold of his hand. "Now that we have time together, I want to make sure it lasts. Is that so wrong?"

"No, I guess not. These are going to be the best years of our lives. I promise you that."

Ava watched with enjoyment. During all the years she had been at the house taking care of all of them, she had never seen Samuel so happy.

"So, what do you say, Ava? I want you to come, too. It's time you had a real holiday."

"I don't know. Let me think about it."

"Nothing to think about. You're part of the family. The staff there is fine with a special dinner. I've just checked with all of them. It's a go. Maybe you can give them a couple of hints about my favorite foods."

"I like the idea. But I'm sure your staff doesn't need me to tell them how to cook."

Samuel laughed. "Well, let's put it this way. They cook for others and it's great, but you cook for me and that's something special."

Ava smiled with a blush. "Glad to hear that. But that won't get you off the hook. You'll still be eating foods that are good for you. Bribery won't work." She laughed.

"Don't I know it." Samuel hugged both of them. "This is going to be the best Thanksgiving ever."

Chapter Twenty

Leo was in the studio waiting for Gracie to come in. They rarely spent any time together since they found out about Lilly and Samuel, and that really wasn't what either of them wanted. It was just the way it turned out.

Actually, it seemed as if neither of them could see they were perfect for each other. If they did, they had a funny way of showing it. Staying clear of each other wasn't a good answer. But for now, it would have to do.

They did the shows and quickly left the studio, rarely talking about anything other than the podcast. The confusion kept them from the frank discussion they needed to have. Was there really a chance for them?

Charlotte, their wonderful, impatient producer was pacing. Nothing new about that. "Do you think someone should clue me in on what's going on between you and Gracie? You two had perfect chemistry, and now you have none. Where is she and why is she always late?"

"She'll be here soon. She won't be a no-show, she's not like that." When he heard those words come out of his mouth, he wasn't sure he believed them. He really didn't know her as well as he would have liked. And there was every possibility she wouldn't be coming in.

"Do you think the listeners notice?" Leo asked with concern.

"If I do, they do. What are you going to do about it?"

There was a long pause, and Charlotte was losing patience. "Leo Tucker, aren't you even listening to me?"

He didn't have an answer, and if he thought a blank stare would be enough, he was wrong. "Yes, of course, I'm listening to you. I heard everything you said to me. I'll talk to Gracie. There have been a lot of changes since Samuel's heart attack. We're trying as best we can. She's still in shock that her father, the man she thought was invincible, isn't."

"I understand that Gracie is his daughter, but I'm not. It's my reputation on the line. I've produced all of your shows, so if they're horrible, that's on me. There will be life after this podcast for me, that is if I don't destroy my career with you two stubborn idiots."

"Has Samuel said anything to you about our shows? He hasn't even mentioned them when I've visited."

"No, that's exactly the problem. Why hasn't he? I guess his recuperation might be making him miss a few steps."

"Now, you know better than that," Leo defended Samuel. "Samuel's as sharp as ever. I just think he's trying to recover so his doctors will let him come back to work. I can tell you one thing, if they don't give him the okay soon, he'll just get up and leave the house anyway."

Charlotte realized she'd pushed too far. "I don't think he should do that."

"Then stop worrying so much," Gracie said as she hurried in after hearing what was just said. "We'll be fine."

Gracie took her place at the mic, settled in, and smiled at Leo. "How are you today?" Her voice was matter of fact.

"I'm good, and you?"

"Perfect. Why wouldn't I be? Just because my father had a little heart attack, why should that change my life?"

She seemed to have quite an edge to her today. Actually, she always had an edge, but it had become sharper after her father became sick. If Leo didn't know better, he'd think if she never saw him again, it wouldn't bother her. That certainly was not his plan.

"We can do this, Gracie. It will be fine."

"Will it?"

Leo nodded. "Of course, it will. You just have to have a little faith."

Gracie knew he was right, but she didn't admit it.

Leo understood, or at least he pretended to. "So, are we going to do this like we mean it?"

"I actually don't know."

"Good enough. It's a start," Leo said, hoping he could break through her indifference. Part of this was his fault. He should have nipped it in the bud when it started, but he didn't. What could he say? His grand-mother seemed to be the root of it all. She was the other woman. And that was a terrible way to view his grandmother.

Leo hated the thought of seeing his grandmother that way. So, he made up his mind that she had always been his shining light, and he wasn't going to let anything change that. She deserved to be happy, and if Samuel was the one that could make her happy, so be it.

Charlotte sat back in her chair. "Okay, guys, let's go for it. Four, three, two, one."

The theme music went on and she looked at both of them, hopeful that the fabulous duo of Leo and Gracie were the ones showing up today. She didn't like the two pretending to be them. That wasn't working.

Leo began. "Hi, everybody. It's Leo Tucker here with Chicago's favorite host, Gracie Maxwell." And this time, when he smiled at her, she smiled back. It seemed genuine.

Charlotte took a deep breath, and off they went, just like nothing happened.

Leo took a letter out of his pocket. "Gracie, I thought before the show begins, you might want to hear what one of our listeners had to say."

"Sure, that sounds good. I love getting messages. Go ahead, I'm listening."

Leo's smile was quite telling.

"Dear Leo and Gracie, you both have helped me in so many ways. At first, when I began listening to your podcast, I thought it was just another podcast in an overcrowded market, but each and every show comes with a sense of caring.

"Some of the callers have made me see things I needed to change in my life that. I had no idea you guys would make a difference for me. I especially enjoy listening to the way the two of you answer the questions with such care and understanding about how important love is and how lucky we are if we find love, not just once but sometimes, we get a second chance.

"I lost my wife in an accident. When she died, I found out she was pregnant. So, not only did I lose my wife, I lost my unborn child too. I couldn't even leave my house for weeks, but then I began to listen to your show.

"After that, I joined a support group, and I met a wonderful woman."

Gracie was listening to every word. She realized how nice it was to hear that she and Leo had helped this listener.

Leo continued. "She lost her husband about the same time I lost my wife. She has two children, and now I'm part of their family. My heart is healing and we are hoping to get married in a few months. It has happened quickly, but when you know, you just know."

Leo knew that feeling. It had happened to him, not once, but twice. The first was his loving wife. After he lost her, he never imagined in a million years that he would ever love anyone again. But, then he met Gracie, and the world seemed so much brighter.

He continued on reading the letter: "I wanted to thank you from the bottom of my heart. Listening to the two of you sharing stories and making us laugh, and sometimes cry, has helped me heal. I'm sure it has done the same for other people too. I never thought love would happen again.

"Thank you for your wit and your charm and for all the wonderful hours of conversation. I took a chance and opened my heart for love, and it found me. Boy, did it find me."

Before Leo finished the letter, Gracie's eyes were filled with tears. It wasn't just the words of the letter, but also the way Leo was interpreting the feelings of the person who wrote it.

Leo continued reading: "May you both be lucky enough to have a second chance at happiness. Love awaits you around the corner. Best of luck and love. Sincerely, Happy again"

Leo could tell Gracie needed a moment. "Thank you for such a beautiful, heartfelt message. We'll be right back after a word from our sponsor. After all, we have to keep the lights on."

He sighed, glad he could get through reading the letter without losing it. He had read it before, and wasn't sure if he had made the right decision about reading it on the air.

Charlette didn't say another word. She just motioned, five, four, three, two, one."

Leo began. "Gracie will be right back. After that incredible letter, we both could use a glass of wine, but that will have to wait until later.

"I'm hoping she'll return. You know Gracie, she might have gone shopping and left me holding the bag." He truly wasn't sure if she left for a moment or the day.

Out of the blue, there she was. "I'm here. Now, that was a tearjerker, even for me. I want to thank Happy Again. It was so brave of him to write such a profound letter. So, now let's hear what Leo has going on. He told me he has news."

"I do. The powers that be made a little change in our schedule. Tomorrow will be the day Gracie and I will talk about families their Thanksgiving stories as well as stories about love and family. Gracie, are you ready for tomorrow?"

"Absolutely. How about you?"

"I certainly am. Family is everything to me." He knew he was pushing the envelope, but he did it anyway.

"It is for me, too. I'm so looking forward to a great big family sit get-together, not that I have that big of a family. Why don't you join us?"

Leo had no idea where she was going with this, but he answered, "I'm not really sure. I'll have to ask my grandmother. Thanksgiving is her favorite holiday."

"Well then, let's do it. Fun is on my list this year."

"Mine, too." Leo's eyes never left Gracie's. He didn't know what she had up her sleeve, but he wasn't going to rock the happy boat. It felt good, and he could only hope it would last.

Charlotte was ecstatic as she glanced at the phone lines that were all lit up. "Yes! They're back," she mumbled to herself. She felt like jumping for joy, but instead, she took a deep breath and smiled. She didn't want to make a scene. But she was silently happy-dancing.

Samuel and Lilly were listening to the podcast, not quite sure what to make of it. Could they share Thanksgiving as a family or would it be too soon to hope for anything like that to happen?

Samuel was feeling lucky to have Lilly in his life, but he knew everything was still up in the air. "Maybe they're ready to accept us. We can only hope."

Lilly smiled back. "At least Gracie and Leo didn't seem as distant as they have been lately. The show went well and that letter — wow. It's great that listeners take the time to let them know how great they are as co-hosts. They do make a great team."

Samuel acknowledged with a nod. "Yes, they do."

"They seemed relaxed, so much so by the end of the show, it did seem like they were somewhat back to normal. Leo isn't too upset with me anymore. He knows the whole story now, and he seems good with it."

"Well, that's good news. He's such a great guy. When he came into my life, everything changed. It wasn't only the success of his books, it was the way he was as a person. He's an old soul," Samuel added with pleasure.

"He loves you, too. And yes, he's always been that way. Even as a kid he had a heart of gold. He was bullied a little, but he always had a great sense of character, and that worked to his benefit as he grew up. I've always been proud of him. After his dad died, his world came undone, and then it happened again with Ellie. He had some issues when his mom left to travel the world like Francine, but he had a great life with us."

"I'll bet," Samuel agreed, understanding what she meant. He wasn't sorry about any of the times he was the one taking his daughters to concerts, baseball games, and even shopping for clothes.

"Guess we knew what we had to do and loved doing it."

"Also, for me, I'm grateful for that day at Manny's deli when we met. Who would have thought a turkey sandwich and a corned beef sandwich would bring such joy to my life? It would be sad if we all can't move forward."

"Leo's disappointment in me hurts, but he was mostly disappointed that I never told him. There was nothing to tell. I had no idea Francine was going to walk out of your life."

"How could you have known? I had no idea we would be getting a second chance. I thought I'd lost you forever. Francine and I had problems our entire marriage, so I'm not sure why I didn't see this coming."

"However it came to be, I'm not sorry we're getting another chance."

"I know the girls will come around. We just have to hope they'll forgive us."

Julianna walked in. "I think we can do that."

Samuel didn't anticipate Julianna being there. "How long have you been standing there?"

"Just a few minutes. I know this has been troubling for you and Lilly. And I also know you didn't mean to hurt us, but I guess it took us by surprise and we didn't know how to feel."

Samuel nodded with a little tear in his eye. He wasn't usually a man that showed emotion. "I'm so sorry. I never for a minute expected any of this to happen. I knew my health was a ticking timebomb, and your mother was never happy, but I never expected it to all happen at once."

"We get it. Gracie and I had a long talk. We know we acted like spoiled little children, well … because we are."

"That's my fault. I did spoil you. But that was my pleasure. I loved every minute of it."

"Gracie and I love you and we both know Mom didn't really make you happy. It would be selfish of us not to acknowledge what a wonderful father you've been, except for the part where you're always telling us you know best. Neither of us like that too much, as you're well aware," she added on a lighter note.

"I know I push a little too hard, but that's just how I'm built."

"We know that. And we also know you tried your best to make up for Mom not being here with us. Luckily, we had Ava. Even when Mom was home, she never really had time for us."

"I'm so sorry she made you feel that way. I should have seen it, but I think building my empire got in the way. I just wanted you girls to have everything. I don't ever want to lose you and your sister. I almost did and I can't let that ever happen again."

Lilly listened, loving the way Samuel felt about his children. She knew she was lucky to have him back in her life. Being with him again was something she had only dreamed of. She never expected she would ever get a second chance.

Samuel felt Julianna's pain. "Your mother does love you both. I think she was just too afraid to be here to talk to you."

"That's giving her too much credit. She still hasn't contacted us to explain any of this. She left it up to you like she always does."

"I really thought she would've called you by now. Maybe by some stroke of luck she will. She was always free to do as she pleased, and I guess that's what she's doing now."

"Gracie and I are running out of excuses for her."

"Just give her some time," Samuel added, careful not to make matters worse.

"Seeing you with Lilly, I see a couple in love." She gave her father a big hug, and reached for Lilly's hand and squeezed it tightly. "If you're both happy, then so are we. I can't usually speak for Gracie, as you know, but this time I think I can."

"That's very grown up of you, and encouraging."

"It's long overdue," Julianna said.

Just as they were finishing up, like the whirlwind she always was, Gracie entered. "So, what did I miss?"

"Everything." Julianna said. "As usual. Late to the dance. Come with me. I'll fill you in."

As they left the room, Lilly kissed Samuel. "You were right. They came around."

"That's my girl." He smiled with pride.

Chapter Twenty-One

Leo wasn't expecting his grandmother, but when he heard the key in the door, he knew he would have some company for dinner, although he was lucky to have Bernie beside him. And to think, when Samuel brought him over, he didn't want any part of owning a dog. But now he couldn't think about not having him to come home to.

Being a writer called for a lot of alone time, but he only liked being alone when he was writing. Otherwise, he enjoyed a good conversation and time to relax with a book or a movie. But after Ellie died, he rarely read, and he didn't enjoy anything the way he used to.

He also never liked eating dinner alone, but since Samuel's heart attack, everyone's schedules were a little bit off, so he found himself alone most of the time. He didn't like that, but he understood that his grandmother wanted to be with the man she loved. *Funny thinking that,* he thought.

"Leo, I wasn't sure if you'd be home."

"Unfortunately, I have nowhere else to be. Sadly for me, after the show, I usually come home, write for a while and then go to bed. A writer's life can be pretty damned lonely." He didn't mean to sound ungrateful, but it did come out that way, and maybe he was, just a little.

Lilly sat down at the kitchen table. "I'm so sorry. I know I kind of left you in the lurch. Do you mind if I join you?"

"Are you kidding? I'm so happy to see you. It's been a long couple of weeks."

"That's for sure." Lilly said as she reached for a piece of pizza. "Lou Malnati's, my favorite."

"I know that. I would have saved it for you."

"So, tell me what's wrong," Lilly said as she reached for her grandson's hand. "I can see there's something more going on here."

"I just can't put my finger on it. I know Gracie likes me, well, somewhat likes me. I'm not exactly sure if we have a chance for anything more than just being co-hosts."

"Have you talked to her about it?"

"Nope, I just can't. When I think I'm getting close, she pulls back. I know she's afraid, but so am I. I thought I didn't care about being alone, but I do. I want to share my life with someone."

"Leo, honey. You have to tell her how you feel."

"That's just it, I don't know how I feel."

"Well, you can start with that. Maybe take her to dinner or better yet, take her dancing or something to have a little fun. Samuel's doing fine. He wants his daughter to be happy."

"I know that, but maybe he doesn't think I'm right for her. Has he said anything?"

"Nothing other than he loves you like a son and always will."

"Really? I didn't even think he knew anything about how I feel."

"Honey, the first time I saw you two together, I could tell. The way you look at her, and let me tell you, the way she looks at you. It's so sweet. I think a lot of people notice."

"Wow, I didn't know I was that obvious. Anyway, did you hear what Gracie and I were talking about on the podcast? About Thanksgiving?"

"As a matter of fact, we did. Samuel and I had an idea about what we could do to make it work, and we could all be together."

"Okay, I'm listening."

"He wants us all to be together in Lake Geneva."

When Leo didn't say anything, she thought he didn't like the idea. "I gather you're thinking it's too early, right?"

"No, actually it might be a good idea. We have to be able to be with each other or we'll all lose out on precious time."

"You're right, honey. I didn't look at it that way, but I guess there really is no other way to see it. Look at Samuel, he never thought he would have a heart attack."

"Right, but what about his doctor? He might not be okay with it."

"He's going for his checkup the day before, and he invited Dr. Leavitt to join us all for Thanksgiving dinner. The doctor has no family in Lake Geneva and Samuel thought the he could use a diversion."

Leo laughed. "Well, I gather Samuel must be feeling better if he's up to another Warrington family dinner."

"What's so funny?"

"You'll see. A Warrington dinner is like a movie. You never know what could happen, but you'll see for yourself."

Lilly didn't want to end the conversation just yet. "I have one more thing to bring up."

"Okay. Let's hear it."

"Don't get upset." She took a breath before springing the news. "We're planning on getting married sooner rather than later."

"Whoa, you two aren't wasting any time."

"So, you're not okay with it? You did say we shouldn't lose time."

"I did, didn't I? Wait a minute, he's not even divorced. What if Francine won't give him a divorce? You know they have had some issues in the past and then she changed her mind."

"Let's see how Thanksgiving goes. I just wanted you to know."

This was Leo's cue to end the conversation. He always knew when his grandmother had finished a discussion. *It's something like Elvis has left the building.* "You know this is going to be difficult for Gracie and Julianna."

"Sweetie, I know that. We're going to do everything we can to make this right."

"What if Francine changes her mind? She's done it before.

Once again, she repeated. "Let's see how it goes."

"Really? Wow, then I guess we're going to have a wedding."

"Let's not mention it just yet. He hasn't told the girls."

"Okay, but you said no more secrets."

Lilly hugged Leo. "I couldn't ask for a better grandson."

"You could, but I think you're stuck with me."

They both laughed, realizing how lucky they were to have each other.

"So, do we have a deal? No talking about it until after Thanksgiving?"

Leo squeezed his grandmother's hand. "We've got a deal."

Chapter Twenty-Two

Jack had been calling and messaging Gracie without receiving any indication she would speak to him again. His plan was to win her back after the fiasco at her house, but if she didn't ever respond, his chances of reuniting with her were down to zero.

He also didn't believe that Gracie and Leo were a couple, but he didn't know for sure. So, with that in mind, he decided he needed to make one more attempt. He had to take one last shot at it, even though he knew it was a long shot. He would call in to the show and hope they took his call. They always took callers, so why wouldn't they take his? Nobody seemed to give their real name when they called, so he wouldn't either. *I'm good at that,* he thought sadly.

Before the show, Charlotte summoned Gracie and Leo for a short conversation. They were both hesitant to have this talk because they knew she wasn't too happy with them. But, they really had no choice — she was here and they were on the air in minutes.

"Listen, guys, you two are like magic on the air. Whatever happened the last few weeks, I don't care about it. It doesn't involve me, but what *does* involve me is how the audience perceives you. Let me tell you, I've gotten hundreds of messages about the two of you."

Gracie seemed annoyed. "What about the two of us?"

"We can go into this another time, but for now, you two are a team and you need to act like it. Got it? Put your personal lives on hold until you're off the air. You both okay with that?"

Leo politely smiled. "Got it."

"What about you, Gracie?"

"I don't know what you're talking about, so no, I don't get it. Leo and I will discuss this another time and definitely another place."

Charlotte knew that was all she was getting, but she added one last thing. "Shake on it."

They clasped hands, but there was no real enthusiasm from either of them. They just did it to keep Charlotte happy. "Okay, guys, it's your time to shine, so don't blow it, please. Remember our deal.

"Five, four, three, two, go for it." Charlotte took a breath and sat down, crossing her fingers that the show would work today. Things were running smoothly, and the last caller asked to speak specifically to Gracie. So, Charlotte put him through to her.

"Hello caller, this is Gracie. And you are?"

There was a pause. "How about if you don't call me anything?"

"I'm okay with that. I know it's hard to talk about families so we're listening. Take your time."

"That's just it, I don't have a family. Though I almost had one."

"Do you want to tell us about it, Mr. Caller?"

"Well, here goes. Boy from Paris meets girl from the States. Girl moves to Paris to be with him. They're in love — deep love. They're soulmates."

Then there was a silent moment. "Are you still with us, caller?"

"I'm here. So sorry, Gracie."

Suddenly she realized who it was, and she was uncomfortable. "Please go on, we're listening." She didn't want to act like she was annoyed, so she turned up the charm. This was not exactly easy for her to do, since that edge about her that Leo enjoyed wanted to show through.

"Boy falls madly in love with the girl. She became his family immediately. He knew she was the love of his life the moment they met. However, he had a few secrets he was planning to tell her, but it never seemed like the right time. Days passed, months passed, and even a couple of years passed."

The caller paused again, and there was silence on the line. This went on so long that Leo was surprised Gracie hadn't ended the call.

"Are you done, Mr. Caller," she asked, still playing the polite hostess.

"No, I need to finish. Her parents didn't approve of

anything I was doing. They wanted her back. She didn't want to go back. Her father told her his version of my life and my love believed her him.

She left me, just like that."

Leo could tell something was too familiar for Gracie, but he motioned that he would finish up the call.

Gracie shook her head no. She could do this. By now, she was hoping he would just hang up, but he didn't. "Mr. Caller, it sounds like you'd rather not finish, and that would be fine. We understand."

"I can finish. I'm good. Okay, I can finish. I should have told the truth, but when you're in love, sometimes you do crazy things. Her father really hated me and he still does. So, to sum it up, the love of my life left Paris, went home to Chicago."

Gracie responded. "If you loved her, why didn't you follow her?"

"Because she had made up her mind, and she was not one to change it. Once she decides something, that's the way it is — good or bad."

"So, why are you here now?"

"I've never stopped loving her and I never will. So, here's my question: Why do you think she won't hear me out? Wouldn't you want to, if you were her?"

Leo didn't take his eyes off Gracie for even a second. He was anxious to hear her answer. But he motioned to help her out, and when she nodded yes, he was relieved.

"Mr. Caller, this isn't about me. Oh, wait one moment, Leo has something to add. Is that okay with you?"

"I suppose."

"Hello, Mr. Caller. While I was listening, a thought came to me. I understand how much you love this woman, but sometimes love isn't enough. I'm sure right now you're feeling like you will never, ever be happy again, but there is a light at the end of the tunnel."

That got Gracie's attention, and she was listening carefully. "Mr. Caller, maybe I can help. I never thought anyone could ever take my wife's place after she died. I was right. But now there's someone in my life who has found a new place in my heart. You, my friend, will find that, too."

Gracie took over. "Leo, that was just beautiful. Caller, what do you think about that?" There was a moment of quiet. "Caller, are you there?"

Charlotte motioned for them to end the show, but they didn't. Leo held up his hand, asking for a few more seconds. Charlotte nodded okay.

"Before we leave this afternoon, I want to thank all our listeners for being there for us. Today was a great example of how many hearts are broken by one single moment. Next time you find yourself in a relationship that has gone wrong or you lose someone you love, stop for a minute and take a deep breath. Love can be just around the corner. Take care, and love with your heart. That can never be wrong."

Gracie left the studio as Charlotte wiped a few tears from her eyes. "Leo, that was lovely." Gracie asked me to give this to you after the show.

Leo opened the note and read:

Leo, please come to my office. I want to talk to you.
— Gracie

Leo was prepared for an argument because he probably shouldn't have said anything. He just couldn't help himself. But when he knocked on the door, Gracie called out, "It's open." When he walked in, she said, "I need to tell you something."

He had thought he was going into the battlefield, but he was wrong. She was standing before him with tears in her eyes. "I think I'm in love with you."

For a moment, Leo was in shock and he couldn't speak.

"Do you have anything to add or am I going to stand here like a fool?"

There was a long pause as the two stared at each other, Leo still grappling for words. Finally he said, "I do have something to say, as you know, I always have something to say."

Gracie laughed. "That's very true, you do."

"You make me laugh, you make me smile, you make me feel as if there's no tomorrow, there's just right now."

Gracie moved closer and said, "Kiss me. You need to kiss me soon, because there is a tomorrow."

Leo could feel his heart beating fast and furious. He couldn't believe this was happening. She looked so beautiful standing in front of him. *How did I get to be the guy who gets the most beautiful woman he has ever seen?*

He kissed her with his eyes open wide. Their lips found each other with a sweetness she would always remember. *This is a guy who literally swept me off my feet. Imagine that,* she thought with wonder.

Neither of them spoke. They were too surprised and happy about what had just happened.

Some days you just have no idea where life will take you. But it was clear that today had taken them to the place they needed to be. Leo and Gracie had made their decision. Time was definitely on their side.

It's All About a Wedding

Chapter One

Gracie had woken up several times during the night in a cold sweat. There she was, falling for Leo Tucker after she swore up and down that she would never fall in love again. She didn't need a man; she needed a career.

However, along came Leo, and her father decided they should do a podcast together about love. She probably should have said no, but she didn't. Then again, if she had, she would have lost her chance to work at Warrington Publishing—and that was not going to happen.

Even Gracie knew she wasn't ready to take on the company, but what was a girl supposed to do when she had ambition? Probably wake up at night in a cold sweat, overthinking.

She hated that she kept questioning herself. She didn't want to be like those silly young women who used to fill up her email when she was still writing as Dear Hannah. Was she one of those women who couldn't let go? After hearing herself repeat the same things over and over, she worried she was becoming the kind of irritating woman she used to laugh about.

She used to feel confident about everything and never had second thoughts. *Where was that Gracie?* she wondered. *Have I lost my identity?*

At work that day, she and Leo had done their regular podcast, *All About Love.* It was hard enough pretending she didn't have feelings for

Leo while they answered callers' questions about romance. If that wasn't enough, her ex, Jack, decided to call in anonymously.

The caller had asked to talk to Gracie. At first, she didn't recognize the voice—but the more he talked, the more familiar the voice became.

"Hello, this is Gracie. Who are we talking to?"

There was a long pause from the caller. "How about if you don't call me anything?"

"I'm okay with that. Take your time."

"It's just that I don't have a family. Though I almost had one."

"Do you want to tell us about it?"

"Well, here goes. A boy from Paris meets a girl from the States. The girl stays in Paris to be with him. They're in love—deep love. They're soulmates. Perfect for each other."

There was another silent moment as Gracie realized who it was. Leo glanced her way, trying to figure out why she had suddenly become agitated.

"Are you still with us, caller?" Gracie asked, hoping he'd hung up. No such luck.

"I'm here. So sorry."

Leo motioned to Gracie that he would take the call if she wanted, but she shook her head and continued.

"Okay, caller, please go on," she said, hoping not to sound as annoyed as she felt.

"They immediately clicked. She became his family. She was the love of his life from the moment they met. However, he had a few secrets he was planning to tell her, but it never seemed like the right time. Time passed and things were going well."

Jack paused again. Silence. This went on so long that Leo was surprised when Gracie didn't end the call. But, for whatever reason, she didn't. It was obvious she was not acting like herself.

"Are you done, caller?" she asked, still playing the polite hostess.

"No, I need to finish. Her parents didn't approve of anything I was doing. They wanted her back. Her father dug up information about me. It wasn't true, but that didn't matter. That was that."

Leo again motioned to Gracie that he could finish up the call. What she should have done at that moment was either give Leo the chance to talk or drop the caller. But she just wanted to get through it and hope she would never hear Jack's voice again.

"Caller, it sounds like you'd rather not finish, and that would be fine. We understand."

"I can finish; I'm good," Jack said. "I should have told her the truth, but when you're in love, sometimes you do crazy things. So, to sum it up, the love of my life left Paris and went home to Chicago."

"If you loved her, why didn't you follow her back?" Gracie responded.

Jack went on with the story like he was the victim. "Well, to tell you the truth, she was the kind of woman who, once she made up her mind, nothing would change it. She wasn't flexible. However, I've never stopped loving her."

"Really, so that's how you see it?"

Gracie was getting a signal from Charlotte to end the call, but she didn't. She knew she wasn't about to be fired; her father owned the company.

"I've never stopped loving her, and I never will," Jack continued. "Why do you think she won't hear me out? Wouldn't you, if you were her?"

That's when Gracie decided he had crossed the line. "Caller, this is not about me so I—"

That was when Leo interceded, and Gracie felt relieved.

"Caller, maybe I can help. While I was listening, a thought came to me. I understand how much you love this woman, but sometimes love isn't enough. I'm sure, right now, you're feeling like you will never be happy again, but there is a light at the end of the tunnel."

That got Gracie's attention. She was so glad he was there to step in, and she was listening carefully.

"I never thought anyone could take my wife's place after she died," Leo went on. "I was right. But now there's someone in my life who has found a new place in my heart. You, my friend, will find that, too."

* * *

When Leo came back to her office after the show, Gracie was so impressed with his words on the air that she kissed him. She realized immediately that she'd made a mistake. She had not planned to be so vulnerable—but, nevertheless, it was a beautiful kiss. Leo was not only a heartfelt romance writer. He was a calming person and, what bothered Gracie the most, she was in love with him. She couldn't take back the kiss, but she could stop their relationship from going any further.

It wouldn't be the first time she lied to herself. Besides, she thought, they were going to spend the Thanksgiving holiday today. If she survived the pressure of it all, maybe she would revisit the kiss. It was undeniable that they had chemistry, and that was the part that made her mad. So many things were going on in her life, and falling in love was not in the cards.

Her father was now engaged to Leo's grandmother, and she'd learned they had been in love for years. That only confused her more. She was supposed to be an adult, but she didn't feel that way. There were too many changes happening at the same time. Sometimes she wished she was just finishing college, with all her hopes and dreams still in front of her. She sometimes wondered if she would make the same mistakes if she could do it all over again. She didn't have an answer.

* * *

She was packing for the weekend when she heard the doorbell ring and decided against answering it. She didn't have time for visitors. She was already late. That was nothing new for her.

The person ringing the doorbell wasn't stopping, so Gracie tossed the few remaining pieces of clothing into her bag and called out. "Ava, can you get it? I need more time."

Then it dawned on her that she was the only one home. Everyone else had left for the Thanksgiving weekend get-together her father was hosing at his new estate in Lake Geneva, Wisconsin. A royally named estate for her father, the king of the family. She laughed to herself; she had always thought of him that way. The only thing missing was his crown.

This was the first year they weren't going to celebrate in their family home. Her father had survived a heart attack, and Thanksgiving was going to be an even bigger event because they were also celebrating his recovery.

She thought of ignoring the bell, but the visitor clearly had no intention of leaving. "Coming," she called out as she ran down the stairs and opened the door.

Leo was standing there, smiling. "Morning, Gracie. I knew you were in there."

"Guess so," she said, trying to sound pleasant when she was perturbed.

He was holding two coffees and white box tied with a thin string, doing his best to balance them. It wasn't as easy as it looked in the movies. He was staring into her eyes, pretending not to have noticed she was still in her girly pink pajamas.

Gracie found it odd how intense his focus was as he stared at her face, a noticeable blush creeping up his cheeks.

She soon understood, realizing her pajama top barely covered her underwear. She crossed her legs and smiled. "Morning. What have you got there?"

"I brought you something I thought you might like. After yesterday's caller, I thought you might need a little pep talk. It was difficult, but you handled it like a pro."

"Thank you. I'm good. However, whatever you have in that box smells wonderful."

"I stopped by the bakery to check on everything. Whenever my grandmother isn't there, she thinks all hell will break loose."

"Did it?"

"Of course not. Everything was running smoothly, but she worries."

"You certainly are one terrific grandson."

"Well, she was always there for me. I could never repay her for everything she did when I was a kid."

Gracie smiled, adding this to the list of Leo's good qualities.

"So, Mr. All-Around Good Guy, what can I do for you?"

"Like I said, just checking in on you. It's pretty quiet around here. Where's Ava?"

"She's cooking up a storm in Lake Geneva with your grandmother, getting everything ready for Thanksgiving."

"She's probably cooking every dish she's created in the last fifty years, but that's Lilly Tucker."

"That's funny because Ava's the same way. You know how my father loves holidays, and Ava has always babied him. It's always been whatever Samuel wants."

Leo laughed. "I know all about that, but I still love the guy."

"That's why my father loves you, too. You give him what he wants, but, mostly, you give him what he needs. He thinks of me and Julianna as his little girls. I'm hoping that will change someday. You give him respect and great discussions. I think I'm a little light in that department."

Leo laughed. He understood Samuel right from the get-go, and he was happy to know that Samuel always felt comfortable enough to let his guard down when they were alone. They were almost like a father and son, but better because they chose each other.

"Your father's the greatest. He pulled me through some rough times, and I'll never forget that."

Gracie smiled, never disappointed by how Leo looked at the world. So appreciative of everything that came his way. She wished she could be more like him.

"So, are you almost ready?" he asked. "You can come with me if you like. I said I'd come early in case they need help with anything."

"As you can see, I'm not exactly ready." She ran her fingers through her messy hair, realizing he had never seen her that way. Few people had.

He was trying his best not to stare. It was definitely a challenge not to admire her radiant beauty. Even without makeup, she was gorgeous. After all, he really wanted to kiss her and tell her that being with him would never be a mistake. He also knew that would scare her, and that was the last thing he wanted.

"I wish I could leave now, but I need to check on everything going on at Warrington," Gracie said. "We keep telling my dad all is well, but you know my father needs everything squared away before he can rest. If he thinks there's a problem, he's usually right."

"You don't think I know that?"

"I think Nicholas has been proactive. Not that I would tell him that. If he knew I thought that, his ego would be even larger than it already is. That guy loves himself—"

"Do you think I could come in?" Leo didn't mean to interrupt her, but it was getting hard to hold onto the coffee and bakery box without dropping everything.

"Oh, I'm so sorry. I guess I'm not a good hostess." Gracie helped him with the box.

She tried to reach for her jacket lying on the chair, just to put something on without making a big deal of the fact she was half-dressed. When she reached for the chair, she nearly fell over. Just as she was about to lose her balance, Leo grabbed her. The muffins fell to the floor, but at least Gracie managed to get her sweater on.

"I'm sure they would have been great," Gracie said, laughing as she tidied up.

Leo was also smiling. "I can get that." He placed the coffee cups down so they wouldn't spill. "I wanted to talk to you about something."

"Sounds serious. I figured you had a reason for coming."

"Well, it is. It's about the kiss."

"Which one?"

"All of them. The one after the show, specifically."

"Oh, that kiss. Right now?" She laughed. "Couldn't this wait? I'm not leaving the country."

"I don't like to keep things that bother me bottled up."

"Come, follow me. I guess I have time for some coffee if I don't make a mess of that, too."

Leo looked around the kitchen, thinking about the last time he was there and how much had happened. "Where's Georgia?"

"She went with the others. We couldn't very well leave her alone."

"I know. My grandmother picked up Bernie yesterday. No stone left unturned."

While they were sipping their coffee, neither said a word, but it was obvious each of them had something to say.

Gracie, as always, spoke first. "I'm so sorry about yesterday. I think I was unprofessional."

Leo was confused, and decided he'd better wait to see where this little meeting of the minds was headed.

"Leo, you know how much I enjoy working with you, but…"

There it was. The "I like you as a friend" speech. Leo took a deep breath, starting to regret coming.

"I was hurt pretty badly, as you know," Gracie continued. "Jack called me last night, which is why I spent the entire night tossing and turning, wondering if I should have said what I said yesterday. I was going to talk to you about it when I got to Lake Geneva, but here you are, sweet as could be, bringing me coffee and…" she smiled, "a few once-beautiful crushed muffins."

"Can I interrupt?"

"Sure. What are you thinking?"

"Oh, something similar." He was lying. Once again, they were both skating around the main subject.

"Okay, you first," Gracie said. She was about to tell him that she wanted to go out on a real date, but she didn't know exactly how to start that conversation—or if it was a good idea to actually want to go out with him. It was all so confusing.

"It was my fault," Leo said. "I shouldn't have come on so strongly on yesterday's podcast. I think I got caught up in the moment. You know, losing Ellie was so traumatic, and the thought of being in love overpowered what I really feel."

Gracie felt like a ton of bricks fell on her. He was going to give her the "just friends" speech. She didn't like it one bit, but she liked Leo too much to push.

"I totally understand," she said. "In fact, that's what I was going to say to you."

Leo faked a sweet smile. "Great. So, we're on the same page."

"Yes, we are." Gracie held out her hand for a shake. "Are we good?"

"Yes. I feel much better," Leo responded quickly as he stood up, ready to make a quick exit. He wanted to hold her in his arms and kiss her again, but he knew that wasn't happening. He wanted to leave gracefully, without making a fool of himself. It was over, and now he knew it. Done.

Gracie was disappointed, letting her pride get the best of her. "So, I guess I'll see you later."

"That you will," Leo said, unable to look her in the eye and trying his best not to sound defeated.

The moment Gracie closed the door, she struggled to keep it together, but it wasn't long before her eyes filled with tears. She was mad at herself and tired of pretending that she was a strong woman. She was sending a good man away because of her own fears.

Even before she got back to the kitchen, there was a knock on the door. She smiled, thinking it was Leo and hoping he had realized she wasn't being truthful. But, when she opened the door, she was surprised by who was standing there.

It was Jack, and she was disappointed. "What are you doing here? I thought we said our goodbyes."

He looked handsome as ever in a white shirt, jeans, and expensive shoes. "Can I come in?"

"I guess so, but only for a minute. I'm running really late."

"I just saw Leo drive away."

"I know. He brought me some muffins."

"Thoughtful guy."

She nodded as he followed her to the kitchen. "Okay, what's so important?"

"I wanted to apologize."

"Didn't we do this before? We said goodbye. You decided to leave America and go back to Paris. What on Earth could you possibly want to talk about?"

"Us. I want you to come back with me, and we can start fresh. I know you still love me, and I love you, so let's do it. This time, we'll do it right. No surprises."

Gracie just stood there, looking at him. "Have you gone crazy? I'm in love with Leo, and we want to be together."

"That's not what he said."

"When did you talk to him? You said he was driving away."

"Last night."

"And what did you say to him?"

"That I know you love me, that I want to go back to Paris, and that, hopefully, you're coming back with me. And that I'll never stop trying."

Gracie just stood there staring at him, wondering where he got the idea that was ever going to happen. "Let me get this straight. You told him that you love me, and I'm considering going back to Paris."

"Not exactly, but he said if that was the case, he would back off. All he cared about was your happiness."

"What's wrong with you?"

"Nothing." He moved closer so he could kiss her, but she pulled away.

Gracie's face flushed, and she took a few deep breaths. "Okay, now I'm only saying this one more time. We are never getting back together. If you were the last man in the world, and I had no money for food, I would starve rather than ask you for a dime. Is that in plain English that you understand? We are done. Kaput, over, never going anywhere together. I don't want to kiss you, see you, or talk to you on the phone. If I run into you on the street, I will walk by you and pretend you're not there."

"You don't mean that."

"I most definitely do. So, why don't you do both of us a favor and just leave?"

Jack started to move closer, but she took his hand and walked him to the door. "Please lose my number."

After she thought about what had just taken place, she decided to call Leo. No wonder he said they were just friends. Before she called, though, she decided whatever she had to say to him needed to be said in person. She also needed time to rehearse.

For the first time in a long time, she felt like she was back.

He had driven Julianna and Nicholas quite a bit, together and separately, especially since Samuel's heart attack. And he was very intuitive.

"They don't seem to click," Alex continued. "They just haven't got that special connection to be husband and wife. Not that every couple has that. I was never lucky enough to share my life with anyone."

"You know it's not too late. Look at me; after thirty years, I'm getting my second chance. Who would have thought?"

"I'm happy for you, but I like my alone time. When I'm home, I like peace and quiet, some takeout food, and an occasional beer. End of story."

Samuel laughed. "Well, you know me. I like a lot of action, and I'm not ready to call it quits."

"I get that. It seems like you and Lilly deserve to have this time together. Both of you worked and worked and worked."

"My heart attack woke me up. I know the pace I was keeping was way too much for a man my age, but I love working. After all, I built this company from nothing. I just can't walk away, but I have a plan that might work well."

"Look, you did an amazing job with the girls. You turned out to be a really great dad. You made a lot of people happy. Your books changed people's lives."

"I'm not sure if my girls see it the same way."

"I've heard them chatting, and they know you were the best. They are very aware of everything you did for them."

"I hope you're right. I was trying to be both mother and father to the girls. At times, it was a lot tougher than working, but at least I had Ava to help. She was just what they needed."

"She's great."

"I know, and I appreciate everything she did. Can you can keep a secret?"

"You're kidding, right?"

Samuel laughed. "So, this is pretty exciting. I bought a small coffeeshop in Lake Geneva with a bakery in the back for Ava. She always wanted to own her own place, and now she's going to have it."

"She must be thrilled."

"Haven't told her yet. You know the girls are grown up, to some extent. Crossing my fingers that they are. It's time for Ava to have a life. She's been a godsend."

"I must say, that's a great idea. She's such a great cook, and she makes the best grilled cheese sandwiches."

Samuel patted his tummy. "I know all about that. Now let's talk about Gracie. You seem to be more observant than me. So, tell me. I worry about her. Whatever she does, it doesn't seem to be enough. I want her to feel happy and content, but she's definitely not."

"I've noticed Leo and Gracie are both a little afraid to let go of the past. It's the way the two of them look at each other when neither of them realizes the other is watching. They match perfectly, but nothing's going to happen until they both realize how they feel."

"Alex, this is a whole other side of you. I'm impressed."

"Don't be. It's just that they have that sparkle in their eyes when they talk to each other. They both seem too stubborn, though, so it might not happen."

"Maybe it will," Samuel said with confidence. "Leo's a good guy. My daughter's a handful, but sometimes that can work. Selfishly, I would love to have Leo as a son-in-law, but it's not my choice; it's Gracie's."

"Not your choice? Where's Samuel Warrington? What did you do with him?"

"You know, a heart attack can do that to a man. I thought I was infallible, but guess what? I'm not. I want to dance at my daughters' weddings. There won't be one for Nicholas and Julianna, though. She broke off her engagement."

"Wow."

"Nicholas is back to business as usual, and Julianna was the one who informed me."

"Meaning?"

"I thought he had changed. I wanted to believe he had. I don't think he's a one-woman man. A man like that is never satisfied."

"So much for him changing his ways."

"He just acted as if he had. I had a feeling that was going to happen, but I was hoping Julianna would be enough. That being said, he's sharp, witty, and one hell of a businessman. He's never said no to me in all the years we've worked together."

"Well, that's something."

"It is. Also, for some reason, he knows that Leo is Nicole Forrester."

"Maybe it's time everyone knew."

"I don't know. It's a risk. I appeased him with more money so he doesn't blow this whole thing about Leo being Nicole."

"You know, Leo would probably be happy if everyone knew. Samuel, it's time. I think the millions of fans will accept him no matter what he does. Maybe even more. Women like a man who's sensitive."

"Maybe so. I just hate to ruin a great thing. He's so popular. He makes a lot of money for us. But you might be right. Has he said anything to you?"

"Every now and then, but not lately. He seems pretty happy these days, but I would think it might be a perfect time."

"Maybe you're right."

Alex smiled as he drove on. "Are you hungry?"

Samuel laughed. "Of course I'm hungry. Especially after that conversation. Maybe you'd like to do a podcast. You have a pretty good grasp of love."

"Not on your life."

Samuel couldn't stop laughing. He was picturing Alex sitting in one place answering calls. "Just kidding."

"Good. Now that we've got that straight, anything else you want to know?"

"Nope, pretty much got more information than I expected, Dr. Alex." They both had a good laugh.

"Find a hot dog stand. I'm pretty tired of my low-fat diet. We need some fun. A man can only stand unsalted food for so long."

"How about this? We'll do that after your appointment, if all is well, before I go back to the city to get Gracie."

"That sounds like a plan. I'm early, so I'll grab a coffee and save my calories for later."

* * *

Samuel arrived early for his doctor's appointment on purpose, just so he could have a conversation with Avery, Gracie's best friend. He was in the cafeteria for a few minutes before she arrived, helping himself to a fresh donut to dunk in his coffee. He was enjoying every last bit of a delicious chocolate donut with gooey chocolate and a few nuts drizzled on top when Avery arrived.

She smiled as she tapped him on the shoulder. "Is that a new addition to the cardiac diet?"

"Good morning. As a matter of fact, I made a promise this will be the last time I have one of these."

"For how long?"

"Until my next appointment. Keep this between us, please. Gracie has me set up with a dietician. Let me tell you, it's not a pretty picture."

"In all fairness, your daughter loves you. She wants you to be healthy. You look great, but how do you feel?"

"Seeing Josh soon. What a great guy. I'm lucky to have him. Never expected to have a cardiologist. I thought I was healthy, but I guess I wasn't."

Avery smiled. "You know the thing about this place. It's not Chicago, but we still have some first-rate doctors and care. I'm sure coming here was a good decision."

"My dear, it was a terrific choice. And they're lucky to have you."

"Thank you. Now, tell me how you really feel. You know your daughter's bark is a hell of a lot bigger than her bite."

"I know. She's a lot like me, so I understand. She always feels like she has to be the best."

"Well, that's true, and she is. When she puts her mind to it, she always succeeds."

"That's accurate unless she gets in her own way."

Samuel's decision about Gracie had been a long time coming. It was only recently that he really took a good look at her and what she was capable of doing. He knew Julianna had never wanted anything to do with the publishing business, which was why he had been so surprised when she decided to work with Nicholas. Her decision to break things off with him had also been quite a shocker, but Samuel now knew how much Julianna still loved Oliver and that she wanted to be there for his daughter. If a life with them in Ohio was what she wanted, Samuel was prepared for that. He was learning that protecting his daughters didn't mean smothering them.

"Don't worry about your daughter," Avery said. "She's going to be just fine. They both will."

"I hope so."

"You set the bar pretty high."

"I don't know about that. I could have done several things differently, but here I am, a happy man who hopes my heart keeps ticking so I can enjoy whatever life has to offer at my age."

"You look terrific, and you sound like nothing ever happened."

"But it did. I've been exercising as much as I can. It's not every day, but I take several long walks a week. It's not as bad as I thought, but I guess I could do more. Maybe I'll start to do it every day."

"Well, that sounds good. Now about your message." Avery cocked her head at him. "You said it was important. What's up?"

"Sit. Please. I'm glad you could fit me in. I've heard you're doing a terrific job."

"I heard some rumors that you might be joining the board here."

"Yes, I am. I decided my semi-retirement isn't up to snuff, so I'm going to become an active member of the board at Geneva North. I want to donate some of my time, not just money."

"Wow. Did that have anything to do with me getting this job?"

"No, you got this on your own. Your reputation got you the job, and I'm proud of you. From everything I've heard, the staff loves you."

"Thank you. Coming from you, that means something."

"Well, I've known you since you were wearing braces and glasses. Seeing you here makes me proud. You've wanted to be a doctor since before you were a teenager."

"Just like Gracie always wanted to run Warrington Publishing."

"Can you keep a secret? I'll let you in on a surprise."

"You bet," Avery said with a grin. "My lips are sealed."

* * *

Lilly was outside walking Georgia and Bernie when Samuel got home. Both dogs were a little off schedule being at Lake Geneva for the first time. They seemed to enjoy the fresh air, and they got along as if they had been together for years. Bernie was a schnauzer, and Georgia was a labradoodle, and both were a bit spoiled. For them, this new adventure seemed to be going smoothly.

Samuel was happy to see that they were getting along famously—especially because he had no idea how the rest of the night was going to go.

Lilly kissed Samuel. "So, do you have good news?"

"I do. Blood pressure is good, and my heart seems to be ticking just fine."

"Thank goodness. I was scared."

"Me too," Alex whispered as he joined them.

Trying not to get the dogs' leashes crossed as they hugged, Lilly sniffed. "I think I smell mustard and, if I'm not mistaken, I'm also smelling pickle."

"I'm busted," Samuel said as he looked at Alex. "I told you she would know."

Alex smiled back. "Not shocking, is it? Anyway, got to go back to the city for Gracie."

"Fine, but don't chicken out on dinner. I want you here."

Lilly smiled at Alex. "Me too."

"Be back soon." Alex drove away, knowing he didn't have a choice. He would stay the weekend, like it or not.

Samuel and Lilly walked around to the back of the property. "You know, Lilly, this is a beautiful place but…"

Lilly gave him a look. "Okay, I know what this is about."

"You do?"

"You don't want to stay here. You want to go back to the city after this weekend."

"Is that okay with you? I know you love it here. But the good news is I planned a trip for us. And it's a surprise."

After the dogs ran inside, Samuel pulled Lilly close to him. "I love you, and I was wondering if you think we've had a long enough engagement."

Lilly laughed. "Long enough for me."

"Good. Then we'll take a long vacation and get married, just you and me."

"What about the girls? And Leo? Shouldn't we ask them to be there?"

"That depends on how tonight goes. I have a few announcements. Either I'll be a great dad or a disappointing dad. We shall see. Also, I have an idea about our wedding."

"And that is?"

"Tomorrow. Thanksgiving is perfect. Tonight, I have a few announcements, and then we party tomorrow. So, my dear, are you ready to do this?"

"I don't have a dress."

"You do. It's in your room. Actually, there are a few options, just in case. I think it's going to be a night to remember. So, tomorrow it is? I have a rabbi coming."

"You love to surprise me." Lilly laughed. "I love that about you."

"And I love everything about you." They kissed.

Their dream was becoming a reality. The rest of their life was about to begin.

Chapter Three

Nicholas Sinclair sat at his desk, wondering if he had made a mistake deciding not to celebrate Thanksgiving with the Warrington family, especially since things weren't going well with Julianna. Marrying a Warrington was supposed to be the ace in the hole he needed to secure his place in the company. That was the closest he would come to being part of the Warrington legacy forever.

Unfortunately, Julianna had other plans. He didn't like being dumped. He even hated the word, but, in all fairness, he hadn't thought about that when he was saying goodbye to any of his girlfriends. Now that he was on the receiving end, it didn't feel great.

Nicholas was not only stunning and charismatic, but intelligent and shrewd. It hadn't taken much time for things to fall into place. Julianna was impressed by all the attention Nicholas was giving her, especially after she left her husband and came back to Chicago. It wasn't as if Julianna was the one he really wanted. Being the smooth guy with an edge, he knew he didn't stand a chance with Gracie, so who better than her younger sister? He was fond of Julianna, and thought becoming her one and only would let him reset the plan. He had pretended to be in love before, and it sometimes turned out better than he imagined. Just not this time; she didn't want him.

This year, Lake Geneva was where they would be celebrating Thanksgiving. It was an amazing place, but as far as Nicholas was concerned, a holiday was just another day. Unfortunately, his family wasn't big on celebrating them—or anything else, including birthdays. His past wasn't anything he liked to talk about.

Of course, this year was special. They were celebrating Samuel's recovery. One heart attack, and everything at Warrington Publishing changed.

Nicholas tried to be humble, but that was quite a stretch for him, especially because nearly everything he ever did was to better himself. He knew he was reaching for the stars, and he almost made it. He was close to walking down the aisle, but he lost his hold when Julianna found out he had lied to her. Maybe he shouldn't have had a roaming eye, but that was who he was.

Maybe he wanted her to find out, because he certainly wasn't discreet. By now, he realized his urge to be with other women was not changing. It was just a game to him.

He probably shouldn't have even been in Samuel's office, but with the office closed for the weekend he assumed nobody would notice. Once he knew the coast was clear, he let himself in and sat in Samuel's chair behind the desk. He had to admit that he felt comfortable at the head, viewing it all as if it would be his sooner rather than later.

He should have felt a bit guilty, wanting to take over the company while Samuel was still at the helm—the man who taught him everything and paid him very well. The man who treated him like a son. The man who helped him in every way he could.

Why would Nicholas be dumb enough to cheat on Samuel's daughter, knowing he would find out? There were so many times when Nicholas could have changed everything by being honest with everyone. He loved his games too much. That, along with his own fear of commitment to one woman, wasn't reason enough to keep him out of Samuel's chair.

Just as he was about to get up for a breather, the door opened. It was Gracie. She looked fantastic, wearing black leather pants and a white wool sweater that showed off her near-perfect figure. Her hair was down and slightly over to the side, just the way he liked it. If Nicholas didn't know better, he would have thought she was there for him.

She was, but not in the way he wanted. That ship had sailed before it ever left the dock.

"Don't get too comfortable sitting at that desk or being in my father's office," she began. "I really don't think that's going to happen."

"Nice to see you too, Gracie. Do you think you could ever come into any office and just say hello? Just once?"

"Let me remind you, this isn't your office. I only came in here because I thought this might be where you were hiding. I thought you might be up to something, and you clearly are."

"Anyway, why are you here?" Nicholas asked, looking as if he had just gotten caught with his hand in the cookie jar.

"I could ask you the same thing. Why aren't you in Lake Geneva with everyone?"

"I'm working. You can just get in your car and be on your way. I'm here because I have some work to do."

"Work or pretending to work?" She cocked an eyebrow at him.

"If I say working, would you believe me?"

"Of course not. That's your M.O. You can tell a lie better than anyone I know."

"Will you ever give me a break?"

"Not going to happen." She smiled in her shrewd but beautiful way. It worked wonders on Nicholas.

Gracie knew Nicholas better than anyone else did. She sat down on the couch and stared at him. "What's wrong with you? My sister loves you, and you know it. Why don't you just end your little game?"

"Maybe you haven't talked to your sister yet, but she told me why she hasn't picked a date for our wedding. Do you want to know why?"

Gracie guessed Julianna hadn't told him the truth, and that he was just fishing for her to spill the beans. She had no intention of being the one to tell him Julianna hadn't divorced her husband yet.

"Tell me what?" she asked in an innocent tone.

"Listen, I know you're not my biggest fan, but—"

"My sister and I love each other. We don't always see eye to eye, but when it comes to you, we decided not to discuss anything that might become an argument. She loves you, and I don't. I'm not even sure I like you."

"Sure you do. You're just afraid to admit it."

"There's that arrogance coming through. I'm surprised my sister hasn't noticed it. She just sees the spectacular view, but anyone who goes beyond that knows looks aren't everything."

"Can you stop for one minute? Am I that bad?"

Gracie paused, but she always liked to have the last word. "Actually, you are. I know you know it, but if you want to pretend otherwise, I get it."

"One thing about you is your inability to get over putting me down. Does that make you feel better?"

Sitting there watching him, Gracie reminded herself how many girls he had been involved with, including her. He was hard to resist, but most of his conquests eventually left him in the dust just as she had. Nicholas had that something extra, but once you got to know him, there was nothing extraordinary about him.

He couldn't come close to Leo. Leo was warm and caring—someone she could love, if and when she decided to give in to her feelings. She wasn't ready yet, and maybe she would never be. By the time she got around to having another relationship, he would have already found someone else. She had no doubt about that.

Nicholas shook his head in disbelief. "Oh, sorry. You like the Leo Tucker type."

"I do. He's a good guy, but I'm not here to talk about Leo. I'm here to talk about you and my sister."

Nicholas stood up and sat on the edge of the desk, ready to tell all. "I'm sure you know about this—but just in case you don't, here goes.

Apparently, your sister forgot to tell me she and Oliver hadn't signed the divorce papers yet, and he was coming to Lake Geneva to see her."

Gracie was speechless. She nodded, waiting to hear his thoughts. "Do you have a plan?"

"No, not really. Julianna also said Oliver had no intention of letting her go. So, there you have it. No wedding in the near future. She broke off our engagement. That's why I'm not going. And since I have nowhere else to go, I'm here working."

"So, you think it's going to be over?"

"I was right. You did know."

"I didn't know he was coming to Lake Geneva. I knew she hadn't signed the divorce papers yet, but I was sure she would. What makes you think she won't?"

"Because she also informed me she wasn't sure how much she really loved me."

"Really, all of this is news to me." She sat back against the leather couch and took a deep breath.

Nicholas laughed. "Looks like you're pretty happy about that."

"I'm sorry." Gracie was trying to be sensitive, but she was elated by the news.

"Well, Gracie, you got your wish. I know you don't want to hear this, but I would have preferred you—though I'm pretty sure you'll never give in to your feelings for me."

"I don't have any feelings for you. I know you find that hard to believe, but it's true."

"You just don't want to admit it."

As always, Gracie liked the last word. "One thing before I leave. You need to get out of this office. You might think you'll be sitting at the helm, but don't be so sure. All eyes aren't on you."

Gracie left without saying goodbye. As she closed the door, she smiled from ear to ear.

* * *

Just as Gracie was walking out of the building, she saw Oliver walking in. She had never met him personally, but she had seen photos. She was ready to walk back in, wondering why he was there, but her phone rang. When she saw it was from Avery, she took the call.

"What's going on? Is everything okay with my dad?"

Gracie felt lucky that Avery had left Chicago and gone to work at Geneva North just about the same time her father had his heart attack. There were so many new things happening in their family, and it was wonderful for Gracie to know her best friend was overseeing her father's care. She wasn't a cardiologist, but just having her at that hospital was helpful.

It certainly wasn't shocking that Samuel wasn't an easy patient, but Avery could handle just about anything. Cases like Samuel's were pieces of cake compared to Friday night at the ER of a Chicago hospital. Nothing phased Avery after that experience—not even Samuel Warrington.

"All is well. I just got an invitation from Josh, your father's doctor. Apparently, your father invited him to Thanksgiving. That's just like your dad."

"Sounds like him."

"Josh didn't have a plan for the holiday, but now he does—and so do I."

"Do I sense a little romance going on here?"

"Don't be silly. We don't have time for anything like that right now."

"Oh, so it's we?"

Avery laughed. "We work together. Nothing more."

"If you say so. From what I remember of Josh when we met, he's definitely someone you might put on your list. He's your type."

"I didn't realize I had a type."

"Everyone has a type."

"But do they always end up with their type?" Avery asked, feeling like she might have been sleeping at the switch.

"I think they do. Look at me. Well, on second thought, don't. I'm not a great example."

Avery laughed out loud. "You're an example. I don't know anyone who's had as many boyfriends as you."

"I picked the bad boys who lie. But that was before. I'm done. I've given up on men."

"You might be staring at love and not even know it. What about this Leo guy? You don't want to be alone."

"We'll talk more at Thanksgiving. So happy you'll be there."

"I had no idea I would be able to take it off. I haven't been anywhere for Thanksgiving in years. In Chicago, I always had to work holidays."

"Sounds great to me. I miss you."

"Are you there already?"

"Nope, I'm still in Chicago. Just left the office."

"What in the world are you still doing there?"

"Tell you later. Alex is waiting for me."

Chapter Four

When Gracie heard her father had cut the Thanksgiving guest list substantially, she was relieved. She had expected the dinner to be a bang-up social event. Whatever the case, she was happy about not having to be part of idle chitchat with people she didn't know.

This holiday was special, but Gracie's thoughts still seemed to get the best of her. She was worried about her father's health, and wondered if a health issue was the reason he cut back. She hoped it wasn't bad news, but knew she would have to wait to find out, because her father always liked making announcements at the dinner table; it was his way of controlling the conversation.

Shortly before dinner, Gracie whispered in her sister's ear. "Meet me in the kitchen, pronto." When Julianna seemed hesitant, she gave her a look of immediacy. "Please."

"Now? Can't this wait?"

"No." She lightly steered Julianna into the kitchen.

"Okay, what's this about?"

"Where's your ring?" Gracie asked. "Being sized? I could have sworn you were wearing it yesterday."

"Can we do this later?" Julianna seemed tense, which was out of character for her. She was usually able to keep her emotions in check, while Gracie was the more transparent sister.

"No, we can't do this later. I went to the office before coming here. Guess who I saw?"

"Don't keep me in suspense. Who?"

"Nicholas. He said you broke off your engagement, and he's heartsick. Well, at least surprised. I don't think he even knows what heartsick means. Anyway, let's have it. Why didn't you tell me?"

"I wanted to tell you in person."

"Here I am in the flesh."

"Well, Oliver is coming here tonight."

"Oh, that's the other thing. Right as I was leaving, Oliver was on his way in. I remembered his face from a picture you showed me. The only other person there was Nicholas."

Julianna seemed a little taken aback. "I wonder why. I hope it doesn't change anything."

"I'm sure it will be fine. Nicholas didn't seem perturbed or anything like that. He was his usual cocky, boastful self. I thought he might be looking for you. Did you go there today?"

"Nope. I'm done there," Julianna said.

"What do you mean?"

"I don't have any intention of working there anymore. I'm going back home with Oliver. I'm going to make it work this time."

"Wow. When did all of this happen?" Gracie took her sister by the hand. "Sit, please. I want to hear everything. Seems like there are a lot of changes happening."

"You're right, but they're good changes."

"Did you tell Dad?"

"Of course. He was the one who helped me decide."

"You're kidding, right?"

"Nope. We had a long talk, and I explained in detail my feelings and how much I wanted to help raise Sophie. Lilly helped me because you know how Dad can be."

"I get it, but why not talk to me?"

"Don't be mad. It seemed like you were already doing a lot of your own soul searching. It wasn't like this whole thing happened weeks ago; it was just yesterday."

"I'm not mad, just a bit confused. I had no idea this was on your mind. But I'm thrilled. I want you to be happy."

Gracie had a big smile on her face as she reached for a couple of glasses from the table and a bottle of wine. "First, we toast. To the day my loving sister dumped the so-called Prince Charming."

Julianna began to laugh. "You really don't like him, do you?"

"He's a smart guy. Do I like him? No, not really."

"I'm so sorry. I should have told you first. I've been thinking about this since I came home."

"I had no idea. I thought you were head over heels in love with Nicholas, which I could never understand. He's not your type."

"Why do you think everyone has a type? Can't we find happiness with someone different?"

Gracie could now take a deep breath, knowing her sister had come to her senses. Nicholas was not the right man for her—or for anyone else, for that matter. He was arm candy, but a marriage to a cheater like him couldn't be successful.

"With all the confusion and Dad's heart attack, plus our mother's hesitancy to sign her divorce papers, I didn't have time to think. Once I did, I knew it would be a mistake. Oliver's a good man, just like Leo."

Gracie's next few sips were more like gulps. "I guess these last few weeks have been a bit chaotic for me, too."

"I was flattered that Nicholas chose me, but when I found out Mom had everything to do with pushing us together, I decided there was no way I could marry a man I didn't love."

"Why would she have done that?"

"It doesn't matter now. I'm just glad it's over."

"And you're sure it's over?"

"I've never been so certain of anything." Julianna raised her eyebrows, giving Gracie a serious look.

"Now, tell me about Oliver. Is he coming tonight or for the holiday dinner tomorrow?"

"Both, but I have no idea why he would go to the office before coming here. Sophie's with him."

"He walked in alone. Sorry, I think I made a mistake by not going back in once I saw him. Nicholas can be cruel."

"Oliver is a successful businessman who can hold his own with anyone. He seemed to manage with Dad, and you know that's not an easy feat."

Gracie nodded. There was probably nothing she could have done anyway. She was anxious to get out of the office without coming to blows with Nicholas. Whether she liked it or not, the two of them being in a room together for longer than a few minutes never ended well.

Just then, their father entered the kitchen through the back door. He seemed to be going outside for a bit of air. "Girls, we need to talk," he said once he saw them.

"We're doing that right now," Gracie said. "Join us."

Julianna seemed surprised by Samuel's entrance. "What were you doing outside?"

"Thinking."

"You need to go outside to think?" Gracie asked with an edge that got to her father.

"Sometimes, but there are a lot of things you girls don't know about me. Since my heart attack, it seems like everyone is trying to figure out everything I do. Guess what? Sometimes, I just do things."

Neither Gracie nor Julianna bought that for one minute, but neither said anything.

"I was going outside to think about you and your sister," Samuel said. "Who else? You two are always on my mind."

"What's the plan for tonight?" Julianna asked.

Samuel smiled. "What plan? We're going to have dinner, and that's all."

"Come on. Come clean. It's never just dinner," Gracie said, feeling a bit too happy. Wine always made her a little mellow, which was a good thing for all.

"Gracie, did you hear the news about Julianna and Oliver?"

Julianna smiled. "Dad, I'm sitting right here. I just started to tell her I'm going back to Ohio to be with Oliver and Sophie."

"As you know, I'm not really busy today. So, if you girls don't mind, I'll listen. Just pretend I'm not here."

Both girls looked at their father. Gracie couldn't help but weigh in. "Is that possible?" she snickered.

"I can *do* that," he replied, knowing Samuel Warrington not voicing an opinion would be impossible.

Realizing he had no plan to walk away, they nodded that he could stay.

Samuel raised his hand. "I understand Julianna's plan, but I wish she could stay in Chicago."

"Dad, you promised to just sit back and relax while we talk."

"Gracie, what do you think?" Samuel asked.

Julianna gave him another look. "Dad, you promised."

"I think Julianna's an adult. If she feels she's ready to go back to the life she started, then she should. I'm all for love winning."

"Good for you," Samuel said. "When did you decide that? Last I heard, you were giving up on men."

"I say a lot of things that may or may not be true."

"Okay, got it, but that didn't last long." Samuel's habit of calling her out used to upset her, but she had mostly gotten over it. Being in Paris for a while helped with some things, but she was still the same Gracie.

"That's what I said about me, but we're talking about Julianna. She's going to make the best decision she can for now. She can always change her mind."

Samuel knew he shouldn't have said a word, but it was time he had some answers. After all, he didn't want his girls to give up on any chance for happiness. He'd made a lot of mistakes in his life, and didn't want them to take as long as he had to find the perfect partner.

Gracie still seemed a little on edge. "Samuel, do you know what your protégé's plans are? Nicholas seems to have his own agenda."

"First, honey, could you call me Dad?"

"Not right now. As long as you joined us, I have some questions that might help me understand what is going on. Nicholas was in your office sitting behind your desk."

"And?"

"What do you mean and? Why was he at your desk? It's your office, not his."

"Could be because I asked him to find some of the paperwork that I hadn't finished because of the heart attack. Is that okay with you?"

"Why didn't you ask me? I'm capable."

"Yes, you are, but he was there when I called."

Gracie took a breath, thinking she should have been embarrassed but wasn't. Julianna just watched. She was a bit amused that they continued on as if she wasn't even there.

"Oh, and by the way," Gracie continued, "did you know he's not coming tonight?"

"Yes. I know. He hates these things anyway. Just for the record, I'm glad Julianna broke it off with him. And I need to say one thing. I love you girls, and you know it, but when it comes to the men you choose, that's up to you."

Both Julianna and Gracie were a little surprised by their father's words, but they were ecstatic. So much so that they high-fived each other.

"Look, girls, tonight is supposed to be about being thankful. I might not have been here to celebrate, so can we talk shop later—or, better yet, tomorrow."

Gracie and Julianna shared a smile before Gracie interrupted the mood. "Maybe this is the best time. Let's put our cards on the table, and then maybe we can have an enjoyable evening for a change. All three of us have some things to talk about. Maybe we can sort them out now."

"Girls, please, give me until tonight. We can rehash my decisions then if we need to."

"You're planning something, right? It's not just a dinner, is it?"

"Maybe a little of both. After tonight, you might be satisfied with some of my decisions. I promise, it will be good for you."

"Okay, Samuel. I'm trusting you."

Julianna smiled, realizing she had made the right decision to go back to Ohio. She knew she wasn't like her sister and her father. They were like two peas in a pod, but the kind of lives they wanted weren't for her.

"Okay, guys," she said. "Enough. Dad, Gracie, let's put a lid on this. You can pick up right where we left off tomorrow. Gracie, you've had one too many glasses of wine, and, as we know, that's never good. We have a dinner tonight, so let's try to have some fun. Oliver has never been with all of us before. Can we act normal, just for one night?"

Julianna hugged her father and kissed him on the cheek. Gracie did the same, then walked up the stairs, realizing she'd better get dressed.

Gracie wasn't in a holiday mood but, after a long, hot bubble bath, she promised herself she would put everything in the right perspective. Her father could have been gone, and that would have been awful. She needed to rethink her mood.

* * *

Luckily, Julianna had dressed earlier because, right after Gracie went upstairs, Nicholas walked in—with Oliver. Julianna took a deep breath. She was beside herself. This wasn't supposed to happen.

Lilly came to the rescue. "Hi, I'll entertain these two good-looking guys. Oliver, it's so nice to meet you, and, Nicholas, I'm glad you could make it." Lilly was always gracious.

"Thanks so much, Lilly, you're a doll," Julianna said. "Ava asked me to help in the kitchen. I'll be back in a minute."

"Wait a minute, Jules," Oliver called out, using his favorite nickname for her. "Someone wants to see you."

There was Sophie, Oliver's daughter, looking so cute in the white furry coat Julianna had bought her last year. It was too big then, but now it fit her perfectly. Julianna opened her arms as wide as she could when Sophie came running toward her. "I'm so happy to see you."

Sofie comfortably wrapped herself into Julianna's arms. "I've missed you so much. Do you like my hair? Daddy's been helping me, but I miss the way you did it."

"I think he did a great job. You look beautiful. Looks like you might have grown an inch or two."

"An inch. Daddy measured me the way you always did."

"Oh, that's great. You know you have a great daddy." Julianna smiled, looking at Oliver. If they were alone, she would have kissed him right then. Her heart was beating fast, and she knew she was going home with Oliver. No way was she overthinking that.

Julianna didn't expect to get emotional, but she couldn't help it. When she left Ohio, she'd thought she could easily forget the life she started, especially after she met Nicholas and fell in love with him. But, at that moment, she began to realize how much she missed the family she had created with Oliver. While she'd enjoyed his attention, Nicholas was never right for her.

She could have stayed and tried to defy the odds, but—even though she wasn't back at home that long—quite a few things changed for her. She thought her father was infallible, but he had a heart attack. She also thought her parents had a happy marriage, but it was perfectly clear they didn't. She never imagined her father would find peace and comfort in Lake Geneva, but he had. Things were changing all around her, and that confused her even more.

Oliver had tears in his eyes as he watched his daughter tightly holding onto Julianna. He was there hoping for a second chance and, watching Julianna and Sophie hug, he realized his future was going to be bright. He had come to the right place.

"If it's alright with your father, let's go into the kitchen," Julianna said to Sophie. "I'll get you a snack."

"Daddy, can I go?"

Oliver nodded. "Go ahead, honey."

Julianna turned back and smiled, thinking this might turn out to be a good Warrington dinner after all.

* * *

Nicholas rarely became emotional, but watching Julianna and Sophie was too much, and he decided to leave. Julianna was far too sweet for him, and, besides that, he knew from their conversation at the office that Oliver wanted her back. So while no one was watching, he snuck out. Nicholas wasn't going back to the office, but he didn't want to be alone either. That was for sure.

He drove around until he found a bar. It was getting late, and he knew the pre-Thanksgiving dinner would be starting soon. He wasn't hungry, but he didn't want to stay at the bar all night. It was snowing, and the roads were kind of slick, so he was still up in the air about where he might end up.

A beautiful redhead sat down next to him. "Hey, are you busy tonight?" she asked, inching too close to him for comfort.

"Yes, I think I am."

"Then why do you look like you lost your best friend."

"Because I might have."

"Hi, I'm Eloise Endicott." She looked him up and down. She was beautiful and smelled fabulous. Nicholas could tell she wasn't new to this kind of behavior, and neither was he. He had been a regular at several bars over the years. He was never shy, and he didn't like the idea of sitting alone. He rarely left by himself.

However, not knowing this bar or anyone there, he began to feel uncomfortable and strange, like a piece of meat. For a second, he felt the same way he usually made women feel when he was out for prey.

"So, what do you say we get out of here? I live close by," the redhead said, stroking his hair. "What do you say, sweetie?"

He smiled at her, thinking about all the times he had said exactly that line. It was almost as if he was eyeing a female version of himself. She had her hand on his shoulder and whispered. "Do you have a name?"

"Nicholas."

"Do you mean like Saint Nicholas?"

"No, just Nicholas. I don't believe in Christmas."

She frowned. "No wonder you're alone. I suppose you don't celebrate Thanksgiving, either."

"I'm just thinking over some of my life decisions."

"Sounds pretty serious to me." She inched her way closer to him.

"I don't want to be rude, but if you don't mind, I'd like to think alone."

"Okay. I get the message. If you change your mind, I'm usually here most nights unless I have something better to do."

"I don't think I'll be back."

Nicholas threw a couple of hundreds down and, before he left, motioned to the bartender to come closer. "Give the lady whatever she wants. Happy Thanksgiving, and have a splendid Christmas. Buy your kids a special gift."

He knew it was time to stop believing his own lies. While watching Eloise make a fool of herself, he had an epiphany. It was time to come clean. He had always told everyone that his parents were never there for him during the holidays, especially Christmas, which was why he didn't care about holidays or any kind of celebration.

He never told the truth because it was painful, and the last thing he ever wanted was people's pity. Nicholas was about four years old when his father left and his mother became very ill. He didn't have any aunts or uncles, or anyone close enough to give him a home after his mother died. With no other options, he was sent to an orphanage until he was eighteen years old.

A group of wonderful nuns raised him and tried to teach him right from wrong. After he left, though, their hard work was all but forgotten. His one takeaway was that hard work paid off, and he worked two jobs to put himself through college. That was when everything turned around.

He won numerous awards and excelled at learning skills that others couldn't. Given his talents and natural ability, he became a sought-after employee. He could run a company with his eyes closed, and did just that, especially when Samuel needed him most. They had always worked well together, and he made a lot of money working with Samuel.

With a past like his, Nicholas never put down roots with anyone. He roamed from woman to woman, never letting his guard down. He was now at a point in his life when he owed Samuel an explanation. He'd lied to Samuel when they last spoke, and said he'd never cheated on Julianna. He knew Samuel was disappointed in him, and he decided it was time to tell the truth—even if he lost his job.

Chapter Five

Leo was on his way to Lake Geneva. He wasn't sure about going, but didn't want to let his grandmother down. She was the one constant in his life; if she was happy, that was all that mattered. And, even if he pretended he didn't want to spend the holiday with Gracie, he would be lying to himself. He wanted to be there with her; in fact, he wanted to share every day with her, but that didn't seem possible.

He couldn't get over the insane vibe he'd gotten when he was at the cemetery. If he had tried writing a scene like what happened when he went to visit Ellie, he might have changed it, because it wouldn't feel real to anyone but him.

But Ellie was always with him, as she said she would be. He might be letting her down. After all, she wanted to rest in peace. If he wasn't so superstitious, he would have walked away from the cemetery and not given it another thought.

Maybe Gracie really felt the same way about him that he felt about her, but he wouldn't know if he kept his distance. He didn't want to push her, but every time they kissed, it felt real, not like something that was just a passing phase. He did more than just care for her; he loved her.

Word around the office was that Samuel's Thanksgiving dinner was going to be a big bash, so Leo was surprised that there weren't more guests when he walked into the dining room. One thing about Samuel—

he could change course in the middle of a sentence. Gracie seemed to be the same way.

Leo waved to some of the others and then took a seat beside Gracie. He couldn't help but feel happy to see her. She seemed happy as well. He wasn't sure if Jack would show up later, but Leo was glad he wasn't there.

"So, where's your date?" he asked.

Gracie gave him a look. "What date? It's pre-Thanksgiving. This is about family."

"I thought you said you and Jack had a heart-to-heart talk. I assumed he would be here."

"You assumed wrong. We did have a conversation. We said our goodbyes, and that was that. He's going back to Paris."

"Without you?"

"Of course."

"Really? I didn't see that coming."

"If he came to Chicago to try to mend our broken relationship, that was never going to happen. I've caught him in so many lies, and the worst part was I tried to ignore it. What does that say about me?"

"It's not about you. You trusted him."

"Why does everyone think you need a partner to have a good life? Maybe I was meant to be alone."

"And maybe you weren't."

"Right, says the romance writer. Does everyone have to have a happy ending?"

"In my world, they do. Love matters. You know how I feel about love."

"We can agree to disagree."

"How about letting me try to change your mind? One bad apple doesn't mean they're all bad."

"Kind of like your characters. I don't think I'm ready. Let's just have a good weekend, and maybe you'll understand a few things about me. How's that for a deal?"

"What kind of a deal is that?"

"The best I can do for now. Let's not put any pressure on either of us to begin something that might not be in the cards. You might think you're ready, but is there a possibility you're not?"

"You might be right. Friends it is." And then he mumbled, "For now."

They shook hands on the deal, but both of them knew they had just lied to each other. Friendship would never be enough.

Chapter Six

Nicholas sat in the driveway for a few minutes before going inside. He had decided that he would join everyone for the pre-Thanksgiving dinner, and then he would stay for Thanksgiving. He probably shouldn't have left but, after many years of isolation during the holidays, he never knew quite how to act when it was all about family.

He never realized what he had been missing. Over the years, he had been invited to holiday parties, but he always said no. It wasn't until he met Eloise at the bar that he even acknowledged that he might be lonely. He kept himself so busy that there wasn't time to think about it.

Sitting at that bar alone made him think of the many things he had refused to do to make himself happy. He had plenty of money, but no one to share it with. Though he didn't love Julianna, he did like inching his way toward becoming part of the Warrington legacy.

He realized he was someone who isolated himself. He never wanted to show any sign of weakness. That was why he was so cautious in all of his relationships. Being on the outside seemed easier. His decision to go back to the dinner was unusual for him, but he still ended up back there.

The moment Samuel noticed his arrival, he motioned for him to walk over. Nicholas wasn't sure exactly how this whole evening was going to go, but their conversation needed to happen. He knew that what was about to take place could go either way, but, in his state of mind, he was pretty sure he wouldn't be working at Warrington after this weekend.

"What made you come back?" Samuel asked as they shook hands.

"You."

"Me? Why would that be?"

"Because it was rude of me. At this point in our lives, I didn't think whatever relationship we have had over the years should end like this."

"Are you quitting?"

"Not if you don't want me to. But there are a few things that I think you should know about me. If we don't talk about them, nothing can ever be right."

"Okay, I'm listening."

"I know we haven't had a heart-to-heart talk for a long time, or maybe forever. I think we're overdue."

Samuel smiled. "Okay. I get it."

"First off, I want to say thank you for all the chances you've given me to make a lot of money, and tell you how much I appreciate everything you have done for me over the years. You've been so inspirational to me. I've learned things from you that I probably never would have anywhere else."

"You're a smart guy. You would have figured out a lot of what I taught you."

"My past isn't exactly what you think it was. I never told you much about it—"

Samuel had to interrupt him because he knew what came next. "Before you go any further, let me tell you what I know."

Nicholas felt as if trouble was coming his way. "Fair enough."

"Your parents weren't rich, and you didn't have any help to get where you are. You were raised by nuns in an orphanage, and you put yourself through school. You have no debt, and you're extremely smart and a fast learner."

"Thank you. I am happy I got to learn from the best."

"I also know you have donated quite a bit of money to the orphanage you grew up in, along with many other charities. That's quite honorable."

Nicholas didn't know what to say. He felt foolish that he had pretended for years to come from a very different background.

"You have a sweet tooth for women and, at this point in your life, I don't think that will change. You and my daughter have come to an agreement, so that's good. She broke it off, and now you're able to have as many women as you want."

"I really am sorry about that. I'm hoping someday I'll find the right one."

"I'm sure you will. Hopefully, you and my daughter have learned just how important that is. However, both my daughters should be off your radar." Samuel raised a brow at him.

"That's a promise. I really am sorry."

"Okay. I'm taking you at your word."

"Are you firing me?"

"Nope." Samuel grinned playfully. "Not this time."

"How long have you known all of this?"

"Since you started working here. Do you think I got where I am without knowing everything about anyone who works for me?"

"But you never said a word."

"That's true."

"If you knew everything, why didn't you ever say anything? That seems strange to me."

"Didn't have to. I have always been a firm believer that everything happens for a reason." Samuel laughed. "You know, there's one thing people may not realize. Any person in my life or my family's life is someone I need to know about. There are no exceptions. It's not only my daughters I have watched. I watch people I care about, and, believe it or not, I care about you."

"I should have told you some of this," Nicholas muttered.

"I understand why you didn't. No need to talk about this again. I would hope we can develop a different kind of trust."

"We can," Nicholas added, feeling a lot better. "So, are we good?"

"We are, but there is one last thing. I believe you are a good person, even though you don't like to show that side of yourself. You need to. If you have anything to say, let's talk about it. Oh, and don't think for a minute I don't know my daughter had a part in this. She can be quite persuasive. But, as they say, no one is perfect. I have plenty of flaws, but I'm working on them. It's never too late to make some changes."

Nicholas sat back and smiled. "Samuel, you're quite a guy."

"After tonight, we'll see. I really hope my vision for the future will work."

"Am I in it?" Nicholas was hesitant to ask.

Samuel smiled. "I certainly hope so."

"You've always had the foresight to make things work. You are Samuel Warrington."

"Sometimes I wish I wasn't. Everyone expects me to know it all, but no one knows everything. My life has had a lot of ups and downs, but I never show my cards."

"Sure as hell seems like you do."

Samuel grinned. "That's the trick of it all. I think we should wrap this up and join the others for dinner. By now, everyone is probably starved. Just so you know, I've invited Eloise Endicott. She's been doing some of my Lake Geneva real-estate transactions, and she was going to be alone. So now she'll be here."

"There's that soft side sneaking out every now and then."

"Let's keep that between us. She's single, and I thought you might want to have someone to talk to after everything that's happened."

Nicholas laughed as he shook Samuel's hand. "You're a good guy. A matchmaker? I'm not sure about that."

"Just being a friend."

"That sounds good to me. I don't have many of those."

"Oh, one more thing. I know you know who Leo really is, but it won't matter after tonight. So, no grandstanding announcement from you about it. Have you got that? Nicole Forrester will be open for discussion later."

Nicholas grinned. "Got it, Chief."

Samuel hoped that everything was going to go as planned. His well-meaning dinners usually had their share of problems, but he was hoping he could avoid those this time.

Chapter Seven

Samuel stood beside Lilly and held up his wine glass.

"Before we begin the holiday celebration, I would like everyone to pick up their glass to start the evening. I imagine my family is wondering why I cut down the guest list. Well, as you all know, I had a heart attack. Even though it wasn't exactly life or death for me, it was life changing. I felt this time with my family was necessary. And when you live as long as I have, you realize family doesn't need to be blood, but it has to be special. Tonight, everyone is here because we have shared memories of life's best moments."

He couldn't help but feel thrilled he had so much happiness ahead of him. A second chance to live and to love the woman he had dreamed about for years. Yet, with all the plans of a healthy man, he was scared. At times, he still felt alone, even in a room filled with people he loved and cared about.

"I almost didn't make it for another Thanksgiving, but here I am. I'm alive. Someone up there likes me." Samuel looked up and smiled. He was good at pretending everything was fine, but he knew he still had a few wrinkles to smooth out. "Of course, I had to make a few promises to the man or woman upstairs, but that's water under the bridge."

There were quite a few laughs and some loud claps.

"Thank you all. Every one of you sitting here made a difference in my life and, if you'll bear with me, there's more to come. I want to thank every one of you who helped in my life and recovery. First off, my doctor, Josh Leavitt. What a prince of a guy. Please lift your glasses, and let's toast to life. As precious as it is."

Gracie watched her sister as she took a sip. She smiled, acknowledging she was happy to see her adapting so well. Things could have been very different if she hadn't broken off her engagement. Marrying Nicholas would have been a serious mistake. For that, Gracie lifted her glass, thankful that if Nicholas wasn't out of her life, at least he wouldn't be her brother-in-law.

Samuel wasn't done. "Okay, time for another toast. Lift your glasses as we toast to the woman who makes me shine—and, also, I might add, makes me feel young. To my sweet Lilly. I just want everyone to know that I'm grateful that she said yes."

Lilly and Samuel clicked their glasses and looked at each other, a fine-looking couple on their way to a beautiful life together.

Then the elephant entered the room; Francine and Wyatt arrived.

Everyone was shocked, except Samuel. His plan was working, and he was pleased with himself. So far, everything was going the way he hoped it would. And to think it wasn't even Thanksgiving yet.

"Francine, welcome. I wasn't sure you were coming, but I'm happy you're here."

"I was intrigued, and I understood the premise."

Both Gracie and Julianna looked at their father, shocked to see their mother enter with no warning. So much for just another dinner.

Samuel put down his glass and took a cleansing breath, the kind his therapist had introduced him to in the hope that he would learn to manage his stress level.

"So much for no stress," Samuel mumbled to himself.

He wasn't exactly the type to listen to advice, which was why he hadn't asked anyone if this would be a good idea. He made the crazy decision himself. Now that he was faced with Francine standing there, he knew there was no turning back.

Samuel loved Lilly and wanted as many good years together as possible, and welcomed the chance to give her everything he possibly could. Before that could happen, he would need to put his cards on the table and see where they fell.

Francine looked beautiful as always. She was dressed in a black Chanel suit, along with her expensive gray pearls—the ones Samuel gave her for an anniversary present years before. They were worth more than some people earned in a year. Her hair was picture perfect, and her makeup was flawless. She looked stunning.

Samuel looked around the room and realized how shocked everyone was to see her. Georgia, his loving dog, ran under the table because she knew something was coming. He called to her. "Sweet Georgia, you can come out. All is well. We won't be having a shouting match."

"That's right, Georgia," Francine added, not feeling quite so confident. "Everything is going to be alright."

Georgia slowly peeked out from under the tablecloth and inched her way toward the doorway. Her reluctance was no surprise. She didn't like when voices got loud and, while everything seemed calm at the moment, she had firsthand knowledge of how storms brewed in the Warrington household, with or without guests.

Francine was eyeing everyone, trying to read the room. She could feel the animosity, and knew she deserved it. "Hello to all. I must say this is a beautiful retreat. Samuel, good job."

Samuel hated when she talked to him like a dog who obeyed her.

"You're looking so well," she continued. "After your heart attack, one might have expected you to look a bit frail, but you look healthy and very happy. I guess Samuel Warrington is still a legend in his own time."

Samuel grinned, trying his best not to say anything that might come back to haunt him. Their divorce was almost final, but that could change in a heartbeat. He was looking forward to the signed papers Francine was delivering.

"Please, excuse us for a moment," he said, then motioned for Julianna and Gracie to follow him.

Wyatt shook Samuel's hand. "Haven't seen you in years. Was this your idea?"

"Yes. I had some unfinished business that needed to take place."

"I imagined it was something like that."

"Why don't you have a seat at the table? We won't be long."

"Are you sure about this?"

"Of course. I've known you longer than Francine has."

"I know, but this is awkward."

"Not as awkward as you think. Just sit, have a glass of wine. In a few minutes, you're going to be a happy man."

"I'm happy enough for now. I just wish this hadn't happened."

"You mean this or the affair you've been having with Francine all these years? I always knew. I'm glad you made her happy, because I never could."

As Samuel walked away, he was grateful he wasn't going to have to deal with his ex-wife much longer. It was finally going to be over, and Wyatt would be the lucky son of a gun who won the prize.

Gracie and Julianna pretended they understood what was about to happen, but they'd had no idea their mother was coming. It wasn't Thanksgiving yet, but they were celebrating something. Their father was acting so strange that evening, trying to act as if things were normal—whatever that might mean for a Warrington dinner.

Despite everything that happened, they loved their mother and wondered why she needed to make such a grand entrance. And why now?

Francine opened her arms to them and hugged them tightly. "I'm so sorry that I haven't been there for you girls. I'd like to make it up to you."

Julianna decided she would speak up or she might never get a chance. "Mom, I love you, but I doubt you could make it up to us at this time. We're still trying to figure out why you left without even a goodbye."

"I had my reasons."

"One thing's for sure. You didn't think of us, like most mothers would. You didn't have the courage to try to explain anything. What kind of a mother does that?"

"Mom, Julianna is absolutely right," Gracie interjected. "Why? Didn't you realize how awful we felt?"

"Of course I did."

"Then tell us why," Julianna said as she wiped away her tears.

"Girls, it wasn't like that," Francine said without shedding a tear.

Samuel interrupted. "Listen, right now, we have a room filled with hungry people who came here to have a good time. Why don't you and Wyatt stay for dinner, and we can talk later?"

Francine was surprised by the invitation. She assumed they were there just to sign the papers and leave. The preliminary work had been completed, but they had a few other things to talk about.

"Francine, I can see your hesitancy, but I think you owe it to your daughters to stay."

"So, what you're telling me is this is another Samuel Warrington agenda dinner."

"I wouldn't call it that, but it will be very enlightening."

Gracie was confused by the whole situation, especially when her mother and father didn't scream at each other. They seemed to be calm and collected, satisfied that their life together was over.

"Dad, why didn't you tell us?" Gracie asked, trying to figure out what was coming next.

"Because she's your mother, like it or not, and she needs to know about my plans for you girls."

Julianna wasn't sure what that meant. She had already explained that she was going back to Ohio right after the holiday.

"Girls," Francine said, "it's my fault. I should have signed the divorce papers days ago, but I didn't. Not that I wasn't sure, but it was purely selfish on my part. We're both ready to move on. It's been a long time since we've been anything close to a family. This is no surprise, and your father and I have found happiness with other people."

Francine handed Samuel the envelope. "Okay, we'll stay for dinner. The documents are signed. We can both move on."

Gracie had no idea why, but her father was acting as if he had something very complicated up his sleeve. She followed Francine into the dining room and sat back down next to Leo. She had very little to say to her mother, but was secretly happy she was there.

"Are you okay?" Leo couldn't help but ask Gracie, though he could tell by the look on her face that she wasn't.

One thing about Gracie was she didn't like surprises. Neither did Leo, and he had a sneaking suspicion that there were a lot of changes in the works. He knew Samuel well enough to know he had an agenda. They had even talked the other day about opening Pandora's box and discussing Nicole Forrester and Leo Tucker. Samuel hadn't objected the way he had in the past.

Gracie took his hand and squeezed tightly.

"I have to admit, whenever I have a problem, you seem to be the one I want to go to. I wish I had your confidence and drive. You always know where you're going."

"Maybe it looks like that, but, trust me, quite a bit of uncertainty shadows me on a daily basis."

"Well, it certainly looks like you've got it together."

"Somewhere between coming back from Paris and now, you stopped fighting. You are a force to reckon with. Where is the Gracie who had it all? I know you can do it."

"It's so funny. I haven't known you for as long as most of the people here, but you know me better than anyone else."

"That's what happens when you love someone." There it was, out of the box.

Gracie turned to him, ready to confess her love in turn, but they were interrupted by her father's return.

Ava motioned for Samuel to come to the kitchen. "You hired all these lovely people, and they've worked so hard—but if we keep rewarming everything, no guarantees."

"So sorry," he said. "Just a lot going on."

"Samuel, you've had a lot going on since the day we met. Believe it or not, I was young then."

He laughed. "Me too. The years have crept up on us, but there will be plenty of changes after tonight. I'm about to make everything right."

"Okay, so we'll start serving, and then you can get on with whatever you've got going. Deal?"

"Fair enough. Deal."

Samuel returned to the dining room, looking around at everyone he loved. "The boss just told me I need to wait a bit before I give one of my big speeches," he began. "So, enjoy the dinner, and please don't leave. This evening is going to be fabulous, and then tomorrow we will celebrate Thanksgiving without me blabbing."

Everyone laughed as Georgia came back into the dining room and sat by the doorway. Even she was waiting for the next shoe to drop. A Warrington dinner was never short of surprises.

Chapter Eight

Dinner went well, and the new staff was impressive. All the food came out perfectly. The hot foods were warm, and the cold foods were just the right temperature. Samuel was pleased. Smiling faces were always welcome, and everything was picture perfect so far.

Francine, on the other hand, had one foot out the door. She was ready to skip out at any time, but Samuel had asked her and Wyatt to stay, so she did. She owed him one last favor.

In the past, she was in charge of all the dinners and the menu. Ava was always a lifesaver for her, and no one ever knew Francine wasn't exactly the greatest hostess. For all the years that Samuel and Francine were married, no one knew Francine couldn't cook more than just an egg, and she didn't even do that well. Ava was a great cook and event planner—everything Francine was not.

Sitting there, Francine felt slightly jealous that she had been removed so easily. She really didn't understand those feelings because she had been the one who decided to move on.

It appeared that everyone, including her daughters, had learned how to live without her. Francine was very good at pretending to be happy, even when she wasn't. She had done it for thirty years, so she had plenty of practice. She decided she would sit there and look beautiful because, at that moment, that was the only thing she was sure about.

Samuel had been doing so much thinking that his brain was tired. There he was in a beautiful new estate with his daughters, his ex-wife, and his beautiful bride to be, along with all the guests who would make this Thanksgiving seem just right. He had always wanted a home away from home with a reasonable drive time so he didn't have to wait for a plane if he was needed back in Chicago.

Things had worked out for the best. However, he knew one thing: he couldn't live in Lake Geneva on a permanent basis. Chicago would always be his home.

* * *

It was time to get the ball rolling. Samuel was quite happy with the way the evening was going so far, and he thought the timing was perfect for his speech. Everyone seemed to be getting along as well as he could have expected, and there wasn't an outburst or trauma that needed his attention. All was quiet on the Warrington front.

"Hello again to everyone," he began. "As I look out at all of you, I see my life flashing before me—and let me tell you, it's quite emotional, but you won't be seeing me crying because I know one thing. I have had a wonderful life and will be embarking on a new one, which I am looking forward to more than anything else. So, no complaints from me."

He smiled as he looked around at all the smiling faces. Alex was there, and he couldn't have been happier. A man needs one friend who he can count on for anything and everything, and that was Alex. He might have been Samuel's driver, but he was as close to a brother as anyone could get.

"My journey is my legacy, and I won't bore you with my past because most of you know it."

Gracie took a deep, silent breath, realizing her father had made some decisions. She was still in the dark as to what they were—not where she liked to be.

"Ava, as you all know, has been the rock who kept my home the perfect place for my girls to thrive," Samuel continued. "She was there when

Francine and I couldn't be. She has helped me raise my daughters, as well as serving the best food ever." He patted his stomach. "I'm looking better these days thanks to some dietary rules that Lilly and Ava have maintained. I know they know I've cheated, but, for the most part, I've been diligent. Another deal I made with God."

He waved to Ava and blew a kiss to Lilly. "Let's hear it for the staff for doing the cooking and preparing everything for tonight. First class all the way. Ava, you run a tight ship. Thank you."

A loud clapping session followed.

"Now that dinner is over, it's time for me to discuss the future. I realize everyone has their own journey, and I have taken that into consideration. I know you all think it was strange for me to have a pre-Thanksgiving dinner, but what would life be like if I was predictable? There's no fun in that."

Gracie wasn't usually uptight when her father talked because she knew what to expect. Since his wedding announcement and her parents' breakup, however, it seemed like nothing was off limits. With the way the night was headed, there were a lot of things that could go wrong, but maybe her father was going to smooth everything over.

She whispered to Leo. "Do you think he's sick or something like that?"

Leo shook his head. "Look at him; he's never looked better."

Samuel laughed, realizing everyone was on edge waiting for his announcements. "Hey, one thing before I continue. Nothing bad is about to happen. This is something that needs to be done. If I could see a few smiles, it would be easier."

All eyes were on him, and he wasn't a bit nervous about his choices.

"I want to say thank you to everyone for all the years of joy and happiness you have given me. Yes, you, too, Francine. You gave me two beautiful daughters I love more than life itself. I know I've been a bit too overbearing, but I promise I'm going to try to give them breathing room."

There were quite a few laughs when he said that. "I mean it. I really do."

Francine gave him a look, thinking maybe she shouldn't have stayed. Everything had always been a production with Samuel, and she'd always disliked that. She was leaving Wisconsin soon enough, and was very glad to be out of his life. She hoped Lilly would be happier than she had been.

"Okay, maybe you were right," Wyatt whispered to her. "We should leave."

Samuel overheard what was going on. "Trust me, Wyatt. Nothing outlandish is going to happen."

Wyatt sat back, ready to see what came next. He was glad he had no stakes in this game—or at least he hoped he didn't.

Julianna caught her sister's eye. "What's going on?" she mouthed.

Ava wished she could have stayed in the kitchen, but she had faith that Samuel would never do anything to embarrass her. He had been the greatest employer anyone could ever ask for.

"Now back to the lady of the hour," Samuel continued. "Ava, I appreciate everything you always did for us, and I want to repay you. You have been part of this family for so many years, but it's time for you to have a life."

Ava, who was slowly sipping a glass of water, gulped it down, realizing she might be out of a job. How could that be good?

"Come up here. I have something for you."

"Me? Samuel? What could I possibly want? I've loved every minute of my time with your family."

He handed her a key ring. "This is for something I know you always wanted."

Ava opened her hand and took the keys. "What is this for?"

"My daughters are all grown, and I will be traveling with Lilly, making up for lost time. You are always so full of life and, as the years have gone by, you have stayed the same positive role model for my girls."

Samuel was as long winded as usual.

"So, to go on with this celebration, Ava, I have purchased a small café in town and you, my friend, will be the new proprietor. This is for all the years that you made us your priority. It's right smack in the middle of town."

"Samuel, I don't know what to say."

"Say you'll promise to keep a fresh chocolate cake ready for all our trips here."

"My deepest appreciation." She hugged Samuel. "How did you know my secret desire?"

"I have my ways."

"I know I'm going to love it. I'm thrilled. What about your home? Who's going to take care of things?"

"Believe it or not, my daughters are grown. It's time."

"Yes, they are great. And they've grown up to be wonderful women."

"You can visit us any time you want, and I promise everything will work out just the way it is supposed to; there's a lot more I have to say tonight."

"I'm so grateful. All the years with your family have been the best years of my life." Ava smiled brightly.

"We're not done. You've yet to take a vacation, so here's your ticket to anywhere you want before you begin renovations to your cafe."

"Where will I go? I would have to go alone." Tears welled up in Ava's eyes as Julianna and Gracie ran up and hugged her.

"No, you won't. We're going with," Gracie said. "I'm sure my father will give me time off."

"Absolutely," Samuel said. "This brings me to the next step of my plan. Leo, can you join me over here?"

Lilly smiled at her grandson, indicating she knew what was coming next.

"You have been like a son to me since we met at Manny's Deli years ago. I'm so proud of your success. It's time the world knew who you really are. I won't put you on the spot to talk right now—unless you want to. Everyone, meet the very successful Nicole Forrester. My favorite author."

There were quite a few gasps, and more applause. Gracie stood up and whistled. "Go, Leo!"

The cat was out of the bag, and Leo was now free. That was exactly how he felt when he gave Samuel a big hug and a few tears of appreciation.

"Leo will be leaving for a while," Samuel continued. "He's going to Paris to accept an award for his new book, *Goodbye Ellie*, which will be published under his own name. It's not the first time he's won a book award, but it will be the first time he will be present to accept one as himself."

Leo gave Samuel a big hug. "You're the best. My grandmother is going to have a great life with you."

"We're going to have the time of our lives. Right now, let's have some dessert and coffee, and then we will finish up with a couple more announcements. All good ones, I promise. Please stay; I would like everyone to hear the rest of the news. A lot of happiness is yet to come."

Chapter Nine

When Samuel had a party, he definitely knew how to do it. That included an array of all the most beautiful desserts that Ava and Lilly knew how to make. They'd spent the previous day in the kitchen, laughing and enjoying each other's company. It was as if they had been friends for years.

One thing about a Warrington dinner was the desserts were always the main attraction. Samuel loved sweets, so there was always a lot of chocolate in the mix. While he cut out most of the foods he loved after his heart attack, he still always had room for dessert, and Ava had learned how to make his favorites in ways that wouldn't interfere with his recovery.

Lilly motioned for Samuel to meet her in the library. Both of them went unnoticed. Together, they had already made some big decisions about their future and what was best for everyone, but Lilly thought about the biggest plan for Thanksgiving Day.

"When are we going to tell the kids about the wedding?"

"Soon, I promise." Samuel was trying to find the right words. He had disappointed Lilly years ago, and tomorrow was supposed to be special. He let her down once, and he certainly wasn't going to do it again.

"What about when the rabbi shows up? A rabbi doesn't just appear at the door."

Samuel was afraid Lilly was getting cold feet. In his mind, he had gone over all the steps he needed to secure their future, but he hadn't thought that Lilly would possibly decide not to marry him. That wasn't even something he'd considered but, looking at her face, something was wrong. Had he rushed things too much?

"Lilly, do you still want to marry me?"

"Of course. I just thought it might be better to surprise the kids in a few months. We could get married on one of our vacations. I'm sure they would be fine with that."

"It seems like Leo is okay with us getting married."

"It isn't Leo I'm worried about."

"Then who?"

"Do you think Gracie likes me?" Lilly asked.

"Of course she likes you."

Just then Gracie walked in. "Sorry to interrupt you, but I think I came in at a great time. Lilly, you're wonderful. Of course I like you. I have liked you since the day we met, when Leo brought me to your home for lunch. You're a wonderful woman, and Leo's a terrific guy."

Lilly sighed with relief. "That's good to hear. I can't help but worry."

"I think I was just disappointed about my parents' life. It's not your fault. I can tell my father's very happy with you, and that makes me happy, too." Gracie gave Lilly a hug. "Whatever you were thinking, there's no problem on my end or Julianna's. We're very happy to have you in this family. You're a wonderful addition."

Samuel smiled, feeling reassured that his daughters were okay with all of this excitement. "I've always believed things work out for the best. After tonight, I'm hoping some of my new plans will make things right."

Lilly smiled. "I have a feeling everyone will be satisfied. Let's go back in. The clock is ticking."

Gracie looked at her father, wondering what that meant. She knew he'd said all the news was good, but she couldn't help wondering if he was trying to hide something. "Dad, please, you can tell me. I know there's more to this story."

"There's much more to come."

"Looks like it's working overtime," Gracie said, wondering if her father might really be sick and trying not to alarm everyone. "I need an honest answer. Are you sick? Is this whole party a smokescreen?"

"No, I'm not." He laughed. "I'm as healthy as I can be. I know you hate secrets. You always liked to know everything before anyone else. Just like when you were a kid, you tried everything to figure out where we hid your birthday gifts, and you searched the entire house before Hannukah until you finally realized your mother and I never brought the gifts into the house. They were always in the car. You never checked the car."

Gracie smiled, remembering those happy times when she had no problems. That was a great feeling. "Okay, I get it, but…"

"No buts. You'll know soon enough."

"Just a heads up, please."

"Not this time. Don't worry, I think you'll be happy. At least I hope you will."

"That's not very comforting." She raised a brow at him.

"Well, kiddo, sorry. For now, it has to be enough."

Lilly reached for Gracie's hand. "Here, come with me. We'll sit and wait together."

Chapter Ten

Oliver and Julianna were holding hands under the table, only to be interrupted by Samuel. "Can you both give me a minute?"

"Dad, can this wait? I think your guests are getting a bit on edge. You know how you spring things on people when they least expect it."

"How can you tell they're on edge?"

"Well, first, Mom is ready to jump out of her skin. Look at her. She's fidgeting with her hair. She always does that when she's uncomfortable."

"I never noticed that before."

Julianna laughed. "Well, that's one reason the two of you have split up. You never pay attention to the little things that people do. Truth be told, you don't always see what's right in front of you."

"That's not true."

"Okay, look at Gracie. She's taking small sips of wine and then blotting her lips so she doesn't ruin her lipstick."

Samuel looked at his daughter and laughed. "What are you talking about? That means she's not a happy camper? Come on, really?"

"She's also not smiling, which in itself doesn't mean anything." Julianna laughed. "But I can just tell. I know she hates when things get confusing."

"Maybe that's true, but she doesn't know what my next move is."

"Bingo. She hates that. You know she likes to be one step ahead."

"I get it."

"That's not the only thing. She's playing with her bracelet. When we were little, she always did that."

"I remember that, but she's not little anymore."

Julianna shook her head and grinned. "Dad, just because we're all grown up doesn't mean we don't feel like children sometimes. You have a knack for taking us back in time. Age has nothing to do with that."

"Point taken."

"Wait. I'm not finished. Then there's Alex, who doesn't want to be here. He's drinking tea. He never drinks tea."

"Maybe he just feels like it."

Oliver sat back in his seat, smiling at how intuitive Julianna was. He'd always thought she was so cute when she did that. He still thought so.

"Okay, I'm not finished. Look at Nicholas. He's pretending to be interested in the woman you set him up with."

"He doesn't need to pretend."

"Yes, he does. He wants you to think of him as perfect. Respectful and tolerant."

"He knows I know all about the things he did and all the things he continues to do. Tolerant isn't how I'd describe him, but I hope he learns to be that way."

Julianna crinkled her nose, the same way she did when she was a kid and didn't like what was being said. "Now you're confusing me. You know all the things he's done, and you haven't fired him?"

"I'm not going to fire him. He's an asset to us, not a liability. I need him at Warrington. He knows how to handle some of our tough venders. He's good at fixing problems, and he's strong when he needs to be. I know he's not soft and cuddly, but neither am I."

"Maybe you need to change a little."

"Maybe I do, but publishing was quite different when I started, and Nicholas is very inventive. He's not like everyone else."

"That's for sure," Julianna replied, happy she didn't continue her relationship with Nicholas. That would have been a divorce in the making. Now she cringed every time she thought of herself as his wife.

"Well, how about this? He's not really interested in his date, but he's still waiting for this dinner to end so he can take her back to his room. She's quite pretty, you know."

Samuel sat down in the empty seat next to his daughter. "This is so insane. How do you know all these things?"

"How do you not?"

"You're beginning to sound just like your sister."

"Speaking of Gracie, look at Leo. He's not talking. Not a word. Nothing. Nada. You know Leo. He talks constantly, but not tonight. He's wondering what you have up your sleeve."

"I can't believe I never noticed any of this."

"That's because you know what you have in mind, and they don't. Having been in your crosshairs several times, I know exactly how they feel."

Samuel got up and started to walk away, but stopped and looked around. He realized what Julianna had said was right. He missed it all. He turned back to his daughter. "Are you sure you're going back to Ohio? Can I change your mind? I had no idea you were so perceptive."

"There you go. You should have known that about me. But I still love you, always will." She kissed his cheek, then grabbed Oliver's hand and squeezed it tightly. "I'm ready to go home. I miss Ohio. My daughter and husband live there." She smiled and kissed Oliver's cheek.

Samuel went back to the front of the room, picked up his microphone, and got everyone's attention once again.

"Okay, everyone. Let's finish this up so we can have a great weekend. I have a lot of plans, but, most of all, I want everyone to have a good time. Someone I love very much pointed out some things I should have seen. Before I go on, let me say my health is fine. Knock on wood. So for those of you who think I'm doing this whole Thanksgiving weekend marathon because I'm checking out, I'm not. Or so my doctors tell me." He pointed to Josh Leavitt, who waved in acknowledgment.

Samuel was excited about his wedding. He felt like a schoolboy. He had thought about Lilly every day for the past thirty years, always hoping they would ride off into the sunset and be able to share their love. Now that reality was only a day away.

"This a short announcement about a huge decision that I hope will be a very welcome one. Tomorrow is Thanksgiving, and Lilly and I will be sharing our vows in front of all of you. The rabbi will officiate a short marriage service and then join us for a wonderful Thanksgiving dinner."

Everyone clapped, and there were a few whistles.

"Lilly, please join me."

Lilly took the microphone and smiled. "I'm kind of a behind-the-scenes person, but I do have a few words to add."

Before she continued, she gave Samuel a loving kiss and took a deep breath. "Tomorrow's our day. Thank you, Samuel, for making my dreams come true. A lot of time has passed, but now, in our prime, we're going to do what we should have done a long time ago. Our life together is about to begin—and I'm as excited as a young schoolgirl. It's time to put this whole puzzle together."

Francine and Wyatt were trying to leave the party without anyone noticing, but Samuel did.

"Francine, please stay. There are a few things I wanted to add."

Francine gave him a slight goodbye wave and left, blowing a few kisses to her daughters, who, as always, were disappointed in their mother's behavior. She didn't know what was next, but she would hear about it another time.

Lilly, who had hoped the evening could have made a difference in how Francine's daughters viewed their mother, saw that hope was gone. However, nothing surprised Samuel as, once again, he watched Francine do the wrong thing.

Samuel went on, trying to make light of the situation, the same way he had for years. "As I said before, it's time to lay out my plan. As you all know, we don't live forever, even though we try to stay in the race for as long as we can—"

He was interrupted by loud clapping. This was a loud bunch, and he loved a good audience. To make it a home run, Gracie put her fingers inside her mouth and gave a few loud whistles.

"I lucked out at a time in my life when I thought a new chapter was impossible for me. I had a life, but now I'm going to have a better one with my new wife. I love you, Lilly."

He was a satisfied man. The world had been his playground. He always wanted happiness for all the people in his life, especially his girls.

"Marriage a second time around is one of the most exciting things that has happened to me in years. We're finally going to get the chance to be together. Lilly and I can travel and enjoy our life without worry. It's our time.

"I was also hoping Francine would have stayed so I could congratulate her on her new life, but she left. I'm going to say nothing more about Francine. The past is the past."

Julianna and Gracie were on edge. Even though their father said everything would be fine, they weren't sure. They knew anything could happen at a Warrington dinner. They held their breath while Samuel continued.

"As you all know, I have never known exactly who would take over after me, but I have two intelligent, hard-working daughters who have been my source of light over the years—"

Gracie whispered to Leo. "Do you know what's going on?"

Leo shook his head. He was also interested to hear the news. While Samuel had confided in him many times in the past, he hadn't mentioned anything about the plans for this pre-Thanksgiving dinner or what announcements would come out of it. Whatever it was, he assumed

Samuel had thought it out. Samuel never did anything just like that; if anything, he was an overthinker.

"I have put Gracie through one test after another, and she handled everything I threw at her," Samuel continued. "I knew she didn't like most of the things I challenged her with, but she did them with a style all her own. She might think I haven't noticed the changes in her and the skills she has obtained. But I have. Everyone around her has seen the transition. And, boy, was I watching, much to her dismay."

As Gracie listened, she thought she was dreaming. She had no idea what her father thought about her choices, but she was glad he noticed.

"Then there's Julianna. How lucky a man am I that I have two daughters capable of becoming part of my legacy? I had planned that both of my daughters would take over the business after my departure, but Julianna is going back to Ohio with her husband and daughter. I'm very happy she has figured out what she wanted her life to be like. And I want to apologize to her and Oliver for nearly ruining a good thing. I have been known to be overbearing—and, for that, I'm sorry."

There was a stillness in the air, but Samuel was determined to get his thoughts out no matter how hard it was for him. His heart attack had changed everything, but he had used his time convalescing at home to figure out what mattered and what didn't.

"Gracie, honey, please come up here."

She was shocked and happy at the same time. "I'm coming."

Before she got up and walked over to her father, Gracie whispered to Leo, "I love you."

Just as quickly as the words came out, she wished she hadn't said them at all. But wasn't that like everything she did? Still, Leo was one of the good guys, and she couldn't understand why she had so hastily tossed his love for her away.

It wasn't Leo's fault she had been involved with several thoughtless men; it was hers. It was time she took the blame and grew up.

Her father was giving her the keys to the castle, and she had better put on that crown and do what he expected. No more crying about what happened before; it was time to be the woman he had decided to trust.

Leo was proud of her, and it showed. He smiled, knowing she could do the job.

"Have you been listening?" he asked her.

"Who, me? Of course. I've always listened to you, even the times I didn't say anything about it. Isn't that what you taught me? It's all a game, no matter what you do. But do it for the right reasons, and don't let anyone tell you that something can't be done."

Gracie walked up and hugged her father. "I had no idea it was my time."

"Well, there's one last thing. I need you to understand the next part of my decision."

Gracie and her sister shared a look across the room. There was always one last thing.

"Even though you're perfect for the job, I'm going to be around for a while, and so is Nicholas. All three of us will run this great publishing house, and we're going to make history."

Gracie didn't know if she should laugh or cry, but she was now an executive. Executives don't cry; they just pout in private. She was excited to run the company, but a lot less excited about working with Nicholas. What was her father thinking?

Chapter Eleven

That night, Gracie found herself unable to sleep, so she cruised down to the kitchen, certain that everyone had gone to their rooms. She was standing at the sink, putting water in the coffeemaker, when Leo walked up behind her.

"Planning on staying up all night? Espresso, no less."

"Actually, I can't sleep, and I got hungry. I'm missing my Starbucks. Can't wait to get back to Chicago."

Leo smiled in his usual charming way. "I like it here. It's so peaceful."

"It's too quiet for me," Gracie said, trying not to have any intimate moments that would make Leo feel like she was ready for a relationship. She wanted to kiss him, but didn't.

Gracie was once again fighting her feelings, worried that a relationship wouldn't work and that she couldn't handle it. Before, she was feeling so open, proud, and happy, making it easy to express herself. Now, she was back to hiding her emotions.

She quickly walked to the refrigerator, peeked inside, and changed the mood. "How about some of that chocolate mousse cake?

"I don't know, sometimes too much chocolate keeps me up." Leo knew what she was up to, and that she was scared to be too close to him. He had written many a scene with characters who didn't want to be romantically involved. He had already figured out every interaction with her, and none of it was in his favor. He was used to it by now, and knew what to do. "I think I'll go back upstairs. Tomorrow will be a long day."

"You can't go. Not just yet. You need to have some cake and some espresso. Can't have dessert without coffee." Gracie smiled and hoped he'd stay. Maybe she'd figure things out if he was there to remind her of how she truly felt.

"Yes, you can. However, I'm too tired to argue with you. I know it's great; my grandmother made it. But it will keep me up for hours, and then what?"

"You can watch TV, a movie, read a book, whatever."

"Do you always have espresso before bed?"

"Sometimes, but I usually don't have chocolate mousse cake. You know this is really special."

"Don't tell my grandmother you like it, or she'll be making it for you even if you get sick of it."

"That's not good advice. I want her to like me. She's marrying my dad."

"She already likes you. She loves you."

"How do you know that?"

"I can always read my grandmother's signs. She's pretty transparent. If she doesn't like you, she never looks your way. That rarely happens, but it's never good when it does."

"That's okay, isn't it?"

"It is, but one thing still bothers me. Even though she's so happy now, I feel somehow like there's still something standing in the way of her happiness. If she hasn't told me about it, I doubt she's told anyone."

"What makes you think that?"

"Well, as a writer, I tend to look at people in a different way. Unspoken words are how we get our characters to react."

"Your grandmother isn't a character."

"Everyone is a character."

"Okay, so tell me why you think that about your grandmother. Does she seem sad or something?"

"That's just it. She is hardly ever sad. Even when my mother left after my father died, she was focused on making my life good. She never complained about anything."

Gracie felt sad as she watched Leo. She knew how upset he got when he thought about Ellie, but otherwise she never saw him upset about anything that came his way. He was the rock on the podcast, the one keeping her steady.

Gracie sipped the espresso and offered some to Leo, but he waved it off. He definitely needed sleep. She could tell he was tired, but she wanted him to stay. She enjoyed being with him, but didn't tell him that.

"I'm still trying to understand your father and my grandmother and the uncertainty of their lives before. How sad must it have been for both of them to feel alone in their marriages? I'm glad they can finally share their love."

"They are kind of cute." Gracie smiled, thinking of them. "My father didn't smile as much with my mother, and she didn't smile at all. Kind of strange how I didn't see the pain they were feeling."

Leo smiled sweetly. "I must admit, I had my reservations. After watching them interact, though, it's beautiful. I think they will both enjoy their life when they travel and have some fun."

"Me too." By this time, Gracie had chocolate all over her lips. Leo wanted to kiss her, but restrained himself and dabbed her face with a napkin.

"And wasn't that great about Ava?" Gracie changed the subject, trying to pretend she didn't enjoy his dabbing gesture or the tingle she felt. She liked being with him, but continued to talk so there was no awkward silence, fearing she'd ruined any chance of Leo kissing her again.

"You know, Ava used to tell us when we were little that she had a dream to own a small café, and now that's exactly what she will be doing. Dreams can come true. Not just in romance novels."

Even though Leo was getting more tired by the minute, he was enjoying Gracie's stories. He laughed. "And that's a good enough reason to come back here."

"I'm going to miss her so much. And my sister's going, too. I'm going to be a mess when they all leave."

"I think you're going to be pretty busy."

Then Gracie brought up the elephant in the room. "What about the podcast?"

"I think your father's got that covered. When he asked me to do it, he told me it was just for a short time. It was fun, wasn't it?"

"You asked to be off the show?"

"Well, no, but I think you're going to be a little busy being one-third of the CEO plan."

"I don't know if it will work out with my father traveling, leaving me with Nicholas. I don't think that's going to be good for either of us. Nicholas and I rarely see eye to eye."

"You can do this. It's what you always dreamed about."

"More like a nightmare. Anyway, how about a little mousse? It's great comfort food."

"Nope, time to go to bed. I'm comfortable and happy."

"Well, that's good. Please stay, because I'm not. I might never sleep again thinking about me and Nicholas having to make decisions and get along. That part wasn't in my dream."

Chapter Twelve

Lilly was up bright and early. It was her wedding day, the day she had waited for long before she had even imagined it was possible. Samuel had agreed not to see her on their special day because she believed bad luck would find her if she got even a glimpse of the groom before the ceremony. She didn't like being superstitious, but she came from a long line of believers.

However, right before she went to bed, she took out a letter that arrived three days earlier, before she left Chicago. She'd thrown it in her bag that day, and had forgotten about it.

Now she read it over and over. It wasn't a long letter, but it was one she had never expected to receive.

> *Dear Lillian,*
>
> *I debated for quite a long time before sending this letter, but I felt it was important. I've searched for you for years and, now that I have found you, I would like to meet. I know that you might have mixed emotions about reading this, and might want nothing to do with me. If that's your choice, I understand, but I had to try.*
>
> *I'm sure you were young and unable to keep me for your own personal reasons. I'm not asking for anything except a chance to meet you. I'm quite financially sound*

and have a good life. But I feel a connection to you, and that is why I am writing this rather than just showing up at your door.

I hope we can meet soon. I also live in Chicago and would be happy to meet you anywhere you want.

I will understand either way, but I hope you will give this some careful consideration. There's nothing more important to me than meeting my birth mother. I have always thought about you, but I never wanted to hurt my mom who raised me. She has passed away, and so has my father. They were wonderful people, and I'm very thankful they chose me, but I still feel the need to meet you.

Please, let me know if this would ever be possible. I won't bother you after this, but it would help me to understand myself a little better. I have enclosed my photo just in case you were wondering what I looked like.

Your daughter,
Stephanie

Lilly crunched the paper tightly, but not enough to rip it up. She held it to her chest and had herself a good cry, then went downstairs to find Samuel. She didn't see him anywhere, so she put on her coat and went outside.

Samuel was very diligent about his morning walk. He waved to Lilly when saw her from the gazebo he had built for her. He was sitting, seemingly enjoying the beauty of the estate. She loved it there, too.

She had the letter in her hand and knew she had to tell Samuel the truth. She never thought she would hear from her daughter, but she'd always hoped she would someday. She had a few tears in her eyes, but wiped them away as she approached Samuel, who took her hand and had her sit beside him.

"Didn't you say we shouldn't see each other today?"

"Yes, but I think there's something we need to talk about."

"It couldn't wait until later?"

"I'm afraid not. I'm not sure there will be a later after you hear what I have to say."

"We've waited over thirty years to get to this place in our lives. Nothing could change how I feel. So, let's have it. We're a team, aren't we?"

"I don't even know where to begin, but I suppose we have to start with the time you broke up with me to marry Francine."

Samuel was confused. "That's water under the bridge. We both lost out on that day."

"It wasn't just us who lost out. Someone else was also involved."

"Francine? That's over, especially after last night. We've finished everything so you and I can have the fresh start we've been hoping for."

Lilly began to cry. "I'm not sure that's possible anymore. I've lied to you, and now I need to tell you something that I should have told you years ago. I made a terrible decision. I've never told anyone about it. Leo has asked me so many times why I seemed sad sometimes; he seemed to sense there was always something missing in my life. But I never told him either."

Samuel had no idea what she was talking about, but knew it had to be serious. "Whatever it is, we can work it out. Are you sick? Something else? We'll get through it. Nothing else matters as long as we get to be together. Just tell me. Please."

Lilly didn't say anything for a few seconds, unsure how he would take the news. There was a chance that everything she wanted was about to go up in flames. In a minute or two, she might be sitting on that bench all alone, as alone as she had been all the years since her husband died.

"We were at the park, and you were explaining what had happened between you and Francine. I was listening, but I was in shock. There I was, a young woman in love, hearing the man I had been in love with telling me he was going to have a baby with someone else."

"I remember that day all too well."

"You were going to do the right thing. I knew you loved me, but that was your choice. Maybe it wasn't the right thing to do."

"What aren't you telling me?"

Lilly took the letter out of her coat and smoothed it out with her fingers. "Maybe this will help," she said as she looked away, not wanting to watch his reaction.

Samuel started to read the letter, and did something no one ever saw him do—he cried. "Why didn't you say something?"

"How could I? You had made the decision to marry Francine, and I didn't want to complicate everything that much more."

"You should have told me."

Lilly nodded, then walked away. When Samuel didn't follow, she knew it might be over. What a horrible mistake she had made. As a young woman, she thought she had no options. She was early in her pregnancy when she told her parents, and they decided what was best for her. They sent her away until she had the baby, who was up for adoption even before she was born. Lilly never saw Stephanie or had any idea who adopted her. The only thing the doctor and nurse told her was she went to a good home. She had no way of knowing if that was true.

If her parents hadn't made the decision for her, she wouldn't have gotten that letter from Stephanie. She would have chosen to raise her on her own. She abandoned her child, and there was never a day in her life when she didn't regret what happened. Now, after all these years, she couldn't wait to meet her.

Samuel called out to her, but she kept walking. Now wasn't the time; she needed a few minutes to breathe. When she turned around, he was gone.

Lilly was sure her dream of a life with Samuel was over, and it was her fault. Maybe she shouldn't have said a word until she met Stephanie, but she couldn't hold onto her secret any longer. This time, her parents weren't around to make her decision, and she was going to make things right.

* * *

Lilly had walked for a long time, and decided to go in and pack. She knew Leo would understand. She hoped everyone else would.

When she got to the door, Samuel was waiting for her. "It's cold, come on in," he said. "We have a wedding to attend."

"A wedding? I was sure you were going to cancel."

"Cancel on my best girl? I love you."

"I don't know if that's going to be enough. Not anymore. I've put you right in the middle of a mess. While I'm really excited to finally meet my daughter, I'm scared. Maybe she just wants to meet me to tell me I'm a terrible person."

"Or maybe she wants to meet someone who did the right thing for her. As hard as it was to make that decision, you thought you were doing the right thing for your baby. Our baby."

Lilly stopped talking and started to cry. "Our baby. Samuel, you had no idea what was going on. It was something I shouldn't have done. Maybe my guilt is overwhelming me because I always knew it was a bad decision."

"Or not. Listen, please, for just a moment. She is *our* daughter, and we will do this together."

"Do what together?"

"I called Stephanie, and I told her we would like to set up a time next week for us to have dinner."

"Did you tell her who you were?"

"Not yet. We need to take this slow. After all, it took a lot of guts to mail the letter. Now that we know, we can help her through this together."

"Samuel, are you sure about this? Because you keep saying 'we.'"

"Yes, of course I am. It is about both of us."

"I'm not sure this is fair to you. You had no idea I was pregnant."

"This is about us. Me and you. But, for the time being, let's keep it to ourselves."

"Do you think this can wait?"

"I do. Knowing Leo, he will understand, but let's be sure before we bring anyone else into this. There's enough going on here, don't you think?"

"I know you're right, but this is coming to a head. For all these years, what I did always haunted me and never gave me a moment's peace."

"But now you never have to feel alone. You're going to meet our daughter. If she's anything like you, she's going to be grateful to finally meet you."

"Do you really think so?"

Samuel held her in his arms, wishing he could take away her pain. "I know so."

"I never thought I would even get a chance to glimpse my daughter. When I gave birth, all they told me was she weighed eight pounds, two ounces. Then they took her away, and I never saw her again."

Samuel felt sad, but he was trying his best to make Lilly understand that he was with her. By the looks of things, he wasn't doing a good job. Seeing Lilly like that was tearing him apart.

"I think I will call her to hear her voice," Lilly said. "I need to do that myself."

Samuel took her by the hand and looked right into her eyes as if nothing else mattered. "I'm finally marrying the woman I have always loved, and today is your day. Please remember, there's always room in my heart for one more."

Lilly was so happy that the truth finally came out. "Are we going to be able to do this wedding without falling apart?"

"Yes, we are. We will meet our daughter together next week. Right now, we need to get ready because I hear there's going to be a wedding fit for a queen and you, my dear, are that woman. So, let's do this. Deal?" Samuel put out his hand.

Lilly grasped it. "Deal."

Chapter Thirteen

Seventy-five people were there, waiting for the wedding to begin. Samuel was running around, trying to make sure everything was perfect. He wanted to give Lilly what she deserved. She was the love of his life and, this time, everything would be perfect.

Rabbi Bernard was a longtime friend of Samuel's; they were college buddies before he changed majors. He'd also known Lilly for years, as well as Francine, so he had a stake in this new union. It was his honor to officiate the ceremony, since he knew the whole story—or at least enough to know he would be bringing together two people who had always loved each other. That was a mitzvah.

While Samuel was making sure everything was going right for the wedding, Lilly was upstairs getting ready. Julianna and Gracie were so helpful, and she was delighted that they wanted to be in the bridal party. She had never had daughters to share things with, but the thought that she would soon have three put a smile on her face.

Lilly took both of the girls' hands and led them to the couch beside the window. It was a beautiful view, and the estate grounds were magnificent, right out of a magazine. Even though it was late November and fairly chilly, it still looked lovely.

Before she spoke, Lilly took out a tissue. She wasn't sure she could get her words out without crying. "I can't tell you what all of this means to me, and I'm not sure words are adequate."

Gracie and Julianna were right there, smiling, realizing how hard of a day this was for her.

"I have loved your father for so many years. I never thought this day would be possible. But here we are, and I'm as happy as a young bride usually is. My age means nothing, because I'm going to be with your father for the rest of my life, and that means everything to me. Having both of you to share this day with me is something that I will never forget."

Gracie was so impressed with her words. She smiled and promised herself she wouldn't cry. She had never seen her father so happy, and that was the greatest feeling ever. All the fights and anger in their home when both her parents were in town had been awful. She was looking forward to a happier arrangement.

And Julianna, who used to be so angry when their mother was gone, realized that was one of the reasons she was going back to Ohio with Oliver. Sophie needed a mom the same way she had. Oliver was a wonderful man with compassion, and a wonderful father. She had never lost hope that she would return to them. Life felt pretty good at that point, and she was certain her decision to have a life with Oliver was the best one she had ever made. Nicholas was never the man for her.

* * *

The florist had decorated the downstairs dining area to make it look like a princess was getting married. Samuel had been in charge of arranging everything. He wanted Lilly's special day to always be the most romantic evening of her life, and nothing less.

Luckily, Alex was a well of information about weddings and parties. He helped with the plans, and Samuel had never realized all the talents that his friend had. Now that he knew, he was definitely going to run everything by him, including all decisions for the estate. Alex had a lot of ideas about how to use space efficiently, and a lot of other things Samuel hadn't expected him to know all about.

Shortly before the rabbi arrived, Samuel asked Alex to have a private conversation. "Can you meet me in the library in five?"

"Can't this wait? You're getting married in a short while. We can talk about whatever it is later. Tomorrow, or whenever. Why now?"

"Because I want to get everything in order so it will be run the way I planned it when I travel. I don't like loose ends."

"I get it. Okay, I'm all ears."

"Alex, you know we've known each other for so many years I've lost count, but I want you to know nothing in my life has been as stable as you. You're not only my driver, but you've been my listening board and best friend."

"I know that. I couldn't love you more if we were blood."

"To me, we are blood, so, please, accept my offer for you to manage this glamorous retreat. I think you're perfect for the job. Let's face it, I can't do everything."

"Are you okay? You've been doling out positions since we got here."

"I'm fine. Just trying to plan for the rest of my life so I can share it completely with Lilly. There are a few things she and I need to handle together."

"Sounds serious."

"It is. Okay, I need to tell someone what I just found out."

"Is it bad?"

"It's actually kind of a wonderful surprise, but it's a secret. Nothing about this to Lilly, okay?"

Alex waited for the other shoe to drop. There were so many things going on at the time. "Okay, let's have it."

Samuel whispered, "Lilly has a daughter."

"What are you talking about?"

"Lilly has a daughter. She was adopted at birth."

"Yours?"

Samuel smiled with pride. "Yes, she's mine."

"When did you find out?"

"This morning. Lilly got a letter from her. No one else knows, so this is strictly confidential."

At that moment, Leo was about to walk in the room to get the rings from Samuel. The rabbi had just arrived, and the ceremony was about to take place. But when Leo heard what they were talking about, he felt a cold sweat. His grandmother had a secret. He stood at the door listening, too shocked to move.

Samuel's face turned white when he saw Leo standing there. "Leo, please. I'm sorry you just heard that."

Leo said nothing, but ran upstairs and knocked on the door to the room where his grandmother was getting dressed. Julianna and Gracie were both surprised when he barged in.

"Leo, what are you doing?" Lilly called out. She had never seen her grandson so upset. "What is it? Is Samuel okay?"

Leo tried to calm himself, but couldn't. "Gracie, can you and Julianna please give me a minute with my grandmother? This is private."

Just as they were about to leave, Samuel came running in, a little out of breath. Alex followed.

"Dad, are you okay?" Julianna asked, glancing over at her sister, who was just as troubled by the urgency of the moment. "What on earth is going on?"

Lilly could tell what had happened by the look on Samuel's face.

"Okay, everyone, just relax for a moment," Samuel said. "I know this wasn't supposed to happen, but if everyone will remain calm for a minute or two, we can all talk about it. Lilly, do you want to tell them, or should I?"

"Go ahead," she said. "You're better at this than I am."

"Let me preface this with the fact that I just found out today, and Lilly found out last night, so we're not keeping some deep, dark secret from any of you. It's something that happened to Lilly before any of you were born. Well, not Alex, me, or Lilly."

Alex proceeded to walk to the door, thinking he shouldn't be in the conversation.

"Just a minute," Samuel said. "Please stay."

Lilly nodded. "It's fine. I can tell by the look on your face that you already know, so just stay."

Samuel poured himself a glass of water and sat down, realizing this was going to be quite a shock to everyone.

Chapter Fourteen

The wedding wasn't going as planned, but it was going to happen. There was a lot going on, and everyone in the dressing room came away with the same feeling. It was a long time ago, and they were going to accept whatever came their way.

The whole wedding party had their say, but that didn't mean everyone understood. It wasn't a pretty picture at first. Everyone was talking at once but, after an hour of heated conversation, the wedding was going forward.

Leo, Julianna, and Gracie were beside themselves, but they knew that Samuel and Lilly were in love and that the wedding should still take place. The service would be small, and the party would go on after they were married, with no one the wiser. The guests would still get the dancing, the food, and some laughs.

Instead of being held in the main dining room, the ceremony took place in the bedroom suite where Lilly had changed from her beautiful, expensive lace dress to one of the other dresses Samuel had ordered. Everyone's makeup was smeared from crying, but with the help of one of the cosmeticians, they began to look human again.

The tears they all shared were part of the process of realizing another family member might be joining them in future endeavors. Then it was time for a short and sweet ceremony.

When the rabbi gave the word, Alex placed the glass on the floor. Samuel broke the glass, crushing it with his right foot, and the guests shouted, "Mazel tov!"

After a few hours, and a lot of deep breathing, the entire family was ready to greet the guests and continue celebrating the wedding.

Leo made his way into the crowd of well-wishers and pulled his grandmother to the side. He whispered, to make sure none of the guests overheard their conversation. He had made a decision. "I love you so much," he said, "but I'm afraid I need to leave for my trip to Paris a few days early. I'm not mad at you for not telling me, but I need a little time to digest what just happened."

"I know, honey. I'm so sorry."

"Did my father ever know?"

"No. I didn't want him to be upset. I had it handled. Until I got the letter, I assumed that my daughter would never want to meet me."

"And I suppose Grandpa never knew."

"No one ever knew except my parents." Lilly kissed his cheek. "I love you, and I hope you have it in your heart to understand what happened."

"I do. I've always loved you, and I always will. I just need some time to process this. This is life changing."

Lilly hugged her grandson, feeling the tension. "We haven't cut the cake yet. Can you stay? Please."

Leo smiled, knowing he could never stay mad at her. She was his rock.

Shortly after the cake cutting, the band played many wonderful songs that Gracie adored. She looked all around, trying to find Leo. He had promised her a dance, but he was nowhere to be found. She had all but given up when she felt a tap on her shoulder. She quickly turned around.

"Oh, it's you."

Nicholas smiled. "Who were you expecting?"

"You know who."

"Leo? He's gone."

"Gone where?"

"You need to ask Lilly."

"Come on, Nicholas. Just tell me."

"Fine. He needed some time, and he went to Paris earlier than planned."

"Paris?"

"He wanted to clear his head." Nicholas laughed. "Your family can get pretty confusing. Don't you think?"

"Then I'm going to Paris to find Leo and tell him I want to marry him."

Nicholas laughed. "You can do better than him."

"You know what? I can't. He's wonderful, and you're not."

Chapter Fifteen

The next day, Samuel was waiting for Gracie in the library. It was already noon, and she had just woken up.

"What was so urgent?" she asked.

Samuel handed her three tickets to Paris.

"What's this for?"

"These are for you, Ava, and Julianna. I heard you were going to Paris to find Leo."

"That's true. Word travels fast."

Samuel laughed. "You know he's a good guy."

"I know that."

"He's in love with you. You know *that*, right?"

"Maybe."

"Are you in love with him?"

"I am. I think I've been in love with him for a while. But why Julianna and Ava?"

"You need witnesses, right?"

"For what?"

"A wedding. Your wedding."

Gracie smiled. "What if he doesn't want to marry me?"

"Read this," Samuel said as he handed his daughter an envelope.

Gracie quickly opened it.

Dear Gracie,

If you're reading this, then my plan worked. There's no award service; I didn't win an award. If you meet me at the fountain, you know the one, I will be waiting there for you. I'll be the one throwing coins in the fountain this time.

Gracie smiled and hugged her father. "I love you. When I come back, I promise to run the company with Nicholas and do everything that I can to try to work with him. If that's what you want, I'll do it. You're the boss."

"No, honey. I fired Nicholas and got him a job with your mother and Wyatt. You're the new CEO of Warrington Publishing. You're the one I want to run the company. You're my legacy. And that's that!"

Gracie smiled and kissed her father on the forehead. "I don't even know what to say."

"Say you'll accept." Samuel knew he had made the right decision when he saw the look on his daughter's face. He knew Gracie was finally happy.

"I will," she said. And she meant it.

Her dream came true. What she didn't know was Ellie was watching from above with delight. She had found the perfect match for Leo. Now she could rest in peace.

The End

About the Author

I'm Marsha Casper Cook the founder and producer of all the Michigan Avenue Media podcasts on Blog Talk Radio.

She has over 25 years of experience in the writing industry with 14 books (five of which are children's books), and 11 feature-length screenplays. Several of her screenplays have optioned by production companies.

My Podcast guests give our listeners info that you might not find anywhere else because many of them choose the topics we discuss. Because I interview people from all walks of life the shows are always exciting.

My latest accomplishment is I am now a contributor to *eYs International Magazine*. To find out more about my shows and my books visit these websites and links:

@Marshacaspercook.com | Linktree
www.michiganavenuemedia.com
http://www.marshacaspercook.com
http://www.marshaskidsbooks.com

All of Marsha's books are available in print, ebook and Audible formats on Amazon.com

www.ingramcontent.com/pod-product-compliance
Lightning Source LLC
Chambersburg PA
CBHW061338310726
48974CB00001B/93